LIFE
after
LIGHT

a novel

E.S. MARIA

ISBN-13: 978-0-9924772-3-3
ISBN-13: 978-0-9924772-5-7

Cover art by Kellie Dennis at Book Cover by Design
www.bookcoverbydesign.co.uk

CONTENTS

DEDICATION

For my family, my brightest beacons of happiness,
You are, and forever will be, my light.

Faith is seeing light with your heart when all your eyes see is darkness.
~Unknown~

PROLOGUE

"I'm a motherfucking eagle! Woohoo!" I scream on top of my lungs.

I'm sitting on the uppermost part of the backseat of my boyfriend's convertible, with the summer air hitting hard on my face, making my skin feel taut. My long, dark hair is flying all over me in complete abandon. It feels so damn invigorating.

I feel so fucking free!

He's driving along Avoca Drive, a route we're so used to, while I'm singing along to "Rock Star" by the N.E.R.D, not caring if anyone can hear my racket.

"Get the fuck down, Hannah! You're tanked, babe," Paul's terse words are inaudible with the same song I just turned up.

"Oh, come on, Grandpa! We just finished high school, and in a couple of months, we'll be having the time of our lives in the big city. It's gonna be amazing!" I scream out again, raising my arms up in complete abandon. "Yeeeaahhh!"

"I'm gonna stop this car if you don't get back on the seat and put your seat belt on. I don't wanna get in trouble with the cops, and I don't want you getting hurt either."

He's already slowing down, indicating so he can pull over. I don't want him to stop, but he's always been a stickler for the rules. With a big pout, I manoeuvre my way towards the front passenger seat, plopping myself down unceremoniously.

"Seat belt!" Paul reminds me sternly, switching off the indicator.

"Ugh! Okay, okay. Relax!" I haphazardly put on my seat belt, just as Paul accelerates again. "Why are you being such a wet blanket, anyway? That party was going off, there were beers everywhere, and yet you only drank two. Loosen the fuck up!"

"I just got this car. My father said he'll take this back if I get any demerit points. You know he'll do it. I need this car to drive us around Sydney, babe."

"*I* can drive us."

"Babe … come on. This is a Beemer. You drive a V-Dub Beetle. I love you more than my car for sure, but your ride is way too girly."

I inch closer towards him, draping my arm around his waist and laying my giddy head on his shoulder. "Hey, I love my Betsy," I grumble, defending my car; then I sigh out aloud, "I'm just really happy, baby. We did it!"

A sudden surge of joy makes me take my seat belt off and jump on Paul's lap. The car swerves from his hands leaving the steering wheel, but he manages to take control.

"Fuck, babe, you're gonna get us killed!"

"No, I won't. There's no one on the road, silly," I answer with a giggle.

The road on the way to Avoca Beach is practically empty at this time of the night so I'm the least bit worried. "Kiss me, Paul," I purr, my arms around his shoulders, my lips pressed on his neck. "C'mon, I'm so buzzed and super horny. Find us a spot, quick. I really want you now."

When I sneak a glimpse, Paul still has his eyes on the road. But I notice his caramel-coloured eyes widen with excitement at the prospect of sex.

My boyfriend may be the kindest, sweetest man in public, and he is … for the most part.

But he is super freaky when it comes to sex.

"I know exactly where to take you. It's this rest stop that no one uses." He speeds up, and I giggle when I feel his excitement growing underneath me.

It must have been a mixture of alcohol and the adrenalin rush that comes with the car speeding that's crushing my inhibitions. I don't remember being so uncharacteristically careless.

But all our lives, we've been the good kids. We're in the popular circle, and, as one of our friends used to say, we looked like Barbie and Ken, but hella smarter, plus I'm a brunette. We've worked hard at school and graduated with top honours. And soon, we're going to Sydney to study law at one of the most prestigious universities in Australia. It's going to be scary but exhilarating at the same time because we're moving out of this small coastal town and making our dreams come true without anyone looking out for us.

But what's most exciting is that I'm going in this adventure with the person I love.

Paul. My perfect man.

He's the person I want to spend the rest of my life with.

I freakin' love him!

And I wanna lick his face right now because he's so delicious!

God, I feel so alive right now!

And I may be super drunk too.

But who cares? This is the best night ever!

I hop on to the passenger seat once again, turning up the music, just as Paul and his libido accelerates the car even more.

"I fucking love you, babe!" I cry out as I grab Paul by the face so I can kiss him hard.

"I fucking love you too, gorgeous," he growls back. And as soon as I let him go, I pump my arms up in the night air.

"Woohoo!" I scream out, looking up at the sky and seeing the stars twinkling above us.

Oh yeah, I'm a mother-effin rock star!

CHAPTER ONE

Present Day

The familiar crunch of the gravel outside our driveway tells me that they've arrived. Mum told me the news last week, and now the day has finally arrived. I feel my heart skipping a beat for a second, then it swiftly drops downwards, making me wrap an arm around my gut, as if I can stop its descent.

I'm nervous ... nervous and a little terrified at the prospect of what's about to happen next.

I'm sitting at my nook right by my window. It has become my little sanctuary, a place for me to sit and take advantage of the morning sun.

And speaking of the sun, even though I can definitely feel its rays warming up my skin, I still feel quite cold on the inside, and my hands are getting clammy and gross.

Wiping the moisture over my jeans, I get off the nook so I can walk out of my bedroom and get this over with. But after a few steps, I manage to catch my foot on something protruding on the floor, and I fall face down on the hardwood floor.

I cry out a litany of swear words in speedy succession.

I didn't even make it to the large, fluffy rug that's lying at the foot of my bed. I hit the floor with my knees and elbows first.

Hello, bruises.

My bedroom door opens, and I hear a loud gasp, followed by the sound of footsteps running towards me.

"Oh Hannah! *Dios mio,* why didn't you call out for me? I could've helped you out."

Sighing, I answer, "Mum, I'm okay. Just let me get up." I try to stand back up after freeing my foot from whatever has caught it, but I feel her hands under my arms as she tries to stand me up. I roughly shake her off of me.

"I said ... I can get up. I don't need help. I'm not an invalid," I tell her in a huff, my frustration reflecting on the harshness of my voice.

"I know, *mija,* but I thought I'll just—"

"Mum, fucking stop! I still have my legs and my hands. I didn't lose them. I only lost my footing and my dignity, okay? God!"

I regret my outburst instantly, knowing my words must have hurt my mother's feelings. But ever since the accident a few months ago, Mum has become my metaphorical punching bag for continuous outbursts and filth that come out of my mouth.

I guess it's one of the perks of a trauma, if it's even a perk—you gain the right to cuss and feel downright sorry for yourself.

But I wasn't always like this. In what feels like forever ago, I was the obedient, charming, and caring daughter. Not the foul-mouthed ingrate that Mum has to deal with on a daily basis.

She doesn't deserve to be treated so badly by someone she cares so much for.

"Sorry ... I didn't mean to go off on you like that." I smooth my shirt down, wincing at the sting left on my elbows and knees. In no time, her hands are holding mine firmly, reassuringly.

"I know, *mi corazon*. You're still adjusting. I understand."

"Yeah ... adjusting. It's fine. I'm fine," I answer back too softly to sound convincing.

How can I convince her, when I can't even convince myself?

Mum carefully navigates my limping self outside of my bedroom, which has been relocated from the second floor. My current bedroom was formerly Dad's study and library, which is a lot bigger than my original bedroom upstairs. I remember when, as a little girl, I would sit at that very same nook by the window, reading or studying, while Dad was sitting at his desk, working.

I loved spending time with my dad. It didn't matter then if we didn't have a conversation. We just loved being with each other's company.

I was a daddy's girl.

Was.

Past tense.

Now, I'm not even sure if he can stand being in the same room with me. Or maybe he just doesn't know how to deal.

He doesn't know how to deal with me.

I'm finding it hard to deal with myself.

Because I know it was all my fault.

I know my actions affected my relationship with him.

I just wish that things would go back to the way they were.

But they will never be the same.

Some losses will never be regained no matter how hard I wish for them to be.

And compared to everyone affected, I lost the most.

My future. My dreams.

My love ...

Him.

I. Lost. Every. Damn. Thing.

How do I go back from that?

Maybe the answer is ... I never will.

"How do I look, Mum?" I ask as soon as she stops walking. She lets my hand go, and I stand before her feeling self-conscious.

"You look absolutely beautiful, Hannah," she answers, sounding choked up.

"Ha!" My fingertips move up to the jagged scar running down the length of my right jawline up to my ear. "I'm definitely looking beautiful, especially with this beauty mark on my face."

It was my attempt at sounding self-deprecating and funny. But I sounded more sarcastic and bitter than lighthearted and witty.

"Oh Hannah."

"Mum! Enough with the *oh Hannahs*!"

"I'm sorry—"

"And the *I'm sorrys* too ... please," I correct the harshness of my tone, pleading softly.

"Oh ... I can't help it, *mija*, but for you, I'll try." Then Mum grabs my hand once again, and we continue to walk out of my bedroom on the way to the front door.

"Okay, stop right here so Brodie can see you straight away."

I keep my feet firmly on the ground, my nerves returning.

The last time I saw Brodie was eight months ago. He's a lead singer and a guitarist in a band called Halcyon. He formed the band with his friends when they were fourteen, and a little over a year ago, they caught a break. Now they're on tour a lot, locally and overseas, promoting their album and being rock gods, but always coming over to visit when he has some free time.

I bitterly laugh to myself. He's the true rock star. Not me.

The front door opens, and my heart thuds heavily with excitement.

"Hannah Banana!" my big brother's deep, booming voice envelops the whole room, and my smile is instantaneous.

"Welcome back, big bro," I cry out as I open my arms wide, beaming from ear to scarred ear.

I'm immediately off the floor as he swoops me up in his arms, roaring happily like a madman. He does this all the time, lifting me whenever he can, even when we were little kids. He has always been so strong, and so tall, and carrying me makes him feel like the Hulk.

It's our thing.

"And you're still light as a feather, li'l sis."

"Whatever. I've practically been a couch potato doing nothing," I giggle.

"Nah! Still a lightweight."

"Shut up! I probably gained over ten kilos. But *you* got *huge!*" I scream-whisper in awe, squeezing his arms and finding no squishy flesh.

"Well, I'm glad you noticed. I have been spending time at the gym. The chicks love it when my guns are out onstage," he tells me smugly when he finally places me back on my feet.

"Gross, bro. But I missed you. It's been so long, huh?" my lips begin to tremble before I can even finish my sentence, suddenly going through a myriad of emotions from happiness, sadness, frustration, regret, and shame.

Unfortunately, shame and regret are now a permanent fixture within me.

"I was there, baby sis. I dropped everything to be there for you, but you probably didn't realise it. I mean you were—"

"Yeah," I cut him off. "I don't want to talk about that. Mostly because I don't remember shit."

I'm lying. I do remember everything. I just don't want to talk about it anymore.

"Okay, but now that I'm here, we'll hang out like old times. And I won't pressure you to talk about it. Only if you want to, okay?"

I nod back, my head bowed. "Mum's waiting for her hug too," I mumble, pushing him off playfully, attempting a lighthearted chuckle.

"Hey, Mum." His heavy footsteps are emphasized on the hardwood floor as he makes his way to our mother.

"I missed you, *mijo!*" Mum croons. "You know you're my favourite son, right?"

"Yes, and only because I'm you're only son." They laugh and I laugh with them. It's a joke we share together. Mum always tells me I'm her favourite daughter too.

She's hilarious like that.

That's why she's our favourite mum.

"Your father's on his way home, dear," she reassures Brodie, without him asking.

"No worries," he answers, and I sense some tension in Brodie's voice. That's one more thing my brother and I have in common. My father and my brother never see eye to eye when it comes to my brother's career choice. For him, being a musician isn't exactly a 'secure job.' Dad wanted Brodie to be a lawyer like him. He resisted from the start. He knew what he wanted to do with his life.

I thought my path was my father's. I actually wanted to be a lawyer, with grand plans to fight for the rights of the abused and mistreated children.

But plans change.

And now he's probably just as disappointed in me. I mean, how else can I explain the way he's been distancing himself?

Dad has been super busy with work in the past months, but I think it's only since the accident that he started working until the late hours. And if he's at home, he's always in his office, which used to be my old bedroom upstairs.

I have a feeling that he's trying to avoid me and the situation I've put myself into. Maybe it's the reality that his well-laid-out plans of me becoming a lawyer like him have now burned to ashes, and it's disappointed him.

Or maybe it's because his sweet little daughter is gone, replaced by a scarred, blind, angst-ridden shell of what used to be his sweet, little Hannah Rose.

I don't exactly know how or when Dad and I lost each other.

But I miss him, and I want him back.

I just wish he'd want me back too, broken or not.

"Guess what? I have a surprise for you both," Brodie announces, making me raise my head in attention.

"It better be something awesome," I answer back, one hand on my hip and the other out, palms up in anticipation, imagining a present that can fit on the palm of my hand.

"I don't know if I can live up to that expectation, but I'll try."

What the fuck?

My blood runs cold … just from the sound of *that* voice.

Not him.

Never him.

Damn it, Brodie.

This isn't awesome at all.

With gritted teeth, I blurt out the first thing I can think of, hatred dripping from every single word, "What the hell is *he* doing here?"

CHAPTER TWO

"Hannah Rose Mackenzie!" my mum calling me by my full name with a heavy Latina accent spells trouble for me. But I don't care. I'm standing by my reaction.

I turn towards her. "I don't want him here."

"It's okay, Mrs. M," I hear him speak again, this time he's closer, my skin seemingly aware of his closeness, and my heart thudding like it's awoken from its passive state.

Brodie seems to whisper something to Mum, and then I hear them walking away, their footsteps getting less and less prominent.

Great! They're leaving me alone with him.

I don't want him to see me like this!

My first instinct is to back away, needing to gain more space between us.

I refuse to have the same reaction I always seem to get when he's close. He doesn't deserve it. The last time I felt like this was when he came to visit a year ago. I was with Paul then, yet my body reacted to this asshole more than I ever did with my own boyfriend.

It wasn't fair to Paul, and it sure as hell wasn't fair to me.

"Look, don't worry, Songbird. I'm not going to stay," his voice is soft, practically a whisper.

And God, he smells so good. Why does he keep coming closer?

"Good, leave. You're good at that, aren't you? Oh, and I don't want you calling me Songbird again," I whisper back with gritted teeth before turning away from him. My intention is to run off in the solace of my bedroom. But he reaches for my arm, and his touch feels like an explosion of tiny little tingles. I try to rid of his touch, but he's holding me firmly, and he's turning me around to face him.

"Please don't walk away from me," he pleads softly.

"Fuck you," I spit back, still trying to get my arm back.

He exhales deeply, as if trying to find his calm, "Okay, I deserve that."

"You deserve worse. Let go of me!"

"I will, but not before I tell you how sorry I am … about … about everything."

"Fine. You said what you needed to say. Now let me go."

"I'm sorry about Paul."

"Fuck you! Let me go now."

"I'm sorry about what happened to you."

"I said, let me go!" Tears that I've tried to hold back are now threatening to fall.

"And for what it's worth, I'm sorry about what happened to us."

"Screw. You. *Atticus*. Screw your bullshit!" The bitterness in my voice when I utter his name should convince him that I mean business.

"Songbird …"

"Call me that again and I'll scream my head off."

He finally lets me go, and the heat from his touch quickly morphs into a cold chill.

"Okay … but I'm here if you need me. And when you're ready to talk, just like old times, I'll be here to listen."

I don't even give him a response. I turn towards the direction of my room, and I walk faster than I should. I just can't stand being so close to him now. Thankfully he doesn't stop me, and all I hear from him before I close my bedroom door is a deep, long sigh.

It's a good thing I'm back in my room, with a thick, solid door blocking him from me. At least he won't see the tears running down my face as I cry out every pent-up emotion that Atticus managed to unleash in a matter of minutes.

Then I hear three taps on my door.

In that ever-familiar, ever-distinct way he does that's meant only for me.

A tiny little code meant for only us.

But that was in the past where it should remain.

And now he's doing it again.

Why?

Fresh tears burst out.

"I know you've been through so much. And maybe that explains the rage and the profanities. But I'd like to think that I was your friend first before … before *we* … happened.
I've never forgiven myself for what I did to you, and I won't blame you if you never forgive me. But I hope you do because I want to be your friend again. What do I need to do to be your friend again?"

The smoothness of his voice and the genuine remorse in it is too much for me to take. How dare he expect friendship from me after what happened between us?

Sighing in resignation, with tears still falling, I answer him, "Don't ask for something I can't ever give you again, Tic. Do what you do best and just walk away."

"That's not an option anymore. Okay, I'll stop calling you my Songbird. But can you blame me? Your voice is perfect. You're my perfect little Songbird."

The hostility that I've been trying so hard to push down surges back up, "Perfect?" I start banging on the door, screaming louder until my throat begins to hurt. "If you still think I'm perfect, then you're a fucking idiot. Leave me alone, *Tic*. Get the hell out of this house! Get out! Get out!"

I hear a pair of footsteps running, with Mum calling out my name, trying to open the door. But they've yet to change my doorknob, which I've now locked to prevent Atticus from coming in.

Then I hear Brodie telling Atticus to give me some space and to leave. He agrees, and I inwardly thank my brother for doing that, but at the same token, my stomach twists, knowing that he's walking away from me again.

I shouldn't be surprised anymore. He's good at that.

Atticus Foster is the master of walking away.

Yes, *that* Atticus Foster.

The same singer, songwriter whose chart-topping rock ballads scored him platinum records and numerous television guest appearances, not to mention a sold-out world tour … the same world tour that my brother's band, Halcyon, is supporting.

This is the same Atticus Foster whose hoards of fans scream his name in concerts. With women professing their undying love and devotion to him, hoping they can catch his eye and have his babies.

That same man that everyone loves, I loved as well.

But I loved him before they all did. He was *my* Atticus.

I always thought his name was different. But it suited him because he was different from any other guy I've met. Sure he was an asshole when I first met him, but then I grew older, and as I got to know him better, falling in love with him became so easy, so inevitable.

He fell for me too … at least I thought he did.

Then he decided that I wasn't worthy of it, and he walked away, leaving me brokenhearted and questioning my self-worth.

If it weren't for Paul, maybe I wouldn't know that unconditional love does exist, and that there are people truly capable of it. Paul made me feel like I was perfect for him, and I believed it because he never failed to say so.

But all good things last, and in my case, it lasted way too soon.

Mum asks how I'm doing, and if I can please open the door. But right now, I can't face her, or Brodie, or anyone else. So in my calmest tone, I apologise for my outburst, telling her I'll take my meds so I can rest up. I also promise to unlock the door once I'm ready.

She knows I will. I've had my moments. This wasn't the first time I've broken down, and it sure as hell won't be the last either.

Eventually, she relents and walks off, and I breathe a sigh of relief when she does.

With a heavy heart, I carefully make my way back to the bright light coming from the window, and I sit on the cushioned nook, leaning against the wall behind me and closing my eyes, remembering how to take deep breaths in the hope that they'll help lighten up this rottenness inside of me.

But who am I kidding? This feeling is permanently embedded within me. And I have to accept it. I have to accept the nightmares, the scars, the guilt, and the regret.

I deserve the punishment.

I deserve it all. Because it's my fault.

It's *all* my fault.

CHAPTER THREE

Six Months Ago

Rubber.

I can smell the stench of burning rubber.

Then I hear someone screaming. I think it's a man's voice, but it's not Paul's. He sounds older, and extremely rattled. He sounds like he's on the phone, and I can barely understand what he's saying. But I do hear enough to understand.

"... accident ..."

"... out of nowhere ..."

"... a truck ..."

"... car rolled ..."

"... she's on the ground ..."

"... he's not moving ..."

He's not moving?

Who's not moving?

Is it Paul?

It can't be.

I try to open my eyes, but my brain can't seem to communicate with my eyelids. I try to speak, but all I can do is cry out in a whisper. I can't even flinch or move a fraction because my body feels like it's made of stone. Then, what feels like some warm, dense liquid trickles from my cheek and down to my chin.

What the hell happened? And where the hell is my Paul?

God, why do I feel so cold?

I can hear sirens coming from a distance; then, the same voice I heard a while ago is now speaking within inches from me.

"C'mon, stay with me. Help is coming, stay with me," he pleads, his voice rough and on edge. I want to look at him and around me, but my eyes can't seem to open, or are they open but I can't see him?

"P-Paul ..." I croak out, wincing at the pain.

"Shh, just take it easy. They're here now ... Over here, mate! Over here!" I hear him yell out. Two more voices emerge, a man's and a woman's, both sound a lot calmer than the first guy.

22

"Hello, sweetheart. Help is here now. What's your name?" a woman speaks to me gently. "You might've hurt your neck so if you can't talk, I'll just ask you to blink once for yes, and blink twice for no, okay? Can you hear me?" I try to speak out so she'd know that I can hear her, but I feel so cold that my teeth are clanking too fast. I try to blink, to open my eyes but I don't even know if my eyes are cooperating.

"Okay good," she says, so I guess I did blink. "You've been in an accident, so we're going to take you to the hospital, but I'm going to place an oxygen mask on you and some blankets to help you warm up and feel calmer."

I hear her call out to someone else about me having the shakes, but what happens next is all vague as I feel myself getting lighter, almost weightless, like I'm floating far away from where I'm lying. The last thing I hear before everything turns black is the lady's voice calling out.

"Stay with me, sweetheart ... stay with me ..."

I'm kissing Paul.
He's kissing me back.
I tell him I want him badly.
But then he lets go of me all of a sudden.
Why doesn't he want me anymore?
Is it something I said?
Then he breaks up with me.
Why?
Now he's driving off, saying he's taking me home.
But he's angry. I just know it ... I can tell.
He's driving fast ... then faster.
I plead for him to stop.
We swerve.
I squint at the glaring lights in front of us.
I hear some screams.
Screams coming from me.
Paul ...

"Paul," I can barely hear myself mumble his name. My mouth feels like it's covered with cotton wool, my throat like sandpaper.

"She's awake. People, she's awake!"

Mum. She's here ... wherever this is.

23

"Oh, thank God. Shhh, not too loud though, Nancy. She's still trying to come to. Brodie, go and get the doctor now."

My dad. Brodie.

He asks to get the doctor.

So maybe I'm in a hospital?

"Hannah, sweetie? Your family's here," Mum's gentle voice is comforting, just like the way she's stroking my cheek.

"Mum … where's Paul, Mum? I need … I need to see him," I mumble, needing to see my mother's face, but struggling to open my eyes. It feels like my eyelids are stuck together.

I hear Mum sigh, and she brushes some hair off my face. "Paul is … I don't know how to say this …"

Her voice sounds heavy and broken, and it's making me nervous.

"Why? What's wrong with Paul? He's okay, right?" I finally manage to open my eyes, but … but it's weird. All I can see is darkness, with only a hint of light coming through. I squint, blink my eyelids faster, slower, hoping it'll make a difference.

But there is nothing. I see nothing. Nothing but darkness.

I try to reach up so I can feel what's blocking my eyes, but there are things attached to me and they're preventing me from raising my arm. "Mum, did they bandage my eyes? I can't see anything."

Mum's hand stills, then she lifts it off my cheek.

"No, your eyes aren't bandaged at all. Can you see my hand, sweetheart?" she asks reluctantly.

I move my head from one side to the other, hoping to see what Mum is doing but failing to even catch a glimpse of what it is. "Are you doing something in front of me? What's going on? Why can't I see anything? Mum? Mum, please what's going on?"

My guts feel twisted up inside.

And I haven't even seen Paul yet. What happened to him? Why isn't anyone telling me what happened to him?

"Good afternoon, Miss Mackenzie. I'm Doctor Navi."

Mum speaks first, panic in her voice, "Doctor, you need to check my daughter. Something's wrong with her eyes. She said she's unable to see!"

I hear my dad's voice, and he doesn't sound pleased, "What? What do you mean, Nancy?"

Then I hear another voice, a woman's voice, speaking in a calm tone, "I think it's best if the family can wait outside while Dr. Navi assesses Hannah. So if you can just wait—"

"No," I cut in, shaking my head, my heart beating way too fast to be normal. "I want my family here. Mum, Dad, Brodie, please don't leave me!"

"I'm sorry, Hannah, but we need Dr. Navi to run some tests without any interference," a female voice obliges. "Your mum can stay, but she needs to be seated. The rest can come back in as soon as the doctor is done."

"We'll be right outside the door, Hannah Banana," Brodie calls out. But his voice sounds a little too bright to be genuine.

"This won't be long," Dr. Navi tells me way too steadily for my liking. When people sound like this, it's usually because they're about to disclose something terrible. I've seen this in the movies and TV shows way too many times. "Would you like Mrs. Mackenzie beside you? Don't worry, I'll speak with the nurse later."

I nod back the best I can, and in no time, I feel my mum's hand enveloping mine. I welcome her warmth, grateful that I have someone loving to hold.

This must be pretty bad if the doctor is making concessions.

Still in that calm voice of his, I hear him speak, "Hannah, you were involved in a car accident. Do you remember that?"

I nod, leaning my head towards the doctor's direction, "Yes."

"You suffered from internal bleeding, and a punctured lung. You also had a fractured skull and a deep laceration along your jaw. On the way to the hospital, we almost lost you because of your injuries. We alleviated your bleeding, but we had to put you on a medically induced coma to prevent your brain from swelling. Your injuries were pretty bad, Hannah, but you fought all the way. It was quite remarkable actually."

"How long was I in a coma?" I whisper, my voice trembling.

"Six days."

I hear my mum sob aloud, but I try to focus on the doctor.

"My eyes. I can't see."

I feel two fingers prying each eyelid, then there's a hint of bright light flashing. But it's dim, like a thick, black curtain is covering my eyes, and I can't seem to push it off.

I hear the doctor clearing his throat. "Sometimes, blindness may occur as a result of injuries sustained to the head. It may be temporary, but unfortunately, it may also be permanent depending on the extent of the damage to your retinas. I'll recommend you to a specialist who can do some tests on your vision. Once your body's ready, you'll be able to do these tests."

I hear my mum sobbing again. The weird part is, *I* feel bad for *her*.

Am I just too overwhelmed to react?

Or maybe I'm just clinging on the hope that it would be temporary.

It has to be temporary. I can't be blind. I have plans, big plans for my future.

And my plans involve Paul.

Paul.

"What about my boyfriend, Paul? He was with me in the car. I need to know what happened to him."

"You need your rest, Hannah," I hear him say, again too calmly for my liking. "We'll talk about Paul when you wake up. Right now, we'll just allow your body to have its much-needed rest."

I'm getting frustrated, but as I open my mouth in an attempt to protest, my jaw starts to feel heavier, and my body seems weighted down.

Did the doctor just make me go all sleepy?

"Paul ..." I croak.

It feels like liquid lead is running through my veins, making me feel weighed down.

And just like that, I black out once again.

CHAPTER FOUR

Present Day

"Han? Hannah Banana? Open up, I've got ice cream!" The loud thumping on my door makes me lift my head from the window. I must have slept without realising it.

Now my bloody head hurts from moving so abruptly.

"Hannah? C'mon you never say no to ice cream."

It's Brodie. I love him, but I don't think I can deal with him right now.

I still can't believe he brought Atticus with him.

"Is he still here?" I manage to croak out.

"Who? Oh …" he pauses, "he left straight after. The ice cream is melting!"

Ice cream. Big bro knows me too well.

I carefully make my way to the door so I can unlock it, moving to the side to let my big brother in.

"Finally! This chunky monkey is starting to look like a chunky milkshake." He walks past me, and I close the door once again.

"Sit with me by the window," Brodie calls out.

As soon as I'm seated, he places the bowl of my favourite ice cream on my waiting hands. Brodie introduced me to this particular flavour a few years back. He said it reminded him of me. I smacked him on the side of his head when he said it, thinking he was trying to poke fun at my expense. I mean, hello?

Chunky = fat and monkey = poop throwing primate.

But then he pointed at the flavour breakdown of the ice cream while he was trying to nurse his head.

I gave him a big hug as soon as I realised the connection.

And as soon as the ice cream touched the tip of my tongue, I knew I found my new favourite.

So this has become our ritual every time Brodie and I are catching up—we do it over a bowl of chunky monkey.

Speaking of bowls, I smile a little as soon as I feel mine. Is it what I think it is? I think Brodie may have given me my favourite bowl too … the same dinosaur-shaped bowl that we used to fight over when we were little kids.

He must have seen me feeling the shape of the bowl with a smile on my face. "Yeah, yeah. Keep it. I'm barely here to use it now, anyway."

Blindness perk number two: finally winning the dino bowl.

"No backsies?" I lift my head towards him.

"No backsies," he chuckles back.

I'm still giggling a little as I carefully manoeuvre the spoonful of ice cream to my mouth, holding the bowl right under my chin in case of dripping.

It took a lot of practice, a lot of messy, frustrating repeats before I was able to manage eating on my own. It felt like I was a baby learning to eat again, relearning how to use the cutlery and making sure I didn't make an ass out of myself. Holding the food helped, but I was determined to use the cutlery and not to eat like I was two years old.

We start eating the ice cream quietly at first, just enjoying each other's company, while I silently thank both Ben and Jerry for this amazing flavour invention.

But the quiet doesn't last long.

"Hey, sorry about Tic. He insisted on going, and if I'm not mistaken, you guys were pretty civil last year."

"We were, until we weren't," I mumble.

"But you were with Paul then," he adds. "What happened last year?"

Paul.

In an instant, my appetite for ice cream is gone. I ignore his question as I set my bowl to the side.

"Do you miss him, Han? Paul, I mean?" Brodie's voice is gentle, sympathetic.

I hate it. I hate the sympathy.

I don't deserve it.

"I don't want to talk about him."

"Mum said you've not visited him even once, and—"

"Mum has a big mouth."

"Hey, don't blame the woman. I was the one who pushed for information. You never answered or called me back when I called you, you never responded to my e-mails or texts. And Mum said she got you that text-to-voice app for your phone."

I remain quiet, my hands gripping the edge of the window seat.

"How come you've never visited Paul?"

Just like that, whatever restraint I had is now gone.

"Because I can't, alright? I just can't! I can't …" I cry out, my voice shaking, with my body following soon after, tears now freely flowing down my face. "I shouldn't."

Brodie's arms wrap around me, but his gesture only makes me feel worse. I push his arms away, leaning my back against the wall. Then I raise my legs up to my chest, wrapping my arms around them tightly. It's a lame attempt at shielding myself from the pain.

"I hate seeing you like this."

"At *least* you can see me," I answer bitterly.

"Don't do this to yourself. What happened was an accident, and it was nobody's fault. You came out of it alive, Hannah. Don't you forget that. And now, you're wasting your time locked up in this room, in this house, doing nothing. You have so much more —"

"Oh, stop it with your speech, Brodie!" I spit out. "I heard it all before. Don't you think Mum and Dad didn't preach about how this is my *second chance* and all that shit?"

"You need to talk to somebody about what you're going through. An expert or something. I'll even pay for it."

"What? To talk to a shrink? I tried it once before and I hated it, so I refuse to do it again. I'm not changing my mind about it. How can anyone understand what I'm going through?" my voice breaks again, and my eyes moisten with ready tears.

He sighs deeply, and again, his arms are around me. But I'm stuck between him and the wall behind me so I have no place else to go.

So I let him hug me.

Because I know it will comfort him, but only him alone.

"No one will understand what you're going through, no matter how much we try," he whispers, "but maybe if you try again to talk to an expert or maybe try to join a support group, they can help you channel this … this grief. Please, Han. Promise me that you'll at least try. I'll even look for one you prefer and drive you if I have to."

"Aren't you going overseas in a couple of months?" I croak out.

"Then I'll drive you in those couple of months."

I close my eyes and let out a deep exhale. "I don't know if I can even get inside a car."

"Mum said you've been inside a car, and she said it helped when you pretend that you're still inside your room."

"A moving room? Sounds credible. Not. But at least I can't see anything that'll freak me out while in the car, right? Yet another blindness perk for me," I attempt a joke, chuckling shakily. "Sorry, that was me being—"

"Awesome. That's you being awesome, Hannah Banana," he laughs with me while hugging me even tighter.

"Can't breathe. Can't breathe," I laughingly pretend to choke. He's hugging me with my knees still up to my chest, and it bloody hurts.

He chuckles as he lets me go, "So, is that a deal? You'll go and see a therapist or at least try to sit in a support group?"

I nod back, wiping my tears and tucking loose strands of hair behind my ear. "Yes, you asswipe! I'll do it. But I can't promise that I'll stay if I don't feel comfortable about it."

"I'm just glad you're giving it a shot. I'll start googling after we finish our ice cream."

"Mine's probably all melted now."

"Melted, huh? Oh yeah. Well, I know that Mum's got a stash of butterscotch schnapps hidden in the pantry. Want to make this ice cream interesting?"

I giggle back, "Ew! It sounds gross ... okay, let's do it. Schnapps me!"

I end up being proven wrong. The combination of the melted banana and choc fudge ice cream with Mum's butterscotch schnapps tastes amazing. Maybe it's because I have more schnapps than ice cream, who knows? But I'm more relaxed now, and in my current situation, that's a good thing.

By dinner, I'm giggling more at Brodie's jokes. Even Dad seems more at ease. And Mum, well, I can hear the happiness in her voice.

We're all here, at the table, eating dinner together, just like old times. The last time we ate together as a family was before the accident. That felt like forever ago.

Life was great forever ago.

I remember our dinners right when I just finished my HSC, and I knew I kicked ass. I was so confident I was going to get the results I deserved that Sydney Uni and their law degree should just be handed to me in a silver platter. Paul was as confident as I was, and we started making plans to go to uni together in the big city during those dinners … even before we received our HSC results.

Paul made it easy for me to get excited about the prospect of going to the university together. That's just part of his endearing quality though. He's the type of guy that can sell ice to an eskimo.

My chest tightens everytime I think of him.

I met Paul at his birthday party because one of my friends was dating one of his buddies back then. Our circles kind of intermingled, but we never had a chance to be personally introduced. He pursued me, and because I needed to get over Atticus, I gave Paul a chance, thinking that if there'd be anyone who'd help me to get over Atticus, it must be somebody completely his opposite. What I never expected was to fall for Paul as well. But looking back, it was just inescapable. With his sun-lightened hair from years of surfing, his tanned, amazingly athletic body, his near-genius brain, his incredibly kind heart, and the fact that he made me a better version of myself … it was difficult not to fall for him. He made it easy for me to love him when I thought it was impossible for me to do so, because his love imposed no conditions … and no questions.

Paul was brought up that way.

My perfect boyfriend.

My perfect Paul.

"Hannah, sweetie? Would you like a cuppa? I'm using our fancy pod thingy that your dad bought," Mum's offer for after-dinner coffee takes me out of my reverie.

"Yes, please. Thanks," I answer back, with a half-smile.

"What are you doing while you're in town, son?" Dad asks my brother.

"Dunno yet. Maybe catch up with friends, chill, maybe do some impromptu pub gigs, hang out with my baby sis," I feel my brother's hand squeeze my shoulder, and I'm thankful that he leaves out the part where he wants to take me to the shrink.

"I heard Atticus came around as well. How is that scoundrel?" my dad asks, chuckling.

"Still a dick," I mutter under my breath just as Brodie continues to have a conversation with Dad.

"Honey, that's not very nice," I practically jump out of my seat at Mum's voice whispering against my ear, "and I don't think the boy deserves that. What did he ever do to you that made you so angry?"

Before I can answer, Brodie suddenly snorts aloud, "I hardly think you can call Atticus a boy anymore, Mum."

"Well, he's like a second son to me," Mum huffs back, "and you two are practically brothers," I hear her voice moving away from me, and I inwardly thank my brother for diverting Mum's attention away from me, and her opinions about Atticus.

Dad clears his throat, "Is Atticus staying at his house?"

"Pfft! No way. He's renting a shack by the beach. I don't even think his dad knows that he's here."

"Right, well, maybe that's a good thing," Mum breathes out. She always has a soft spot for Atticus, and has been quite protective of him, especially after learning about his asshole of a father.

That's because Mum doesn't know about Atticus and I and what he did to me.

And if she ever found out, I wonder if her opinion of *him* will change.

"You right?" Brodie nudges my shoulder.

I raise my head towards him, half-smiling, "I'm just tired. I think I might just go to bed. Excuse me." I push the chair back to stand up, carefully walking in the direction of my bedroom.

"Let me help," my brother pipes up.

"I know the way to my own bedroom, big bro. I'm cool," I let out a sigh, smiling sheepishly. "Thanks, anyway. 'Night Mum and Dad ... Brodie."

Mum gathers me in her arms. "I guess that's a no on the coffee. Goodnight, *mija*. Rest up."

I hug Mum back and give her a kiss on the cheek. I know she's only giving me a slight reprieve before she hounds me with questions about my mood tomorrow.

Whatever. I'll cross that bridge when I get there.

As soon as I'm inside my bedroom, I start taking my clothes off so I can take a shower. Today has been a roller coaster emotionally, something I don't really need, especially with what I've been going through these past months.

Damn it, I can still smell Atticus's scent on me.

Why did he have to smell so good … so familiar … so heartbreaking?

These are the times when I truly wish I could see something, anything … that is, anything but *him*.

When Atticus invades my dreams, the first thing I'd envision is his tall, lean-muscled physique, his unruly dark blonde hair, and his tattooed arms … just as I last saw him last year. But then, just as I would try to approach him, he would raise his aviators to hide those green eyes of his. Then he would turn around and walk away from me.

Away from us.

Without saying a single goodbye … without any explanation.

It broke my heart over and over again as that vision of him played out on auto-repeat. It felt so real because it was.

I didn't expect for that pain to cut so deeply. But it did, and it's all on him.

And it hurt so damn much.

And no matter how much I wished Paul could take all the hurt away, it kept reemerging in the worst possible moments.

Now I'm paying for it. And I'll never stop paying for it.

Hannah, inhale through your nose, exhale from your mouth.
Breathe, think happy thoughts, breathe.
And repeat.

After a couple of minutes, my fingertips are skimming along the wall right next to the door. When I finally locate the button, I press it down firmly and music instantly envelops the bathroom—loud, angry music that seems to seep inside my skin and take over the remains of my senses. It does what it is supposed to do: push off the negative thoughts in my head.

My dad knew how much the music helps, so he got someone to install a waterproof sound system in here. They also installed a phone inside, in case I needed help while I'm in here.

Blindness perk number four: getting utterly spoiled by my parents.

Even though my dad doesn't know what to do around me, he still makes sure that I have a bathroom that caters to my special needs. But sometimes I think he goes a little overboard. My bathroom has heated nonslip floor tiles that have different textures for me to identify which part of the bathroom I'm in. The shower is open, with no curtains or sliding doors, just a tiled half-wall that serves as division between the toilet and the shower. The taps, switches, and power points, like in my bedroom, have been labelled with a series of dots to help me identify what they are.

Blindness perk number five: learning Braille.

And that's me being sarcastic. Learning Braille took a lot to get used to. And sometimes it would frustrate me when not a single dot would make bloody sense.

But I knew that if I want to be more independent, I needed to learn this new skill, and learn it damn well.

A large sink is set on a benchtop that goes along the length of the wall. This serves a dual purpose: it helps me figure out where I am in the bathroom, and the bench space means I can place my stuff on it without the risk of the said stuff falling off on the floor or in the toilet. Dad made sure there are as few corners as possible to avoid the risk of me getting injured. And Mum comes in regularly to make sure my things are placed on the same spots so that I know where to find them.

I have nothing kept in this bathroom to keep me hair-free. Mum has the unenviable task of shaving my legs. I know. Ew. But she said she wanted to make sure I'm confident enough with using sharp objects like shavers before she'll let me anywhere near them.

But I have a feeling Mum thinks I might be borderline suicidal.

I'm not. Really, I'm not.

Yes, I'm bitter, moody and I cry way too much. I also refuse to go out of the house which makes the whole thing about Mum shaving my legs, completely pointless.

These past months I refused to see my friends. When they came over to see me, when they tried to call me, I told my Mum to tell them that I wasn't ready yet. It never felt that it was right for me to move on. I knew it was the right thing to do. My poor mother had to give them the same excuse every single time.

And what would I talk about with them, anyway? Our conversations would probably be about them feeling sorry for me, or worse, they might even blame me for the accident.

I didn't need them for that. I could do a decent job blaming myself.

As the months progressed, my friends' visits and calls became progressively scant. They had all moved on to study in their respective schools, and start their lives as university students. So the visits stopped altogether, and the calls are now practically nonexistent.

And as much as I'm relieved that they stopped trying to make contact with me, I'm also saddened that they've given up on me.

Years of friendship down the drain, and all because I was afraid to answer their questions, and was too proud to have my blindness turn out into a crutch.

The haunting voice of Marilyn Manson fills up my ears, and I have to laugh as I'm brushing my teeth.

Beautiful People. I was one of them.

One of the beautiful people.

Queen fucking bee.

At least that was what everyone told me.

And that included my now non-existent friends.

I spit out the minty remnants in the sink, wiping my mouth with the back of my hand, and grazing the scar on my jaw.

Who in the hell will think you're beautiful now, Hannah?

CHAPTER FIVE

What in the hell?

"Wake up! Wake up! Wake up!" Brodie's voice is way too loud right against my ear, and my bed is bouncing up and down so much that I'm close to being tossed off my own bed.

"Stop it! Did I not lock that damn door?" I groan, taking the pillow underneath my head and placing it over my ear, hoping to block my idiot brother out.

"Good morning to you too. Wake up, sunshine. I'm fixing breakfast, and then I'm taking you out."

"You must be out of your mind. Get out!" I cry out, sounding like a whining baby.

But I don't care. He needs to leave me the fuck alone.

"We're going to the beach. You need to get some vitamin D, breathe in fresh air. We'll walk. C'mon!" Brodie takes my arm and drags my limp body off the bed. "It's either you cooperate or I'm dumping you in the shower and switching on the cold water. Up to you, Hannah Banana."

"Fuck. Off!"

"Okay, your call." He lifts me up like a sack of potatoes, and knowing my brother, he'll follow through with his threat.

With gritted teeth I cry out, "Let me down! Fine, I'll go. I'll hate it, but I'll go."

"Oh, come on," Brodie answers as he finally allows me to stand up on my feet. "You're hanging with your big bro. You'll love every single minute of it."

"No, I won't, but I'll go because you'll just annoy the shit out of me if I don't. Now get out of my room so I can get ready ... *please.*"

He ruffles the top of my head, messing what feels like a bird's nest even further. I slap his hand away, and he snorts a laugh.

"Breakfast in fifteen, yeah?" he yells out as he walks away.

When I hear the door close, I exhale deeply but couldn't help the corners of my lips from lifting up.

Brodie can be annoying as hell, but despite this, and the fact that he's three years older, we've always shared a closeness usually reserved between good friends.

That closeness was tested, however, when he found out about Atticus and me.

We just started getting serious when Brodie found out. He wanted me to break things off with Atticus, told me how ambitious he was, that his music was his key to moving out of his house, and away from his abusive father for good. I told him that I knew what I was getting myself into, that he couldn't control my decisions, and that Atticus had been upfront with me from the beginning.

The latter was a lie, but my brother didn't have to know that.

But I knew Brodie well. He will never stop guilt tripping me until I broke it off with Atticus.

So I told my big brother that I'll break it off with Atticus.

I lied to Brodie to get him off my back.

I also lied to Atticus, and I told him that we had to keep things a secret because I didn't want Brodie to find out and interfere between us.

Brodie believed my lie, and so did Atticus.

I thought back then that I was being clever, even finding some form of adrenalin rush from all the discreet acts of endearment, the sneaking in my bedroom window, and the raunchy text messages coming from our made-up aliases.

But I had to keep things under the radar because the alternative wasn't even an option for me. I was falling so hard for Atticus, and I was falling so quickly that I didn't even have a chance to rein it in. And the sad part about it all, was that it made me foolish enough to realise that I was on the road to making the biggest mistake of my life.

I thought that if Atticus felt that what we had was real and tangible, he would change his mind and never leave me.

So when he left town, no matter how much I wanted Brodie to choose my side, I couldn't force him to do so because that would mean admitting that I lied to him and to Brodie, that whole time.

Atticus may have shattered my heart, but I wasn't going to allow that to threaten the bond I had with my big brother as well.

And maybe it was a good thing that I never said anything because while Brodie was in the city, he reunited with Atticus, and they managed to continue on their friendship. They even busked right after each other at Pitt Street Mall ... his band Halcyon and Atticus Foster.

One day while Atticus was playing a set, a well-known music producer who was shopping with his family saw his performance, and he wanted to hear more. He loved what he heard, and not long after he signed him up.

He mentored Atticus and helped produce his first album using his original songs. It didn't take long before his first single hit the charts and became a staple on mainstream radio. One thing followed after another and now he's touring all over the world, promoting his album, with Halcyon supporting him in each and every show.

Yeah, Halcyon got signed up too by the same record company. Brodie and his mates even had to defer from their university degrees just so they could go on tour together. But if their success continues, I seriously doubt that they'll consider going back to their deferred courses anytime soon.

When I first heard Atticus's song on the radio, it was bittersweet. His song was called "Underwater," and as soon as the DJ announced the title, my chest tightened, and I didn't know if I should cry tears of sadness, anger, or pride.

I knew the song so well.

That was our song.

Our story.

He sounded just like how he did when he sung it to me before—raw, gritty ... beautiful.

He sang about how loving her was like coming up for air because it made him feel alive ... how he wanted to drown in her loving arms ... how she felt like his lifeline ... and how he knew he needed to let her go so he wouldn't take her underwater.

That line threw me. It wasn't part of his original song. The original line was that he knew he couldn't let go, and that he wished they could hide underwater.

I always wondered every time I heard the song, whether he changed that line to send me a message, or did he change the line to make it catchier?

Here I go again.

I rub my forehead back and forth roughly, frustrated that I'm back in this cycle.

Atticus is not the man I should be thinking about.

I'm not being fair to Paul.

Paul. My heart constricts painfully at the mention of his name.

But I need that pain.

Sometimes I need that reminder that I don't deserve to move on after what I've done.

After a quick shower, I dress in denim cut-offs and a T-shirt. Mum organised my closet according to clothing types so it's easier for me to figure out what to wear. I can tell separates just by feel and from memory. I told my parents not to buy me any new clothes since it'd just confuse me. That was only half-true. I love my mum and all, but her taste in fashion isn't exactly up to par with my own. In other words, she wears mummy clothes, clothes bought from stores catering for women aged forty and above. I think the shops I actually used to go to, scares her a little. It must be from the tiny amounts of material used on the said clothes.

These are the times when I wished I had my girlfriends with me again. I trusted their taste.

I don't even bother searching for shoes to wear. My favourite pair of thongs is right next to my door. That'll do.

After giving myself a good pat all over, hoping I look decent enough, I square my shoulders and leave my bedroom.

Breakfast, then, outdoors.

You can do this, Hannah.

You got this.

I can't do this.

After consuming Brodie's signature pancakes, the one dish he can cook to perfection, he tells Mum that he's taking me to the beach. And judging by Mum's sharp intake of breath, she's completely shocked that I agreed to it. Her immediate reaction causes me to doubt my decision, and now I think that maybe it's a stupid idea, that I'm not ready to venture out, that I might hurt myself, that people I know will see me and either laugh at me or worse, feel sorry for me.

I seriously can't do this.

Shit, why did I—

"I think it's a great idea, Hannah," Mum's voice cuts through my thought process. "Actually, I think it's about time. If all it took was your big brother convincing you, I would've told him to hop his bum in a plane and fly back home, even for a little while."

I notice a hint of melancholy in her voice, and I know I'm the reason for it. I hurt her feelings. She's been trying to get me to go out with her, even for a little while, but I adamantly refused each time. My brother's been here for a day and I'm already heading out with him.

I wasn't ready then. But for some reason, I feel that I'm ready now.

Well, not really, but I feel like I want to at least try.

"We're just going to the beach, right? I mean, I wouldn't know ..." I trail off, getting a little anxious.

"Of course you'll know, silly. You want me to throw you in the water, or bury you halfway in the sand to prove it?" he snickers, patting my shoulder lightly.

"You're an idiot," I answer back. "Do anything like that to me and I'll never trust you again."

"Relax, lil' sis. I was just kidding. I just want you to stop looking like a fuckin' vampire."

"Language," Mum sternly warns Brodie.

"I meant freakin' vampire," he protests unconvincingly.

"I said, *language*," Mum insists, and I can't help but snort out in amusement, "and that goes with you too, young lady. I know you're both adults, but spare your mum the heartache and at least try to take the profanity down a notch when you're home?"

"For you, Mum, I'll try," Brodie answers back sweetly ... a little too sweetly.

"Oh, *you're* trying alright," and as expected, Mum picks up on it. I can't help but smile, as I listen to them go back and forth.

"Have fun today, *mija*." I feel Mum cup my face, turning me so she can lay a gentle kiss on my cheek. My smile widens as I nod back.

"I'll *try*," I answer, showing her my cheeky smile.

She snorts back, "Oh, don't you start with me too." With a quick hug, I hear her walking away.

The sound of a mug landing on the table, makes me jump, then it's followed by Brodie's voice, "Ready, li'l sis?"

The first thing that hits me is the salty-fresh sea breeze. As soon as I fill my lungs with the all-familiar scent, my skin starts tingling all over.

Both of my hands are firmly on Brodie's forearm as he slowly navigates me across the sand. The squishy feel of the sand, something I'm used to feeling almost every day and have taken for granted, feels amazing in-between my toes.

The smell, the gentle lick of the breeze on my skin, and the sensation of my feet being buried in the soft sand as I walk, instantly take me to childhood and teenage years spent at this very beach.

I never realised how much I missed, how much I can remember, with something so simple as feeling the sand in-between my toes.

This is the same beach where Brodie and I used to bury each other in the sand, the same beach I learned to surf, the same beach my friends and I went to hang and muck around … and the same beach that has a pathway that leads to rock formations where Atticus and I used to kiss in secret.

My fingertips instinctively touch my lips. I can still remember the feel of his lips on mine, even after years had passed.

Even after Paul.

I suck in my breath, and the same fingers now bend into a fist.

Stop it, Hannah! You shouldn't be thinking about Atticus. Ever. What about Paul? He should be the only man in your broken-ass brain. Not Atticus or Tic or whoever he is. Ever.

Brodie must've sensed my anxiety because he places his hand over mine. "You alright?"

"Yeah," I lie, nodding back, "I'm alright. It just got a little overwhelming there for a minute."

"Do you want to go home?" he asks gently.

"No. This … I'm actually enjoying this. I should've done it sooner."

Brodie doesn't answer back. Instead, he takes my hand and wraps the same arm I was clinging to, around my shoulder, giving me a comforting squeeze. I keep my arms to my sides, unable to hug my brother back.

Because I know I'll just break down if I did.

Damn it.

"So," I continue, "the waves are sounding pretty good."

Small talk. That'll take his attention off me.

"Yeah, the waves look amazing. I miss this," he breathes out.

"You should've brought your board," I muse, slightly tilting my head up at him.

He takes his arm off and replaces my hand back on his forearm so we can walk. "Next time. Right now, I just want to hang out with my Hannah Banana."

"And this is coming from the same brother of mine who used to get me in trouble with Mum so I could get grounded and he could have the surf to himself. Since when were you this sentimental?" I ask incredulously.

"Since that day when we almost lost you," he answers, his voice booming, but choking with emotion.

Shit.

Without a second thought, my arms wrap around Brodie's waist, and his arms instantly circle around my shoulders. He holds me tight, I hold him tighter. And we both let the tears fall.

After several minutes, which felt more like forever, we finally let each other go, wiping our tears almost immediately.

"Fuck this," I mutter.

"*Language*," Brodie answers back, copying Mum's tone.

I laugh and he laughs with me.

We laugh with complete abandon.

And just like that, the heaviness in my chest lifts.

Laughing is so much better than crying.

Somehow along the way, I've forgotten how good it feels.

After the beach, Brodie convinced me to go to our local café right next to the beach, a place I haven't been to in months. I insisted that I wanted to go alfresco because I didn't want to remove my sunglasses for obvious reasons. Now I'm able to keep my sunnies on without looking like a douche.

"Okay, so I got you a cinnamon-apple muffin and a cappuccino. That's cool?"

I nod back a yes, only smiling slightly. I'm nervous. This is my first public outing since the accident, and because I have no clue how I look like on the outside, I feel … no, I know I look like shit that got shitted on. If my friends do see me, my only consolation is that at least I won't see them and the looks of disgust and, or pity towards me.

I'm putting that down as blindness perk number six: being completely oblivious to other people's judgemental stares.

42

With two hands, I carefully take a sip of the coffee. It's been a long time since I've had a proper cuppa, and after the initial shock, I think my taste buds are thanking me profusely.

"So, I'm just curious, is it complete darkness? What you see, or what you don't see, I mean," Brodie asks, sounding both curious and hesitant at the same time.

I shrug back, "Usually it is, but sometimes I see some light coming through. Then I can work out some shadows and shapes. I can differentiate if it's daytime or nighttime by the kind of light coming through as well."

"Have you thought about getting one of those walking sticks? They might come in handy too."

"I do have one. I just prefer not to use it since I can make my way around the house anyway."

"What about if you want to go out?"

"You know that other than my trips to the specialist, I've never really been out. A walking stick just makes it too real for me. It's like, *yes, I'm blind, and I have this walking stick to prove it.*" I screw my face in a wince, picturing people who know me, as they're pointing their fingers at me, whispering to each other … pitying me, maybe even laughing at me.

I know I sound vain. But the truth is, I never cared about my appearance before until the ability to look at myself in front of the mirror was taken away from me.

"But you've always been so independent, Hannah," my head tilts towards Brodie at the sound of my name. "Don't you wanna gain that back? Everyone else's opinion can just go to hell."

I start fiddling with my coffee cup, shrugging back at him.

He's not wrong. I used to value my independence. In fact, I took pride in it.

Past tense.

How can someone like me be independent now?

"Hannah?" I hear a high-pitched, almost childlike female voice call my name.

"Yes, that's me. Who's that?" I answer, scrunching my brows together as I lean my head towards her direction. This feels like I'm talking on the phone, since I can't connect the voice to a face.

"It's … it's Nicki. Nicki Colt. We went to high school together."

Fuck. I'm shit with names.

43

I *used* to be great at remembering faces.

Blindness disadvantage number twenty: Virtually everyone I have ever met are back to being strangers to me.

"I'm sorry. Nicki, is it? It's kind of hard for me to place a name with a face now, and I'm super bad with names," I explain regretfully.

"That's okay. Uh, we used to be in Legal Studies together? I just wanted to say I'm sorry, you know, for the accident."

That's when a vision of a black-haired, tiny girl with pale skin and glasses appears in my head. She was the quiet one and very studious. But her voice when she did talk made her sound like, well, a mouse. Unfortunately, this made her a target by Vivian, someone whom I can probably call a former friend since she never made an effort to come over, nor did she ever call me after the accident.

She christened her *Nicki Mouse* ... as in like Mickey Mouse.

It's lame-ass. But the intention to hurt was there.

I always disagreed with the name-calling, and I called Vivian out about it. A couple of my closest friends, Patricia and Brooklyn, disagreed with the whole 'mean girl' mentality as well. But because we were part of the popular circle, anyone outside of it thought we were all the same.

And now one of Vivian's victims is talking to me.

And she doesn't sound angry. She sounded sad. And she wants to say sorry to me.

Whether it's genuine is beyond me.

She must be laughing on the inside, seeing me like this.

"Hannah?" Nicki's tiny voice calls me tentatively.

"Yes ... I-I remember you now. Thank you," I answer distractedly, hoping she'll move on soon without me pushing her away.

"You look great though. I mean—"

"You don't have to tell me shit like that," I interrupt, cutting her off. "I know I look awful."

"Hannah ..." Brodie warns. "Nicki, Why don't you join us?"

I turn my head at my brother's direction. *What the hell is he doing?*

"Oh, it's okay. I'm only here to buy takeaway coffee. Thank you. But ... but I wasn't lying, Hannah. You *do* look great. And I understand what you're going through. I can relate. I know this may sound presumptuous, with us not really friends and all, but I just

44

want you to know that if you need to talk, I'm here for you."

My brows furrow in a scowl. "How can you relate? Have you lost someone so suddenly? You didn't lose your eyesight, obviously."

Wow, I'm a bitch.

"Yes, but I ..." I hear her let out a frustrated sigh. "Look, our community's pretty small, and I know it's none of my business, but I've heard that you didn't go to uni, and a friend of mine who knew one of your friends, told me that you weren't even accepting visitors for months. I know what you've been through was rough, and I'm sure you think you're better off pushing people away. But I went through something very similar too. I thought no one would understand, but I was forced to go to a support group. Now I think it's one of the best things I've done. Who knows, maybe you—"

My brother cuts her off, "She'd love to go, Nicki."

"Brodie!" I screech at my brother. How dare he decide for me?

"Here, type the details of the support group you go to in here." I faintly hear the sound of phone unlocking, most likely Brodie's.

"Oh my God. I can't believe Brodie Mackenzie's letting me type on his phone. Sorry, I'm a big fan. I'm gushing," I hear Nicki sputtering as I hear the sounds of Brodie's phone keyboard being pressed in fast succession.

I remain quiet, silently simmering.

"Well, here you go. I really hope to see you there, Hannah. And oh, Brodie, I heard Atticus Foster is back. It's great to see that even rock stars like you and Atticus are still grounded. Um, any chance of you guys doing a little show or something? I'm sure the locals, especially a lot of the girls, would love it. You and Atticus have a huge fanbase here. Huge!" Nicki's swoony voice surprisingly rubs me the wrong way.

I reach for my muffin and stuff my mouth, hoping it'll stop me from saying anything derogatory.

How the hell can Atticus still make me feel so territorial?

I'm sorry, Paul. I didn't mean to.

Damn it, Hannah, keep it together.

"Thanks. I've forgotten how fast news travels around here. I'm actually just here for my family, but you never know, Tic and I might get an itch to play."

"Wow, I hope so. Well, I don't want to take up too much of your time, so, " Suddenly, I feel two tiny arms wrapping themselves around me, and a waft of flowery cologne reaches my nostrils as she whispers, "It's great to finally see you, Hannah. It really is. You were one of the good ones. I knew you defended me over the others, and I'm grateful for that. I hope that in my little way, I can help you out too."

I don't know why. But her words bring me to tears, and my chest tightens as well. Not because her words hurt, but because I pushed so many people away, that the only kind words I've heard in months other than those from my family, have come from someone I'm not even friends with. And even if it doesn't take all the pain away, it helps, somehow.

Still choked up, all I can manage is a nod, unable to lift my head to at least give her a smile. I hear Brodie thanking her as well, before I hear some shuffling and soft footsteps walking away. After a short second, I feel Brodie's hand cover my own, and he gives it a squeeze. He doesn't have to say anything.

In some weird, cosmic way, I have a feeling that he understands.

By the time we get home, I'm already exhausted, and my head is throbbing nonstop. It's yet another wonderful side-effect of the accident. After thanking Brodie for finally dragging me out of the house, I excuse myself so I can have a little nap … something I know I need but dreading to do, because even though I hope to dream of Paul, somehow I think a certain asshole ex will take over.

CHAPTER SIX

Four Years Ago

"Did you see how Danny was staring at you? That guy wants in your panties for real," Patty teases as soon as the doors of the bus close.

"Shut up, Patty! Are you serious? That guy's a joke. He collects girls like he collects … well … panties probably. Brook, can you back me up on this one?" I tug at the arm of my other best friend—the more balanced, practical one.

"Seriously, that guy is super immature," Brook interjects as we make our way to my house. "Hannah's not an idiot. She's not gonna wanna waste her v-card on that jerk-off."

"That's probably what he does a lot too … jerk-off," I giggle back nudging Patty and Brook at the same time.

"Gross! Please don't go there," Patty gags. "I do not need that shit in my head."

"You guys wanna come in?" We pause at the end of my driveway. Patty and Brook live on the same street as I do, and we usually hang out in each other's house to study, to watch TV, or to stalk the boys we like on Facebook and Twitter.

We're fifteen years old. We love boys. That's how we roll.

"You guys comin' in?" I ask.

"You reckon, um, Brodie's home from school already?" Brook asks shyly.

I roll my eyes at her, saying, "Beats me. I'm not his fuckin' keeper."

"Maybe you should be. Have I told you how cute your brother's become?" Patty adds.

I lift my forefinger at both of them, feeling like I want to wretch. "Uh, first of all, ew. Second, how the hell should I know? He's my brother. He'll always look like a boofhead to me."

"Fine! Whatever," Patty snorts. "I need to go home anyway. It's Mum and Dad's date night so I have to babysit my little sister."

"Brook, are you coming up?" I ask, raising my brows.

"I'll go home first and show my face, but I'll come over in thirty minutes or so."

"No worries. See ya, babe." We give each other hugs before I start heading up the steep driveway to my house.

"I'm home!" I yell out loud enough so Mum can hear me. I usually find her in the kitchen at this time of the day, preparing our after-school snacks. She loves to do that, so I cannot find the heart to stop her. Lifting my shirt up from my skirt's waistband, I'm walking past the living area on my way up to my bedroom so I can change into something more comfy, usually a pair of shorts and a singlet, before snacking with Brook, and I'm already unbuttoning the top button of my shirt when I hear someone clearing his throat, making me screech and jump out of my skin. "What the fuck?"

I turn towards the direction of the source and find a boy lounging on our couch, sipping a can of soda and looking like he owns the place.

"So she swears like a sailor."

"And who the hell are you?" I ask, with my arms crossed and chin up.

Because unlike him, *I actually* own the place.

Well, technically my parents do, but still.

He stands up slowly, taking his time. And as soon as he is completely upright, I swallow hard.

Geez, he's tall. Tall with muscles. Not the weightlifter kind, because he seems only slightly older than me, but the *'Oh yeah, this is genetic cos I don't really work out'* kind.

And he's cute. Far cuter than any boy I've seen in my school.

Dark blonde hair with green eyes. And I think I see what appears to be a dimple on one side of his face as he smiles.

But there's no warmth in that smile. Only smugness … like he just caught me checking him out and he's the least bit surprised.

He's also wearing a school uniform, except that his isn't from the same school as my brother's.

"I'm Atticus. And you're still staring," the smug boy speaks once again, making me blush.

"And why are you here?" I raise a brow, cocking my head and ignoring his last remark, doing my best to look annoyed instead.

Because I am. He's beginning to annoy me.

"He's here because I invited him to hang out," Brodie answers as he walks out of the kitchen.

"Here you go Tic, for later." My brother tosses another can of soda at him, which he catches with ease. "So … you've met my charming little sister, Hannah. She's off limits, just so you know."

I scoff him off.

As if I'd even go there. I'm more pissed that he gave Tic my name.

Seriously … *Tic*?

"Does Mum know you have a stranger in the house?" I ask instead.

"I met your mum and she's nice, and I'm not a stranger anymore. We know each other's names."

My brother laughs it off and motions his head up to his room, and they start heading in that direction before he whispers to me, "Tic's a pretty kick ass guitar player. Be nice to him. I'm trying to convince him to join my band."

"Yeah, whatever," I snort in response. Brodie's plan of forming a band is a joke. Sure he's an amazing guitar and piano player, but he'd been talking about this for months and months and still, nothing.

As soon as Tic passes by me, I call out, "See ya, *Tic*," making sure I'm extra sarcastic with his nickname.

"Only my friends call me Tic. We're *not* friends," he answers back as he follows Brodie up the stairs.

"Yeah, well, I don't wanna be your friend anyway. And your nickname sucks!" But I'm a bit too late with the retort. Brodie's bedroom door bangs shut even before I finish my sentence.

Damn my slow response rate.

Ugh.

What. A. Douche.

CHAPTER SEVEN

Present

"I got it. I got the details for the support group, Hannah Banana. I rang ahead. They have a session tomorrow morning at ten." I'm close to finishing my breakfast with Mum and Dad, when I hear Brodie's footsteps stomping down the stairs with the announcement.

"Yaayyy for you," I answer back with not an ounce of excitement.

"Oh, honey. This is great! You're actually gonna do this," Mum sounds more excited. Of course she would be. She'd been trying to get me some help, someone to talk to, but it was either I adamantly refused to go, or I reasoned myself out of it. Eventually, she just gave up.

And now, even with me reluctantly saying yes to Brodie, and him arranging everything, I know in my heart that I can't go through with this.

"Excuse me, I'll just be in my room." I push my chair back and walk the same route carefully to my bedroom. I hear Mum's protest, but thankfully, Dad tells her to leave me be.

How can I even attempt to move on with my life, to start to heal, when I have absolutely no right to do so? What about Paul? He wasn't given a chance either.

If Paul can't move on, I owe it to him to hold on to the guilt. That's what I deserve. I deserve to suffer for the rest of my life.

God, I need to distract myself from all this angst.

Music. Yes. I need to drown myself in music. Taking the phone out of my pocket, I unlock it, speaking the name of the radio app. After a second or two, the app is playing songs from my personal playlist. I climb on the bed and lay my head on the pillows, placing my phone right next to me and increasing the volume to an almost deafening loudness.

I'm beginning to feel relaxed, my nerves beginning to calm down. That is, until I hear the first notes of the next song.

"For You I Will" by Teddy Geiger.

The song instantly takes me back to his eighteenth birthday party over a year ago. It was held in their house, possibly the biggest one in Avoca Beach, located on top of the cliff with uninterrupted views of the vast ocean. It was the party to end all parties, and it was going off in a big way. Everyone who was anyone, was there. His parents, both successful lawyers, had decided to stay overnight in the city. They trusted Paul, and why wouldn't they? He may be an only child of an affluent couple, but he's far from being an irresponsible asshole.

I was standing at the balcony, taking in the views. It was beautiful, calming. Even with the DJ playing loud dance music inside, when I looked out into the ocean, everything seemed to quiet down. Everything was still.

Suddenly, I felt two tanned arms wrap themselves around me, my hair was swept to the side before I felt his lips pressed on my neck.

"Hey," I sighed, as I closed my eyes for a second, relishing how it felt. "Your party's a success. No surprises there."

"Hey," he murmured against my neck, as he held me tighter. "This is my favourite part of the party so far, and I want to enjoy it."

"Which part?"

"This, just holding you. I haven't had a chance since the party started, so I'm not letting you go anytime soon. Maybe ever."

I couldn't help but giggle, "Babe, you're the host. This is your eighteenth birthday. Mingle, drink your ass off, have fun."

"Can you hear that song?" he asked as he refused to move, his arms still around my waist.

"Huh?" I leaned my head towards the house, where a slow song had started to play.

"I asked the DJ to play this as soon as I have you by myself. His timing is exceptional."

"What song is this?" I heard the singer melodically say that he'd pretty much do everything for the girl he loved, no matter what it was. It was a familiar song, although I've never really heard all the words.

"It's called 'For You I Will,'" Paul twirled me around, just as my heart started beating faster. His blue eyes stared at me with so much emotion that it overwhelmed me, and all I could do was stare back. "Hannah, I can't sing for shit. And the last thing I want to do is embarrass myself or you. So I'll just let this guy sing for me."

"Sing about what?" I whispered.

"That I love you, Hannah Mackenzie."

I gasped, literally gasped after I heard his words. But before I could respond, he continued, "Please don't feel pressured to say it back. I don't expect you to. I know how much that asshole broke your heart, and you told me plenty of times before we started dating that you wanted to take it slow. But I don't know, it's my birthday, I have had a few drinks already, and I wasn't planning on blurting it out like this. But I can't help it anymore. And because I'm in a selfish mood, I want you to know that in a way, I'm grateful he left you because even when you were with him, I loved you. And now that we're together, I feel that you should know that I would never, *ever* break your heart. I'd rather die than hurt you the way he did."

I opened my mouth to speak, but he pressed his finger on my lips. "I'm not done yet," he smiled sheepishly. "If you don't feel the same, well, I'll do my best to understand. Please don't feel pressured into saying it back. That isn't my intention at all. I just—"

My hand instinctively covered his mouth. "Now you shush. Stop talking. It's my turn to talk."

He tried to speak in protest, but it was warped from the pressure of my hand, which I pressed harder until he got the message.

"I love you, Paul. I. Love. You. Too. Okay? So stop explaining yourself. You're breaking into a sweat," I smiled sweetly and released his mouth so I could wipe an imaginary drop of sweat from his brow.

Paul didn't waste time. He instantly held me tightly in his arms, and his mouth pressed with my own. His kiss felt like a promise fulfilled, beautiful and sweet, even gratifying.

"Best birthday ever," Paul whispered in-between kisses, his mouth forming in a grin before turning the kiss into something more passionate. And I let him. Because he deserved it.

That was the moment when I realised he deserved a perfect girlfriend.

So after the party, after everyone had left his home and we were all alone, after just two months of him patiently waiting, I finally became that perfect girlfriend. I gave Paul all of me.

I gave him the Hannah he loved, the Hannah who was perfect in his eyes, the Hannah who was willing to love him the way he should be loved, a love fitting to a person who may be considered in every sense of the word, perfect. So I gave him perfect. The perfect girlfriend, the perfect love.

And as I'm lying in my bed, with the memory of Paul's birthday filling my confused head, a loud sob escapes me, and I begin to weep. My body curves in a foetal position as my heart tightens so hard, it feels like it's about to reach its pain threshold.

For even though I gave Paul what I know he'd been waiting for, my body and my heart, I was nothing but a fraud to him. Because even though I professed my love, my heart still pined for the one person who broke it into a million pieces.

Paul was the last person who deserved that.

And that made me no better than Atticus.

So how can I even think of moving on when I clearly have no right to do so?

By doing something I've been avoiding to do for months.

Because I was afraid … and I still am … of what's going to happen next.

But I need to see Paul.

And finally find the courage to apologise to him.

CHAPTER EIGHT

Two Years Ago

It's been two months, three days, seven hours, and forty minutes.

Not that I'm counting.

Maybe I am.

My friends have been telling me I'm better off without him, that this is the best thing that can ever happen to me.

Atticus is a loser, a good for nothing insensitive dick-wad, who only wants me for one thing. And now that he finally got what he wanted, he left me without warning, without even saying goodbye.

I deserve so much better, blah, blah, blah blah.

White noise. All of them.

The truth is, this is as much as my fault as it is his. He warned me from the start. But I was too blinded by my feelings for him that I accepted our doomed relationship.

But maybe my love wasn't enough for him to stay.

His life was already complicated, and when I gave him myself for the first time, I probably complicated things further, and it freaked him out.

I'm not going to deny that I'm upset because I am. Very. Extremely.

I'm gutted.

He walked away after taking something precious from me.

I wish I can hate him the way he deserves to be hated.

But I can't. No matter how much I want to rid myself of this feeling.

I was in so fucking deep with him.

He was my first kiss

He was my first love.

He was my first time.

He was my first *everything*.

Until he became my first heartbreak.

No, strike that. This feels more like an atomic bomb to my heart, leaving it completely shattered beyond recognition. There's no way anyone would want it now because, well, it's ugly and irreparable.

All I need is for him to come back. He doesn't have to be with me because I can never trust him again. How can I, when everything that happened between us was probably a lie.

But I need him to come back because for once in the whole time that I've known him, I want him to answer one question honestly: "What the hell did I do wrong, Atticus?"

My friends manage to do the unimaginable.

They trick me into going to a party. And now they're off dancing, leaving me alone to fester.

I can fester just fine at home. I don't need to be here to do that.

As soon as we turn the corner, and I hear the music, it becomes clear who's hosting the party.

Paul Simpson.

The only heir to arguably the largest house in all of Avoca Beach and inevitably, the heir to Simpson and Simpson, a law firm owned by his parents.

I see him around at school all the time. He's the type of guy that stands out. We do have mutual friends, and my girlfriends find him super cute. But I'm never really interested. And the only guy who manages to get me more than interested left for fuck knows where.

Maybe I should leave. I'm not ready for this shit.

I'm not ready to have fun yet. I'll just bring everybody down.

"So, does it kick ass?"

A voice right next to me takes me back to the present.

"Excuse me?" I ask, trying to push back my irritation as I turn to the culprit who interrupts my thoughts. But whatever it is I want to say is stuck in my throat when I realise who he is.

"That place you went to just now. I just noticed you seem to prefer to be wherever you were instead of here," he's smiling at me, but with no hint of malice. His smile is sincere with a tiny hint of cheekiness.

He's cute. His bright eyes are practically twinkling.

Damn it, I really don't want him to be cute right now.

But this is his party. I can't be rude to the host.

"Sorry, I didn't even realise I was that obvious," I smile back, though I think I look more like I'm wincing in pain.

He sits next to me on the couch. "Is there anything I can do to make this party more fun for you?"

"Oh God, don't worry about me," I shake my head, laughing with embarrassment. "You should have fun in your own party and not worry about a gate crasher like me."

His brows seem to scrunch together. "Who said you weren't invited?"

"Dude, you don't even know who I am."

"Of course, I do. You're Hannah Mackenzie," he confirms, smiling his smile again.

My eyes widen in surprise, "You know my name?"

"Do you know mine?" his eyebrow cocks up, his smile getting cheekier.

"Paul Simpson. You own this house I'm currently in right now. And it's your birthday party, so Happy Birthday," I answer laughing sheepishly, possibly blushing as well.

"Ah, thank you," he nods back, his smile showing off a set of perfect teeth. "Well, there you go. Awkward intros done and dusted." A server walks by with a selection of drinks. He picks up two cups of beer. He hands me one and raises his cup to me, tapping them once in a toast.

"To new friends," he declares.

"To new friends," I repeat softly, unable to help the smile on my face.

He stands up after we take a sip, but not before bending down again and this time, his lips are merely centimetres from my ear.

"Just so you know, this isn't my house. It's my parents'. But I must admit this house never looked this good until now." He straightens up and raises his beer cup at me before walking away to mingle.

In most cases, that might come off as cheesy … sleazy even. But when Paul says it, it feels sincere, like he actually means it.

For someone whose sense of trust was ruined after Atticus, Paul seems to be able to do the opposite.

But I shut down that feeling straight away.

Fool me once, shame on you. Fool me twice, shame on me.

After taking one long sip of the beer, I get up from the couch so I can see myself out. I only live a couple of streets away. I can manage.

By Monday's lunch break, everyone is talking about Paul's party. I keep to myself while my friends discuss the events that happened hours after I left. I'm surprised they are still talking to me at all since I left without saying goodbye, and I didn't answer their calls or messages the following day. In a way, I think they understand why, but I'm sure they wish I got over my 'mourning period' sooner.

People grieve differently. Some people take it harder than most. I'm just one of those people.

Yay for me.

"Did you hear what I just said, Han?" Patty prods her manicured finger on my arm in a way that annoys me.

"What?" I ask, now irritated.

She rolls her eyes before smiling mischievously at me. "Paul was looking for you last Saturday night. Apparently you guys were just talking, but then you upped and left straight after. I think he took it personally." She nods her head in the direction of a group of guys seated a few tables from us. I know that group. *Everyone* knows that group. I mean, my group is pretty popular too. And I'm not even going to be humble about it. We're relatively high on the food chain. But if you're a bunch of hot guys who are champions in team sports, your group will no doubt be amongst the most popular ones.

And Paul's looks and amazing physique stand out from the said group. I've seen him at the beach, surfing once in a while, and man, those abs don't lie.

I don't even realise that I've been staring at Paul, who's currently listening to his friends' chatter. But even in the distance, I can see that he's staring back at me.

I turn around to check if there's anyone behind me, but my back is facing the wall. He is definitely looking straight at me, and he's not even attempting to hide it.

Oh, boy.

I look away, trying to act nonchalantly. It's a good thing he's far away enough not to see the way my cheeks are blushing.

"Holy shit, he's coming over!" Patty suddenly grabs my forearm, squeezes it, then shakes it roughly.

"Chill, woman," Stan, her boyfriend, intervenes and takes her grabby hands off me.

Just then the bell rings, signalling the end of our lunch break.

Relieved at the opportunity to escape, I stand up and grab my stuff so I can head out the door.

Wait? Why am I running away?

Why should I feel guilty about finding another guy hot?

I'm single, and only bloody seventeen years old. After the manner I was dumped, I need an excuse to feel like I'm attractive to someone again. Maybe, Paul would be the guy to do that.

Screw it. I'll take my chances.

So I slow my pace, until I finally stop walking. Then I turn back around to where I came from. But as soon as I do, I get into a head-on collision with someone's chest.

And as soon as I get my bearings back, I open my eyes again.

Okay, so judging from the tie, this is a guy's school uniform.

And judging from the hands clasping my upper arms, this guy is quite strong.

And as soon as I look up to his face, judging from the way he's smiling at me, I realise that I just face-planted on Paul's chest.

Shit on a stick.

"You better decide if you're coming or going so I know if I should chase after you or wait for you," Paul says with laughter in his eyes as he reluctantly lets me go.

"Why would you do either of that?"

He places his hand on the back of his neck, and his smile turns awkward, "Because I want to ask you out on a date."

His bluntness takes me aback. And my eyes widen in surprise. "Wow, you didn't even beat around the bush with that one."

Paul laughs, looking up at the ceiling as he does, "Yeah, well it took me a while to work up the courage to even ask you."

"What?" I scoff. "You're kidding, right? I've seen you hang out with other girls."

He shrugs, looking sheepish again, "I have an endgame."

"Really?"

"Yeah. You."

"Me?" I ask, confused and pointing at myself.

"I'm going to be honest with you, alright? The other girls weren't serious. They knew it, and I knew it. But it's different with you, that's why it took me this long to ask you out."

"We only met last Saturday," I tell him pointedly.

"It doesn't mean I haven't been paying attention to you long before last Saturday."

"Oh. How long ago are we talking about here?" I ask softly, finally realising that other students are passing us to get to their classes and possibly listening in.

He winces, "Since year eight. But I think you were preoccupied with someone else. You probably don't even remember that we danced on your sixteenth birthday."

My breath hitches. He was there, on my sixteenth birthday, possibly with mutual friends. But that was around the time my attention was focused solely towards one person.

Maybe if I paid attention to Paul instead of Atticus, my heart would probably still be intact.

Noticing the hallway almost empty, I start backing away from Paul. But not before grabbing a piece of paper and writing my number.

I grab his hand and place the paper on his open palm. "Pick me up Friday at eight." Then I turn around to hurry to my class.

"See you then!" he yells out.

It's only when I'm already seated that I realise the lack of fireworks when we touched. But I dismiss it in an instant.

Fireworks are way overrated anyway.

CHAPTER NINE

One Year Ago

"Happy first year anniversary," I whisper against his ear before handing him my present.

"Happy first year, baby. I wonder what this is." He pretends to shake the square-shaped, thin, gift-wrapped present he's holding.

I can't believe it's been a year since Paul and I got together. One year of no insecurities, no fighting, no mistrusts, and no dramas.

I love it.

He knows about my past, I know about his. He knew from the onset that it would be harder for me to open my heart than it would be for him. And yet, he's been patient and he never pressures me to give him more of myself than what I can commit.

But without his patience, without his unconditional love, I might not get to where I am now.

He makes me *feel* again. And although the fire he brings out inside of me isn't immediate but more like a slow burn, I feel that it's exactly what I need right now.

I had the raging inferno with Atticus. With him, it was instantaneous, like living every day like it was our last. I gave him all of me without thought, without caution. And when he left at the time I needed him the most, I was left burned beyond recognition.

But I'm gaining myself back. I'm healing. And I have to thank Paul for that.

I didn't know this kind of love existed until this man came into my life and showed me.

It was inevitable.

I've fallen for him.

I love him.

And boy, he sure loves me.

"So can I open this now?" Paul asks, looking adorable excited and super handsome at the same time.

"Of course, babe. Hope you like it. It's kind of a big deal to me that you do so I'm feeling kinda nauseous right now from the nerves," I say, chewing my lower lip nervously as soon as he rips open the packaging.

My fingers start playing with my new bracelet, his anniversary gift to me. It's a beautiful, silver Tiffany bracelet with a small teardrop charm. As soon as Paul hooked it around my wrist, I understood why he chose it for me.

He promised me when we first started dating that he would do his best to only make me cry happy tears.

And this bracelet confirms his promise.

How did I get so lucky?

"It's a CD," he tells me, eyes wide with childlike excitement.

I nod back, pointing at it, "Read the note on the disc."

He kisses me sweetly on the lips first, before turning the case so he can read my handwritten inscription, 'Happy one year anniversary, Paul. This is the best way I can think of, to show you how much I'm thankful that you're in my life. I love you. Yours, Hannah.'

He turns back to me and wraps his arms lovingly around my body, giving me a kiss filled with love, even gratitude. After a few moments, we break for air, not caring if the patrons in this posh restaurant are witnessing our PDA.

"C'mon, let's go. I want to listen to this in the car." He waves his hand politely at our server before asking for the bill.

As soon as he settles the bill, we walk hand-in-hand towards his brand-new car. He just got his provisional licence, after passing the driving test in just one try. His parents bought him a BMW convertible, but on the condition that he'll drive safely. Since he's had the car, he's been nothing but super safe with it. I'm just wondering where he'll put his surfboard though. He loves surfing, and I constantly tease him that he loves to surf more than he loves me. But I stop the moment he plants a kiss on my lips.

He inserts the CD in the player and presses the Play button. The first chords of the guitar begin, and my nerves go into overdrive straightaway. It's an unfamiliar tune, and I can see Paul's brows scrunching in the middle.

That is, until he hears my voice.

"Oh my God," Paul whispers.

I stay quiet, staring at him and trying to read his reaction. It's been a long while since I last played my guitar, even longer since I last penned a song. There were way too many good memories that turned bad attached to my guitar, that I even considered selling it. Sure, the pain of a heartbreak inspires many artists to paint, to sculpt, or to create songs. But when my heart broke, I could barely look at my guitar, let alone function to write music.

But Paul made me want to play again. His love inspired me to put pen on paper and write him a song. And seeing his reaction change from puzzlement, to recognition, to awe was enough for me to know that maybe I did good.

"This is you. This is you, singing … and playing the guitar!" Paul says, elation spilling out of his voice, making my nerves dissipate and my mouth to form a wide grin.

"I know it's not an expensive present. But I wrote this for you … because you inspired me to want to write songs again," I explain softly, my voice shaking.

He doesn't respond immediately, only staring at the screen where it shows the title of the song, "Dear Mister." But as the song ends, he lifts his head up and turns to me, and his eyes tell me everything he's unable to speak of.

"So, do you like it?" I ask nervously as silence surrounds the car. "It's a bit rough, isn't it?"

"Rough? I fucking love it, Hannah. The song, your voice, and the way you play the guitar … everything about this song is beautiful! Come here, cheeky girl," Paul cups the back of my neck and pulls me closer as his lips press against mine. I can still taste the chocolate cake on his lips, and the taste, plus Paul's lips, make this kiss even more delicious. He moans as his tongue meets my own in a dance we've become familiar with.

He suddenly pulls back, catching his breath. "Wait, just so we're clear. I'm that Mister, right?"

His question makes me giggle because his tiny bout of uncertainty is pretty damn adorable. "What do you think?"

Paul raises his brow, "It's me, yes. But kiss me anyway just to confirm that it is."

So I do, over and over again.

He drives me home after listening to my song so many times that I begged for him to give it a break. Sure it's my song and all, but even I have a threshold when it comes to repetitions.

I notice the lights in our backyard are on, and I can hear people talking and laughing. This is pretty unusual for my parents to have visitors at this late an hour. Usually by this time, my parents would be upstairs sleeping. They don't bother waiting up for me, since they know I'll either be with Paul, or my girls, if I ever go over my 11 p.m. curfew. My parents trust them the most.

Unless …

"Are you coming inside?" I ask Paul as soon as he switches off the engine. "I think Brodie's home. You'll finally get to meet him," I add excitedly. I haven't seen him in ages since he and his band Halcyon went off to Sydney to work on a record deal.

Paul looks wary, "Are you sure, I mean that's your big brother, and he's friends with your ex—"

"That was the past, and that's where it belongs. And my brother loves me. He knows I'm happy with you, so he has no choice but to be happy with you," I interrupt, then open the car door before turning back to him. "C'mon," I give him my best coquettish smile, raising my brows suggestively, "we can make out in my room after."

He seems to deliberate his next move before sighing, "Okay. Let's do it. I'll cop it from your big brother. But only because you're giving me a good incentive."

I giggle as we step away from the car together. He parked right up the driveway, thankfully. I don't think my legs will survive walking up the steep driveway with these heels. They make my legs look killer though, but they're killing my feet too.

I take his hand as we walk around the side of the house, where the side door is thankfully unlocked. I want to surprise my brother by sneaking up on him.

The laughter and the chatter become louder as we get closer to the backyard. It sounds like there are girls with them. I roll my eyes, hoping they aren't groupies. Desperate groupies give me the shits. Before we're visible, I stop and face Paul, pulling his head down so I can kiss him. The heels get me closer to Paul's height. Without them, I'd have to tiptoe and still manage to only face his chest.

I stretch my head as we reach the corner of the house, and I immediately see Brodie, Derek, Shane, and Mike sitting around the bonfire with a big cooler filled with beer next to them. A couple of girls, a redhead and a blonde, are sitting on Derek and Shane's lap respectively. Brodie's back is facing me, so I try to sneak behind him. Shane and the girls see me first, so I raise my finger up to my lips to shush them. There's a hint of alarm in Shane's expression, and his eyes drift back to the house, then back to me. But I put it down to him being surprised and having to keep his trap shut.

As soon as I'm close enough, I cover my brother's eyes, but I blow my cover as soon as he mouths off a few choice expletives.

I release him, and he jumps up from his chair, turns around and lifts me in a tight bear hug. He loves showing off his strength, but it's easy for him since I'm practically half his size.

"Hannah Banana!" he yells, eventually putting me down. His eyes travel to Paul, who's possibly surprised at his reaction, but smiling politely regardless.

"And is this the famous Paul Simpson?" Brodie offers his hand, and Paul accepts it, shaking it firmly. Paul's confidence impresses me since he *was* nervous just a few minutes ago.

"It's great to finally meet you," Paul tells Brodie. "Hannah talks about you a whole lot and just so you know, our little town is pretty proud of your band's success."

Brodie's eyes light up at the compliment. That's what so impressive about Paul. He's a charmer, and he has a way with words.

It obviously worked with me.

"So what brings you home, big bro?"

He shrugs, "We're taking a break from recording. The boys are getting antsy. So I suggested a weekend spent at home should help us recharge," he pauses, exhaling deeply, "By the way—"

"Wait, hold that thought," I plant my hand on Brodie's shoulder, halting him from continuing. "I'll just introduce Paul to the rest of the boys."

He opens his mouth, but closes it straight after I brush past him with Paul in tow.

I give all three of them a hug, introducing Paul as I go. The girls I find out aren't groupies, but Shane's and Derek's girlfriends. I think I'm more surprised that these two commitment-phobes are actually in a serious relationship.

Don't get me wrong, I love these guys like they're my brothers. On top of that, they're amazing human beings, but man, they are idiots when it comes to girls. I'm just glad two of those girls saw past that and took them seriously.

I notice the boys looking at each other uneasily, and I guess it's weird seeing me with a guy who's not ... God, I shouldn't even be mentioning his name.

"Well, we'd love to stay, but it's our anniversary, and I'd like to spend it with my boyfriend instead of you all." They erupt in congratulatory cheers and playful banter. "So if you don't mind, we'll be inside the house." I wave and blow kisses at everyone, all while walking backwards on our way to the house. I even wave at the girls, who seem quite nice and friendly. Pointing at Brodie, I add, "We'll talk tomorrow."

Brodie opens his mouth again, but I'm already waving him off with Paul, excusing himself as well. I'm actually excited that I get to fulfil my make out promise with Paul.

Just then, the boys' attention focuses behind me, dread written all over their faces. Thinking my parents have awoken, I'm about to follow their gaze when the voice I never wanted to hear suddenly speaks my name.

"Hannah?"

That voice. Deep ... husky. The type that hits me right in the guts.

Damn it.

Now I get why those guys looked panicked ... or were they looking guilty?

Traitors.

Why didn't they warn me?

I stare them all down, just as I grab hold of Paul's hand. I need to gain strength from my boyfriend before I can even attempt to face *him.*

And when I finally do turn, I wish to high heaven I didn't. His hair seems a little longer, with a slight fuzz covering his jawline. He's wearing a dark T-shirt that shows off his now full-sleeved, tattooed arms. His eyes, green and intense, focus only at me like we're the only two people here.

Shit.

I shouldn't have stared into those eyes because it doesn't take long before they begin to draw me in. Now I'm losing myself in them ... again. It's like I'm back to being the hopeless girl that has a serious crush on an unattainable boy. My breathing starts to hasten, and my heart starts beating like it's about to jump right out of my chest.

He's the only person able to make my heart do that.

I used to love it. Now I fucking hate it.

He doesn't deserve this kind of reaction from me.

I just wish he didn't look or smell this good. That doesn't help matters at all.

Over a year ago, I would've given anything to see him again even for one last time. I have questions that needed answers … and a hand that could do with some slapping.

"Hannah?" I hear my name being whispered again, but this time it's from Paul.

It thankfully brings me back to my senses.

So I tighten my hold on Paul as I start leading him back in the house.

"Atticus," I nod back curtly as we walk past him, but not before noticing his jaw clenching as he sees me holding Paul's hand.

What does he expect? That I'd drop everything and everyone just for him?

As we take the steps up to my place, I can feel my hair rising, and my skin tingling. I know he's watching my every move. I always know when his eyes are on me.

Good.

I'm going to take great delight in knowing Atticus is witnessing Paul and me, hand in hand, walking up the steps to the house. I hope he also sees us go up the stairs and into my bedroom.

I hope he knows that I'm going to make the hell out with Paul.

I want him to realise what he lost, what he could've had.

So why in the hell do I feel so damn guilty right now?

CHAPTER TEN

Present Day

This is the first time in a long while that I'm waking up with a sense of purpose.

I get out of bed; take a shower; dress up in jeans, T-shirt, and sneakers; and tie my hair in a ponytail.

I don't know how I look, but on the inside, I feel good. Still not great, but I'm starting to feel like I'm ready to restart my life again.

I hear a knock on the door, followed by Brodie calling my name.

"You ready, Hannah? Have some breakfast before we go, yeah?"

"Okay," I grab the CD on my night table. Something I prepared the night before. Then I open the door with a smile on my face. I'm surprised at how oddly nice it feels. I haven't been smiling this big in the mornings for a while now. "I need you to take me somewhere first. No, actually, make it two stops."

"Are you sure about this?" Brodie's worried voice isn't doing much to alleviate the bundle of nerves that have accumulated inside of me. I felt so confident on the way, but now, I'm so close to backing out, that all I need is a small sign telling me this is a bad idea and I'll tell Brodie to do a U-turn.

"No. I didn't know exactly what to expect on the way. But we're here, and I know it's something I need to do if I ever want to move on with my life. I need some kind of closure, Brodie."

He sighs, "Okay. But I'm walking with you."

I nod, chewing on my lower lip. He steps out from his side of the car and collects me. Holding both the CD and a recent purchase from my first stopover securely in one arm, I hold my brother's arm tightly as he leads me up the path to where I need to go.

"We're here, Hannah," he whispers and halts his steps, and in an instant, my stomach turns and twists repeatedly.

Don't chicken out now. You can do this, Hannah. You have to do this.

"Brodie ... I'm ... I'm actually scared." A knot feels stuck in my throat, feeling too overwhelmed that I'm starting to break in cold sweat.

"I'm not going anywhere. I'll give you your space, but I'll *be* here with you. Just breathe, Han. Breathe," he tells me firmly, reassuring me by placing his hand over mine.

I try to breathe slow, deep breaths until my shot nerves begin to calm down.

"Okay," I nod, "I'm ready. Please lead me to Paul. Oh, and thanks for giving me some alone time with him."

"Of course, Han. But call for me if you need to, and I'll come over. Alright, here he is." Brodie gently takes both of my hands in his, and as soon as he lays them on the cold, smooth surface, whatever composure I had left begins to disintegrate. My legs start to buckle, my whole body shakes uncontrollably, and like a dam with cracked and damaged walls, my tears spill out with no resistance. The bouquet of white roses I bought from the flower shop feels like lead making it near impossible to place on top of the headstone.

All the sadness, the loss, the grief, and the guilt ... I feel them all at once like a sharp, but jagged stab to the heart—one painful strike after the next. The agony is too hard to bear, but I know I deserve every single blow.

I'm now slumped, deflated, knees-first on the grass, tracing each letter of his name with my fingertips.

P-A-U-L ... D-A-M-I-E-N ... S-I-M-P-S-O-N ...

The pain is more excruciating with every letter I trace with my trembling fingertips, so excruciating that I wish I'm able to physically rip my heart out to if it eases the pain.

I don't want this reality.

I don't want this truth.

"Oh, Paul. I'm so sorry. I'm so, so sorry," I whisper, trying to imagine him merely inches from me, but the sadness in his imagined features is torturous. I clutch my chest, sobbing furiously, my head bowed in great sorrow.

"I'm so sorry for what I did. I'm sorry that I made you so upset. I know that I should've visited you sooner. But I just ... I can't accept that you're gone. And you know it's not just that, Paul. I'm also ashamed of what I did to you ... to us. I *know* it's my fault. It's *all* my damn fault. I caused that accident. And now you're gone, and

I didn't … I didn't get a chance to say goodbye. They told me I was in a coma. And by the time they let me out of the hospital, you were already buried. Now it's too late and I'm scared that you'd never forgive me because I failed you so many times. You were so angry with me that night. You had every right to be. I'm sorry. It wasn't fair to you at all."

I stop to catch my breath in-between sobs. And that's when I feel my brother's hand on my shoulder, squeezing it gently in an attempt to comfort me.

Brodie whispers, "If this gets too hard, then I'll take you home if you want to."

"No," I answer back, shaking my head. "I have to do this. It's taken me this long to find the strength to do this, and I'm not leaving until Paul hears me out. Please, just give me some space again," I beg.

He sighs, and he gives my shoulder another squeeze before I hear the shuffle of his feet on the grass as he's moving away.

I turn back to the headstone, closing my eyes and imagining him sitting in front of me again. "I miss you, Paul. You were the perfect man. And you made me feel like I was your perfect woman. You were patient with me, and you loved me the way I know I didn't deserve to be loved. I just wish that I got another chance to see you again, even just once. But I'm paying for my sins now. The accident made me lose my eyesight too. They said that the chances of my vision coming back are basically zero. I'm blind now, Paul. But I'd gladly stay blind, if it means you get to live. God … I don't want to remember you like this. You deserve so much better than this, Paul. And now you're gone because of me," I know my voice is rising, hysterical, but I can't stop it. I need to find a way for Paul to hear me beg for his forgiveness.

"Han, stop!" Brodie interrupts me again. "No one is blaming you for what happened. How the hell can this be your fault? If Paul were alive, you know he won't blame you either. He lov—"

"You don't know what happened between us before the accident. He *hated* me, Brodie. What if his last thoughts before he passed was that he *hated* me for betraying him?" My voice trails, and an uncontrollable surge of grief takes over me once again.

"What do you mean by that?"

I shake my head, "We got into a fight. I … I fucked up."

"Han," Brodie kneels beside me, his arm around my shoulders. But I shrug them off.

I refuse to elaborate. I can't afford to have my brother despise me as well. I am the villain in this story. I caused this fatal clusterfuck, so I cannot justify being consoled in any way.

"What ... what does his epitaph say?" I croak out, my fingertips feeling every ridge and curved lines, trying desperately to feel a letter, a symbol ... something, after his name. I'm still learning how to figure things out with my fingers and right now, I can't seem to figure this one out.

"It has his date of birth, and um, the date he died. But you know that date already," he pauses for a moment, and I close my eyes, trying to hold the tears that have been flowing since my outburst.

"There is also a small inscription. It says: *Gone far too soon, but loved forever. Heaven earned another angel.*"

"That's beautiful," I whisper.

"Yeah, it is. There's also a cross and flowers on the side," Brodie adds.

Without thinking, I reach for the headstone, and I hug it tight, eyes still closed, forcing myself to think of all our happiest memories, hoping I can somehow show Paul what we had. Because no matter what happened in the end, I loved him, and will always love him. Then, I place the CD I've been clutching so tightly, and I lean it against his headstone. My fingertips are back on the epitaph. I want to feel the raised letters that spell his name again.

"You'll always be my Dear Mister, Paul. You *will* be loved forever ... not just by your family, but also by me. No matter how bad we left things, please know that I will always, always love you. You are a big part of me, Paul, and I will do whatever it takes to honour you and your legacy." I take a few shaky breaths, preparing myself for what I'm about to say next.

"But Paul, I need to try to move on now. And I hope that in time, you'll eventually learn to forgive me, just as I'll have to learn to eventually forgive myself."

With one lingering kiss on the cold, smooth stone, I stand right back up, unsure but somewhat ready to take a hopeful step towards healing.

The drive to the community centre feels like the longest half an hour of my life, especially when you cannot escape from your damn

70

thoughts by distracting yourself with the view from outside. Brodie switches on the radio to fill the silence that has taken over the car since we left the cemetery. I closed my eyes earlier and pretended to sleep. It is the last thing I want to do, but I'm just not open to any form of conversation.

I'm still pretend-sleeping when Atticus's song, "Songbird," starts playing on the radio. Apparently, according to the DJ, it remains at number one for four consecutive weeks now.

Woo-freakin-hoo.

I know the song well. I know the song too damn well. So every time I hear it at home, I switch stations or just switch off the radio altogether. But because I'm pretending to sleep, I can't just press the car player's button to switch it off.

Eventually, the car slows down to a stop, and Brodie starts nudging my shoulder to wake me up.

"Hey, sleepyhead. We're here."

I slowly shift my position, faking a yawn as I stretch my arms out.

"Ready?" Brodie asks.

"I don't know if I'm ready. All I know is that I'm here now," I mumble.

Brodie sighs before opening his car door. After a few seconds, my door is open, and he helps me out, offering his arm to guide me inside.

The old, musty smell is familiar as we enter the hall. I remember this place well, having done after-school activities and attending birthday parties in here when I was a little girl.

Who knew that something as depressing as a grief support group meeting can happen in the same place as something so joyous and innocent as a children's birthday party?

The world is ironically fucked up like that.

"There are some snacks here, Han," Brodie changes direction and starts walking to what seems like the right side. "Want something?"

I shake my head. "No, thanks. Not really in the mood to stuff my face before I have to talk to a bunch of strangers about Paul's death."

"Suit yourself," Brodie answers, and starts walking me forward again.

71

"Hannah?" another voice calls my name, and I hear soft footsteps on the hardwood floor, growing closer. "It's Nicki. Oh, wow you made it," she says enthusiastically.

"Is it just me, or do you sound a little too excited to see me in here?" I ask, raising my brows.

"Oh, I'm … I'm just glad you're giving this a chance," Nicki answers, and I can't help but note the embarrassment in her voice.

"Sorry, I was being sarcastic and that was uncalled for," I say, as I reach out for her hand. She helps me out and takes mine instead.

"That's okay. It was the same with me on my first day here. But it'll get better. Eventually, you start looking forward to it, surprisingly enough."

I don't know if I'll ever look forward to this, but I just nod instead.

"Well, it looks like you're in capable hands. I'll come back in an hour, yes?"

I hesitate before nodding back, whispering, "Earlier would be great … you know, just in case."

"You said you'd give this a chance," he utters in monotone.

"Fine," I grit my teeth. "I love you bro, but I'm kinda hating you right now."

"I love you too, Hannah Banana. And you don't hate me." He plants a kiss on my temple before saying goodbye to both Nicki and me.

"Come, let's go grab some seats." Nicki walks me forward, and it feels kind of awkward holding the hand of someone I barely know.

But I want to take the first step to healing, whether I deserve to or not.

I hear scraping of chairs, which probably means people are getting seated. Then I hear a guy speak. He introduces himself as Gary, the moderator of the group. He thanks everyone for coming, saying that he's happy to see new faces with the familiar ones.

Then he tells us about his experience of losing someone. A drunk driver killed his own daughter as she was crossing the street. She was on the way to the beach with her friends, and they were just at the crossing waiting for the pedestrian light to turn green. Most of her friends couldn't be bothered waiting, so they made it across by running from one end to the other when the traffic got lighter. But she was always cautious, and she decided to wait until it was her turn to cross. She had the right of way, crossing when the green light appeared. But drunk drivers can't differentiate right from wrong, and apparently this one had a blood alcohol level of 0.140, a damn high level, considering it was just around midday. He speeds through the red light and crosses the intersection, running her over and killing her instantly.

He didn't even stop.

It was a case of hit and run.

She died at a very young age of thirteen.

The police eventually captured the driver through traffic and CCTV cameras, but the driver's arrest and subsequent conviction didn't change anything. His daughter was dead, and she's never coming back.

But what truly shocked me the most was that he forgave the driver.

Yes, what that irresponsible driver did, caused the life of Gary's daughter, but according to him, it became easier for him to deal with the loss by being at peace with the cause. Holding onto her daughter with anger won't bring her back. But through forgiveness, Gary and his wife were able to finally let go of the crippling pain from losing her. They held on to the happy memories instead. They celebrated the life she lived, knowing that this is what would give their daughter peace as well … seeing her parents happy and living their lives once again.

I don't know how many times Gary had told his story, but he's either crazy or he truly wants to help others survive their loss, because I'm sure it's never easy reliving the whole experience over and over again, just to be able to show the rest of the support group that if he can move forward, so can we.

I chew hard on my lower lip. I know how hard it was to forgive the person who caused his daughter's death. But it seems like as soon as they did, it helped him and his wife move on with their lives.

But what if the person who suffered the loss was the main reason why that person died in the first place? If I forgive myself, will I find my own peace as well?

Will that be what Paul wants?

There was no clapping after Gary had finished retelling his story, but only murmurs of positive reinforcements from the rest of the group.

"So, does anyone want to start?" Gary asks the group.

There's a slight pause amongst the group. But then I find myself raising my hand, "Um, I'd like to start."

"Wow. That was ... thank you ... for sharing," Nicki says as soon as the session is finished, placing her hand over mine, which is currently gripping her arm for guidance.

Wow, indeed. I can't believe I spoke up. I can't believe I opened my mouth and my voice came out, forming words with clarity that even I think is quite surprising. I never expected to cry, but I did. But then again, I never expected to speak up anyway, but I did. It's just that for some reason, knowing that I'm in a group that share similar stories of grief, loss, and remorse made me more comfortable to speak up.

I opened up and told the group my story. Not everything, but just the core, the parts that kept repeating in my head. People listened, and they made reverberations of sympathy, and they spoke words of support and encouragement. But God, I've never been thankful that I'm blind until then. Hearing them sympathise and relate is one thing, but seeing their reactions to my experience would be harder for me to handle. It's human nature to judge people in our own little ways. It's just who we are no matter how much we protest against it.

But opening up felt liberating.

I can't believe I did it.

"I thought I better speak up before I start overthinking it and chickening out," I answer, shrugging.

"Well, I'm glad you did. Maybe if you came here before you were ready, your first session might not have gone so well."

"Maybe," I shrug, answering softly.

I didn't even think about that.

"Let me walk you out. Maybe your brother's already here."

"Okay. Oh, hey, thanks for being there. It's nice, you know, having someone familiar with me," I tell her, feeling a little embarrassed. I never had to thank anyone for being there for me. I could always count on my old friends to be there for me always.

Until I drove them away, that is.

I hope it's not too late though. I hope that in time, they're still willing to be my friends.

But this leads me to wonder why the hell Nicki didn't leave with the rest? "Hey, um, hope you don't mind me asking, but how come you stayed here? Why aren't you pursuing a degree somewhere?"

"Well … my dad used to run a business … I'm not sure if you've heard it … Colt's Corner?"

"Oh my God, Colt's is your father's? Of course he is, duh! I love that café! I used to go there a lot."

"Yeah? That's good to know. Well, even when I was younger, I used to help Dad out, and he taught me how to run the place. But I was usually at the back, in the kitchen, you know, because I love to cook."

I smile, now remembering how tiny and skinny she was. Who would've known she loved cooking from her physique?

"Anyway," she continues, "when he died, my mum considered selling the café. She didn't really get involved with the business because she was running the household, so she thought selling was for the best. But I refused, like full-on refused. I told her I could run it. Dad showed me how, and it would be like doing it with my eyes closed … oh sorry, I mean—"

I laugh out aloud. Seriously, she's cute. "It's okay, please continue."

"Mum said she'd give me three months to run it. She helped with the money matters, but it was mostly up to me. Three months became four, and now we're getting closer to six months, and the café is still going strong. The locals make it easy for me to run the café because they keep coming back. I think it's mostly out of pity. But I'll take pity if it means revenue, you know?"

"Wow, so you've totally foregone your tertiary studies to work?"

"For now, yes. Eventually, I'll hire someone to manage when I'm away to study, but I'm happy with my decision to take the reins."

I turn to her, smiling admiringly, "Well, good on you."

"Thanks. Oh, I can see a car driving up. It might be Brodie coming up the road. Nice car, by the way. Would you like me to wait with you?"

"He must be driving Dad's car. But it's cool. You don't have to wait. Thanks for letting us know about this group. It was … today was an eye-opener." She sucks in her breath, and that's when I realise the unintended pun.

"Ah, I stepped into that one, didn't I?" I smile, shaking my head.

"You sure did," she giggles. "I'm gonna help with the cleaning up inside. Maybe you can come over to Colt's when you get a chance."

"Well, I suppose I can fit it in my super busy social schedule," I answer dryly.

She giggles again, "Your sense of humour still kicks ass, just like in school. Well … I gotta go now. Hey, um, do you mind if I gave you a hug?"

Her request surprises me, but I smile and raise my free arm as in invitation.

She hugs me first. "You were so brave in there. And your strength was inspiring. You'll get through this. I know you can. And when that time comes, you *will* move on."

I kept my composure when I finally spoke up about my grief on Paul's death, but what Nicki said, hit me in the kindest, yet most painful way.

My life went from being perfect to shattering into unfixable pieces, just like that. Paul lost his life because of me. How the hell can I possible move on from that?

And yet this person believes that I can.

This really nice girl from my former high school believes it.

Even my family believes it. They keep telling me so, even if I refuse to listen.

Maybe *I* really need to start believing it.

I wipe my tears as quickly as I can before we pull away. After a quick sniff, I manage a small laugh before saying, "Thanks. I hope so too."

"I *know* so, Hannah. Oh, and by the way, there's a bench right behind us if you want to sit down."

"Thanks, but Brodie will be here shortly, so I'll just stand," we loosen our hold on each other before saying our goodbyes.

I'm standing alone for a few seconds before I sense someone approaching.

"Brodie? Thanks for coming before the session ends like I asked you to … dipshit!" I tell him with all the sarcasm I can muster. Then I raise my hand so he can take it in his, but as soon as his hand touches mine, the strong jolt of electricity I feel is all it takes for me to figure out he's not my dipshit brother.

Atticus.

"No! What the fuck?" I shake his hand off of mine.

"It's Atticus, Han. You don't have to panic."

"Oh, really? No way!" I retort sarcastically, "Where the fuck is Brodie?"

"You knew it was me? You ... you still feel it too?"

Oh shit. He can't know he still affects me like this.

"I can smell your stink from here."

"Hannah."

"What *the fuck,* are you doing here?" I bark out, but he cups his hand over my forearm, and the feel of his fingers on my bare skin is too much.

So I pull away, trying to distance myself. But with the bench behind me, I have nowhere else to go.

His touch should feel like betrayal and lies. It shouldn't make my skin tingle like this. And my heart should most definitely not beat like this.

"I asked you a question, Atticus. What are you doing here? Where's Brodie?" I ask roughly through gritted teeth.

"Your mum accidentally had a big slip down the stairs at your place. Brodie was home, so he took her to the hospital."

My hands cover my mouth, "Oh my God!"

"Don't worry. Brodie said she's fine. He just wants to make sure she didn't damage her knee. Your dad had some court thing, so he couldn't pick you up. Brodie didn't know anyone else who can take you, so," he sighs, "here I am. I'm sure he considered how bad this would seem."

"Well, I'm not getting inside the car with you," I cross my arms, and I stand firmly on the ground.

"I promised your brother that I would drive you home safely."

That makes me laugh, and I make sure it sounds bitter. "And since when do you ever hold on to your promises?"

"Look, okay, I won't touch you if you don't want to, no matter how ridiculous you are being, right now, but can you please just take my arm so I can take you to my car and drive you straight home? You can say whatever you want inside the car, but I am still taking you home," he exhales loudly, and I can just picture him raking his dark blonde hair back in frustration. And he's speaking in a lowered voice, making his voice sound both raspy and gravelly.

I wish he didn't sound like this, because as much as I'm overcome with anger right now, on the inside I'm turning to mush.

Damn him and that sexy voice of his.

"I heard loud voices … is everything oka—oh. Oh, shit. Atticus Foster," Nicki's voice changes from concern to pleasantly surprised.

Of course. He's a freakin' heartthrob.

He was getting this kind of reaction from girls even before he made it big.

I need to be out of here, and away from him, fast.

"Can I ride with you, Nicki? Please say you can take me home?" I ask desperately.

"Uh, well, sure. I just need to finish up. I can leave in ten minutes?"

"Okay," I nod back, "sounds good."

"No. Sorry, Nicki. No offence, but her brother asked *me* to pick her up and to take her home, so that's exactly what I'm doing." I jump out of my skin when I feel his hand on the small of my back. It almost takes my breath away.

So I swipe his arm off.

"Leave me the hell alone!" my voice gets louder, and I forget that there might be other people around us.

"Alright, that's it. I'm sorry you have to see this, Nicki."

And without warning, he wraps his arm around my thighs, bending me over his shoulder, before hoisting me off of my feet.

He's lifted me! He's bloody carrying me up on his shoulder!

He starts walking, and I hear Nicki speak words of protest, but Atticus refuses to stop.

"Let me go, Atticus!" I scream, pounding my fists on his back.

"I will. As soon as we're at the car," he answers calmly, like carrying me over his shoulder, fireman-style, is a usual occurrence.

I hear the bleep of a car's alarm being switched off, followed by the car unlocking. Then, surprisingly true to his word, he stops, and he lets me stand on my feet.

But he's still holding me around my waist.

I don't like that I like it.

Maybe I need to do something about it.

I place my hands on his chest, uncertain fingers curved against his pectorals. I wish I didn't notice that even through the material of his thin, cotton T-shirt, his chest feels harder and more defined. His breathing catches, going shallow as my hands slide up to his neck.

And as much as I want to deny the feeling, it thrills me inwardly to know I can still affect him like this. Then my hands rest on his jaw, and his breathing gets heavier, his chest heaving deeply. I ignore the way his stubbled jaw makes me feel on the inside, trying to push off the memory of how sexy that looks on him.

"Hannah," he whispers, his warm breath tickling my wrists.

And in one quick move, I slap him.

I slap him as hard as someone like me could, thankful my hand actually hits its target.

"Fuck," he mutters. "Okay … okay, I deserved that."

"You deserve a lot worse," I spit back.

I hear him open the car door, and his hand finds its way on the small of my back once again. "Get in," he says curtly, the hand on my back gently nudging me in.

"Get your hands off me, and I will."

"Fine. There!" His hand is off me in a heartbeat, but my stupid body seems to cry out in protest at the loss of his touch.

I hastily get inside his car, noticing the lack of roof. Then I notice the all-leather, bench-style seats. I reach for the dash, feeling its smooth, streamlined fittings.

Is this what I think it is?

I cannot believe it.

"Did you get yourself a sixty-seven Mustang convertible?" I ask in awe, turning to Atticus as soon as I hear him stepping inside.

"You just felt the car and you figured out the exact model?" he asks as he starts the engine and pulls out of the car spot.

I laugh out, "Are you kidding me? This was your dream car. Whenever you had a chance, you told us *why* you wanted this car. You even had photos of this car model in your bedroom …" I pause, unable to continue, as I feel the rush of blood on my cheeks.

"Yeah," he says softly, cutting through the awkward pause, "as soon as I got my first decent royalty cheque, I decided to make this car my first purchase."

"What colour is it? Red? Black? You always seemed to like those colours."

"This was red when I bought it, but I had it custom-painted to blue."

"Why would you do that? You told me before that if you were able to buy this model Mustang, it would either be red or black. Why'd you change your mind?"

79

"Have I told you how beautiful you look, sitting inside my dream car? It's as just how I've always pictured it in my head ... just like how we talked about back then."

Wow, did I just hear what I think he said? I'm completely unprepared for the butterflies fluttering in my stomach because of it.

But he's just distracting me.

He's so damn good at that.

"You didn't answer my question. Why'd you change the colour of this car to blue? Not that I care or anything. I'm just curious."

"I'm entitled to change my mind."

"True. Hey, you changed your mind about us, so this would've been a walk in the park for you," I answer bitterly.

"Wow ..." Atticus whispers after a slight pause. I know that felt like I stabbed him right in the guts with that one. But my heart and my mind sometimes don't agree with each other. And right now, my heart is winning, and it's angry and feeling quite stabby.

He doesn't say anything further, so I speak up instead, "What do you want from me, Atticus? I moved on. You knew I moved on. But then you came back and saw how happy I was, and it pissed you off. So you pursued me again, and almost broke off my relationship with Paul. Then guess the fuck what? You left again! So I'm asking you. What do you want from me, Atticus?"

"I've only ever wanted you, Hannah. Only you." He tried to hold my hand, but I swiftly move my hand away.

"I can't believe I fell for your lies the second time around. Paul actually *loved* me. He wanted a future with me. He didn't get scared, and he didn't run off when things got a little complicated."

"Damn it, Han," he whispers, his voice sounds choked up, "if you only knew ..."

"Knew what, *Tic*? Knew how naïve I was to fall for you? Trust me, I know now. I found out the hard way, remember?"

Atticus lets out a frustrated growl, "I changed the colour of this car to blue because I wanted it to match the colour of your eyes! There, I answered your question, okay?"

A knot starts to form in my throat, "Wait, what? That's ridiculous. You're lying!"

"Am I? Because when I saw this car after it was repainted, I knew I made the right choice. I used to get lost in your eyes, Hannah. Your dark hair and blue eyes haunted my thoughts every single day. Even to this day, nothing's changed. Your eyes are just as beautiful as—"

"Stop it! Just stop," I shout out, raising my hands up to emphasise my point, "*Everything* has changed, Atticus! And you left me. You. Left. Me. Twice. So you don't get to say any of those things to me anymore."

"I know, and no amount of apologies will be enough. But Hannah," he says as I feel his hand close over mine again, and this time I'm powerless to resist, "I just want you to know that leaving you was the hardest decision I've ever had to make. But I had to do it."

Of course, he warned me. I was the stupid one.

I finally find the will to pull my hand away. "And I just want you to know that I don't believe a single word you just said. *Oh, poor Atticus*. All the fame, fortune, and women, obviously must've messed you up real good, haven't they? Please. It's what you've always wanted, isn't it … to be rich and famous? That was obviously more important to you than what we had. And all the while back then, I actually thought you'd wait for me like how we talked about. Instead you got impatient and greedy. That makes you a gigantic asshole in my book."

He sounds like he's about to say something, but immediately stops himself. Instead, he breathes out a curse and slams his hand on the wheel. I knew then that I must have gone too far. Maybe it's a good thing I can't see his reaction. As much as I want to make him feel the same hurt he gave me, I know that seeing his reaction to my cutting words will most likely break my heart too.

We spend the rest of the drive home in awkward silence. Atticus doesn't switch on the radio, which makes it all the more awkward between us. Sometimes I feel my skin tingling, and my heartbeat starts accelerating. I only really get this feeling whenever Atticus looks at me.

I always know that he has his eyes on me by the way my body reacts. I don't even need to see him to confirm it.

Even in those times when I wasn't sure about how Atticus felt about me, there was always that constant force between us—that strong sense of awareness of each other. We didn't need to see each other to be aware that we were in the same room. It was like our attraction for each other became our sixth sense.

I never thought it was something that I missed until now, when it dawns on me that I never had this kind of unexplainable magnetism with Paul.

I just wish I didn't feel this pull with Atticus right now because it's confusing and scaring the hell out of me.

As soon as I feel the car drive up at an angle, I breathe out a sigh of relief, knowing I'm finally home, and Atticus and I can go our separate ways.

"I'm home now, aren't I?" I ask, as I unbuckle my seat belt.

"Yes," he answers.

"Okay ... bye."

With shaky fingers, I open the car door, and step out carefully, ignoring Atticus when he tells me to wait.

Pfft. As if.

After closing the car door, I carefully navigate my way around the car. I'm a little nervous, and my arms are stretched out in front of me, as I curse at myself for not bringing my walking stick. I've never really walked outside of the house on my own, and even though my parents replaced the steps leading to my house into a ramp, I still need to make my own way there.

I am in the middle of saying a silent prayer that I don't stumble and make a fool of myself in front of Atticus, when all of a sudden, I feel myself being lifted off my feet again. I shriek out as Atticus starts walking steadily, his arms holding me securely underneath my legs and against his chest.

"Let me down, Atticus," I cry out, but for some reason, my protest sounds feeble, and my heart is racing way too fast.

"I said let me—"

"No."

"What do you mean, *no*? I don't need your damn help!"

"I'm not doing this for you, Hannah. I'm doing this for me."

"What? You're making no sense." I make an attempt at punching his chest, but his chest feels harder than before, and even back then he was ripped!

And how did my arm end up around his shoulders?

I let go of him and cross both of my arms across my chest.

"I want to help you, Hannah, but you pretend like you don't need it. And I've dreamt of holding you since the last time we ..."

"Shut up and let me go!" I scream out with gritted teeth.

"Well, fuck it. I'm carrying you whether you like it or not."

"This is kidnapping!"

"I'm carrying you to *your own house*."

"You're carrying me against my will!"

I suck in some air as soon as I feel his warm breath against my neck, his lips so close to my ear that he's practically kissing it. "Against your will? I can read how your body reacts when I'm around, Hannah. It's something you know we're both good at."

He halts his steps, and even with the background noise, I can still hear his heart beating strongly, fiercely even.

It matches how fast my own heart is beating right now.

But I'm angry. That's all there is to it.

And then he tilts me in an angle so my feet can touch the ground.

Oh. This is what I wanted, then why do I suddenly feel disappointed?

"Where are your house keys? I can open the door for you."

House keys? Oh, shit! No one's home!

"I don't have a set. Why would I have my own set of keys? Do I look like someone who needs it?" I grab my phone from my purse, stating my brother's name clearly so I can make the call.

"Hannah? Did Atticus pick you up? Where are you?" Brodie asks as soon as he answers the phone.

"How's Mum?"

"She's fine, but her ego's a little bruised. She ran down the stairs, tripped, then fell. We'll be home in an hour or so. She wants to go to the shops first for some groceries, then we'll be home."

I can feel Atticus standing close. The energy between us is making my skin feel prickly. So I turn away from him, and I cup the phone, whispering, "You and I are going to talk later. You're an asswipe, you know that, right? Ask Mum where the spare keys are."

"Oh, shit, I didn't think that far ahead. Hold on …"

In the background, I hear Brodie ask Mum about the keys. Before long, he's back on the phone, "Remember those two large pots with the little plants on top of them? If you're facing the front door, go to the left one, lift the small pot. The spare key's at the bottom of the pot. You still remember the alarm code, right?"

I close my eyes in frustration, "Yes," I answer, "but FYI big brother, my eyes don't work? How am I supposed to do all of that?"

Without asking, Atticus deftly grabs the phone from my hand. "Hey bro, I'm here. I'll help Hannah. What do we need to do?" He's too close again, and his scent, the same one that makes my insides clench, is becoming extremely harder to ignore.

"Okay," he speaks again, "got it. Don't worry, I got her."

I. Got. Her.

Stop it, heart.

Stop getting all giggly.

Remember what he did to you.

My reprimanding is interrupted by Atticus taking my hand to return my phone.

"Stay here," he says firmly, before squeezing my shoulder gently. I hear some rustling, then the sound of ceramic making contact with hardened clay. After a few more seconds, I hear the door opening and finally, the tiny beeps from the alarm code being entered on the keypad.

Then his hand takes mine once again.

And my amnesiac heart gets all giggly again.

Stupid heart.

"Come on, let's go inside," he says, as he leads me inside my own house. As soon as we are, I pull my hand away and start making my well-treaded path towards the kitchen.

"I can't believe my brother trusted you with our alarm code when you're the last person I'd trust. I'm going to make sure that it gets changed as soon as possible," I scoff, "Oh, and you can leave now. You don't need to stay," I make my voice louder as I walk away from him. I don't need him here. I know my way around the house.

But when I hear the door slam, my whole body jumps in surprise, then slumps back down in defeat.

I never thought he'd actually go and leave me here on my own … without even saying goodbye.

Again.

Wow.

Why do I keep allowing myself to feel *anything* for Atticus when he goes and leaves me as soon as he gets the chance?

I'm such a loser.

Literally.

I close my eyes and let out a deep exhale.

"Fuck him," I mutter under my breath.

No. Say it out loud, Hannah, no one's here.

Oh, yeah. That's right. No one else is here.

So I take a deep breath, and I let it rip.

"Fuck you! Fuck you, Atticus! Fuck you, and your stupid guitar, your stupid fame, your stupid money, your whorish groupies, your lame-ass green eyes and how you look at me with them … but must of all, fuck you and the way you keep leaving me! You're an asshole, *Tic*! You're a gigantic love-sucking asshole, and I hope you get a million kinds of STDs from all the stupid sluts you've ever slept with, and it gets so bad that your dick falls off!"

Yes! Mother. Fucking. Yes.

But, oh my goodness!

I never shouted so many swear words in my whole entire life. Ever.

But it surprises me how liberating that feels. And what surprises me even more, as I sniffle and wipe my tears away, is how overtaken I am with all kinds of emotions.

I'm crying a little, laughing a lot, guilty crying and angry laughing at the same time.

I've gone mad.

It's been a roller coaster of a day: from finally visiting Paul and having the guts to apologise to him, being brave enough to share my story with the support group, and letting the whole universe know how Atticus has truly hurt me, is completely and utterly liberating.

I can even feel my whole body tingle because of it.

But now my throat hurts and my head is throbbing.

I overexerted myself and now I might be developing another migraine.

I turn around and reach for the fridge handle, then using my other hand, I carefully feel each bottle cap sitting on the bottom right shelf so I can read each label in Braille until I find the one with the OJ. I carefully pick up the plastic bottle and place it on top of the benchtop right next to the sink before closing the fridge. Then I reach for the cupboard handle behind me and grab one of those unbreakable cups.

Most of our plates and glasses have been changed to unbreakable plastic crockery. I suppose after being responsible for a large number of glass and porcelain breakages, my parents decided to switch to these unbreakable, not to mention the *el-cheapo*, plastic plates and drinking cups for everyday use.

It makes me feel like I'm a preschooler again.

Awesome, right?

I place a drinking cup on the drying section of the sink, then, after twisting the cap off the OJ bottle, I tilt it down while wedging the lip of the cup just underneath the opening of the bottle.

"Need help with that?"

I scream in shock, and my hold on the juice bottle is gone, and it falls in the sink with a thud.

"Oh, shit," he says a little too close. His arm brushes against my belly as he retrieves the bottle from inside the sink, and it makes me jump back from the shock of contact.

Hold on.

Oh no.

Oh. No.

My hands cover my instantly reddened cheeks, and I start backing away, slowly, then, quickly. I have to get out of here, back to my room where I can close him off and the humiliation I'm feeling right now.

He heard my rant.

All this time, Atticus was right there, and he would've heard quite clearly, my expletive-ridden rant about him.

I start to turn away, feeling sick all of a sudden from the knots forming in my stomach. But Atticus grabs my hand, and I feel the surge of embarrassment all over again.

"Let go of me," I choke out, my hand inside his, balling into a fist.

"I won't," Atticus stretches out my curled-up fingers, then places the same cup in my hand. "Here. You wanted a drink, right?"

"I-I …" I shake my head, unable to form words like I ran out of the ability to do so.

"Go on," he whispers back, and I feel him step closer, "drink up."

My throat and my lips suddenly feel dry. So with slightly shaky hands, I take the cup and sip its contents very slowly.

After I'm done, he takes the cup from me while I stand on the same spot, rigid, and in shock.

"You … you were here all along?" I ask him, my voice rough from my now raw feeling throat. "So you heard everything?"

"I couldn't bring myself to interrupt. You were kind of on a roll there."

"Oh my God!" I cry out, cupping my mouth with both hands and knowing my face is now as red as an overripe tomato.

"I thought you left. I heard the door slam shut," I reason out painfully.

"Of course, I shut the door … from the inside. I don't feel comfortable leaving front doors open. That's just inviting trouble."

"But I didn't hear you!"

"It must've been the shoes I'm wearing, I'm not sure. Plus you already concluded I left, so …"

"Oh my God!" I cry out once again covering my face in shame. "I'm sorry."

"Are you saying sorry for what you screamed out? Or sorry I didn't leave?" his voice is surprisingly calm, with no trace of anger in it whatsoever.

I gulp down. "No … I don't know," I answer, my voice still muffled.

"Then don't apologise for it." Atticus is still standing so close that my skin is becoming hyperaware of his closeness.

"I deserved every single word. Though I really, really hope my dick doesn't fall off. I kind of love that part of my body."

"Oh my God!" My skin feels as hot as coals, and my reaction seems to be on auto play.

I don't know what else to say!

Why is Atticus making me feel like this?

Then his hands are touching mine, urging my hands to uncover my face.

And for some reason, I'm letting him do it.

"I fucked it up tremendously between us, didn't I?" Atticus asks softly, his hands still holding mine, his fingers now tangled with mine.

"Yes, you did," I answer shakily, my head bowed.

"I want another chance with you, Hannah," he tells me in a voice full of yearning that it tugs at my heart, unwilling to let go.

But I shake my head, "How many chances do you need? How many times will I let you hurt me?"

I feel the hair on his face brush my temple.

He's so close, his lips touching my cheek.

"I still love you, my little Songbird. I never stopped. "

His breath is warm against my cheek, and I hate that it's getting me distracted from the resentment I'm supposed to feel for him.

I need to remind him how *I* feel.

"You can't say those things to me anymore. Paul showed me what real love is. You, on the other hand, you broke my heart, stomped on it, then rubbed my face in it … twice."

I take my hands back and with all my might, I push him away from me.

"Go home, Atticus. For real this time, please just go."

"No. I'm staying," he sounds determined, and the image of him, with his eyes growing dark with intensity fills my head.

When he wants something, he never stops until he gets it.

And back then, all he wanted was me.

That was, until he decided he wanted fame and fortune more.

Does he expect me to say 'Thank you' now that he's back to wanting me?

"Fine! Stay here, then!" I turn away from him, so I can hide out in my bedroom. I've had enough of him, and the way he continues to affect me.

"Where are you going?" Atticus asks right behind me.

"Fuck you," I cry back.

"Alright, that is it!"

Before I can even have time to respond, he places his hand on my shoulder and spins me around, cupping my face with his hands.

"Atticus, what are you—"

His mouth.

It's on my lips.

Atticus is kissing me.

I try to protest, but the pressure of his lips against mine, muffles my voice.

And I'm just standing here, not pushing him away.

Because at this very moment, every single cell of my body is at a standstill from the shock.

He pauses ever so slightly, like he's waiting for my reprisal.

But then his kiss changes, from hard to gentle, furious to hesitant, as he continues to gauge my reaction.

And yet, I am still stoic.

It's a complete contradiction to what's happening inside of my body. My brain is screaming for me to stop him, but my body is refusing to listen, as is my heart, which is now racing so fast that I can hear the blood rush through my ears.

I feel like a bomb just waiting to detonate.

Then my face does something incomprehensible.

My eyes drop shut, while my lips are starting to open for him.

My body is reacting to Atticus in the way it always has … instinctively.

I hear Atticus whisper my name, and I feel his breath tickling my lips, sending tiny shivers all over my body. I respond by tilting my head up, inviting him closer.

He takes my gesture as an invitation, and he moves one hand from my jaw and takes my hair tie off, letting my dark hair loose. He tangles his fingers in my hair, pulling my head closer. Then I feel the tip of his tongue skim beyond my lips, making me hum as it finds my own.

"God, Hannah," Atticus whispers, "I missed this so damned much."

I'm aware at how my brain is waging a war against my body, telling me how wrong this is on so many levels. But as I feel a thrill running through my entire body, just from hearing those words, I know that my common sense is getting shot down in flames.

I almost forgot how Atticus is a lot taller than I am, so I fist his shirt, pulling him even closer.

It's either this, or I climb him like a tree.

And I'm so close to climbing him right now.

He wraps his arms around me, palms flat against my back, curving my body upwards, our bodies pressed so tightly that I'm sure he can feel my heart beating just as strongly as his own.

My hands are itching to touch his hair. I used to love running my fingers through the smooth, dark blonde strands, and now I wonder if he's cut his hair, or if he's grown it even longer. But just as I'm about to find out, I hear the familiar sound of the front door opening, followed by the sound of two people talking animatedly.

Mum and Brodie!

And just like that, my brain has whooped my heart's ass and is now keeping it under lock and key.

What the hell am I doing kissing Atticus like that? Have I not learned anything?

I break off the kiss, pushing Atticus off with all my might. And judging from the sound of his protest, he's actually surprised by the sudden rejection.

"Don't you ever try to kiss me again, you hear me?" I whisper harshly at him, making a show of wiping my mouth in distaste. Then with my heart still beating too fast to control, I push past him, needing to distance myself from him as far away as possible.

"Guess who's back from the hospital with a massive bruised ego?" Brodie calls out as they join us in the living room.

"Oh, shush, you," Mum answers back, chuckling not long after. I can just imagine her playfully smacking my brother's shoulder, before pinching his cheek like he's still a little boy.

It makes me smile, until I realise how much I want to actually *see* Mum doing that to Brodie.

Ignoring the pain caused by the tightness in my chest and keeping the smile plastered on my face, I remark, "Now I know where I got my clumsiness from."

"Sweetheart, don't listen to your brother. I only fell because I got some news that got me truly excited. But we'll talk about that later," Mum embraces me warmly before kissing my cheek.

"And Atticus, my dear, thank you for keeping Hannah company." Mum lets go of me, and I can imagine her with her arms outstretched, about to hug Atticus. "See? You're a big star now, and yet it doesn't bother you to come out of your way and do us a favour, like picking up my daughter."

"It wasn't a big deal, Mrs. M. When it comes to Hannah, I'd—"

"He was actually about to leave, Mum," I cut him off firmly.

After a moment of awkward silence, he answers back, "Uh, yeah. I better head out. It was good to see you're okay, Mrs. M."

The scent of his cologne, the same one I used to love on him, hits me as closes our distance. I brace myself for what he's about to do next, jumping when I feel his hand on my shoulder.

"Bye, Hannah. It was great catching up. We should definitely do *that* again. Actually you know what? I *insist* that we catch up again. Soon, hopefully."

Then he gives my shoulder not one, but two pats.

Two pats … the type of gesture you give to an acquaintance, or even a pet, before you say goodbye.

What was I expecting anyway? A hug? A kiss?

God, he pisses me off!

Not long after, he takes his lingering hand off me, and then he says his goodbyes to both Mum and Brodie. I hear the door slam shut, just as Brodie announces he's going to the kitchen, leaving Mum and me behind.

Mum grabs hold of my hand, squeezing it gently. "Brodie told me what you did this morning before you went to the support group session. I just want to say I'm bloody proud of you."

Proud ... of me?

I feel like a fraud. How can someone be proud of a fraudulent human being?

I'm suddenly overcome with a strong emotion, an emotion I'm so used to nowadays. And just like that, tears well up in my eyes. But these aren't tears I want to shed because I'm proud of myself.

In fact, it's the complete opposite.

The tears now falling are tears of shame, of guilt, of self-loathing.

I finally found enough courage to visit Paul's final resting place, finally apologising to him in person for causing this tragedy to happen in the first place. Then the group session was my first step in my attempt to move on, to heal.

And then I just undo whatever progress I had by kissing the one person who, albeit unknowingly, initiated the whole chain of events that ended with my boyfriend dead and myself blinded.

Hence the self-loathing ... because as much as I want to blame Atticus, I know that what happened that night, six months ago, was no one else's fault but mine.

This was all on me.

So again, I'm forced to ask the question: If Mum knew about it, would she still be proud of me?

CHAPTER ELEVEN

I love my mum with all my heart, truly I do. But there are times when she can really be taxing.

Like earlier, for example, as soon as Atticus finally left, I wasn't in the mood to talk at all. I was already having a hard time processing what just happened between Atticus and me, so forming words into sentences was not something I was really keen on partaking. But my mum ... she could be very persistent if she wanted to. So I told her everything she needed to know about the group session, but excluded everything else that might result in her blood pressure rising, for good measure.

She also asked me why I was so hard on Atticus, and why I couldn't forgive him in the first place. Okay. That surprised me, not only because she might be aware of what went on between the two of us, but also why it had taken this long for her to ask.

Back then, I liked how Atticus and I were keeping things on the down low. It was our choice to make our family think we weren't together because we both knew that we had an expiration date. So we kept our relationship under wraps, something meant for only between us, complete with sly glances, hands linked under the table, read-between-the-lines jokes, the adrenalin rush from stolen kisses, and him climbing in and out of my window for our secret make-out sessions. It felt like Atticus and I were living in our own little bubble, just floating carelessly with the wind, enjoying the wild ride without outside interference.

But bubbles are fragile, and the possibility of our bubble bursting was a notion we weren't keen on entertaining.

I loved our bubble ... I loved Atticus being in that same bubble with me.

I loved him. And I thought he loved me.

But one day, that bubble burst.

And all because Atticus could no longer stand being in the same bubble as I did.

My heart burst like that bubble.

Stupid, fucking bubble.

Now I hate that bubble. I wish I never allowed myself to be in it in the first place.

And to add more to the drama, I found out that people actually knew that we were together after he left. My brother was especially livid, telling me that I should've known better, that he warned me beforehand, that I shouldn't have been so naïve as to think he'd actually commit to me.

It hurt me at first when Brodie kept his friendship with Atticus. But I had no right to tell him what not to do.

Why would I stop Brodie from being friends with Atticus when I was the stubborn one who refused to heed his warning and continued a relationship with Atticus in the first place?

I didn't plan on committing with anyone for a long while after Atticus left me, but then I met Paul and something about him made me want to give love another chance. He made me see that my brother might actually be right—that maybe I did deserve better.

And I did get better.

But then, sometimes life decides to serve you a big bowl of irony with a whopping side of cruelty.

Because just when I was finally happy with someone whom I knew loved me unconditionally, I did something completely stupid to fuck it up, and I ended up losing everything as a consequence.

My head is beginning to pound, and I can feel blood literally swooshing in my head.

This can't be good.

I have to stop reliving all the shit in my past.

I need to get some rest.

Wiping an escaped tear from my cheek, I leave my nook by the window and drag my feet towards the bed. But just before I hop on, my big toe hits something from underneath.

After getting over the initial sting, I bend down to reach for the culprit.

I have a feeling it's the same culprit that tripped me on the same day Brodie came home.

Since losing my eyesight, it has been a common thing for me to bump into, or to hit something in my path. I can't even imagine how many bruises or cuts I have accumulated over the months. But it isn't the little accidents that hurt me, but the hard fact that this has become a big part of my reality.

It doesn't take me long to figure out what hurt my toe. The feel of the smooth leather and thick stitching instantly gives me a mental picture of exactly what it is.

My stomach clenches as my fingertips find the handle, and without thinking, I hold onto it and pull the whole thing out of my bed.

I remember telling my mum to hide it. Even though I can't see it anymore, somehow, I don't want my brain imagining it in its old spot next to my bed, like where it used to be when my bedroom was still upstairs.

But now, for some reason, I'm pulling the whole thing out, my fingers knowing where to go as they lift up the clasps that keep its content sealed and protected. My heart starts beating excitedly as I lift the lid up, immediately feeling the smooth surface of the body, the neck, all the way up to its head.

Buckley.

My guitar. Yes, my guitar has a name, and his name is as beautiful as he looks, just like the fallen singer who shares his namesake.

Brodie thought it was ridiculous to name my guitar like it was a pet or something.

Atticus, on the other hand, told me that if it helped me connect with the instrument better, then there was nothing wrong with giving it a name, though apparently, it would typically be given a girl's name.

He named his, Betty.

I can't believe I used to get jealous of Betty … how I wished back then that Atticus held me the way he did his acoustic guitar.

But that was none-the-wiser, fifteen-year-old me.

That's why I gave my guitar a boy's name. I did it foolishly in the hopes that Atticus might get jealous too.

He never got jealous.

Like I said, foolish.

But I had Buckley in my arms almost every day.

I thought I'd never play Buckley again when Atticus left me, but Paul inspired me to continue on.

And now he's gone …

I shut my eyes tight as soon as I feel my eyes start to moisten.

Paul would've wanted me to continue playing. He loved hearing me play music. He wouldn't have wanted me to stop.

And if I can just be honest with myself, then I'll accept the fact that I've never been this excited to touch my guitar again.

Holding onto the fret board, I gently lift the whole thing out of its case, folding my legs so I can sit comfortably, before positioning the instrument the way I always had.

Before I knew it, I begin tuning the strings.

My dad bought me this guitar because I wanted to keep up with my brother. Brodie looks so cool whenever he plays. Plus girls who play guitar seem pretty bad-ass as well. But Brodie has a gift, and he is so good. He actually needed just a handful of lessons, and he was already playing like a pro. Not only that, but he plays a mean piano as well.

I'm not, on the other hand, a natural. Even after going to my guitar lessons, the flow just wasn't there. The idea that I wasn't good at it, frustrated me. I was a consistent top five student, and I excelled in sports and the arts.

Maybe that's why I became frustrated. I really, really wanted to be good at playing guitar, and I was getting impatient.

I was so close to accepting that maybe I'd never play guitar the way I wanted to.

That was, until Atticus stepped in.

I shake my head, then I let out a deep breath.

I need to get that man out of my mind, and I know that the thing to do is just to shut out everything and anyone else.

So, like I always used to, I close my eyes, letting out a deep exhale … and then I strum.

CHAPTER TWELVE

Four Years Ago

"So Hannah," Patty annoyingly tries to catch my attention by tapping my shoulder with her pointe finger, "aren't you going to tell us who your brother's new friend is?"

"Huh?" I ask, immediately annoyed by her question.

"You know, that guy who was leaving your house with Brodie the last time Brook and I came over for dinner? I know I've never seen him in school, so he's not from around here. Give me the goss, woman!"

Patty, Brook, and I are at the local shopping centre to watch a movie and to find something to wear for Viv's birthday party. The day has been going well so far, until Patty decides to annoy me with her curiosity.

Since meeting that jerk Atticus for the first time weeks ago, I just refuse to acknowledge his presence each time he's at our place to practise with my brother. It's a good thing that they practise in the shed, which my dad converted into a soundproofed mini studio so that Brodie and his fledgling band can play without disturbing everyone else in the neighbourhood.

My dad tolerates my brother's playing, since he knows he's really good at it. But it doesn't mean he's going to tolerate having the police called by our neighbours because of noise pollution.

Anyway, I used to enjoy watching the band practise and sometimes, I'd take my guitar and I'd play some songs with them. When Atticus started practising with the group, most of the time he would just ignore me. But when he did acknowledge my existence, he would either stare at me with annoyance, or he'd tell a joke at my expense.

I haven't been in that converted shed with Brodie and the boys for over a month now.

"He's just some guy Brodie met while he was busking at the other side of the centre."

"Really? What's his name? I think he's cute. No, hot. Really hot."

Why is Patty so keen? I love her, but right now, she's really starting to piss me off.

"His name's Atticus. But Brodie calls him Tic. Any more questions?"

"Like an insect Tic?" Brook asks, chuckling.

"Yeah, but no *k* at the end. Oh, and FYI, only his *friends* can call him that," I add sarcastically.

Brook squints her eyes at me but doesn't say a thing.

"So what's he doing with Brodie?" Patty continues her interrogation.

I roll my eyes at her, before shrugging, "He plays great guitar and sings pretty well, if you like that tortured, brooding type of sound."

"Oooh, I bet he is, you know, tortured. That's super sexy. I bet he's good at other things too," Patty says with a dreamy look in her eyes that makes me want to throw up my lunch.

"Gross. Don't say shit like that. You don't even know him, and neither do I. To be honest, I don't think he's a band type of a person. He's only close to Brodie but hasn't really connected with the rest of the band. Maybe he's just one gigantic asshole."

Brook sighs, "Why are the hottest guys the biggest assholes?"

I don't answer her question, distracting myself with checking out the clothes in the store we stepped in. I really don't want to waste my breath talking about Atticus anymore. It turns out to be a good thing, since I find a couple of cute dresses that I know would be perfect for the party.

Saturday arrives in no time. We're at Viv's sixteenth birthday party, and it's going off just as she said it would. Though Viv and I aren't a real fit in terms of personality—she's a bit of an entitled bitch, and I don't like entitled bitches—we somehow became friends because her brother Mike plays the drums in the unnamed band my brother formed.

One of the guys from school sneaked in some tequila, and offers me a shot. I shake my head no, but Patty and Brook insist I take at least one shot to loosen up, seeing as they have taken a couple of shots each already. It's not like I haven't tasted alcohol before and enjoyed it. Also, parties like these would always have something to help 'loosen up' someone. But I've always been the designated good girl' though. And by 'good girl,' I mean I don't get shit-faced drunk at parties so people can talk about me the next day. I want to be aware of everything and anything. So, even though I did eventually succumb to the one shot offered to me, I shoo the guy away as soon as I'm done.

"C'mon, let's dance. This is my song, people!" Patty screeches, rising up from the couch with her hands in the air. Judging from her slurred speech, Little Miss Lightweight strikes again.

She pulls me up, just as Brook leads us to the makeshift dance floor near Viv's swimming pool. Her family hired a DJ, one of the best ones in the Central Coast, and the music is admittedly too hard to resist.

We're dancing, giggling, showing off intentional god-awful moves, when three guys from our school approach us. Patty seems to know one of the guys, Stan, who focuses on her. Brook and I sneak a wink. I've seen this guy staring at Patty before, and it looks like he's finally found the guts to come up to her.

Two of his friends start dancing with Brook and me. The guy I'm dancing with is Mal, who's a bit on the short side, with spiky hair. Brook's dance partner, on the other hand, is tall and lanky. But I must admit, they can dance, and quite well too, like b-boy style cool. Eventually though, Brook and I end up just standing there, watching with the rest of the guests, and cheering them on when our supposed partners begin an impromptu 'battle.'

Having enough of the show, I excuse myself to look for some food. I've only had a soda and a shot of tequila, and my stomach is beginning to act up from hunger. I finally manage to find a table laden with enough fancy finger foods to feed an army, or in this case, a big group of teenagers.

I grab myself a chicken satay on a stick, presented so nicely in a skewer stick and squared banana leaf. The chicken already has peanut sauce on it, which I seem to have forgotten, as a good portion of the said sauce is now on the bodice of my brand-new, light blue, vintage-style dress.

Shit.

Does this stain?

Shit!

I look around for some serviettes, but just as I find the last two on a holder, a much bigger hand grabs them before I do.

Shit!

"You don't need two of those, you kn—" I turn to the jerk who took my serviettes so I can give him a piece of my mind, but I end up almost choking on the chicken I'm chewing.

"Well, if it isn't Brodie's charming little sister, Hannah."

Blood rushes up to my head, and I feel my cheeks burn.

He's the last person I want to see, let alone while in the middle of an embarrassing clothing situation.

Was he even invited? He doesn't even go to the same school as we do.

He must be gate crashing the party.

Ugh, figures.

I roll my eyes at him, and I try to walk off, hoping to go around him. He blocks my way. I try his other side, but he sidesteps me.

"What the hell? Let me through, Atticus!"

"I can't let you walk away without looking presentable."

"What?" I look up at him with that smug smile of his, anger building up inside of me.

Then he produces the serviettes, "Here, have these."

I stare down at the two pieces of serviettes he's holding, unsure if I even want to take them. I don't want him to think he's helping me out, or that I'll owe him.

"Are you going to take these or not? Or do you want me to wipe the sauce off myself?" He raises the serviettes closer to my chest, a smirk on his face.

Is he serious?

I swipe his hand away, and the serviettes fall on the floor. "Don't even try," I warn him, giving him the hardest look I can muster.

Using his surprise at my response, I attempt to walk around him again. I need to get away from him … like, as far away from him as I can.

"Wait," he finally says.

And then he's touching my hand.

His fingers are gripping my own fingers.

It makes me gasp from the shock. Not just from Atticus holding my hand, but also from the way my body is reacting from the touch.

This is like nothing I've ever felt. My skin is tingly, and my heart feels like it stops beating for a long minute.

Is this even normal? This can't be normal, right?

My eyes drift down to our linked fingers. For some reason, I can't seem to untangle myself from him. My eyes travel upwards, and I catch him staring at our hands too.

And now those eyes are staring back at me.

He's not cute. Don't think he's cute, Hannah.

Who am I kidding? Patty's right. He's freakin' hot!

Oh God, please don't look at me like that, Atticus.

"Ah, there you are!" Viv's flirty singsong voice cuts through the tension, and whatever the hell you call what just happened between Atticus and I is thankfully broken.

I pull my hand away first.

He doesn't protest.

But he's still staring at me, and just like when our hands were linked, my skin starts to feel prickly all over again.

He opens his mouth to say something just as Viv steps in, between us. She's not even facing me, she's facing Atticus, effectively becoming a wall separating me from my nemesis.

"There you are!" Viv wraps her arms around Atticus's shoulders in greeting, and a sudden urge to throw up overcomes me. But I'm still standing still, my feet superglued on the floor.

Viv turns to see me still there, and she doesn't even attempt to mask her annoyance, like I'm disturbing her time with Atticus, "Hey, Hannah, I think Patty and Brook are looking for you."

"Okay, thanks for letting me know," I answer back too cheerfully.

I'm sure they aren't looking for me. But I take that as a very blatant cue to leave.

And as I turn to leave, I can feel eyes on me. And judging from the way the tiny hairs on my arms and the back of my neck are rising, I know exactly whose eyes they belong to.

I breathe a sigh of relief as soon as I find the closest bathroom. I lock myself inside, and I lean against the door, only noticing that I've been breathing heavily like I just came from a triathlon.

So, judging from Viv's overzealous welcome, Atticus is definitely invited to the party.

But why would he be invited to this party? He's probably eighteen like Brodie, so this isn't exactly his age group. Unless he's with Viv …

Just stop, Hannah!

Stop thinking about Atticus, and his reasons for being here, and ... and the way he makes me feel giddy with his staring and touching ...

"Aargh! Get a fuckin' grip, Hannah!" I growl under my breath, my hands fisted as I shake them in frustration.

I push myself off the door and walk a few steps to where the sink is. I turn on the tap, and using my fingers, I try to wipe off the satay residue from my bodice, noticing a couple of drops fell on my chest.

And to think, Atticus was about to wipe it off! He probably just wanted to cop a feel!

Or what if he was just teasing me, trying to see how far I'd let him go?

Shaking my head at how close I was to letting him win, I roughly wipe off the sauce drops on my skin, before checking myself in the mirror.

I mean, *hello*, I don't even have big boobs, why would he want to touch them? Now Viv's boobs, on the other hand, developed early, and they are ginormous for her age. She knows they'll serve her well, judging from the stares she gets from most of the guys at school. And if she weren't so scary, other girls might actually try to call her out for flaunting them so much.

I'm sure Atticus wouldn't mind wiping sauce out of those boobs.

Damn it! Stop thinking about him!

The song from outside, though dulled down from being inside the bathroom, thankfully distracts me. They're playing my favourite song, an oldie but a goodie, "Crazy in Love" by the Queen B herself. It's probably the only song I've perfected playing on the guitar, mostly because the acoustic chords are easy. But I only really play at home and only sing when I know I'm alone. Compared with my brother, or even Atticus, my voice is kind of weak. I can't afford the humiliation if people start laughing at my singing voice. So seeing as I'm all alone in the bathroom and with the volume of the song up, I begin to sing along with it, trying in vain to copy Beyonce's moves in the music video. At least I can laugh at myself for looking ridiculous.

Queen B can keep her crown. I'm definitely no threat here.

After the song is finished, I check myself in the mirror one last time, not caring anymore if I have an oily spot on my blue vintage-looking skater dress.

All I need to do when I leave this bathroom is be on the other side from where Atticus would be, and I'll be able to enjoy the party.

There seems to be a lull in-between songs, so without thinking, I start singing my cover version of the same song under my breath while washing my hands, continuing on as I dry them off, up until the time I open the bathroom door. But I stop mid-chorus, screeching in shock.

Atticus is leaning by the wall right next to the bathroom door with his arms and legs crossed, a mild surprise on his face.

"Fuck, Atticus! Why do you keep on doing that?"

He regards me with amusement, "Okay, I'm just gonna ignore *that* reaction. Has anybody told you that you have an amazing singing voice? Sweet, but has grit. It's actually beautiful, Hannah. Who'd ever think that a voice like that comes from this?" He waves a hand from my head to my toes, looking like he's about to break into laughter.

My eyes widen in shock, and my mouth is gaping open. But I can't utter a single word.

From what, Atticus?

He seemed so sincere, that for a second there, I actually felt my heart skip a beat.

But then again, this *is* Atticus.

He's always like this with me—ignoring me one day, insulting me the next.

When it comes to me, he's just mean.

A damn bully.

This is just like him to find a reason to make fun of me, to mock me.

It bloody hurts.

And just when I thought I can't embarrass myself even further in front of him, the very last thing I want him to see happens.

My eyes well up, my throat chokes up, and even when I shut my eyes to stem the tears from flowing down, one escapes, then two.

I swiftly wipe them off, and I swallow hard, telling myself firmly to not give him the satisfaction of seeing my tears.

When I finally have the guts to look him in the eye, he surprises me even more.

He actually seems concerned … surprised, but concerned.

"Uh, I'm sorry, Hannah. I didn't mean to—"

"What did I ever do to you, Atticus?"

He seems puzzled.

Is he serious?

"What did I do to you to make you want to make fun of me like this? You don't even know me. Not that you even bothered to," I try to reign in the shakiness of my voice, but I'm still choked up, and I'm putting all my energy into not showing him another tear again.

He opens his mouth, but I cut him off, "Is it because you think that since I'm Brodie's little sister, then it must mean I should be treated like I'm some annoying runt? Well, you don't know me. But I know you. You're a bully, Atticus. A big bu—"

All of a sudden he cups the side of my face and leans forward.

What the?

And now he's kissing me.

Oh dear God.

His lips are pressing against mine. His lips. On mine. He pulls back, but only barely, and I'm too much in shock to move away. My widened eyes are staring right into his green, soulful ones. I never realised how long and thick his lashes are, and at the risk of sounding like a cliché, my insides are turning into liquid goo when I look into those eyes. His breathing seems laboured as he slightly pulls away, and I can't help but stare down at his full, bowed lips, the same lips and the same dimple that probably gave the sexiest smiles to the girls he flirted with but never directed at me. Now those same lips are literally a breath away from me. I lick my lips in silent yearning, hoping that Atticus will give me another taste.

"I'm not a bully," he speaks in whispers. But I'm too mesmerised by his lips, his voice, his effect on my body, both inside and out, that I answer by tilting my head up and letting my lips touch his.

"Fuck it," Atticus groans as he meets my need with his own, crushing my mouth and devouring me, plunging his tongue and tasting me like a man deprived and hungered for days.

That's when whatever control I have left, leaves me, and I'm kissing him back, eyes closed, heightening my other senses—the way he smells like soap and ocean combined, the sound of his moaning when I pull his lower lip to suck it gently, how delicious he tastes when my tongue dances with his own, the way my skin feels like every single pore is emitting tiny little fireworks.

This is like … I can't even think of any conceivable way to describe this, except it's primal, hungry, and I'm afraid to say it, possibly borderline addictive.

How can someone who loathes me the way he does, kiss me the way he does?

But that's just it. This is Atticus. My big brother's close friend. He's older, and he's a jerk towards me. And now I'm kissing him in a party where there's a chance we'll get caught.

What if Brodie catches us? Is he even here?

He'll break off his friendship with Atticus, then Brodie will just hate me for it.

Shit! My own brother will hate *me*!

This is wrong on so many levels.

Or maybe that just adds to the thrill. Maybe that's the reason why this feels so damn amazing.

But, no.

Just, no.

This isn't like me at all.

So I break off our kiss, ignoring the way my body seems to scream obscenities at me. And with whatever strength I have left, I push Atticus off and away from me.

He's breathing heavily, I'm breathing heavily.

He looks surprised, I'm beyond shocked.

He's staring at my lips with his brows knitted together, and I can't stop staring at him, staring at me.

He leans forward without warning and tries to kiss me again, but I'm quicker now, and I push him back. I push him back so hard that he loses balance and holds on to the wall for support.

"Don't you do that ever again," I tell him with gritted teeth, stepping back a few steps to increase our distance apart.

"Are you sure about that?" Atticus asks, his eyes now boring against mine, like he's trying to read my mind.

And now I'm questioning my decision.

Am I really sure? That kiss was ...

Then a slow, sly smile rises from his mouth.

That self-satisfied, smug grin of his is back.

He's been playing me all along, and I fell for it.

"*Ugh*, you really are an asshole!" I yell out at him before stomping away as fast as my feet can take me. I don't even care if I feel his eyes on me. All I know is that I need to be as far away from that demon seed as I possibly can.

I eventually find my friends, and they are waving at me to sit next to them. I notice the DJ onstage is gone, and now a drum kit, amplifiers, and microphones are being set up.

Then I see familiar faces onstage: Brodie setting up front and centre, Mike on the drums, Shane and Derek on bass and guitar respectively.

What? My brother's band is playing here?

"Did you know about this?" Brook asks.

I shake my head, "No. This must be the surprise Viv was telling us about. Brodie didn't even mention it."

I notice another microphone stand being set up beside my brother's. That's when my heart starts to thud a little faster.

Oh no.

And there he is, walking up the stage, acoustic guitar on hand.

Atticus *fucking* Foster.

And now I'm torn. Torn between wanting to be here to watch my brother's first ever 'live' show, and wanting to leave because of the asshat newcomer in their band.

"Girl, you look like you want to kill the new guy," Brook whispers to me. "It's either that or you want to make out with him."

How did she ... am I that obvious?

I feel my cheeks warm up, but I throw Brook an evil eye, and she shrugs innocently at me.

Well, guess what, *Tic*? I'm staying. I'm holding my ground. I am invited to this party, and people in this party know who I am. He can play his guitar and sing like he's supposed to, then he can leave, and while he does, I'm going to show him how much he sucks.

We're sitting very close to the stage, at one of those cocktail tables with bar stools. He will definitely see me.

While tuning his guitar, Atticus raises his head and finds me at once. I make a show of crossing my arms, my chin up high ready for a challenge.

It's on Atticus, and you're going to lose.

He raises his brows, then turns to the rest of the guys and whispers something to them. They look at him quizzically, and after a few more words from Atticus, they eventually seem to agree with whatever he's saying.

Brodie then approaches the mic, "Good evening, everyone. Most of you may have seen us around. But if not, my name's Brodie, and I'm lead vocals and guitar, Shane is on bass, Derek's on guitar and piano, and that crazy bloke behind the drum set is Viv's brother, Mike. She asked her brother if we could play some songs for her party. And because Viv apparently gets what she wants, plus she said she'll pay us, we agreed." That makes the guests laugh, even I let out a chuckle.

"We also have a great addition to our band. This fella right here is Atticus Foster. He'll be huge one day, mark my words. But so will we, so just remember, you saw us live here first!" More applause and nonsensical cheering ensues.

"We'll be playing a mix of covers and originals. Our first song is an original, and it's called "Amplify." Oh, and by the way … We. Are. Halcyon!" And they're off, playing a song I've heard them practise so many times and bringing everyone to their feet. It's a great song to start with, and everyone is screaming and dancing like crazy—me, included.

Halcyon. I like. I better make sure to tell the band.

A guy I know from class, Charlie, approaches me, and gives me a quick hug, congratulating me on Brodie's band kicking ass onstage. He hangs around, and we start chatting about random shit. Once in a while, he has to lean a little closer to hear me speak, since we're quite close to the speakers.

As I'm watching my big brother play onstage for the first time, I can't help but feel a tinge of pride. Sure it's a party gig, but it's a start. I know I need to lock this moment in. So I grab my phone, and I take several photos of him and his band in action. The whole band is in their element, their attention either on the instrument they're playing, or they're feeding off the crowd's reactions.

I love the photos so much that I show the girls, even Charlie, who asks if I can put the photos up on Facebook so he can check them out again later.

When I finally put the phone down, I'm startled to see that out of all the members of the band, one of them is solely focused on me.

Atticus is staring right at me. Eyes intense … hard … angry? I don't know what his problem is. Does he not want me to take his photos?

The song ends, and I break the stare, sitting back on the stool and sipping my drink nonchalantly and ignoring Atticus.

Patty sneaks in beside me, tapping me on the shoulder and whispering, "Was it just me, or was Atticus just eye-fucking you the whole freaking time?"

I turn to her in shock, "What? Oh, don't even … that asshole hates my guts as much as I hate his!"

Thankfully, Halcyon continues to play on, and they deliver a good mix of covers and originals. I try to make sure that my focus is on my brother or my friends, and not on the boy playing beside him, no matter how hot he does look onstage, or the way he keeps looking in my direction.

Because if I do look at him, I'll just be taken back to that kiss he stole … the same kiss I wish I didn't enjoy so much.

"Hey folks," they just finished another song, and now Atticus is speaking.

What does he want to say now? And why do my guts feel this twisted?

"I just want to say, first of all, happy birthday, Viv, and thank you everyone for being amazing. For our last song, how about we slow it down a notch?" I hear some girls screaming how much they love Atticus, and I can't help but roll my eyes straight after.

Atticus winks in their direction, and I roll my eyes again.

Then he continues, "Let's see if you can figure this out." He smiles at the crowd, his dimple in full view, and I swear I hear some girls scream some shit that any girl our age shouldn't.

Seriously?

You wanna have his baby?

What is this, an MTV reality show?

Why those idiotic catcalls piss me off is beyond me.

Shouldn't I be pleased that there are other girls vying for Atticus's attention so he can finally stop torturing me?

Atticus looks at the rest of his bandmates, then nods. He steps closer to the mic, then strums once. The crowd cheers on as he strums the same note again, strumming continuously until I begin to recognize what he's playing.

Suddenly, I can hear a series of fast beats. But Mike isn't playing the drums. I place my hand on my chest and realise that it's actually from the way my heart feels like it's beating out of my chest.

Why is he doing this? Why is he playing another sick joke on me?

My chest is heaving up and down, panic slowly morphing into anger. And with his eyes now fixed on me, he starts singing the first verse.

He is such ... a ... jerk.

"I *cannot* believe he's singing "Crazy in Love" with just an acoustic guitar! He just made that song sexy. That's it. I'm buying his album when it drops."

But I ignore Patty's comments.

Atticus did this on purpose.

I can't believe he's continuing to torment me.

Is he just plain cruel?

Well, I'm not going to hang around anymore. He can take "Crazy in Love" and shove it up his ass.

I turn to both of my friends, "Hey girls, I'm sorry but I think I'll go home. I'm feeling pretty tired, and I think I ate some bad chicken."

They sound off their protests, but I give each of them a quick peck on the cheek and a tight hug, telling them I'll call tomorrow. I'm about to walk away when I remember Charlie's still standing next to me. I'm about to tell him I'm leaving when an idea hits me.

I turn to the stage, and just as I thought, Atticus's eyes are back on me, his eyes betraying the smugness I loathe.

Good.

Before I can stop myself, I pull Charlie down to me for a kiss. It takes him by surprise, hence the sloppiness of it all. This kiss, however, is not meant to be anything else but for a show.

And just as soon as I kiss him, I pull away, leaving him even more stunned. And for a tiny second, I actually feel bad for using him as a pawn.

But the need to piss Atticus off has overtaken me. I don't even look back at the stage to see Atticus's reaction anymore. I leave the party and walk the two blocks home, satisfied that I, Hannah Mackenzie, finally has the last laugh.

CHAPTER THIRTEEN

The next day, after a night of unwanted dreams about Atticus and the bewildering events of last night, I decide to clear my mind with a morning surf before breakfast.

I look out my bedroom window, where I'm lucky enough to have a decent view of the ocean. The condition seems perfect for catching a few good waves, so I quickly splash on some sunscreen, put on my wet suit, run down the steps, and yell out to whoever's awake that I'll be gone surfing. Then I grab my board and make a dash out of the house before Mum chases after me.

I can't help but smile as I breathe in the fresh, salty air, feeling exhilarated as I watch the waves pounding the coast. There are already a handful of surfers in the water, so I waste no time in getting in on the action.

After a couple of good runs, I notice a swell that looks too good to pass up. So I paddle as quickly as I can before someone claims it. I'm only a few seconds into riding, when something goes wrong. A rogue wave makes me lose my balance, landing me head-first down the pit. I try to swim back up, but another wave pounces over me, dragging me further down. My chest is beginning to feel like it's burning, like it's on fire, the desperation to breathe becoming a desperate need. With whatever power I have on my legs, I push myself up until I finally reach the surface, trying desperately to hold onto my board, but failing miserably. From my peripheral vision, I see another wave about to pummel down on me, and with no energy left, I know I have to bear the brunt of it.

Just then, I feel two strong hands lifting me up and placing me on top of my board.

"Hold on," he barks, and I do what he says. I'm too exhausted to turn and see who it is, and my eyes are hurting from the prolonged sting of salty water. Then I feel myself being pushed forward, with him lying just over my straightened legs as he paddles us to safety.

He jumps off as soon as we reach calmer waters, and I manage to open my eyes in a squint, just as he's wading beside me.

The first thing I see is dark blonde hair, possibly darker from being wet, and framed in a halo from the brightness of the morning sun. Though I can barely see his face, for me, he seems like an angel—my guardian angel—and I'm not even sure if what is happening is for real, or if I'm just imagining this. But there's a certain calm that envelops me, like I'm truly in safe hands.

Did I drown to death, or was I actually saved? Is he a lifesaver? Must be.

"Am I …" I start to ask. But he shushes me gently as he finally nudges my board to the shore. He's kneeling beside me, not leaving my side, pulling my tangled mass of hair away from my face.

"You scared the hell out of me out there, Hannah," he whispers, relief evident in his voice.

He knows my name? Is he someone I know?

Though still weak, I try to push myself up, with him offering his arms as some form of leverage.

And these arms are muscular, hard, and connected to shoulders that are equally robust. What looks like a tattoo of some sort appears to adorn his right arm, but I can barely make out the shape from my vantage point.

He shifts his position, and that's when his face finally comes to light.

Atticus.

And suddenly I'm overcome with a mixture of different emotions. I feel elated that he was the one who pulled me out of the dangerous undertow. But I also feel embarrassed at my show of weakness and trepidation because I'm afraid he might use this incident as ammunition against me.

My chest feels tight again, and I'm feeling totally breathless … but for a completely different reason.

"You … did that? You saved me?" I barely whisper to him, not realising that my hands are still grasping his arms. "Thank you. I-I don't know what else to say."

He brushes his fingertips against my cheek as he regards me with tenderness I've never seen coming from him. "You don't need to say anything. It was just sheer luck that I was surfing here with a couple of friends this morning. I saw you when you got in the water. No one else took that wave for a reason, Hannah. I'm just relieved that you're okay."

"Oh. Don't let me keep you. By all means, you can go back in there."

He scoffs, "I'm not leaving you, and I'm not gonna let you go back in there, at least not for today."

I turn away, doing my best to ignore the way my heart skipped a beat just then.

"So you don't have any smart ass remark to say about my wipeout, or will you think of something later?" I ask, still looking at the ocean.

From the corner of my eye, he shakes his head, "No, of course not," he tries to catch my eye, and I relent. "Look, Hannah, I'm sorry about what happened last night. I acted like a dick, and it was completely uncalled for. If I can take them all back, I would."

Oh.

My heart dips from the hurt, as memories from the party begin to invade my thoughts again. And without thinking, I pull away, conjecturing, "I see. I guess you'd wish you can take back kissing me, huh?"

That takes him aback, but he just shakes his head, resignedly placing his hands on his lap.

"I'm sorry that I put you in that position. I know I shouldn't have kissed you. That was a momentary lack of good judgement on my part, and I won't put you through that again."

I don't want to feel hurt from his apology. I mean, he sounds like he means it. And isn't this what I wanted to hear from him after all?

Then why does him regretting the kiss feel like I've been bashed with a rock and left for dead?

"Okay. At least I know for sure now that it was a mistake. You almost made me think that you liked me," I answer with a laugh I can only describe as phony. "But after that stunt you pulled onstage with you mocking me outright, I knew then that you still didn't."

I turn my attention back to the ocean. Atticus may have saved me from drowning out there, but right now, I'd rather be out there than feel this bittersweet torture I'm receiving from him.

"Hannah," he holds me by the arm, and the way he speaks my name makes me turn my attention on him, "I never said I don't like you. And I'm sorry if this whole time, I made you feel that way."

I swallow the lump in my throat, surprised with his admission.

"Brodie has become a good friend of mine," he starts, and I put my hand up to try and stop him.

"Atticus, you don't have to explain," I say to him, but he just takes my hand by the wrist and gently pushes it back down.

But he's not letting go of it either.

"I do need to explain. I owe you that, at least," he sighs, before continuing, "Brodie had seen how I was looking at you from the first time we met, so he repeatedly told me to keep away from you. You even heard him say it, right? He sounded like he was joking when he said you were too good for me, but I know deep down he believes that. And he's right, I'm no Prince Charming."

This is what being blown away feels like.

Is Atticus implying that he likes me?

No way.

Before I can stop myself, I counter, "But I don't want a Prince Charming."

The way his eyes seem to glisten at my answer makes my heart flip. But it's gone, just as soon as it appears.

"You're too damn perfect to deserve anything less."

No, I was wrong. *This* is what being blown away feels like.

"I'm not perfect, Atticus. I'm flawed just like every single person that exists on Earth."

"You're not like every single person that exists on Earth," he says.

I swallow hard, trying to halt the way my chest is expanding.

He just keeps one-upping the way he's blowing me away.

"Atticus—"

"That's why I know I should keep my distance."

What? Bullshit.

"Hold on, so what are you telling me? That after all the times you mocked me, practically bullied me, you're actually saying that you liked me all along? And because you like me, you have to keep your distance and push me away? You know how twisted that sounds? But what about those slutty girls who cling on to you when you practise at my place, or the ones *you* can't seem to keep your hands from? Don't tell me you don't like them either because that will just confuse the hell out of me."

"You kind of sound like you're jealous," Atticus seems amused.

Jealous? Now I'm beginning to get pissed off.

"I'm not," I lie, shaking my head vigorously.

"Do you have any idea how much I want to kiss that jealousy of yours away?" He deliberately stares at my lips, watching intently as I unwittingly run my tongue across my now dry lower lip.

"But you won't kiss me because you'll just regret it, right?"

He smiles and with his lips and that damn dimple, he doesn't have to do much to make me swoon. He places his hand gently on my thigh, making my insides twist. "So, you basically just admitted that you're jealous."

"Screw you." Embarrassed, I try to get up, but his hand feels heavy on my thigh.

And I'll be lying if I say that I don't like how it feels.

"What if I ask for your permission to kiss you? Will you let me?"

I stare at his eyes and see no sign of smugness on them. Instead, I see apprehension, even a hint of vulnerability. Atticus is nervous about my answer? He can kiss any girl he wants, and they'll probably say 'thank you' for his trouble.

"If I say yes, will you?" I answer abruptly.

"Yes," he whispers under his breath, and before I know it, his lips are upon me, justifying his answer. I feel a sense of desperation in the way he thrusts his tongue inside, licking my lower lip and drawing it to him. I open my lips further, and I welcome the taste of saltiness of his lips, as well as the sweetness that must be unique of him. I gasp when he suddenly lifts me onto his lap, holding me closely, tightly, making me wish I'm not wearing this stupid, thick wet suit. I can feel his masculine body with my wandering hands. He's still slick from being in the water, and just as I imagined, he's built amazingly for his age. Now my whole body wants to feel him skin-to-skin. I moan in frustration, hugging him as tightly as I can instead, my small breasts pressing against his hard chest.

"You taste so damn sweet," he murmurs against my now moistened lips before devouring me again.

"But you taste like someone I don't deserve." And like an internal switch within him suddenly flickers off, he stops kissing me, hissing a curse word under his breath, and pulls away immediately.

But then he stares back at me with solemn eyes. "I don't think I can disrespect your brother's friendship like this. I can't allow anything else to happen between us."

The mere mention of my brother has the same effect as being thrown a bucket of ice-cold water. I let him go, and I slump back on my board.

He's right. My brother will never agree to this—with me, seeing Atticus—his close friend and Halcyon band member. What if things don't work out? Other than music and this stupid attraction, what else do we have in common?

"So you're happy to just leave it like this? You kissed me twice, pretty much admitted you like me, and then decide to just put a halt to it?"

"Hannah, it's more complicated than that," he looks past me, avoiding my gaze.

"You just made it more complicated by kissing me in the first place."

He turns back to me, eyes harder this time. "My music comes first. It's the one thing I'm good at, and it's what's gonna get me out of here and out of my hellhole of a life."

He breaks his stare, eyes downcast as he focuses on the sand instead. He seems caught out, like he admitted more than what he'd wanted to.

But I want to understand. I want to know why he seems so lost and so determined to leave.

I never ask Brodie about Atticus. Most of his friends are open to me about anything, sometimes even a little too open to the point of awkwardness. But Atticus is different. He's never friendly with me, and I'm not sure about getting to know someone who seems to hate my guts.

Is that a front?

I never want to get to know someone more than I want to get to know this boy in front of me.

"Why do you want to leave Avoca Beach? It's beautiful here."

He laughs, but humour doesn't reach his eyes. "You think I live in this part of town?"

"But you're always around since you became friends with Brodie, so I just assumed ..." I trail off, not exactly knowing what to say to him next.

Atticus shakes his head, "I'm not a local, Hannah," he sighs and starts holding onto the sand and letting it slip from his fingers, "and if you knew where I lived or who I live with ... well ... hanging out with Brodie and the band, and being able to play music ... and seeing you ... make existing bearable."

My heart tugs at this admission, the pain in his eyes is too distinct to hide.

114

"Atticus, you can talk to me. I'll listen." I reach for his hand, a comforting gesture that is meant to reassure.

He stares at my hand over his, but he doesn't answer back. Then he surprises me when he links our fingers together. My hand is practically swallowed by his much larger one. That's when I notice the callouses on his fingertips, possibly from years of playing guitar. I can't help but run my fingertips over each one of them. I feel each hardened bump, knowing now that he earned each one from years of practice, having been self-taught, just so he can hone his skills into perfection.

I feel his gaze on me, feel the warmth creep up from my neck to my face. When I turn to meet his gaze, he untangles our fingers instead and places both his hands on his knees.

I follow his movements, wishing Atticus's hands are touching mine again.

"Can you teach me how to play guitar?" I ask out of the blue. "You're gifted, Atticus. It would be great to learn from you."

"What? That came out of nowhere. But don't you play the guitar already?" he asks while looking amused and puzzled at the same time.

"Yes, I can play. But have you *heard* me play?"

His eyes widen in realisation, "Ah, yes. I've heard you play a few times. That was more than enough in my opinion, no offense or anything."

I laugh with embarrassment, "See! So do you still think I'm perfect? I'm a shitty guitar player!"

He laughs at that, and I can't help but stare at his face in awe. I really do like his laugh, especially when it's with me and not at my expense.

"Well," he nods, pointedly staring in all seriousness, "your amazing voice practically balances it out. You're on the cusp of perfection."

What he said takes me back to last night, and my smile falls flat.

"Why did you make fun of me last night?"

He exhales aloud, "I wasn't, Hannah. You really do have a beautiful voice. I was being truthful about that, and I'm sorry for being such a dick. But I'm just … I don't know how to act around you."

"Why?" I ask softly. "I'm just me."

He regards me for a few long moments before he turns his gaze back at the ocean, licking his lips in contemplation.

"Okay, I'll teach you how to play."

Overcome with sudden joy, I suck in a breath, covering my mouth so he won't see my stupid grin. "You will? You won't regret it. I promise."

He chuckles, "I never taught anyone before. What if I become an even bigger jerk to you?"

"So, do you want a diplomatic answer or an honest answer?" I ask, trying to be cheeky.

"So, do you want me to teach you, or will you be bringing that smart mouth of yours?" he asks back, almost succeeding at looking insulted, if not for the glint in his green eyes.

Still feeling playful, I answer back, "I'll be good. Please, Mister Foster. Teach me everything you know. I'll be your willing student," I plead in a breathy voice, biting my lower lip.

"Don't do that," Atticus answers warily, shifting his seated position.

"Do what?" I ask with big innocent eyes.

He lets out a resigned sigh, "Just … I'll teach you because you do have promise talent-wise, and I want to make it up to you for being such a giant douche bag. But only if you agree that we'll keep this as platonic as possible."

I try to push the sudden disappointment away, knowing that kissing Atticus again is probably now an impossibility. But he's offering an olive branch, and if it means being able to hang out with him, then I'll accept his terms.

"So, does this mean we're finally friends?" I ask.

He rolls his eyes before nodding, "Yes. We're friends. But only if you let me call you Songbird or Canary, depending on my mood."

"Why?"

"Because it sounds cute on you."

Rolling my eyes at him, but secretly thrilled that Atticus associates me with the word *cute*, I offer him my hand, "Songbird is okay. Agreed?"

He takes my hand and we shake on it, "Friends," he confirms. And even though my skin prickles from the contact, my heart can't help but dip into a dull thud from disappointment.

Damn, stupid *feels*.

We agree to have my guitar lessons after school on Tuesdays for an hour, and if he's free, before he practises with Halcyon.

"So how much do I pay you?" I ask, standing up. He follows suit, waving at people surfing and gesturing to them that he's leaving.

"I'm not charging you anything," he says.

"It's okay though, I want to pay you." I have to ask Mum and Dad, but I'm sure it'll be okay with them. They like Atticus, and I've seen him helping out Mum clean up at the kitchen. Those were the times when I wondered why he was never that nice to me.

He exhales loudly, "Please don't insult my ego. I can't accept your money."

"There must be something I can do for you. I can't just take something like your precious time and leave you empty-handed."

"Your cookies."

"Excuse me?"

Please let that not be actual cookies.

"You can pay me with your Anzac cookies or your famous Mars Bar cookies." His sudden enthusiasm of my baked goods is infectious, making me forget my disappointment that he wasn't referring to any of my body parts.

I can't believe how Atticus is seriously making me such a horn bag.

A *virgin* horn bag, but a horn bag nonetheless!

I can't help it. Just looking at him makes me think of highly inappropriate things … unladylike things.

Things reserved for the bedroom.

I'm starting to rethink if having guitar lessons with Atticus is a good idea at all.

"Hannah?" He's gently shaking my shoulder, and my glazed eyes focus back on him.

This is bad. *Very bad.*

"Okay. You can have my cookies!" I blurt out.

He looks at me with surprised amusement.

Very, very bad.

"Great. First lesson's at your shed on Tuesday at 4.30."

I nod back, "Uh, yes. Okay. Done. Can't wait."

He smiles back in response, and my stomach twists when he bites his lower lip to hold his imminent laughter. He stands up and runs across the sand to grab what looks like his T-shirt, then he jogs

117

back to me and offers his hand, "C'mon, I'll walk you home."

I hesitate for a second before taking his hand and standing up. He takes the board from me and holds it using his other arm.

But him taking my hand is getting me all sorts of confused.

Atticus starts walking, and I walk a step behind him. When he tugs me closer, I can't help but stare at our linked fingers in utter confusion. He must have noticed it because he raises our linked hands up.

"What? Friends *can* hold hands." He throws me a coy smile for good measure. All it does is get me further perplexed.

But as soon as we reach my driveway, he removes his hold on me and gives me back my board.

"Hey, um, you wanna come in for breakfast or something?"

Atticus looks up at our house, his face unreadable. Then he turns back to me and shakes his head.

"Nah, it's cool. I have to get back to my place."

"And where is this place you're referring to?"

"Up north."

"And how do you get to your place up north?"

"I bus it."

"Bus it? Seriously, Atticus, where do you live?"

"Roscoe," he answers dryly, expressionless.

"Roscoe? As in two lakes over, Roscoe? And you come all the way here just to go for a surf?"

He shrugs and looks far in the distance.

What are you not telling me, Atticus?

"Well, I'm really glad you do," I tell him, placing a hand on his shoulder. "Please, just stay for breakfast?" I insist. "I'll even cook it for you as my thanks for saving my life earlier."

He hesitates, before finally nodding his head, "Okay."

"Oh, and um, don't tell them about what happened while I was surfing, alright? I just don't need them to worry unnecessarily."

He nods, "If that's what you want, then sure."

I flash him a big smile in return. He takes my board again, and he walks up the driveway ahead of me.

And I swear, that just as he's passing me, he bites his lower lip again to suppress another smile.

Mum calls out to me as soon as I open the front door, immediately followed with reprimanding me for not telling her I was going and for not bringing my phone.

Seriously, she worries too much.

But worry changes to surprise once we round the corner to the kitchen and she sees Atticus walking right behind me.

"Atticus! Oh. Good morning! Brodie's upstairs playing his video game, I think. We just had our breakfast, but I don't mind fixing up something for you and Hannah."

"It's okay, Mum. I'll cook," I tell her with a kiss on her cheek.

"But look at you in your wet suit. You'll get sand all over my kitchen, *mija*!"

"Oh, sorry. Okay, let me change, and I'll be right back." I walk past Atticus, giving him a smile, which he returns, killing me with that dimple.

As soon as I make it up the stairs, I hear Mum offer Atticus a towel to wrap around him and his wet board shorts, which is a shame because wet shorts clinging on Atticus's legs and bum is kind of my idea of visual heaven. But Mum is such a clean freak, bless her heart.

I shower in no time, changing into a dress. I don't even know why I choose this particular short, flirty number. I don't want Atticus to think I'm intentionally dressing for him. But I'm spending too much time up here already. I should be cooking breakfast for my knight in shining armour, right now.

Have I seriously just referred to him with some cheesy description?

What the hell is going on with me?

By the time I head back down, I can already hear Brodie and Atticus talking, laughing, and sounding like they're mucking around.

Uh oh. Brodie.

I walk inside the kitchen, and Mum is nowhere to be seen. It's a Saturday, so I can only assume that she's upstairs getting dressed so she can go out and do her grocery shopping. But all thoughts of Mum disappear as soon as I zero in on Atticus. He's sitting on a bar stool next to the kitchen bench, and he zeroes in on me as well, his eyes running from my head to my toes and back, leaving a trail of tiny prickles in its path.

I try to stay unaffected as I walk straight to the fridge, opening it and grabbing some eggs.

"What's this thing Mum said that you're cooking breakfast for Tic? Do you know what it means when you 'cook breakfast' for a guy?"

I turn to him, puzzled. When it finally hits me, my mouth gapes open, and my expression turns to horrified. Thank goodness Mum isn't here to hear this!

"Hey, keep your head out of the gutter and leave her alone. She's just thanking me for ... for uh, agreeing to help her play guitar better."

"What? First of all, you're *defending* Hannah? Second, Han, you had lessons. And I taught you too. How come I got shit for my efforts?"

"That's 'cause you're a shit teacher who can't teach shit," Atticus answers, and I watch as he playfully punches Brodie's shoulder, with Brodie retaliating with a punch of his own.

Boys.

"Okay, okay. Enough. So are you staying for this breakfast or what?" I ask Brodie pointedly.

"Nope," he answers, shaking his head before turning to Atticus, "Hey, you wanna play some Forza while she's cooking?"

"I was actually planning on *not* being a douche to your sister and helping her out."

"Well that's something I never thought I'd hear or see from you," Brodie says, genuinely looking surprised.

"I like to keep everyone on their toes."

I'm already grabbing a frying pan at this time, which means I'm facing away from them, which means they can't see me blushing.

"Suit yourself. I'll be upstairs trying to get over how you chose to help my little sister cook, rather than race cars with your mate."

"You'll get over it," Atticus laughingly answers back.

I turn around just as both of them are getting up from their bar stools, with Atticus laughingly pushing Brodie towards the stairs.

And once my brother is in the next room, Atticus turns around and walks straight towards me, eyes never leaving mine. He stops only inches in front of me.

"I don't mind if you wanna play Forza, Atticus." I take a couple of steps back, making a point to go to the other side of the kitchen to get a bowl to mix the eggs in.

I need to keep my distance from this boy who's making my heart beat way too fast for comfort.

"I want to help." He takes the bowl I'm holding, momentarily grazing his fingers with mine. I can't deny what his touch is doing to me. But now he's smiling, and it's that megawatt, dimpled smile he uses to guarantee any girl's attention.

I used to wonder how it would feel to be at the receiving end of Atticus's smile.

And now I know.

And now I wish I didn't.

Because I'm melting.

I'm. Melting.

"Uh, you know how to cook?" I ask him, quickly grabbing the milk, cheese, salt, and pepper. I need to keep moving around. I need to be anywhere but in his immediate vicinity.

"I know enough to survive," he pauses, then shrugs, "I've got no choice." His explanation makes me want to ask further, but instead, I watch as he places the bowl on the space close to the sink and starts cracking the eggs. He cracks them with one hand, a skill acquired through practice.

I can't help but move closer and watch in awe as he uses all of the ingredients without even asking me if he's doing it correctly, whisking like it's nobody's business. Then he places his hands on my shoulders and gently nudges me to the side, winking at me before switching on the gas burner.

"Wait, I offered to cook for you in return for guitar lessons. Why are you taking over?" I tap on his shoulder, trying to get his attention.

He turns to me, but only to ask, "Where's your butter?"

"Um, I asked you a question?"

"So did I," he brushes past me, and opens the fridge. "Never mind," he says, butter dish in hand.

"Hello?" I block his path, and he screeches to a halt.

"I'm cooking the eggs. Just deal with it!" I grab the butter from his hand and put a pan on the gas burner. He tries to grab the butter off me, but I stick my elbow out to stop him, moving from side to side to further block him off.

"God, woman. Relax!" Atticus laughingly tells me, and the way he calls me *woman* makes me feel giddy all over. Then he makes it worse by planting his chin on my shoulder as I pour the eggs on the hot, buttered pan.

He may be doing this as an innocent gesture, but the way he smells of sea and his own personal musk, the same way he smelled last night, is making me feel things that are far from innocent again.

"Uh, if you wanna help, you can toast a few slices of bread?" Without thinking, I turn my head toward him, not realising how close he actually is. Before I can stop myself, my lips accidentally touch the corner of his mouth.

Oh shit!

Cheeks now hot, I jerk my head away and face the eggs like nothing happened.

"Sorry," I whisper out. What if he thinks I did that on purpose? Why did he have to place his head on my shoulder in the first place?

"Well, the eggs are done," he says, straightening up and switching the burner off. He doesn't speak about my major blooper, instead grabbing the loaf of bread from the fridge and walking over to the toaster. He's standing mere inches beside me, acting all nonchalant. But the coy smile he's trying to hide is enough for me to wish the earth would swallow me whole.

He didn't want to kiss me anymore. He only wanted us to be friends.

Now he thinks I'm probably obsessed with him, trying to sneak in a kiss.

I try to concentrate on plating the eggs, and just as I'm about to carry the plate of cheesy scrambled eggs, he quickly closes our gap and drops a kiss on my cheek.

No warning, no hesitation, leaving me stunned, mouth agape.

"Now we're even," he says with a crooked smile on his face.

Oh.

The corners of my lips turn upwards in a slow smile, but I bite on my lower lip, not wanting to ruin the moment by saying something inane.

I hear footsteps coming from the stairs, and I take that as my cue to move away from Atticus.

Dad comes in the kitchen, dressed casually in shorts and a plain T-shirt. He smiles when he sees me, but his eyes widen when he sees Atticus a couple of steps behind me, toasting some bread.

"Good morning, Han … Atticus," he kisses the top of my head, but not before I notice how his eyes are trained only at Atticus. "Taking a break from playing video games, Tic?"

Atticus looks guarded as he tries to answer, "Uh, I'm just —"

"He's just helping out, Dad," I finish for him.

It's true anyway.

Sort of.

"Okay," my dad shrugs, but the way his eyes follow Atticus warily makes me a little nervous.

122

He gets over it thankfully, turning his attention to me. "Did you go surfing this morning?" Dad asks, grabbing a fork and helping himself with a mouthful of my scrambled eggs. He nods in appreciation, "I actually wanted to check out the waves myself. I could've come with you."

Knowing what just transpired at the beach earlier, I take a moment to make sure I answer back without making Dad worry about me.

"I didn't stay for long. The waves started to get choppy."

"Ah, okay. Maybe next time then?"

"For sure, Dad," I answer back, beaming up at him.

We haven't surfed together in quite a while, and I know he misses it. I do too. When his practice became busier, so did he. This meant his weekends were spent in his office and not with his family.

"Maybe we can go later? The waves might improve by then," I tell him.

I hear a loud clang from behind me, and when I turn around, I notice Atticus looking at me, spoon in hand, with a frown on his face.

I ignore him and turn back to my father. "So, what do you say, Dad?"

His expression lightens, and flashes me a smile, "I'm in! After I take your mum grocery shopping, we should go check it out, yeah?"

"I'll be here when you get back," I nod back enthusiastically.

He gives Atticus a brief wave, and Atticus hesitantly does the same. "Well, enjoy your breakfast. I just need to clean up some crap in the garage. Tell your mum when she's finally ready that I'll be out there, okay? I swear your mum takes much longer to get ready as she gets older."

"Dad! I'll tell on you," I answer back, laughing.

"No, you won't because you love your daddy," he yells back as he makes his way to the front door.

"Whatever, Dad!"

"Wait, I'm ready!" I hear my mum's voice call out for Dad. "See you kids. Be good!"

When the door closes, I distinctly hear Atticus breathe out loudly.

"What was that about?" I ask Atticus straight away.

"I can't believe you'd want to go back out there. You should be resting for the rest of the day."

"Pfft," I scoff, "why would I delay going back out? I'm not going to let what happened scare me."

He shakes his head, "I don't know if you're just really, really brave, or really, really stubborn. Maybe I should come with you."

"Just because you saved my life once doesn't mean you have to feel obliged to be my fucking knight in shining armour. That's not your job to do."

He turns to me, eyes hardening, "You're right. It isn't."

I squint my eyes curiously at him and decide to turn things around. "And anyway, I noticed how you reacted with my father. Don't tell me he makes you nervous."

He goes back to his task and shrugs.

"He's just used to you hanging out with Brodie while you piss me off in general," I continue, chuckling softly.

He picks up the plate of toast and stands next to me, smiling back sheepishly, "Was I really that much of an asshole to you?"

"You weren't that bad. Most of the time you just ignored me, so technically, you probably didn't mean to, but if I'm being truly honest, it sucked."

"Hannah, I—"

"It's okay," I chuckle softly. "We kind of kissed and made up, right?"

I wanted to be funny, and try to laugh that off as a joke, but he's not laughing with me. Instead, he regards me so intently that my laughter simmers down. Then he raises his hand and grazes my cheek with his fingertips.

Man, why does my body react to him like this?

My breathing turns shallow, and I can't take my eyes away from his. I see the inner torment in them, like he's trying to figure out what is the right thing to do next.

But I heard him loud and clear at the beach.

He wanted me, but he couldn't have me.

His music is his priority.

"Our breakfast is getting cold," I turn away from him, removing myself from his touch.

He just stands next to me, and it takes him a moment before he walks to the other side of the table so he can focus on his breakfast.

As we're eating, I try not to notice how he looks up from his plate to watch me. When I try to catch him, he goes back to eating

124

like nothing happens. It's weird how my body responds to him: my hands don't feel steady, and my fork keeps dropping because of it, my skin feels hot and cold at the same time. I feel almost feverish, but instead of feeling sick, I actually feel invigorated.

What is he doing to me?

Is he feeling this way too?

Is it natural for me to feel like wanting to touch him no matter how I know that it can turn out to be my undoing?

He's confusing me.

I'm confusing myself.

I get up and turn away from him, needing a break from all the weird thoughts his presence is doing to me. I grab a large bottle of OJ from the fridge, pouring myself a glass. When I place the glass on the table, I realise that I haven't offered him one.

"Oh, sorry. Would you like some water or juice? I can get you your own …"

Then he surprises me when he reaches for my glass and drinks from it, shrugging, "It's cool. We can share." He offers me a crooked smile, and I look at him and at the glass he drank from, suddenly feeling thirsty.

So I sit back down, and I take the glass and drink, knowing that my lips are on the exact place his lips were just on.

What's gotten into me?

Will I do whatever it takes to feel his lips on me again that I'll succumb to this?

But when I look up, Atticus is staring at me, his eyes watching me again, and he's not even trying to hide it this time.

"What is it?" I ask in a shaky breath.

He doesn't answer me straight away, but his gaze is steady.

"I was just thinking," he finally answers.

"About?"

He bites on his lower lip, brows creasing as he regards me thoughtfully, eyes fleeting from my eyes to my lips, "I'm just thinking about how much I want to be that glass of OJ right now."

My breath hitches. "Don't say things like that," I answer back.

He shakes his head, "I know. I'm sorry."

"It's not that. It's just … just don't say things like that if you can't back it up."

"You know I can't, Hannah," Atticus exclaims, and I can't help but notice the pained expression on his face. He pushes his chair back and stands up, opening the back door leading out to the garden.

I push my own chair back and follow him out. He's seated on the top step of our deck, eyes looking straight at the shed on the other end of our garden.

I don't know why, but I step back inside the kitchen, reaching for the row of hooks next to the door. I grab the keys to the shed, and I walk back out, and take the handful of steps down. I stop as soon as my feet are on the grass, turning to Atticus and offering him my hand. His gaze moves from my outstretched arm to my face, and he's probably unsure of what's going on.

"Come on," I tell him encouragingly, taking the initiative and grabbing his hand instead. He stands up, and he lets me lead him towards the converted studio. I unlock the door, and he waits for me to step inside before him.

"Why did you take me here? We're not practising today," Atticus points out, his hands to his sides, looking a little vulnerable and all kinds of cute at the same time.

"I don't know," I answer, "but you just looked like you needed some distraction."

"But I didn't bring my guitar."

I chew on my lip as I look around the room, where Brodie's and the rest of the band's instruments are resting idly on their stands. The boys just leave their instruments in here, but Atticus would often bring his guitar home.

"You have a lot of instruments to choose from in here."

His eyes light up, and he walks over to one of the spare acoustic guitars and lifts it off its stand. He places the strap over his head, cradling the guitar across his chest, knowing fingers wrapping around the fret, while the other set is poised over the strings.

I never thought I'd be jealous of an inanimate object. But I'm feeling exactly that as I watch Atticus sit on one of the high stools, tuning the guitar with his eyes closed. I'm sitting on the couch, legs crossed, hugging a pillow while I watch him.

"Do you have any requests?" he asks, face lit up with his dimple showing.

"Oh, are you singing for me? Well, I don't know. You decide," I answer, smiling back, hoping I'm not ogling too much like those groupies he hangs out with.

126

He looks away, thinking, then he gets up from his high stool and decides to sit mere inches away from me on the couch. He's too close, and if I was self-conscious before, I'm more so now … and he's the one holding the guitar and about to sing me a song.

Or so I thought.

"How do you feel about singing *with* me?"

"Huh?" I push myself further away from him, my back against the armrest of the couch.

"Last night, I know you thought that I was making fun of you when I heard you singing at the party," Atticus rakes his moussed-up hair back. "I wasn't, Hannah. I was being honest with you. But you did surprise me because you never sang with us when we practise."

I shrug shyly, "I'm not confident like you guys. And do you think I'll sing in front of you? What did you say before? Oh yeah, *we're not friends.*"

He looks down at the guitar, but I still notice him wincing.

"So … just to be clear, are we really friends now?" I ask, tilting my head to gauge his reaction.

A glimpse of his dimple making an appearance tells me he's smiling. Finally, he raises his head and nods once, "I'd be honoured to be your friend, Hannah Mackenzie."

"Great," I beam, "so can I call you Tic like Brodie and the other boys do?"

"Sure. But I'm partial to you calling me Atticus."

"Why?"

"I don't know. It just sounds nice when you say it."

There goes my skin tingling again.

Stop it, skin.

I try to make it look like what he said isn't affecting me. "Right, so friends talk about a lot of things and are honest with each other. Will you try to be honest with me at all times?"

"It depends. We're friends but we're not close friends yet," he teases.

"Dick!" I laugh as I fling the pillow at him, and it hits him right on the face, wiping the smug smile off him. I'm laughing aloud now, tilting my head back with abandon.

Me: One, Atticus: Zilch … Nada … Zer-

Bam! The same pillow hits me on the face as well.

"Ow!" I yell out, covering my nose with my hand for protection.

"Oh my God, I'm sorry!" Atticus gently removes my hand and checks me for any injuries.

Luckily there's none. I can't say the same about my pride though.

"See? I just don't fucking know how to be around you." He's cupping my chin, rubbing my cheek with his thumb, his eyes intense, frustrated and even guilty.

My heart clenches for him, so I reach up for his wrist, holding onto it, and I answer softly, "Yeah, I think I agree. But you can just be yourself … you know, the nice, less asshole one, and we'll be fine."

That damn dimple is back as he cracks a smile at me.

I wish he would stop smiling at me like this. It makes me want to be selfish of that smile, overprotective even.

His smile makes me want to have it all to myself so no other girls can catch even a glimpse of it.

But he's made it clear that he and his heart-stopping smile will be out of my life as soon as he can figure out how to leave this town for good.

Maybe I should say something to wipe that smile off his face so I don't have to see it.

"I'm okay, you can sit down now. I, um, actually wanted to ask you something about last night."

"Yeah? Okay, what is it?" he asks, eyes meeting mine once again as he sits back down.

Good … there's distance between us again.

"Why were you outside the bathroom listening to me last night?"

Yup, that did it. Smile's gone.

"I just wanted to make sure that you were okay. I didn't intend to stay when I saw you go inside the bathroom, but I don't know, for some reason I did. Then I heard your voice singing on the other side, and, well … shit, Hannah. Your voice is incredible."

"What? No, it isn't." Blood seems to rush up to my cheeks, and I'm sure it's glowing bright red.

He regards me thoughtfully, but doesn't respond. Instead, he seems to play with the strings of the guitar, then, he goes into a tune that sounds familiar.

Then he sings the first line … about how he doesn't know me, but he wants me. He nods to me encouragingly, inviting me to join him with a smile that shows off that dimple. That was it for me, and without thinking, I open my mouth and start singing.

I start singing the familiar words with him, my heart beating fast and loud, that I'm sure he can hear every single thud.

We sound awkward at first, until we start singing in sync, and by the time we're singing the chorus, it's like we've been singing together for years.

"Falling Slowly"

God, I think I'm falling faster than that.

By the time he strums the last notes, our eyes are glued to each other. He places the guitar down on the floor, but he doesn't break contact. He moves closer, inch by inch, and I refuse to move, my whole body cemented on my side of the couch.

When I feel his warm hand on my glowing cheek, his face coming closer as he dips his head down towards me, I know that I need to just *feel* him, just as I need him to feel me.

So with one last shaky exhale, I close my eyes, and I *feel*.

The way he touches me … warm … gentle … comforting.

The way he whispers my name … soft … low … endearing.

And finally, the way his lips feel on mine … sweet … tender … amazing.

So. Amazing.

A whimper escapes me as I succumb to him. When his tongue pushes past my lips, he moans as it meets my own. His other hand moves to my back, spanning his fingers across it as he urges me to come closer. My arms circle around his shoulders, and I pull him closer as well, until our chests are pressed together, and our legs tangled.

Are all kisses like this? Do they always feel this good? Am I supposed to feel this rush every single time a guy kisses me?

Or is it because I'm kissing Atticus?

"Atticus?" I whisper against his lips, "what are we doing here?"

He pauses, pulling away slightly, intense green eyes looking straight at me, "I don't know. But all I know is that I don't want to be your friend at all."

Oh … wow.

That hurts … so much.

"Okay," I answer back, blinking back my tears, "and I don't want to be your friend at all either."

129

"Good, because what I'm feeling for you right now goes beyond friendship, and it's fucking scaring the shit out of me."

Just when I thought he blows me off, he says something like that and blows me away instead.

"I'm—I'm scared about this too, Atticus. I know you're going to leave town, and I don't want to be the one to get in your way."

Atticus reaches for my hand, holding it upright with his fingertips pressing against my fingertips. Then he laces our fingers together, bending closer to kiss each bone on my knuckle, melting my resolve even more with every kiss.

"This wouldn't have happened if I hadn't kissed you last night. Hannah, I can't promise you forever with me. All I can offer you is right now, and I'm not sure if that's enough."

I try to swallow the pain from Atticus laying his cards all out on the table. He told me what he's capable of giving me. The question is if I'm willing to accept it.

"I'm fifteen years old, Atticus. I'm not expecting forever. Yes, maybe you shouldn't have kissed me, but you did, and it changed everything." I touch his cheek, my thumb brushing the groove where his dimple would appear. "So I accept the *right now* that you're offering me, and I accept it willingly. In fact, I want us to take things slow. Maybe this whole thing is moving too fast, and we need a little time to just get to know each other first."

"Are you sure about this? The last thing I want to do is to hurt you," Atticus says softly.

"You won't hurt me, Atticus because I won't let it happen. I know what I want and that is you."

"I need you to be sure about this, Hannah because once we—"

I fist his shirt so I can pull him closer, "Shhh! No more talking, Atticus. Just shut your mouth and kiss me already."

CHAPTER FOURTEEN

Present Day

It's been a week since that day Atticus ambushed me from that group session.

A week since he literally carried me for refusing to go with him.

A week since he drove me home in his dream car.

A week since he drove *me* mad with anger.

A week since he kissed me.

A whole damn week since Atticus brought to life something I thought had died since the accident.

Myself.

And since that week, Atticus has been completely under the radar. Brodie told me that he has locked himself in the house he's staying in, busily writing songs or whatever and didn't want to be disturbed.

Not that it matters. Maybe it's better that he hasn't shown up at all, because whatever spark Atticus ignited inside of me, has now become overshadowed by one thing: guilt.

Guilt has been my constant companion since the accident. Followed closely by remorse. Both of them have been my two closest friends ... or enemies. I don't even know anymore.

Pretty much after Atticus kissed me, thoughts of Paul, the love he had for me, and the pain I caused him in the end have begun to torment me once again. It's like my subconscious is punishing me for allowing Atticus to affect me the way he used to.

Playing the guitar is helping me regain some form of internal peace. But I can only play so much before Paul is back in my thoughts. It always starts with our happier days, but then it morphs into the way I broke his heart, which tragically ends into the accident that cost him his life.

Right now has been particularly awful, like out-of-control-crying-practically-the-whole-day, awful.

And checking the date on my phone made everything clearer.

Paul and I would've celebrated our third year anniversary today.

Is this Paul's way of sending me a message?

I have to visit him. I need to at least try and talk to him, and get things off my chest. It used to be so easy talking to Paul. He never mocked me, or made fun of what I had to say. We also nurtured each other's dreams and have been each other's rock.

I have never stopped loving Paul, and what disturbs me the most is the realisation that in his final breaths, he thought that I never loved him at all … that I lied to him that whole time.

But I didn't lie. My love for him was real, genuine. I may not have been capable of giving him my whole heart, but I was foolish enough to think that I'd heal completely in due course, so I gave him all the love I could muster.

If only I could literally turn back the clock, then I can reassure him that he was loved, and will always be loved by me.

Maybe it's not too late for me to tell him. Maybe he's still willing to listen. I just have to try.

I can't punish myself like this for the rest of my life.

"Brodie?" I yell out as I leave my bedroom, walking stick in hand, having dressed up in whatever I can grab, unsure and uncaring if I looked like shit. At least it would match my mood.

"Brodie!" I yell out again.

"Hannah? Brodie stepped out about an hour ago," Mum tells me as I near the kitchen.

"Oh," I answer back, unable to hide my disappointment. "Do you know how long he'll be out?"

"He told me he's catching up with that friend of his who now owns Peak. You know, that nice, little bar just at the Esplanade? I think he's helping out with open mic night gig?"

"Sounds cool," I reply distractedly.

"Maybe I can be of assistance to you?" Mum asks expectantly.

I consider it for a few moments. If I ask Mum, I'll also run the risk of getting bombarded with questions. But what I need to do now, cannot wait.

"Um, actually, yes. I was gonna ask Brodie if he can drive me to the cemetery so I can visit Paul …" I explain, feeling a little awkward and shifting from one foot to another.

"Oh … of course I can drive you. Wait here while I clean up and change my clothes." I hear the tap open, so I decide to wait for her in the living room since it is closest to the front door.

Not long after, Mum announces, "Okay *mija*, I'm ready. Let's go."

The ride to the cemetery consists of Mum trying to sing along with whatever's playing on the radio, which when sung with her accent never fails to make me smile. Her accent is not as pronounced as *Abuelo's* and *Abuela's*, but they usually become more obvious when she's singing, or upset and telling us off.

Mum's family migrated from Mexico when she was twelve years old because her parents decided that they wanted a better life for her and her two sisters. They were Sydney based, until she met my father while studying an education degree. Dad was studying law then and was in the library to do some research when he saw Mum studying with her friends as well. My dad was not a hard core romantic, but he knew right there and then that she was it for him. So he walked up to her, not giving a damn about the possibility that he might make a fool of himself. He tapped Mum on her shoulder and introduced himself as her future husband. My mum laughed him off at first, but saw something in him that piqued her interest.

Mum said that her decision to go on that first date with this weird Aussie college boy was the best decision she ever made.

Thanks to Dad's decisiveness and brazen behaviour, he eventually married the girl he saw his future with.

I always loved hearing their story. Especially since love at first sight doesn't always happen to everyone. But even after going through two devastating broken hearts, I still have some belief that someone out there is waiting for me. I knew from the beginning that my future was never going to be with Atticus, though I naively wished that it were because I loved him with everything I had.

And looking back, I may have fallen for him since that first day he pissed me off.

But our story started out the wrong way, and maybe that became our downfall.

And then Paul came into my life in a way so similar to how my parents met. I thought I had my chance at forever with him, and I was so determined to keep my perfect boyfriend that I swept the pieces of my still-broken heart under the rug and away from view.

Out of sight, out of mind.

But those pieces didn't stay hidden forever.

And unfortunately, they decided to show themselves at the worst possible time.

After a number of minutes driving in a straight line, I feel the car making a right turn. I count the number of turns after that, trying to memorize the route in my head.

I know it's a silly thing to do. It's not like I can drive myself here or anything.

The car finally slows to a stop, and I feel Mum's hand cover my own.

"Hold on, I'll collect you on the other side," she tells me.

My hands start to feel clammy from the nerves. I've been here before, and the first time was the worst. But now I'm back, not only to apologise again, but just to talk. I used to love that about Paul—how easy he was to talk to, and how good he makes me feel after venting out to him about random stuff. My problems never fazed him. He was the calm to my chaos. And if the situations were switched, I used to do the same for him too.

But sometimes, I feel like he drew the shortest stick from the stack. I was the lucky one because he loved me regardless of my shortcomings. And compared to him, I had plenty.

He was perfect, and he made me perfect by association.

But even perfect people have their limits.

Mum opens the passenger door and helps me out before walking me towards Paul's plot. She tells me that Paul was cremated, a fact I failed to ask as I went through my various stages of grief. They have a family plot, and apparently it's beautiful, with luscious, green grass and white flowers surrounding the headstone. Most of Paul's cremated remains were scattered in the ocean because that was where he'd usually be found when he was still alive. But they kept a part of him here so that his loved ones had something more tangible to hold onto.

I wish that I were there when they performed the scattering of the ashes. But I had no right to … he didn't even want to have anything to do with me in the end.

The truth hurts so much that I clutch my chest tightly.

Mum finally stops walking so I can untangle my arm from hers.

"We're here," she says, "I'll go back to the car, and I'll wait for you there. If you're ready to leave, just wave up at me, and I'll come and get you, okay?"

"Thanks, Mum. And I'm sorry for the hassle," I tell her softly.

"*Mija*, it's no hassle at all. I'm your mother, and being your mother is what I'm good at, okay?"

I smile back, trying not to choke on the tears, "Okay."

She kisses my temple, and I feel the breeze on my skin as she turns to walk back to the car.

It takes me a long moment to collect my thoughts, feeling nervous and speechless all of a sudden. I had the words memorised in my head, but now they're all muddled up and unrecoverable.

Stepping forward, I reach out for Paul's headstone.

"Hi, Paul," I whisper. "I just realised that I forgot to get you flowers. I'm sorry about that." I pause to sit down, legs crossed, my hand is still on what I've been told is black marble. Memories of those times he bought me flowers come flooding back, and I can't help but smile.

"Remember when you used to give me flowers? I knew that most of the time you didn't really buy them. They were the same flowers you had in your garden. I hope you didn't get in trouble for doing that, but I want you to know that I loved them all. They were all beautiful, though I sure hope your garden recovered from all the thieveries."

I'm chuckling softly, though my eyes begin to water. I squeeze my lids shut, breathing slowly through my mouth to calm myself down.

"I can't get that night out of my head, Paul. I can't get over how much I must have hurt you. After everything you've done for me, for us … I don't know why I said what I said. We were going to have a great future together, and I fucking messed up. I. Messed. Up. Now I can't take it back."

A few stray tears fall from my eyes, and I swipe them from my cheek. "I just wish I got the chance to tell you that I love you before you left. You will always have a place in my heart that nobody can take. You knew that I didn't want to fall in love again, but gosh, you were so damn charming. You made it so easy. I miss our conversations. I miss how our life was so good together. I just miss … you. But I know what I did, and I know I messed up. You probably don't want to hear this again … but I thought I got over him, Paul. I really thought I had no more love for him. But don't worry, I'm not going to speak his name. We both know who I'm talking about, and you heard me babble this explanation before … before the …" I let out a shaky exhale, my chest tightening with anguish.

"I don't know how to move on from here, Paul. You always were the decisive one between us. I just … I just need some sort of sign that it's okay for me to move on, and I'll figure out the rest. I'm just lost … and I'm scared," I pause for a few moments, trying to collect my thoughts.

"Is it okay if I come visit you once in a while? Someone has to drive me here though, and unfortunately, Brook and Patty can't come with me either. I'm sure that they're studying in the city as planned. It sucks though because I pushed them away. I didn't want them to feel sorry for me.. I guess I thought that they wouldn't want to be friends with me anymore since I'm scarred and blind. Maybe cutting my ties with them was the best thing to do. Yeah, I know, it's so superficial. I can imagine your eyes rolling," I chuckle softly.

"But you know what? They'll visit their families since the school holidays have started. Who knows, maybe I'll get a chance to catch up with them, right?"

The constant silence fills the gap in-between my one-ended conversation with Paul. But I don't care. In some cosmic way, I can feel his energy surrounding me, and it's peaceful … calming. I reach down towards the bottom of the headstone, and breathe a sigh of relief when I feel the square, plastic case with my CD still inside of it.

"I'll wait for a sign, my Dear Mister. I'll wait for you to tell me it's okay to move on. I owe you at least that much."

I press two fingers against my lips, and then I touch them against the headstone.

"I'll see you around," I whisper with a smile, wondering if he's chuckling on the other side from the obvious pun. I stand back up, waving my hand up like Mum said.

"Are you ready?" I hear Mum say after a few moments.

"Yeah. And I'm kind of hungry."

Mum laughs, "Not a problem. I'm treating you for lunch in that restaurant we used to go to when we had our girls' day out."

I frown at the thought, "I'm not sure about that. People we know will see us."

"And so?"

"Mum … I don't know. I mean, people might stare at us, then, ask you questions. And I don't even know if what I'm wearing is suitable."

"You look beautiful as always, Hannah. And you're dressed quite nicely. So I don't want you making any more excuses, okay?

Now if only you'd go to that appointment I tried so hard to get, then you can work with a guide dog …"

I shake my head, sighing, "I know it wasn't easy to get an appointment with them, and you fell from the stairs and everything because you got way too excited when they confirmed an appointment. But I don't know if I'm ready to go through with getting my own guide dog."

"Why are you hesistant, Hannah? It will help you be more independent, isn't that what you want?"

"It is, but I don't know. It just feels like that's it for me. Like I've thrown in the towel and accepted defeat," I pause for a second, trying to think of a good compromise for my mum. "Okay. I'll go to that appointment at the Guide Dogs Association with you. I'll listen to what they have to say, and then we'll go from there."

Mum suddenly gives me a tight squeeze, "Thank you, *mija,* that's all I wanted. And don't you start with me about accepting defeat. You are not defeated, Hannah. You have Spanish and Scottish blood running through your veins so you have that fire in your belly. What you're going through right now should only feed the flame."

I smile at Mum's highly emotional rant. I just love her spirit. And she's right. Maybe I should stop treating this as a handicap and make good use of the second chance I've been given.

"Alright, calm down. Message received. But right now though, the fire in my belly is making me hungry. Okay, let's eat out, but can we go to Colt's instead? I want to introduce you to my new friend."

Colt's Corner is packed according to Mum. No surprises there. It always is. But as soon as we step inside, I hear Nicki's voice call out my name, followed by two small arms giving me a hug, which I happily return.

"Oh my God, Hannah! You're here!"

I break into a smile, "I am! And I've brought Mum. Mum, this is Nicki Colt. She was in my year, and her family owns this café. She, um, is actually the one who invited me to join the support group I went to because her father—"

Mum thankfully saves me from finishing my uncomfortable statement when she cuts me off with her reaction, "So, you're the one responsible for convincing my daughter to finally join a support group. Thank you, dear child, I am so happy you approached her on that day. And I know who your father is. I remember how he was always very nice and very proud of this place."

"Well, that's actually why I stayed, so I can help run his café. I'm planning to pursue my degree when I know I'm comfortable with leaving this place even if it's only temporarily. Oh, what am I doing? Let me get you seats!" We start moving, with Mum guiding me around the tables until I'm finally seated.

"Thanks, Nicki. Mum said your café is pretty full right now."

"Yes, but I'll make sure you guys have a table whenever you come around," Nicki tells us.

"You are such a sweet girl. I'm sure your father is looking down on you from heaven, thinking how lucky he is to have a daughter like you."

"Thank you so much, Mrs Mackenzie. That means a lot," Nicki says, sounding all choked up, "and can I just say that your daughter was one of the nicest girls in school. We just didn't run in the same circles, but she always had a smile on her face, and she was … she was very kind," her words make my chest hurt because I remember being that happy girl, always carefree, with a big smile on my face.

It's crazy how things can change in a matter of seconds.

My melancholic thoughts are broken by Nicki's voice, "Okay, so ladies, who wants to hear the specials for today?"

After a delicious lunch, Mum decides that a spot of shopping will be a good way to burn off what we just ate. I am hesitant at first, but other than my friends, I used to love a shopping day with Mum. And if I want to continue to move forward with my life, I need to start by reconnecting with Mum again. All I have to do is get over the obstacles I've imposed on myself.

Sounds good on paper, but harder to achieve.

Come to think of it though, nothing great ever comes from anything easy, right?

CHAPTER FIFTEEN

The days leading to the weekend came and went with me taking more steps forward. Mum took me shopping again yesterday, and Brodie has been taking me to the beach in the mornings. It's great to hear the sound of the waves crashing, and sometimes, I just lie on the sand, listening to an audiobook, while he surfs. I miss surfing. And maybe someday, I will again. But now, I can't even bring myself to waddle legs deep in the water, let alone go for a swim. As much as I know how good a swimmer I am, or how adept I am in the surf, not being able to see the waves coming, or not seeing whatever it is underwater makes me feel way too vulnerable for comfort.

But one thing I'm happy to do with Brodie is play music. He asked me two days ago to help him practise for his surprise acoustic performance at Peak. I was admittedly surprised at this request, thinking Atticus is around, why not ask him like he used to before? I have a feeling that this is a pity practice, like he thinks that I would jump at a chance to play with him again.

Don't get me wrong, I did jump at the chance. But I drew the line when Brodie said that maybe I should sing a couple of songs onstage. I mean, I want to move forward … but with baby steps … not gigantic leaps.

I haven't asked my brother how long he's staying. I know he said a couple of months, but his is the type of job where you go where your agent books you. They're still new in the industry, and they are supposed to be doing radio gigs to promote the band. As I'm playing guitar alongside my brother in our makeshift studio, I can't help but wonder if I'll go back into my shell when he leaves, or will I take the chance and step out into the world on my own.

And what about Atticus? Is he still around? And why am I even thinking about him again? But there has been no sign of him. He hasn't dropped by as far as I'm concerned. And it's not like I'm going to ask Brodie if he's paid him a visit.

139

When Atticus left me all those years ago, I noticed how Brodie seemed relieved that Atticus broke it off with me. Sure he was pissed, but the relief was definitely there in his eyes, and I couldn't forget that. I never talked to him about it though. Now it feels like it is too late to ask Brodie about the whole thing. All I know is that in those rare times when he actually talked about Atticus with me, he said that Atticus only cared about his music and nothing more.

I already knew about this when Atticus and I got together. I knew more about him than I've let on with anyone else. Atticus opened himself to me ... showed me who he was and where he came from, and why he was who he was. And yet, I still loved him, foolishly thinking that maybe it was not just his music that could save him. I could save him too. Because even though I knew that he cared about his music, I also knew that he cared about me tremendously.

At least that's what I believed in.

But I guess my brother was right all along.

"Are you sure you don't want to try singing even one song onstage?" Brodie asks after practising one of the songs he's playing in the acoustic session.

"You're kidding me, right? I mean in case you haven't noticed, I'm not exactly stage material."

"What the fuck are you talking about?"

"Erm," I wave my hand up and down myself, "have you seen me lately?"

"Erm," he says sarcastically, "have you seen Stevie Wonder onstage?"

"Oh, come on, don't compare me with him. He's a fucking legend. He's phenomenal. I'm a scar-faced, wannabe guitar player with an average sounding voice. Granted, blindness might actually work to my advantage since I can't see anyone laughing at me, or looking on with disgust. Believe it or not, my hearing is actually more acute now, and if I hear nothing but silence after I finish baring my heart and soul in front of them, I'm going to be shattered, Brodie. I honestly wouldn't know what I'd do in that scenario except cry my eyes out. "

"How can you even be certain that'll happen? Yes, I know it sucks that you lost your sense of sight, but then you go and tell me your hearing is a lot better now. So if that's the case, how come you can't hear how good your voice actually sounds? I mean, come on, are you serious? Atticus was right, you know. You've no idea how good you are … how *amazingly* talented you are."

My eyes start to water, and I turn away, sniffing sharply as I blink the tears away.

Atticus said that? He actually thought I was good at this? When he left, I concluded that he was just bullshitting me all those times. And now my brother, the same guy who I know was totally opposed to what Atticus and I had, is now agreeing with him?

This is rendering me speechless.

"Will you at least do one song? It'll be with me. Yes! Sing a song with me. It'll be cool. Brother and sister tag-team taking on the world! Okay, well, at least Avoca Beach, anyway."

I snort out a laugh, "We'll see … maybe."

"You gotta tell me now. I have to organise my playlist."

"Geez, pressure much? Fine, I'll sing … uh … a cover of "Strong" by London Grammar on my own," I answer way too quickly for comfort.

Shit! That's not an easy song. Why did I say that? And why did I say I'm singing alone when I had my way out of that?

Baby fucking steps!

"Yes … yes! That is perfect! Your version is fucking epic! You're gonna make this one song your bitch. Trust me."

"I won't. It'll be a freakin' disaster!"

"So you're either really, really deaf or fishing for compliments. But too late, I'm adding that to my playlist. You're gonna be amazing, Hannah Banana."

"I'm going to need shots both before and after that one song, Brodie. Then I'm probably going to kill you for making me do this. Straight after your set, you're done for."

"Good luck with that because you have to find me first," Brodie laughingly teases me.

My eyes widen at his answer, and I feign a hurt look on my face.

"Oh shit, was that too soon? I'm so sorry, Hannah," Brodie places his hands on my shoulders, his voice sincere and apologetic.

I answer with the only way I know how … the same way I used to get back at him when he used to annoy the hell out of me.

Without warning, I give both of his nipples a hard twist. Hard enough that he feels the burn through his T-shirt, making him screech in agony.

"Didn't need my eyes to do that, dickhead!" I laugh out aloud.

"Tell me again why I'm doing this? I can't go on, Brodie. This is insane!" I nervously whisper to my brother while we're sitting in the booth closest to the stage. I'm already on my third shot of tequila, hoping this liquid courage will actually work.

"You got this, Han," he reassures me. "You should be loosening up by now. How many shots have you had, anyway?"

"First of all, no, I don't 'got' this. I have *never* sang, nor have I played guitar onstage. This will be my first, and possibly my last performance. And this tequila's not working! Are you sure you gave me tequila?"

"Hey, if this will be your last performance, which I'm highly doubtful of, then bloody make it count!" Brodie sighs. "Look, the place is packed, and most of these people know who we are. They're not here to judge you or me. They're here to have a good time. Why don't you just give them a little bit more credit, huh?"

"I know. I'm just … I don't know," I mumble. The noise buzzing from the crowd muffles the sound of my nervous heart beating, but I can still feel it thumping.

Okay … now I feel nauseous. Oh, boy.

"Oh my God. Hannah?" a familiar, sweet-sounding voice calls my name.

That voice. How can I *not* know who owns that voice?

"Brook?" I turn my head to the direction where the voice comes from, feeling equally astounded. "Brooklyn Sanders, is that you?"

"Oh my God!" she cries, then her familiar scent hits me, followed by familiar arms wrapping around me, and not letting go. "I can't believe it. I mean, I was hoping to visit you at your place while I'm here for a break although I never really held any hope that you'd want to see me. But you're here, and you can't escape me now!"

"I'm so sorry, Brook. I was in a really bad place after Paul … and now I'm blind …"

"I know, you don't need to explain," she tells me. "We all felt Paul's loss. We all grieved with you, Hannah. And we understood that you needed time."

I say nothing, as I close my eyes, feeling my chest clench. I remember vividly the shame I felt, self-loathing after our accident. It led me to drive off everyone I cared for. I hated myself for what I did, and I was too scared that they'd see through my grief and find out that I was the cause of it all.

"But hey, you've been given this gift of a second chance, Hannah. And I'm sure Paul would want you to use this gift and continue to *live*."

I choke on my tears, nodding. She's only been here for less than five minutes and she already knows how to make me feel better.

"I'm trying to live again, Brook. But it hasn't been easy. I'm just thankful that Brodie's here right now." I reach for my brother, giving his shoulder a good squeeze.

"Hey, Brook," I hear Brodie speak apprehensively.

"Hey …" Brook hesitantly answers back.

Even through the tears I'm wiping off, I notice the tension in their voices. It seems weird, but my gut feeling is telling me there's more to it than meets the eye between these two.

Am I just being paranoid, or do I need to look into this further?

I try to set the thoughts aside for now so I can try to enjoy the fact that one of my best friends is actually here, and she has forgiven me.

And very soon, she'll watch me make a fool of myself.

Shit, I can't believe I'm still going through with this!

Just then I hear a guy's voice introducing himself as the host. He thanks everyone for coming to Peak and for supporting the club's first ever open mic night.

That's it, I can't play the guitar now; my hands are too clammy!

"And now to kick things off, we have a surprise for all of you," the host says. "We have a guest here at Peak, who's also a friend of mine. But he's not just any guest. He's the lead singer of this little known band called, what was it again … Halcyon?" The crowd erupts in cheers, with the girls high-pitched screaming filling the space so loudly that it's practically deafening.

"Let's welcome home, Brodie Mackenzie, everyone!" The crowd roars once again, and if I weren't so damn nervous, I would be joining them too.

"That's my cue. Meet you up there later, sis," he whispers, giving my temple a quick peck, and as the cheers become louder, I know that he's now onstage. Brook is now holding my hand, and I give her a squeeze—maybe a little too tightly.

"Why are you trying to numb my hand?" Brook asks, chuckling softly.

"Sorry, I'm just nervous," I answer, wincing.

"Don't be. You'll kill it on stage, I'm sure of it," she reassures me.

Wait. I thought this was supposed to be a surprise? I thought no one knew I was playing except for Brodie?

"How did you know I'm going up there?"

"Uh …" she pauses, and I turn towards her with curiosity.

"What's going on, Brook? How did you know I was playing?"

"But you might get mad at me. Please promise me you won't be mad."

"Why do I not like where this is heading?" exhaling aloud, I continue, "I was the bad friend between us so of course I won't be mad. So … out with it."

"Okay, here goes … Brodie and I are—"

"Dating?" I cut her off.

"What? You know?"

"It's funny how losing my sense of sight made my remaining senses a lot stronger."

"I asked him not to tell you yet until I'm here. I wanted you to hear it from both of us. Are … are you angry?" Brook asks, sounding genuinely worried.

I reflect on her question and realise that I'm not. How can I be?

Shaking my head, I answer, "No. I'm pissed off that he kept it from me, but it's only because I would've given both of you my blessing sooner."

"It's all new, Hannah. And it only really started by chance when I bit the bullet and contacted Brodie so I could ask how you were doing. One thing led to another. I wasn't really sure how you'd take it."

"Well, you've been crushing hard on my brother since you started wearing a bra. Until now, I still can't figure out why."

"I wasn't that obvious, was I?"

"You were," I chuckle. "But my brother wasn't exactly subtle when he started noticing you. I just didn't want to say anything before because I didn't want things to get awkward between you two if my suspicions were incorrect."

144

"Damn, all this wasted time, just because I never thought Brodie saw me that way."

"Are you happy though? Are you both happy?"

"I can't speak for your brother, but I'm so happy, Hannah."

"Then nothing's wasted." I hold her close to me, squeezing her tight.

"Oh man, enough about me and Brodie. How about after the show, you and I have our own girl time and just catch up?" Brook squeezes me in an embrace again. "I missed you so much."

"I missed you so much too. But seriously though, I just want to know if you're ready for what comes with dating someone like Brodie. I mean I love my brother to death, but he was just on tour and he'll be on tour again. You're just starting your degree so you'll be busy too. Atticus left me for his music, Brook. I don't want you to feel the hurt I felt."

"I understand your concern, and I love you for it. But we're still figuring it out. And who can really tell? Maybe this will be different, maybe it would end up in a heartbreak, who knows? But I'm willing to find out where this takes us."

Brook sounds choked up, and I feel a twinge of guilt for making her feel like this.

But she's right. Love's like a lottery. Sometimes you just get lucky and hit a jackpot. Sometimes, your luck just runs out.

"You're right … I totally agree."

"Thanks, Han. Thank you for being so understanding about this whole thing." Brook gives me another hug, and manages to squeeze the guilt out of me and replaces it with joy.

She's always been such a wonderful hugger. I never realised how much I missed that about her.

We both turn our attention back towards Brodie, now singing the acoustic version of Halcyon's hit song, "Amplify." I can't help but feel that bubble of pride at how a song written in the old shed at home has now become one of the most played songs on the radio.

By the middle of his second song, my stupid nerves decide to make a comeback, making me nauseous with anxiety from an onset of stage fright. I know I'm supposed to come up on stage soon after Brodie has finished with the second song. He'll do some sort of introduction before he accompanies me towards the stage.

"You're shaking, Han. And your hands are getting all sweaty," she says, as she playfully wipes my palms on my jeans.

"That's because I have to be on stage soon. I'm a nervous wreck!"

Brook chuckles softly, "Well, stop it, woman. You're beautiful and super talented, and you look absolutely perfect in your skinny jeans with that off the shoulder top. And did I mention how killer your boots are? Oh, wait!" I hear Brook rummaging through what I presume is her purse. "Good, I brought it with me." She turns my head towards her, holding my face secure by the chin. Then I feel something moist running over my lips, followed by the distinct taste of strawberries.

"What the hell?" I ask when she's done. "Is that lipstick?"

"Nope. It's just a nice, tinted lip gloss. Your lips will look absolutely fantastic under the lights."

I suddenly remember the side of my face that needs to be hidden. So I sweep my hair on my right shoulder, fluffing it up a little so my scar is covered.

"What are you doing?" Brook asks.

"What do you think? I don't want these people to freak out when they see this," I tell her, cheeks reddening from the imminent embarrassment.

"No one will freak out when they see you. Your scar's not even that obvious. Don't worry. And if someone says something, I'm going to fucking punch that person in the throat, then your brother will hold that person down so I can carry on with the punching."

I can't help but laugh at sweet Brook's threat of violence in the name of loyalty.

This is why I never should have pushed my friends away.

Moments like these make me realise how much I took my friendships for granted.

But I have no time to feel any form of regret. As soon as I hear Brodie starting on the introductions, I know I have to man up and put my game face on.

"Ladies and gentlemen, thank you for deciding to stick around after a couple of songs. But right now, I'd like you to indulge me with some amount of your time so I can welcome to the stage, my sister and sometimes best bud, Hannah."

I hear murmurs from the patrons around the bar, with some laughing at Brodie's intro. But all it's making me want to do is melt into the leather of the booth's seat.

"Most of you don't know it, but my sister actually plays guitar as well. Mind you that unlike her big brother, she wasn't very good at first." There is some laughter scattering around, and I know this is Brodie's light-hearted attempt at humour is his way of making me feel comfortable enough to take the stage.

But I'm still nervous … nervous about how I'll sound, how I'll play my guitar and how I'll sing that cover.

Brodie continues on, "Nah, I'm just kidding. She plays like a pro. She's also writing her own songs and let me tell you, they are pretty sick. But …" I hear my brother exhale through the mic, "something happened six months ago that changed everything."

My stomach twists in knots, and I try to keep my composure as I push past the anguish.

I can't break down in here.

"All I want to say is that my sister went through hell and back, and I've never admired anyone's tenacity more than I admire hers. So it will be an honour if she joins me onstage for one song tonight. Ladies and gentlemen, give it up for my sister, Hannah Mackenzie!"

As Brook helps me out of the booth, amongst the cheers from the audience, I get an instant epiphany.

It's all clear now.

Paul.

The first thing I feel as I'm guided on the stage is the warmth of the lights on my skin. Though some of the light is seeping through my eyes, the warmth tells me exactly how bright it is.

The next thing I feel is a rush of adrenalin flowing from inside of me, and my heart racing.

With Paul's smiling face in my thoughts, I reach for the microphone, my guitar across my chest.

"Hi, everyone, I'm Hannah. I just wanna say you guys sound amazing, and thank you Brodie, for the kind intro," I chuckle softly, the crowd joining in with encouraging cheers.

"I was supposed to do a cover song for you tonight. But I thought, since this is open mic night, anything goes, right?" I hear the crowd clap in agreement, instantly boosting my confidence. "So, I've decided to deviate from my original choice so I can sing you an original song instead. Is that alright?"

The crowd roars once again, making me smile back at them.

Now I'm beginning to understand why my brother loves to perform.

"I wrote this song for a special person in my life. Well, it was actually for our first anniversary. I didn't have a lot of money to spend, so I decided to write him this song instead. When he was taken from this world way too soon, I … I took it quite hard. And even though I'm still on the road to acceptance, I consider the time I've spent with him as a blessing because he truly was that … a blessing, not only to me, but also to the people who knew him well. And wherever he is right now, I hope that he's listening because every word in this song is dedicated to him. This song is called 'Dear Mister.'"

And as always, I take one deep breath, I close my eyes and I strum.

After I hit the last note of the song, the crowd erupts in a high-spirited cheer. I respond with an awkward bow, endorphins making my heart pound. Brodie comes up to me and whispers that people are standing up, clapping, whistling, and asking for more.

My eyes fill up with tears.

I did it. I can't believe it. The crowd is still clapping, their sound thunderous.

I don't know how to describe how I'm feeling in this very moment. But one thing's for sure: what just happened is beyond invigorating.

I wish Paul could see this. I wish he were here so he would know without question that he would always have a place in my heart.

"Thank you. Thanks, everyone," I bow my head several times, humbled by the crowd's continued, positive response.

"Give them a wave, Hannah Banana," Brodie whispers.

I do what he says. He asks me if I want to sing another song. I shake my head no.

I want to leave the stage on a high.

It feels like I've just exorcised my inner demons, like I've finally bid my goodbye to the guilt and regrets. Like this is me, telling Paul that I'll be forever grateful to him for the way he loved me, but it's time to start a new chapter.

I told myself before that I wanted to move forward with baby steps.

But after tonight, I've finally realised that sometimes, moving forward means throwing yourself off a cliff, and trusting that the universe will help you land right on the very spot where your new journey should begin.

Still on the weirdest high, I give the audience one final wave before Brodie takes the mic and my guitar, thanking me for an 'epic' performance, before ushering me back off the stage and onto Brook's waiting hands.

At least I thought it was Brook's.

But this person feels way too much like the very last person I expect to hold me.

"Atticus?" I call out, my hands instantly on his arms, then on the sides of his face, my smile fading.

Well-muscled arms, a light scruff on the face … and that scent—that same scent I used to love smelling on my clothes and skin.

Oh God. This is the last thing I need right now.

"Hi," he says.

"You're here," I answer back.

"I wasn't going to miss this, Hannah. You were phenomenal up there, just like I knew you would be," he says.

I hate how sincere he sounds.

His touch makes my skin tingle, so I push myself off him. I don't want him to feel what his touch can still do to me.

Stupid body chemical reaction.

"Why are you here? No one told me you were coming," I whisper harshly to him.

"You're surprised, I understand. But let me take you to your booth first so we can talk." Atticus places his hand on my lower back, and carefully guides me around the crowd and into the booth.

"I don't think we really have anything to talk about. Where is Brook?" I ask.

"She was filming your performance so your parents can watch it, but now she's giving her boyfriend some water. Don't worry, I'm not kidnapping you; I offered." I hear the leather squeak, and the cushion dips on one side.

Great, now he's sitting next to me.

And not only that, he heard me sing about Paul!

"Why are you here, Atticus?" I ask again.

"I was invited."

"By whom?"

"Nate, the owner. And Brodie."

"Did you know I was singing tonight?"

There's a slight pause, "Yes."

"Did Brodie tell you?"

"What's with all the questions, Hannah?"

"I think you know why. Maybe it's a good thing you heard me sing that song."

"Because you wrote it for Paul?"

I don't answer, but I do slide away from him, needing the distance so I can think straight.

"That was a beautiful song, Hannah. I'm sure that would've made Paul very happy." Atticus reaches for my hand, startling me and making me gasp.

"He *was* happy. I wrote that song for him on our anniversary," I answer back sharply, unsure why Atticus stating Paul's name gets me on the defensive. "Why are you still sitting here with me? Why don't you go and find somebody else to piss off?

"I'm *just* sitting, Han. I'm not out to fight with you. This is a free country after all."

"Well, you can't just show up whenever you want to and expect me to act like it's okay."

He snorts, then I hear glass slamming on the table, "Still hating my guts, I see. I knew that coming was a risk, but nothing could've stopped me from watching you tonight. And I'm glad I came because you were a fucking breakthrough."

What he said ties me up in knots. Then I hear some shuffling, before a cool whoosh of air on my skin tells me he's no longer sitting next to me.

I hold my hand up, "Wait ... I don't hate you, Atticus. You don't have to go, okay?"

"It's for the best." His scent hits me as I feel him coming closer. Then he lays a kiss on my temple, "Keep on singing, Hannah. This is your path. You have the power to inspire people with your music."

Oh.

I should be pissed off with him for just showing up whenever he wants to, wherever he pleases. But then he goes and says these kind words to me.

It's not fair how he keeps breaking down my walls like this.

I grab onto his arm, "Don't go. Look. I'll hear you out. Maybe we can go somewhere quieter to talk?"

"Of course. Where do you want to go?" Atticus asks me, the

relief in his voice evident as he takes my hand, standing me up with him.

"I'll just let Brook know, then, we can go."

Atticus takes me to where I assume Brook will be. By this time, Brodie's finishing his last song of the night, but as soon as the rest of the crowd sees Atticus in plain sight, I start to hear girls shrieking and gasping his name, followed by murmurs of delight that Atticus is sharing this space with them.

He squeezes my hand to get my attention, "So where would you like to—"

"Atticus!" Whatever he was going to ask me was cut off by Brodie calling out to him, "Where are you going, mate? I was just about to introduce you."

My brows scrunch together, "You were going to play?" I ask him, feeling confused.

He sighs, "Uh … yeah, but I don't have to. I want us to have that talk."

"Ladies and gentleman, who in here would like to hear Atticus Foster sing us a few songs?" Brodie yells out, and the crowd answers with a roar like they're about to bring the house down.

I hear Atticus whisper a harsh curse.

But the loud volume of the crowd calling out for Atticus is reaching fever pitch.

I can't take him away from this. He lives for this, doesn't he?

"Go. Sing." I let go of him, gently pushing him on the shoulder. "I'll wait."

"No, it's okay. I don't have to," he answers, placing his hand over mine.

"A-tti-cus! A-tti-cus!"

My whole body reverberates from the thunderous claps and booming cries of the people demanding a performance from their local star. And as much as I'm flattered that he would prefer to turn away from this pandemonium so we can talk, I'm not going to be selfish when it comes to him. I have no right to.

"Do you really want to deny this mob of your music?" I ask him in my loudest possible voice. "It's okay, Atticus."

"But if I get up on that stage, will you stay and listen to the song?" he asks, his lips close to my ear, making my insides clench. And even through the loudness of the maddened crowd, I can still hear the vulnerability in his voice, and it tugs at my insides.

"I'm a blind woman in what sounds like a packed bar full of possibly drunken patrons. Trust me, I've got nowhere else to go alone."

He chuckles, his lips still by my ear, and as much as it makes my insides clench when I recall how his face lights up in laughter, I can't help the sadness that comes with not being able to physically see it.

"Well, I'm not gonna take any chances," Atticus wraps an arm around me, and my heartbeat spikes. Then he pauses, and with hands on both arms, he urges me to sit, where a chair is waiting for me.

"You're front and centre, babe." And before I can dispute the endearment, he kisses my cheek, and whispers, "I only need to sing one song. Then we can go."

I shrug back, "Okay."

The crowd erupts once again, and I imagine Atticus must be getting on the stage.

"Thank you, everyone! You guys are too kind to this Central Coast busker from Roscoe."

I can't help but smile. He *has* come a long way from busking in just a short amount of time. And even though I was a casualty on his way to success, I can't feel any resentment for his hard work.

"I wasn't really sure if I should be singing tonight. The calibre of talent has blown my mind, and frankly I'm kind of developing a complex here," he pauses, waiting for the laughter to die down. "Brodie is amazing as usual. And … and as for his sister, Hannah? She … well, this budding singer, songwriter is just something else. She truly inspires me," he pauses, and I bow my head down, unwilling for him to see that I'm blushing.

He continues, "So, how about we give them a hand?"

The crowd applauds, and I hear catcalls of *"Go, Hannah,"* making my cheeks turn a deeper shade of crimson.

I've never touted myself as a singer or a songwriter. I always thought my path was to become a lawyer just like my father. But the accident has given me a second chance to choose the path that truly makes me happy, and making music *is* that path where I feel I'm at my happiest.

Now I understand Brodie and Atticus even better.

"The song I'm about to perform is something I wrote just recently, while I was holed up in my shack. It might sound a little rough, but I think this is the right time as any to share it, so bear with me, yeah?" The crowd screams in approval, and some random woman yells out that she wants to be holed up in the shack with him as well. I try to ignore the urge to punch that woman in the face because really, I have no right to be jealous. Atticus and I are over, and all I'm willing to offer him is my friendship.

"I'll take that as a yes," he responds. "This song is called "Once Again.""

As soon as Atticus starts singing and I hear the poignant emotion from every single word, my chest begins to tighten up, and I feel like I'm losing my breath.

His song is about second chances, and that not everything is what it seems.

I don't want to believe this is about me ... or about us. But it's hitting home, and it's hitting hard.

You want him as your future,
But your future's standing here.
Think your heartbreak has no cure.
I'll be your medicine, dear.

That verse confirms it. It's the final blow, and it cuts through my skin and into my heart, leaving me with shivers and goose bumps all at the same time.

And that's not even the worst part. The worst part is how my brain is rethinking my offer of friendship towards Atticus. His words are waking emotions that I forced into slumber, and now it's making its presence known.

I don't want the song to end, but on the other hand, I also want him to stop singing the song because I hate the power it's starting to have over me.

The audience loves the song. Their reception is overenthusiastic to say the least. But as for me, I can't even bring myself to clap my hands. I'm too stunned by the song to even function properly. A hand squeezes my shoulder, and I tilt my head up to figure out who it is.

"Wow, Han. He's not holding back, is he?" it's Brook, and even she sounds in awe.

I am too. I'm fucking speechless.

"Thanks, everyone!" I hear Atticus say. "You've been amazing

… and loud! Very loud. But I have to call it a night, guys!" Most of them clap, but some of them sound their disapproval. Then I hear the host speaking on the mic, trying to appease the crowd with a round of free drinks.

"Hannah? Are you ready?" Atticus is now in front of me.

Good question. Am I? I don't even know what to say after *that*.

Is this going to be another leap for me?

Any doubt I have on my next leap with Atticus is drowned out by the hard thuds of my heart and my blood rushing to my head, drowning any remnants of hesitation I have left.

"Brook? Is it okay if you tell Brodie that I'm going with Atticus? He'll take me home."

"Oh … ooh! Yeah, sure. Well, good night, kids! And let's catch up soon, Han. Now let me find my boyfriend. Gosh, it still feels weird saying it aloud!" The thrill in Brook's voice is hard to mask, and I must admit that it matches the thrill I'm feeling inside.

"So … where would you like to go?" Atticus asks hesitantly as he takes my hand and helps me up.

"Your place," I answer way too quickly, but I stop myself from retracting my answer.

"Hannah," he sighs, "I'm not sure if my place is ideal for us to talk. How about —"

"I don't wanna talk anymore. We can do that after maybe … I don't know."

He pauses, and I know for sure that he's staring at me with a stunned expression.

"Okay … okay. If that's what you want." He's still holding my hand, and as he guides me through the hyped up crowd, he whispers, "Hold tight." And I do, my other hand clinging to his arm.

The fresh air on my face and the way the noise from the bar now sounds muffled, tells me that we're finally outside.

"Where's your car?" I ask him.

"Tell me what's on your mind right now, Hannah."

My heart is beating so fast, and my insides are tightening like never before. If only Atticus could see all of these things happening inside of my body, he wouldn't have to ask me about it.

"I know that I wanted to talk earlier. But then you sang that song. Maybe it was for me, I don't know, but now …" I stop walking and I turn to face him, reaching both of my hands to cup his face, "now, all I can think about is you and me …" I feel my heart rise to my throat. "And I want you, Atticus."

"That song *was* for you. They have *all* been about you, Hannah. But I didn't do that with the intention of getting you into bed with me."

My heart falls back down with a thud, and I go on defensive mode, "So are you telling me that you don't want me? Is it because I'm blind? Or is it because of the big-ass scar on my face? I must look so fucked up to you right now."

"No … Just … Just. Stop. It's not any of those. Haven't I been clear about how I still feel about you?"

"Maybe you haven't," I spit back, still stinging from the initial rejection, but I continue after a shaky breath, "Since I've already made a fool of myself, I might as well not stop now. So let me just give it to you straight, okay? I want you, Atticus Foster. You sing about wanting another chance with me … then help me remember you. Let me remember how you *feel*. That is my decision, and if you can't bear to do it, please just take me back inside Peak."

So that's it. My pathetic attempt at seducing the person who broke my heart in the first place, has turned into a pitiful act of pleading.

This is humiliation at its finest.

This must be what rock bottom feels like.

Atticus takes me by the elbow and starts walking, but not speaking a single word. My heart sinks even deeper, and into an abyss that has become increasingly hard to get out from.

"Are you taking me back to Peak?" I ask, on the verge of tears.

He stops walking again, and I do the same. But what I hear next is the familiar beeping of a car alarm being switched off, then a car door opening.

"Get in," Atticus commands, and he guides my body inside, placing a hand on the top of my head as I step inside his car.

I stretch my arms up and feel the car roof above me. And before me are the same clean lines I felt that day he manhandled me from my group session.

I hear the car door opening from the other side, and as he gets in, the enclosed space allows me to enjoy the way he smells. I don't know what it is about this guy's scent that gets me every time, but it does. God, it *so* does.

I instinctively turn to face him, and just as I do, his long fingers cup the sides of my face, and he kisses me.

His lips on mine, warm and moist, and his tongue as it enters my mouth is hesitant yet persistent. It feels perfect, and I have no choice but to give in. The first time he ever kissed me, I was completely unprepared for it, but I knew that clearly, my body was. Now they are in sync, as my thoughts are filled with images of Atticus's green eyes darkening with desire for me, and my core clenching in response.

Atticus pulls away, his breathing laboured, "My place."

"Your place," I answer back, just as breathless as he is.

He untangles himself from me, and I reach for the seat belt, my heart racing and my cheeks feeling flushed and warm. But my hand reaches for his arm, halting his movements.

"No rush. Please … just be careful," I utter meekly.

Then I feel his hand on my cheek, and he kisses me chastely on my lips, "I promise."

He starts the engine and drives off.

The ride is quite short, and from where I remember Peak is, which fronts the beach, Atticus's *shack* must be just around the bend.

"Do you remember that house close to the rockpool? You know, that blue and white beach house which I said I'd own when I became super famous rock star?"

He's parked the car, and we're just walking up what I assume is the path to the house. Then I hear him unlocking the door.

I chuckle softly, "Yeah. I remember. It was just the right size. Not too big, but it had a killer balcony. Wait, don't tell me this is it? Did you …?"

"I'm just renting it for now. The owners decided to move up to Queensland. They're not interested in selling this. Well, for now, anyway. I'm thinking of making them an offer they can't refuse."

"Really? Why would you buy a house here when you're travelling all over the world? Why not make the city your home base? Do you think it's practical to plant roots here?"

"You ask way too many questions," he replies lightly, "but I want to be upfront with you from now on. Yes, I do have an apartment quite close to the city, and that's where I stay if I'm not touring. But I want to be able to have a place to run to when shit gets too real … somewhere I know I'll be happiest in."

"So Avoca makes you happy?" I grin at him.

"No. I'm happiest where you are."

"What? That doesn't make any sense," I laugh it off nervously, feeling my stomach flutter.

"I know it's hard to believe considering what I've done to you … to us. But Han, it will always be *you*. So even if I'm not physically with you, just knowing you're in the same vicinity as I am, it gives me a sense of calm that I can't fully explain."

Oh.

"But—but you were never around. You only came back that one time over a year ago."

"I came back a lot more than once. But every time I did, you were with Paul. The first couple of times were hell because I told myself that I couldn't rebuild a bridge I destroyed myself. So I stayed away. But that time last year was my weakest moment. My jealousy won over common sense. And when my common sense finally took over, I ended up hurting you all over again."

I jump when I feel his warm touch over my scar. "Then I found out about the accident. Hannah, I …"

His voice trails off, and I don't know what he's about to say next.

All I know is that I don't want to talk about that or anything else anymore.

At least for tonight.

"How about … how about we talk about this tomorrow?" I whisper, "Please, I just want you to kiss me again."

I tilt my head up as an invitation, and with one choked groan, Atticus dips his head and meets my waiting lips. Both of our lips open eagerly, welcoming each other's tongue in a desperate dance. I go up to the tops of my toes, needing more of his beautiful mouth, if that's even possible. But he does one better, making me gasp as he grabs the back of my thighs so he can lift me up.

"God, Hannah. You taste like how I dreamt you would," he mumbles against my hot mouth.

"You dream about me?" I ask in a whisper, unable to hide the grin spilling on my face.

"Fucking always," he growls back.

He's walking forward, and I feel myself bouncing slightly as he goes up the stairs.

I move my lips to his jaw, nibbling down his neck, making him moan. I know for sure that his green eyes are now getting darker, and the expression on his face will be focused … even aroused.

I'd give anything to see that.

Just imagining the expression on his face makes me want to combust. What started as a slow burn when I first heard his song at Peak is now turning into a raging inferno.

He stops walking, and with my legs still wrapped around his waist, I hear him opening a door.

"Are we in your bedroom?" I ask softly as he walks once again.

"I hope this isn't too presumptuous for you?" he asks, letting me go so he can close the door.

"No. This is just perfect." And before I know it, he swiftly turns me around making me gasp. Then he fists his hands in my hair and pulls me closer, tipping my head up so he can smash his lips on mine.

This kiss is not as gentle as earlier. He's kissing me like a man deprived of oxygen, and I'm kissing him back like I have all the air he needs. He sucks on my lower lip; then, he leaves kisses on my jaw … that scarred jaw.

Oh no!

I move my head subtly, hoping this movement will make his lips move downwards, or back to my waiting mouth … anywhere but there.

But once again, I feel his lips retracing their steps, and he starts leaving tiny, torturous kisses along my scar.

This time, I'm not so subtle when I turn my head away, but he gently cups the unscarred side of my face so I have no more room to move.

"Don't, Hannah," he whispers against my cheek, "Let me."

"No! It's disgusting. It's ugly," my voice rises, as tears of shame threaten to flood my eyes.

How can he even think that this awful scar is worth touching, let alone worth kissing?

Feeling sick to the stomach, I push him away, stepping further away from him.

"Why would you kiss my scar like that? Can't you see it's horrible? Every time I feel it, I'm reminded of that night when Paul died because of me. *This*, Atticus is a part of my fucking punishment! I'm cursed, and I can't do anything about it."

158

"*Nothing* about your face is ugly, Hannah. And you are *not* cursed. What you think is abominable is actually a reminder of your survival, of your resilience ... of your second chance. It's a gift. That's why I want to kiss your scar because, believe it or not, I'm thankful for it. To me, it's a stunning addition to the amazing person I'm still completely in love with."

I'm stunned, my mouth agape, but I can't utter a single word. Instead, my tears begin to fall.

Atticus sees the beauty in my ugliness, and the positive in all of my negativity. It's a sentiment I'm not allowed to deserve.

"Hannah," he whispers and my body goes rigid as I feel his arms wrap around me, "please don't cry." He tilts my head up, and I close my eyes. It's a stupid thing to do. I'm blind after all. But I can't let him in … I can't face him. I'm too afraid that maybe, somehow, he'll see how undeserving I am of his words … his song … his love.

Oh my God.

He just said he's in love with me.

Still. He said *still*.

Atticus is wiping the tears off my face. I reach up to hold onto his forearms.

"You said you still love me," I manage to choke out.

"Songbird, I never stopped."

My heart feels like it's about to explode. "Please … can you just kiss me? Please?" I plead softly.

He does, with no hesitation.

And he's kissing me passionately, lovingly.

Then his hands make their way downwards, his fingers finding the break between my top and my jeans. And as soon as I feel his fingertips on my bare skin, I gasp.

"Unbutton my shirt," he says with a voice thick with desire.

"Okay." I nervously reach for his chest, trying to feel what type of shirt he's wearing, but I can't seem to think straight, my heart racing, and my fingers trembling.

"Trust what you feel," he says, and he guides my hands over the middle of his shirt.

My fingertips graze the opening of his button-down shirt. I carefully open each button, surprised at how deftly I'm doing so. When I feel that I've unbuttoned all of them, my fingers seem to have a mind of its own as it spreads his shirt apart.

His breath hitches, as does mine, when my fingertips touch the warm skin of his chest. I push one side of his shirt further, hopefully exposing the side of his chest where his heart lies. Then I place my hand over it, promptly feeling the strong beating of his heart.

Unable to help myself, I take one step forward, until my lips are a hair's breadth away from his chest. I take in his scent, masculine, clean—very Atticus. Then I close my eyes and press my lips right on the skin where his pulse is beating.

"Hannah," he moans. But I refuse to stop, tasting him as I move upwards until I reach the middle.

"What are you doing to me?" he roughly whispers.

"Same thing you're doing to me," I whisper back, my lips not leaving his skin.

With a pained groan, Atticus lifts me up and roughly lays me on his bed. I feel him hovering just above me, using his knee to open my legs wider.

"My beautiful Songbird," he says, as he pushes strands of hair from my face.

I almost choke on a sob. I feel the heartfelt sincerity in his voice, and it's the sweetest torture. I reach up to wrap my arms around his shoulders, pushing him down so I can press my lips against his. When his tongue pushes past, I lightly suck it, earning me a guttural groan. Then I feel his hands move down to the hem of my top, gripping it. And just as he tries to pull up my shirt, I raise my arms over my head to make it easier for him. Before long, my top is gone, followed by my shoes, then my jeans, leaving me only in a pair of my underwear that I'm positive is unmatched. I feel the chill of the salty sea breeze coming from what I assume is an open window, but it's when his now naked body is on top of mine, do I feel tiny goose bumps on my skin.

"Hmm," he says, his fingertips lightly grazing my skin, arousing every sense I have at my disposal, "Feeling chilly, or is this because of me?"

"Both," I breathe back, biting my lower lip, "but mostly because of you."

"Hmm," he repeats, before I feel his lips on the curve of my breast, as he nibbles his way upwards and back to my mouth. He kisses me so passionately that my legs wrap around his waist, lifting my hips up to gain some friction. He knows what I need, as he dips his lower body down and begins undulating his hips right against my already throbbing apex.

And he's hard … hard and amazing against me.

I don't need my eyes to remember how incredible he feels against me.

Somewhere along the way, our underwear has been shed, leaving both Atticus and I completely naked.

"I wish I can see you," I croak out.

Atticus shifts positions, and I feel the bed dip right next to me.

"Use your hands to remember me, Hannah. It's just like you playing the guitar ... close your eyes and strum." Atticus takes my hands and places them on top of his bare chest.

And so with my heart beating out of my chest, I lift myself off the bed and swing my leg over his torso, placing my palms flat on his chest to find my balance.

"God, I'm not gonna last long with you on top, baby," he tells me in a pained voice.

I place a forefinger over my lips, "Shh, I'm trying to concentrate here."

And with one deep breath, I close my eyes and 'strum.'

It seems weird that I feel the need to close my eyes when I play guitar. But closing my eyes helps me focus, giving me a mental picture of the placement of my fingers, and a clearer memory of the notes from the music sheets I've memorised.

And now, as I use my highly sensitised fingertips to reexplore Atticus's body, I close my eyes and start to rebuild an updated picture of him … piece by piece … part by part. I start from his arms, feeling every sinew, every muscle. He feels larger, with muscles more pronounced. My heart breaks a little when my fingertips graze over the scar on his upper arm, courtesy of his piss-drunk excuse of a father who swung a broken beer glass at him in anger for not giving him his busking money. The glass shard missed his face, but his upper right arm bore the brunt instead. And from my memory of him last year, his one tattoo is now joined by many more, as his whole right arm is now adorned with beautiful works of art. I remember him telling me the story of each and every single tattoo, and I actually felt a tinge of hurt when I realised that none of his tattoo stories included *our* story. But I pushed the disappointment away. I was committed to Paul at that time, so I had no right to ask Atticus why our story wasn't worth a tattoo.

But in one night, I managed to forget my commitment to Paul, thanks to Atticus and his power over me.

God, I'm a bad person. I'm *such* a bad person.

"Come back to me, Hannah," Atticus's gentle voice pulls me back to him.

"I'm here … don't worry, I'm here," I tell him, as I move my hands to his hair, which feels longer, but still soft and silky. Then my fingertips travel to his face, hovering over his eyes: green with speck of gold from memory. He has the kind of eyes that you can easily get lost in, just as I have done so many times before. His sculptured jaw is now covered with what feels like a short beard. I'd give anything to see him with it, and if the visual I have in my head is the same as what he actually looks like, I know for sure that he looks sexy as hell. Then my forefinger glides along his lips, and I squeal when he nips at my fingertip. But he makes up for it when he holds my hand and kisses the same forefinger. I have to bite on my lower lip to stop myself from moaning. Both of my hands are now tracing the length of his neck, and I smile when I feel his pulse thudding faster. Knowing his excitement is building to fever pitch makes my insides clench. When my hands sweep across his chest, Atticus lets out an uneven breath, and I smile to myself, knowing that I'm slowly undoing him. But it's my turn to let out a sigh as soon as my fingertips are reacquainted with Atticus's abs, because now, they feel more cut, more pronounced than the six-pack I remember.

"You've been working out," I tell him, trying to sound cool so he won't notice my drooling.

"Gotta take out my frustrations somewhere, right?" Atticus answers, sighing jaggedly.

My brows scrunch together. "Frustration over what?" I ask, licking my lips while I trace the deep grooves just above his hipbones, wishing it were my tongue tracing this sexy, sculpted line instead.

"Frustration over not having you." Atticus suddenly grabs me by the waist and flips me on my back. The sudden move makes me gasp, and I'm excited beyond belief.

Before I can utter a single word, Atticus smashes his mouth on mine with an intensity that makes every bone in my body turn to mush.

"I want you so badly, it fucking hurts. Please make this pain go away, Hannah," he pleads with me while pressing his hard self against my wetness.

I nod like a crazy person, "Yes, Atticus. I need you too."

He reaches past me, and I use this chance to taste the skin on his chest, unable to help myself. Seriously, how can someone taste this good? He groans, just as I hear a drawer opening and closing, followed by what sounds like a foil wrapper being ripped open.

Atticus positions himself in-between my legs, and as he whispers my name, he enters me fully with one thrust, knocking the air out of me.

"Oh my God," I cry out, tilting my head back from the pleasure, as I savour the fullness of him inside of me.

He laces our fingers tightly, raising our linked hands above my head as he continues to thrust inside of me—slowly at first, but growing stronger, faster, deeper. My moans mingle with his own as the pressure building inside of me grows to explosive heights.

Because I feel everything.

I feel him. I feel them all.

And wow, Atticus is waking all of my senses and they are in full alert: his sounds of satisfaction, the feel of his hard body against mine, and light chest hair tickling my torso, his taste … if sexy has a taste, then Atticus tastes just that: sexy. And finally his scent, mixed in with the scent of sex is just complete sensory overload.

And damn, how he feels inside of me cannot be put into words.

It's too much. It's way too much for me to hold on.

"Oh … God ... Atticus!" I screech out as the throbbing inside of me becomes too much to bear, and I come. Hard. So hard my whole body convulses in its aftermath.

It doesn't take long before Atticus follows, and as he comes, I pull him down so I can kiss him, loving the reverberation of his groans as they become more intense.

And then he's still, as I am, and the only sounds that break the silence are our hearts beating strongly in unison.

"Wow. Wow," he whispers against my lips.

"Yeah, wow," I answer back.

That's the thing about orgasms. As you wait for euphoria to settle, your brains seem to stop functioning altogether.

He buries his head against the crook of my neck, and his breathing is ticklish on that sensitive spot. "Sorry. I tried to lower my pace, but I just couldn't hold it in any longer. I've been dreaming about this moment for so long that I've gotten impatient. But I'll be a lot better the second time around, and I'm fucking ready. Just say the word."

I try to hide the grin on my face when I answer, "Hold on, tiger. Second time around? You're getting awfully cocky, aren't you?"

He kisses my neck, and I giggle even harder when he finds that super sensitive spot. "When was I ever *not* cocky?"

"You got me," I giggle some more.

A moment passes before Atticus whispers back, "I sure hope so."

CHAPTER SIXTEEN

Hannah's Sixteenth Birthday

It's true.

My life pretty much rules right now.

I just turned sixteen, and my amazing family is throwing me an epic birthday party at the local Surf Club, and everyone I've invited are here and having a great time.

But most of all, Atticus Foster, arguably the hottest, most promising singer, songwriter that has ever graced this coastal town, is performing at my party.

Oh, and have I mentioned that Atticus Foster is my boyfriend?

My. Boyfriend.

Mine.

Sure, I insist that we keep it a secret from my family, not because I'm ashamed of him but because I don't want Brodie or my parents to interfere. I know they'll try to talk me out of a relationship with Atticus because they don't want me to get hurt when he leaves. I have a feeling though that they've figured us out already, and they're just waiting for us to confirm it.

I mean hello? My family's not dumb. There are only so many times we can find excuses to 'practise' in the shed together. And, my guitar playing has improved so much that having Atticus over for more 'lessons' is now becoming harder to justify.

But after tonight, I plan on telling the whole world what Atticus Foster means to me.

God, it feels so good to be able to finally do that.

Who knows? Maybe if Atticus sees how much I'm committed to him, he will do the same and decide to stay, or at least wait for me until I graduate so we can move to the city together.

Hopeful much? Maybe.

Or maybe I've finally realised that I don't want to live my life without Atticus in it.

And speaking of the hot devil, I'm watching him as he's setting up onstage. Strands of his longish dark blonde hair have fallen on his face, and he haphazardly rakes them back.

Hmm, maybe I should go over there and help him.
Nah, he's got this. I'll just stand here and enjoy the view.

Brodie's band Halcyon has just finished their set, and it's now Atticus's turn. He scans the hall, and finds me immediately. He ignores the group of girls from my school who are trying to catch his eye, jutting their chests out to make their boobs look bigger. It annoys me, and I know I shouldn't be upset on my own birthday party, but this is one of the reasons why I want everyone to know that Atticus is mine.

But maybe I'm just being an idiot.

Atticus might have been a total player before but ever since we got together, his wandering eyes are focused only at me.

And he confirms it when he gives me a wink before flashing the smile that puts his dimple on full display. Thank goodness I'm sitting down, otherwise my legs would probably give out. I hear Patty whispering for me to keep my legs crossed and to restrain myself from throwing any piece of my underwear, or myself, at him mid-performance. I just giggle back in response.

The only people who know about my true relationship with Atticus are my best friends, Brook and Patty. They understand where I'm coming from, and why I have to keep things under the radar, at least for the time being.

And once in a while, they help me out by covering for me so I can go out on a proper date with Atticus. Sometimes we even go somewhere as far as the city so there won't be any chance of us being seen by someone we know. There, he treats me to lunch, then we watch the talented buskers at Pitt Street Mall. I always tell him that those buskers have nothing on him, and it's true. But on the inside I'm dying a little, because as much as I'm fully aware that our relationship may have an expiration date, a part of me is still clinging to that hope that he'll change his mind and stay.

But on the other hand, it will be a huge disservice to society if they don't get a chance to hear any of Atticus's songs. He's an amazing songwriter for such a young age. He writes with genuine emotion because the music and the lyrics he creates are borne from his own life story.

Atticus places the strap over his head and plants his sexy bum on the bar stool right behind him.

This is where he belongs—onstage, but definitely somewhere a whole lot bigger than a surf club hall.

He's bound for greater things.

Maybe it'll make me the worst girlfriend in history if I stand in his way.

"Oh God, look at how he's looking at you, Han. He looks like he wants to eat you up!" Patty tells me lightheartedly.

I can barely respond to her observation because I'm too busy melting under Atticus's gaze.

But that's his effect on me. His smile or even the way he looks at me feels like we're the only two people in the room. Anything or anyone else doesn't matter.

It takes all of my self-control to stop myself from bum-rushing the stage and getting into fourth base with him in front of everyone.

He doesn't know about it, but tonight, tonight is the night that I'll give *it* up.

By *it*, I mean my virginity.

Just thinking about it gives me butterflies in my stomach—nervous, excited butterflies.

Atticus has been extremely patient, never asking me to do anything further until I'm truly ready. The thing is, we've been together for over six months, and I know that it must've been hard for him to hold back, especially since he's used to girls throwing themselves at him.

I know what blue balls are, and I'm sure he's suffered his share with me.

But Atticus is hot as fuck. I'm not even going to mince my words. And I'm only human. We *have* done other things.

We've also seen each other naked. But that was also one of the reasons why I was scared to take that next step with Atticus—his size. I mean, what if he won't fit? And what if I won't be able to live up to his expectations and he'd think I wasn't worth the wait after all.

And yet, in those times when we've come close, and I'd tell him that I couldn't go any further, he'd stop and would tell me he understood, and that he wouldn't go any further until I was very sure that I was ready.

That alone, made me fall even deeper in love with him.

And somehow, that was what made it worse as well.

Atticus knows that I love him. I never have any qualms in saying that out loud to him. But when it comes to him expressing his feelings for me, the closest he'd ever been was by singing me covers of songs during my 'lessons.'

And yet I swooned every single time. And there were instances when I'd even pretend that he wrote that song for me. My imagination could be quite convincing when I wanted it to be.

That was another reason why I held back from giving myself completely to him—I was afraid that he really didn't feel the same way as I did … that he really didn't love me as much. He was too closed off, and I couldn't understand why.

Then one day, out of desperation, I followed him home. I followed him all the way to Roscoe, and when I knocked on his door, I saw the shock on his face. And the fear he had that his father might find out about me was enough for him to finally let me in.

He took me home on the same night. And the very next morning, he returned and finally told me everything.

Atticus was raised in a house where love had never seen the light of day. His mother died due to severe blood loss as she was giving birth to him. His father was devastated and never got over it. So much so that he became resentful of his own baby, his very own son, and he decided to leave him in the care of his mother, Atticus's grandmother. He told me how his grandmother was nurturing, and she did everything she could to care for him like he was her own. When he grew older, Atticus found out that his father barely sent them any child support, spending his money on booze instead. His father was able to hide his drunken state from his employer for some time, but awful habits have a tendency to catch up on you. He came to work one day still reeking of booze. His boss told him to go home, and he got punched for because of it. Atticus's father was fired right there and then.

His father never went for counselling, or sought help from professionals. His therapy came from the likes of Jack Daniels and Jose Cuervo.

Then it went from bad to worse for Atticus.

His grandmother was loading a few grocery bags in the boot of her car one afternoon, when two men attempted to steal her car. She tried to fight back because that's how she was, according to Atticus. She was a fighter, and she fought to raise Atticus in the best way she knew. But, as she fought against one of the carjackers in the driver seat, her shirt got stuck to the door and she was callously dragged for over a hundred metres down the road, before stopping to finally free her from the car. But by then, it was already too late. She died on the scene due to the extent of her injuries.

Atticus was at school when it happened.

Her grandmother was on her way to pick him up.

Atticus was picked up by the police instead.

He was only ten years old.

By then, his father found another reason to resent him even more. When he was brought back to his father's home, his father made damn sure that he reminded Atticus of the repercussions of causing the deaths of his wife and his mother. The physical, mental, and emotional abuse towards Atticus continued on until now. I asked him why he never ran away from home, or why he never reported his father to the police. He had relatives living in the next town over, and maybe if they realised how bad his father was treating him, they could take him in. But he said that back then, he couldn't blame his father for all the beatings. Somehow, he had it in his head that he was actually responsible for the deaths, but I'm sure that it was his father's brainwashing that made him think so. Unfortunately, the abuse damaged him so much, that as he grew older, he began to shut down emotionally, and started lashing out at school. He didn't have many friends to begin with, but when he started picking fights, he pretty much lost all of them.

Thankfully, the music teacher who broke off a couple of his fights, saw the bruises Atticus tried to hide, as well as the pain hidden behind the anger in his eyes. He approached him and asked if he was interested in learning an instrument. He said that music could be a way to channel his negative energy. On the day he first picked up the school guitar, it changed his life forever. His teacher told him he was a natural, but that he was still holding back. So he encouraged him to try to put his feelings into words, which wasn't easy for someone so closed off like Atticus. But his teacher believed in him so he started believing in himself. Eventually, they managed to transform his words into song form.

So, at thirteen, Atticus had written his very first song, "I Am Here." The first time he sang the song to me, I was in tears. I felt his pain. I felt what he wanted to express.

Using the money he saved from small jobs here and there, he managed to buy himself a preloved semiacoustic guitar. He practised whenever his father would pass out drunk, locking his door just in case he'd wake up and decide to shut him up with a belt.

And when he got better, his confidence grew with it. So he busked at the nearby shopping centre on the weekends, and on Thursdays when it was open until the late hours. He was so good, singing covers and one or two of his original songs that he managed to collect enough money to buy a decent guitar. And when he was of age, he used his savings to cover up the scar on his arm with a tattoo: a badass phoenix.

He opened up a bank account and kept the rest of his money away from his house, in case his father got wind of his savings and tried to get it from him. Even though he was all grown up and could physically fight back, Atticus never did. He knew that hurting his father will never end the cycle of abuse, but would just make him no less different from his abuser.

One random Saturday, Brodie and his mates, all members of the Halcyon, chanced upon him busking. They were so impressed that my brother knew he just had to get to know him.

They eventually became good friends, and that was how I met him.

And even though Atticus and I started off on the wrong foot, I wouldn't have it any other way.

I'm in love with him.

I'm in love with my beautiful, damaged, but gifted man.

If only his past didn't make him incapable of saying those three little words back.

Maybe after what I have in store for us tonight, he will finally declare how much he loves me.

Yeah, I know that it's probably the worst thing that I can ever do. I've probably read way too many romance novels, that I'm naïve enough to think that men sweeping women off their feet truly happens in real life. It's not like he hasn't been very clear since the beginning that he's leaving for the city to focus on his music career. Music has always been his 'out.'

But he's still here, and he's still with me.

That must mean something, right?

"Hello, everyone," Atticus's deep, rough voice cuts through my sombre reverie. The waiting audience whoops in response, their arms up in the air.

"So ... I was asked by the lovely birthday girl herself to sing a few songs for you all tonight. She also asked nicely, so it was easy for me to say yes," he chuckles softly through the mic, with his eyes looking straight at me. The intensity of his stare makes my insides clench.

"Before I start, how about we give Hannah a huge round of applause?" And to my surprise, everyone does, and my best friends start hugging me tight. Atticus gives me a wink, making me smile even wider.

And just before the noise dies down and with his eyes focused on me, Atticus begins to sing.

Watching him in his element is awe-inspiring, something I don't think I'll ever get over witnessing. It's like watching a star shining so brightly that it obscures everyone else around it.

It's beautiful.

This is where he belongs. I've known that all along. But watching him and his effect on his audience confirms it. He truly is meant for bigger things.

But now I'm struck with a worrying thought. If I give Atticus my virginity, I wouldn't need a crystal ball to predict that it's going to make me fall more in love with him. And I must really be naïve to think that he'll magically change his mind and decide not to leave because he's also fallen so deeply in love with me as well.

I lose either way.

Maybe I should hold on to at least one part of myself that's still intact.

I can't give him my virginity and my heart at the same time.

I need to at least keep one thing I still have control to.

After all, my heart is already a lost cause.

Atticus wraps up his third song, and I clap my hands, feeling my chest expand with pride. But the smile I'm wearing has now been marred by this unexpected dilemma.

He takes it all in, and I love that even through his show of confidence, there's still that look of surprise in his eyes, like he can't believe that a large group of people appreciate his music. I hope that when he does make it big, and I know he will one day, that he'll never lose that sense of humility.

I notice Atticus pulling the stool closer so he can sit down, his guitar resting on his thigh. He adjusts the microphone lower to his seated level and addresses the audience again.

"I wrote this last song a little while ago, but this is the first time I'm singing it for anyone else. But I think that out of all the songs I've written or have sung tonight, this would have to be hands down, *my* favourite," then Atticus lifts his gaze back to me.

Maybe it's the way he keeps looking at me with so much sincerity, but my skin starts to prickle and my back straightens up in attention. I raise my drink to him, and I flash him an encouraging smile.

When I asked him if he could sing some of his own songs for my sixteenth birthday party, he promised to sing four … all originals. But he said that the only way he could sing them was if he'd be directing them only to me. He said he wasn't ready to see the guests' reactions, in case they hated the songs. I wanted to shake some sense into him for not believing in his talent. But, on the other hand, I might have loved him a little bit more for seeing me that way.

"Well, this song is for her. *Only* for her. This is called "Songbird.""

I almost choke on my drink in shock.

Songbird. His song is called "Songbird"!

He strums the first notes and I think I stop breathing. But as he sings every lyric, every line, all I can feel are goose bumps on my skin, and my heart beats so hard it feels like it's lodged itself in my throat.

The song is about me … and about us.

But it's when I hear the chorus.

That's it for me.

I just let my tears flow.

> *You saw beauty in the scars;*
> *You're like my dream coming true.*
> *Songbird, you got me fallin';*
> *I've fallen in love with you.*
>
> *Sing me your sweet lullabies;*
> *They keep the nightmares away.*
> *I want to drown in those eyes;*
> *My songbird, I'm here to stay.*

This must be what it feels like to die and go to heaven. Because every word from "Songbird" is killing me in the best, most amazing way. It feels like an out-of-body experience, like I'm actually floating on air.

He loves me.
And he's here to stay.
!!!!!!

I want to rush on the stage and hold him tightly in my arms. I want to kiss him like no one else is around us. I want to feel his breath on my skin. I want to take his clothes off and …

… and what?

I want to make love to him.

Oh my God, that confirms it.

Oh my God! Oh my God! Oh my God!

I can't believe how a single song can become such an incredible turning point for me.

Atticus. Loves. Me.

And.

He. Is. Staying.

He said it in a song … a song he wrote for me.

I can't breathe. Need air.

I feel his eyes on me as I stand up, ignoring the curious reactions from my friends. I walk past the large crowd as they applaud Atticus's song. I don't wait for him to finish, needing that air so badly. The skin all over my whole body is tingling like crazy, and I feel like I need to giggle and cry at the same time. I finally make it outside, and I turn towards the beach, taking off my platform heels so I can feel the sand on my toes.

The cool grains of sand swallow my feet, and the smell of salty, ocean air calms me down and keeps me centred.

The dance music from inside the hall is my signal that it's time for me to blow out my sixteen candles. But before I do, I need to just breathe in and out and compose myself.

So I do the same ritual that helps me start the process.

I close my eyes, and I just breathe deeply.

"I'm sorry if my last song scared you off," the sombre tone of Atticus's voice makes me jump and tugs at my heart at the same time. I turn around and see the hurt in his face.

Oh no.

This is not what I want him to feel.

I quickly walk up to him, and I wrap my arms around his waist. He sighs aloud, but thankfully, he hugs me back.

We fit so perfectly.

I'm falling so hard.

With my head still against his chest, I assure him, "Your song didn't scare me. It was … God … it was so beautiful."

I tilt my head up to face him, smiling, eyes still glazed, "I still can't believe you wrote me a song."

"I can't believe you walked away."

I shake my head, "I didn't walk away from you or the song, Atticus. It was either this, or I rush that damn stage and offer myself to you like a living sacrifice."

He chuckles, the full moon illuminating the relief on his face. Then he cups my cheeks with both hands, "This sacrifice you speak of … does it in any way involve you slowly undressing in front of me?"

I nip on my lower lip, my eyes locked in his, "Hmm, I was actually thinking more like sacrificing my virginity to you."

He chuckles again, before what I just said finally hits him. His face turns serious in an instant.

"Wait, where are you going with this?"

I take his hands off my face, replacing them on my ass cheeks instead, "I'm sixteen now. Legally, I'm of age. You getting where I'm going here?"

His eyes widen, and I can't help but notice the spark of excitement in them, "Are you sure?" he whispers to me.

"Do you love me, Atticus Foster?" I ask softly. "Please … I want to hear you say it."

A smile so tender lights up his face, and he whispers back, "I love you Hannah Mackenzie. I think I fell for you long before I even realised it was love." He kisses me lightly on the nose, "I'm sorry it took me this long to tell you. I'm fucking slow like that."

I brush my thumb against his cheek, the gentle gesture a complete contradiction to how explosive I'm feeling on the inside. "You're not slow. You were too hurt. But I'm here, and I love you," I brush my thumb across his lips, "and after this party, I want you to make love to me."

His mouth gapes against my thumb, and my core tightens as his breath tickles my skin.

"If this is truly what you want, then I'll take care of it. But I want you to know that there's no pressure, okay? You have from now 'til after the party to cha—"

"Shush," I cut him off, pressing my forefinger against his lips, "I am not changing my mind from now, 'til ever. This is happening

174

tonight. Question is, are *you* ready?"

He raises his eyebrows in mock surprise, and his smug smile, the one that drives my hormones crazy is back. "I waited over six months for this, Han. Why don't you look down my pants and tell me."

My eyes widen at his brashness, and I swallow hard as my eyes travel downwards.

Wow. He wasn't joking.

I know exactly what his junk looks like when he's ready. Our make-out sessions had made me an expert on his *readiness*.

It's too good not to touch. Even if it's just a feel and squeeze over his jeans. But just as I'm about to reach for him …

"There you are! Quick, Han, cake time!"

I jump away from Atticus in panic, and I see Patty rolling her eyes at us, trying hard to look cross.

"Okay, babe. Thanks!" I answer back, cringing at Atticus's expression—a smile that's a cross between apologetic and someone getting kicked in the nuts.

I smile apologetically, whispering, "Don't worry, I'll do my best to make you feel better tonight." Then I give him a quick kiss on the lips before walking back to the hall.

"Fuck me," I hear him mutter under his breath.

"I will," I call out, giving him my sexiest cheeky wink, laughing at his gaping expression.

"Here she is, everyone!" Patty announces over the music, as I step back inside the hall. She gives me a knowing smile as she veers me in the middle of the makeshift dance floor. And I mouth a discreet *thanks* as she starts backing away.

The light suddenly shuts off, and a collective gasp fills the air as Brodie and his friend Shane carries a sculpted cake of a girl riding a wave with a surfboard, with sixteen candles illuminating the whole masterpiece. The way the surfboard and the girl, who thankfully bears a resemblance of me, riding the crest of the wave, practically defies gravity.

Brodie leads the singing as soon as the kickass cake is right in front of me.

"C'mon, blow the candles, Han! This cake is damn heavy!" Brodie orders.

"Language!" Mum's clipped response sends everyone laughing, me included.

I close my eyes and make a wish, but instead of a wish, I thanked the universe silently.

I had my wish already—Atticus loves me, and he's staying!

I quickly blow all the candles, and just as the crowd erupts in hoots and cheers, the disco lighting goes back on, and the music blasts from the speakers again.

I scan the crowd for Atticus, wondering what he meant by 'I'll take care of it.' Not finding him anywhere in the hall, I let my friends drag me onto the dance floor, and we dance while eating a slice of my chocolate fudge-flavoured birthday cake.

Yum.

A guy I see around school gives me a birthday greeting and asks if he can dance with me. I think he said his name is Paul. He's super cute in a surfer kind of way, and I'm flattered that he's even asking me for a dance. But everyone knows he's a player. I've seen him with a different girl almost every week.

I wish I was more gracious with him while we're dancing but I'm way too distracted by my rock god, tattooed boyfriend, who, by the way, is still nowhere to be found.

Where the hell is he?

When the song ends, I excuse myself from Paul, vaguely noticing the wounded look on his face. But I quickly push the guilt away. I have a boyfriend, and I love him so much. So damn much that I am willing to give him my precious v-card.

I'm sure Paul won't have any trouble finding someone else to dance with.

It's been a little over an hour since I blew out my birthday candles and guests are beginning to say their goodbyes. I'm starting to worry, checking my phone constantly. I left him a couple of messages asking where he is, but he hasn't replied yet. The last thing I want is to freak him out by getting all clingy and sending him a hundred texts.

Patty and Brook are chatting with me about some shit that went down outside the hall between two girls from school. They found out they were dating the same guy and shit got real. I'd normally be all over this like seagulls to a piece of chip, but all I can think of is Atticus and why he hasn't called me.

I'm close to asking Brodie to help me find him when I feel my phone vibrate. I breathe a sigh of relief when I read that it's actually from Atticus: *Ask your friends to cover for you overnight. Then meet me at the parking lot near the public showers.*

By this time, my nerves are shot. But I turn to find my friends, and beg them to help cover for me so I can meet with Atticus and hang out with him for the night.

And because they're my best friends, they went along with my plan.

After telling Mum that I'm tired and that we're having a girls' sleepover at Patty's, all three of us head outside the hall. Patty calls her boyfriend to take her and Brook home. We go our separate ways so I can meet with Atticus. I'm scanning the surroundings looking for him, when I notice a tall figure approaching me. The light in this parking space is a joke, but the swagger in his walk confirms who it is.

"Hannah," Atticus calls for me, raising an arm up for me. I run to meet him, skin prickling with an excitement I only ever feel when I'm in his presence.

As soon as I'm pressed against his body, he smashes his mouth against me, kissing me deeply, tongue pushing through my lips like it's on a mission to obliterate me. I reach up to touch his cheek, but as soon as I do, Atticus lets out a pained wince.

I pull away, now concerned, and that's when I see a bruise turning purple on his jaw.

"Oh my God, Atticus. What happened? Did you get into a fight?"

He shakes his head, pulling away completely. But he keeps silent as he takes me by the hand and leads me up towards the main road.

"Atticus? Talk to me!" I block his path, leaving him with no choice but to stop walking.

He exhales aloud and roughly rakes his hair back, but he walks around me, "Don't worry. It's just my dad. I forgot my wallet so I went home to get it. Unfortunately, I hid my wallet a little too well that I totally neglected to bring it," he laughs bitterly, taking my hand so I can walk with him.

"So he did that to you? He hurt you? Why?" I'm practically tripping over myself, trying to match his stride in wedged heels. But he's closing off again, and it hurts me to see him like this.

"Atticus … Atticus, please … tell me what hap—"

"He fucking wanted money, and when I said no, he did what he

177

was good at …" Atticus closes his eyes, and I watch him with concern as he tries to breathe out the anger and the hurt.

How a father can hurt his own flesh and blood like this doesn't deserve to be called a parent.

"I'm so sorry Atticus. I feel like this is my fault. You wouldn't have to go back home and cop a beating from that … that *man*. We need to ice that. Do you want to go to my place instead so I can ice your bruise? We don't have to do … you know … If you just wanna talk or something," I reach up to touch the darkening bruise, but he catches my hand and presses his mouth against my fingertips, sending tiny shivers up and down my spine.

"It will always be up to you, Hannah. I don't want you to feel obliged to do anything you don't feel comfortable doing."

"When you said you were taking care of it. What did you mean by that?"

He looks away, "I, uh, booked us a hotel room. Well, it's more like a room at the motor inn. Unfortunately it's nothing fancy, but it's what I can afford. We don't have to go. You might not like the place. I can still cancel it."

I pause from walking, and I look up to his face, and see my man's usual confidence on the decline.

Gosh, this boy … this beautiful, vulnerable boy.

I love him so damn much.

"Take me there," I tell him softly.

His eyes widen, "Are you sure?"

"I don't care if it's a hotel room, a motor inn, a cave, or a small patch of grass. If it means spending tonight with you, wherever it is will be perfect for me."

His look of disbelief turns to awe. "I want to kiss you so badly," he whispers.

"And I don't want you to stop when you do, so take me there now … please?" I insist gently, giving him my sweetest smile.

He returns the smile and takes my hand so we can start walking again. Avoca is a tiny coastal town, so it doesn't take long before we're both standing at the entrance of the motor inn. I've passed by this place many times, and this is the first time I've actually taken it all in. It's got a simple façade, but it fronts the beach, so its location is perfect. We can hear the waves crashing from here.

Nervous tingles awash my whole body, and it bursts when Atticus squeezes my hand, urging me to follow his lead. We walk past the front office, passing one door after the other, where a couple of cars are parked in front of them. He turns his head to me, giving me a smile that calms my nerves slightly. Several more doors down, and he stops in front of door number sixteen.

"Sixteen?" I ask him incredulously, laughter bubbling on the inside.

"It was available. I couldn't help myself," he shrugs, smiling sheepishly as he produces a key from his pocket with a keychain that matches the number on the door.

My heart beats faster and harder as Atticus opens the door and says, "I might have gone overboard on the whole taking care of it thing, so …"

And as he steps aside to let me in, I gasp, hands over my mouth, eyes wide open, taking it all in.

The room is lit using just the lamps, giving a softer ambience inside. On the table sits a bottle of what looks like champagne that's been chilling in an ice bucket with two flutes beside it.

And the bed—there are rose petals scattered on the bed.

Rose petals!

Who the hell does rose petals on the bed?

They're beautiful. More than anything I even asked for. I never asked for any of this. I just wanted him. But he goes out of his way to do all of these; even getting himself beaten up by his father just so he can give me something I'll never forget.

What did I do in my sixteen years to deserve someone like Atticus Foster in my life?

I hear him closing the door and locking it. "Happy Birthday, Hannah Mackenzie," he says.

I turn around to face him, a ready smile on my face. But when I see him standing there, holding three red roses with one hand, and wearing a smile that is a polar opposite to his usual smugness, I choke on my tears.

He offers me the roses, and I accept them, smelling their fragrant musk, "I made sure I bought extra for the bed. I don't know, the smell kind of reminded me of you. Is it too cliché?"

"Never, baby," I laughingly cry, bunching his T-shirt with my free hand, I pull him down to me, crushing my lips to him. He moans against my mouth, his hands sliding flat on my lower back, pulling me against his body. His tongue touches my own, and I open my lips wider, needing more of what he's offering. He tastes so wonderful, so addictive.

But then I realise how much of a mess I must've looked like.

I don't want to remember our first time together with him thinking that I looked like a hot mess.

And his bruise ... my poor baby!

I untangle myself from him and immediately see the frown forming on his handsome face.

"Let me just freshen up a bit. And while I'm getting ready, we should ice that bruise of yours."

Before he can say anything, I'm already in the bathroom retrieving one of the face washers. Back in the room, Atticus is still standing on the same spot, hands in his pockets, eyeing me curiously.

I head straight to the table, giving him a sidelong glance, smiling to myself as I place the flowers next to the wine bucket. I try to pick up a few ice cubes, but I can't seem to hold onto most of them. That's when I notice that my hands are a little shaky.

My focus is on trying to make this ice pack for Atticus that I gasp when I feel his hand on my stomach, and my hair being swept to one side. Then his lips press gently on that sensitive spot on the crook of my neck.

"Hmm," he sounds off, and the vibrations of it, travel right down to my core.

I try not to notice how my legs are almost giving way as I face him with the makeshift ice pack.

"Here, place this on your cheek." I lift it up and see him trying not to wince when the cold meets the purpling bruise.

"I just want you to know, before we do this," I continue, "that what you did tonight: from that song you wrote, from hearing you say those three little words, and going the extra mile to make this night special, are something I'll never forget for the rest of my life."

He brushes his knuckle against my cheek, and I close my eyes to feel the way his skin feels against mine.

"I love you so much, Hannah. I don't know what you've seen in me, and no matter how I made it so hard for you to love me, you still do. And God, you love so freely. I just want you to know that I'll always put you first, okay? I'll always put you first. No matter what happens. Always."

Then he kisses me. He kisses me in a way that he never has before. It's a kiss of love, of gratitude, of passion, of pain, of hunger … of everything.

This kiss is everything.

I love his everything.

All thoughts of freshening up are thrown out the window, as each piece of our clothing is thrown on the floor instead. He takes the lead, and I let him. He's kissing me everywhere, in places he's familiar with, and in places that he knows will make me cry out his name.

He's made me come before, but tonight, it doesn't take me long before my blood is pumping, and I'm writhing in complete abandon, out of breath and in utter bliss.

I'm still catching my breath when he crawls on top of me, using his knee to open me wider for him.

He takes a condom from the bedside table and readies himself, his eyes never leaving my own.

"I'll be gentle. Trust me?"

I nod back, circling my arms around his shoulders, "I love you. Of course, I trust you."

And then he's inside of me, inch after inch. I hear him exhale an unsteady breath, but by now, I'm squeezing my eyes shut, wondering if I can actually adjust to his size, and trying to anticipate the pain I hear about so much.

"Open your eyes, Hannah. I'm right here."

I blink my eyes open and focus them back to him, and I'm taken aback by how he's regarding me so tenderly, reassuring me without words that he's true to his word, and he won't hurt me.

Then in one swift thrust, I feel the sting, making me arch my back as air seems to be pushed out of my lungs. He presses his mouth against my own, deepening his kiss with every thrust until all I can feel is pleasure.

Atticus lifts his head up and cups my face with his hands, watching my face as he rolls his hips, making me feel sensations like nothing I've ever felt in my life.

"You're so beautiful," Atticus tells me, his eyes roaming over my face like he's seeing me for the first time.

I brush my thumb against his bruise, my heart aching for this wounded, broken love of my life.

But all of my thoughts dissipate when his thrusts increase in momentum, and I close my eyes, moaning as the pressure inside of me intensifies and overflows.

"You feel so good, Hannah ... so worth the wait. Just like I thought you would be," Atticus whispers against my neck, his breath tickling my skin. Then he nibbles the crook of my neck, squeezing my breast with one hand.

That's all it takes.

And I explode into a million pieces.

"Oh my God!" I cry out, my fingernails digging into his back as my body trembles from unspeakable pleasure.

"Hannah," he cries out. He follows me soon after and climaxes with me, head buried in my neck, whispering my name over and over again.

It takes me a few moments to collect my thoughts, and so does Atticus. And then he lifts his head and looks straight at me, brushing strands of hair that have stuck to my face. He regards me with an unreadable expression, and I begin to wonder what's on his mind.

"Well, how was it?" I ask him quietly.

"I should be asking you, Han," he answers, half-smiling.

"It was more than what I expected."

"Did I hurt you?"

I shake my head, "No. It stung at first, but it felt great after."

His half-smile turns to a self-assured grin, "I'm glad."

"You haven't answered me yet. How was it? I mean, you're far more experienced than I am." I look away, unable to avoid the stupid pain of knowing I wasn't his first. It sucks just wondering what number I fall under on his list of conquests, but for some masochistic reason, I needed to know what he thought.

"Look at me, please, Han," he uses his forefinger to turn my attention back to him. "You were incomparable."

"What does that even mean?" I ask, my heart beating out of my chest.

"It means you pretty much ruined me for any other girl."

"Shut up." My eyes widen in shock, and I think my heart literally jumps out of my chest from happiness.

But it is short-lived. "Wait. Does that mean you're planning on hooking up with other girls?"

He shakes his head, smiling kindly, "Baby, you misunderstood me. It means I wouldn't want to hook up with anyone else because *no one* will ever compare to how good you make me feel. And I'm not just talking about what we did tonight. You make me feel like I actually do have a place in this world. You make me feel so fucking loved."

"That's because I do love you with everything I have, Atticus."

"I love you so much back, Hannah."

"Thank you for waiting for me … and for deciding to stay," I add, as a tear falls from my eye.

He doesn't answer. Instead, he touches his lips with mine, and we kiss not with hunger or desperation, but with contentment and complete abandon.

Atticus is staying.

He's. Staying.

And he loves me. He *loves* me.

Best. Birthday. Ever.

I don't remember the moment I actually fell asleep.

However, as I'm coming to, squinting from the light spilling from the crack on the curtain, I do remember the events that happened before I did.

Maybe that's why I can't wipe the smile off on my face.

I hope Atticus knows that he's responsible for that.

Speaking of my hot as fuck boyfriend, I wonder if he's up for round two?

Damn, I'm such a slut!

Hmm, I'm sure he'll love it.

I reach over to his side of the bed, wondering when I actually untangled myself from his embrace.

I love his embrace, and I want more of it.

But as I slide my hand over, all I can feel is the rumpled blanket and the pillow with an indentation from where his head would've been on.

Puzzled, I open my eyes wider and sure enough, the bed is empty. I look around and notice that all of his clothes are gone as well.

Maybe he went out and got us breakfast.

I can't help but smile again at the thought. It makes me feel all sorts of warm and fuzzy. Duh, of course my sweet boyfriend wants to surprise me!

That's when I notice a small piece of folded paper on his bedside table.

Aww, a love note!

I'm smiling even wider now as I get up to reach for it.

But as soon as I read Atticus's handwritten note, my blood turns cold. For what I thought was a gesture of love, turns out to be a sledgehammer to the heart, painfully breaking it into tiny shards.

Hannah,

You will always and forever be my beautiful Songbird. But even though I'll love you until my last breath, I now know that you deserve someone so much better than me. I'm so sorry ... Atticus

CHAPTER SEVENTEEN

Present Day

No ... no! No, no, no, not again!

I wake up with a crazed sense of déjà vu as soon as I reach for Atticus's side of the bed, now empty and feeling awfully cold.

This means he would've left quite a while ago.

What makes things worse is that there's no way for me to confirm my suspicion.

I think I'm going to be sick.

"Atticus? Atticus!" I cry out from the top of my lungs, trying to hear any kind of sound to convince me that he hasn't done it to me again.

But I don't hear him calling back to me in response. I can't even hear any footsteps approaching. In fact, I can't hear anything outside of this bedroom.

Suddenly I feel a cold chill run down my spine.

I can't believe it.

I fell for this again.

Atticus sings me a song, and like a fucking rat to the Pied Piper, I become overemotional and gullible, offering myself again to the one person who I should know by now will never deserve it.

I'm such a damn fool!

My eyes are now pooling with hot tears as I stumble out of this unfamiliar bed, trying to get my bearings in this unfamiliar room so I can find my clothes, as well as my purse, which has my phone and my walking stick. But in my panicked state, I can't picture how this room looks like in my head, and I can't remember where I placed any of my things.

This is so humiliating—I'm stark naked, crawling around the floor trying to find my clothes and possessions because the man who I thought bravely poured all of his feelings for me in a song is still not brave enough to face me the next day. So he walked out and left me here ... again.

All alone.

What did I do in my nineteen years to deserve this from Atticus Foster? What did I ever do to *him* to make him hurt me like this? Haven't I gone through enough already?

"I'm such an idiot. Such a naïve, stupid, fucking idiot!" I scream out through gritted teeth.

Tears are spilling down my face and blood is pumping in my ears, but I don't give a shit anymore. All I know is that I need to get the hell out of here and out of Atticus's life forever.

And this time I mean it. I'm done.

I'm just. Done.

There is nothing left of my heart to break and yet Atticus still manages to scavenge whatever pieces he can find and break *those ones* as well.

After several attempts at feeling my way around the room to look for my things, I finally manage to find what feels like my jeans and a top, then my underwear soon after that. I hastily dress up, not caring anymore if the clothing is inside out.

Where the hell is my purse?

I remember dropping it next to the door. And I think my shoes are in that vicinity too.

Now standing up, I stretch my hands out so I can figure out where to go. But just when I thought I'm almost there, something on the floor stubs my toes and I trip, my whole body flying forward.

But that's not enough, *oh no*. The universe decides to one-up me again because as I'm sprawled on the floor, I hear the bedroom door opening, which by the way, I'm only inches away from.

"Hannah? What happened?"

Atticus.

What?

He hasn't left me.

The tidal wave of anxiety, anger, and relief becomes too much, and I completely fall apart. I curl into a ball on the floor, sobbing, unable to stop no matter how much I want to.

I hear him coming closer, and soon after, he's carrying me back on the bed, my head on the same pillow I was just laying on several minutes ago.

"Are you okay? Did you hurt yourself?" he asks, as he brushes away strands of hair stuck on my wet face. But I swipe his hand off me.

"Where were you, Atticus? I was calling for you," I ask him in between snivels. "I thought you left me again."

Damn it, saying those words out loud becomes my undoing. I fucking hate this. I turn away from him, trying to muffle the sobs with the pillow.

"I just got us some breakfast and coffee from the café close by. I didn't leave you, Hannah." Atticus lies down behind me and wraps me in his arms, holding me tightly. "I'm never going to do that to you again. I'm so sorry," he whispers against my ear trying to comfort me.

But I break from his embrace, unwilling to surrender to how amazing this truly feels. I try to find the furthest side of the bed, and I sit up from there, knees up to my chest in an effort to block him off.

"Then why did you leave me before then? What did I do to make you leave me without even talking to me about it? Was I that awful?"

I feel him shifting positions, but I flinch as soon as I feel his hand on my leg. "Please don't do this. It was never about you, Han."

"I wanted to hate you when you left me, Atticus. I really did … so badly. What you did cut me so fucking deep."

He whispers my name, and I wish I could see his reaction.

Blindness disadvantage number thirty-three.

"I don't know if you'll believe me or not, but as overused as this reason was, I never wanted to hurt you. That was the last thing I wanted to do. But after that night … after you … you gave yourself to me, I felt like I've become this greedy son of a bitch. You were this beautiful, funny, smart girl with top honours in school, coming from a well-to-do family. You had your future paved nicely before you. I was from fucking Roscoe, who went to a rough school, and the only way I got to eat was if I busked or ate at your place because my father was a drunk who thought parenting involved a good belting—"

His voice is becoming shaky, broken—just like I knew his childhood was. I saw it for myself back then when I followed him to his home that day.

The need to touch him … to comfort him … is too great, and I find his shoulder, leaving my hand there, unsure of what to do next. My heart jumps when he takes my hand and gently presses his lips over the palm of my hand.

But that's all he does. He doesn't do anything further. He just tangles his fingers with mine, and lays them on his lap.

He continues, "I just knew that night that I didn't want to be the one holding you back from who you wanted to be. So I took the coward's route, Hannah. I knew that then, but I had to do it. I know that I left you in the worst possible way, and that I hurt you deeply because of it."

"I woke up and you were gone, Atticus. And the measly note you left, telling me how I'm better off was a load of crap. Just admit it. You left me, not because of my dream, but because of yours. It has always been because of your dream. And once you'd taken what you wanted from me, you probably thought I wasn't worth hanging around for anymore. There was nothing else of me that you wanted. And now, I know for sure I have nothing more to give you."

"Stop. Just. Stop." I feel him shifting positions, and he takes my other hand and holds them both so tightly, and he continues on with a voice full of conviction, "You had and still have so *much* to offer, Hannah. And if that was what you thought this whole time after I left, then that was on me. I'm sorry."

"But Paul came and turned things around," I reply back bluntly. "He loved me more than I could ever dream of."

"Yes … I know. And the last time I was here, he made pretty damn sure that in no uncertain terms should I ever go near you again."

My head inclines to the side, and my heart starts to beat out of my chest. Did Paul know what happened back then? Is that why Paul never told me any of this. "He confronted you? How come I never knew about this until now?"

"I mean I can't blame him anyway. His reasons for confronting me were valid. So I told him he had nothing to worry about."

"But we kissed that time, Atticus," I whisper harshly at him. "Or have you forgotten? Maybe you just didn't care. You were telling me how it was going to be different between us, and I believed you. Then you up and left me again. And now this!" I pull both hands away, "God, Atticus, you played me for a fool the second time around and that was *on me*. That was *my* fucking fault! Do you have any idea how hard it was to keep that from Paul? I didn't want to keep secrets from him, but I had no choice. I loved him, but I betrayed him by not only kissing you, but also believing that *we* had another chance!"

"Hannah …"

"What was your excuse the second time around, *Tic*? What was it? Did you have another girlfriend waiting for you in the city? Was it the promise of more money from the record company? Or was it because you just *love* to play me?"

"It was none of those. Please, you have to believe me when I tell you that I left for the right reasons," he pleads.

This is hurting so bad. Why did I think it's a good idea to talk and reopen old wounds, and relive how awful I was to Paul … and how awful I allowed Atticus to treat me?

"Then what is it? What's your reason leaving me the second time around?" I ask, my voice shaking.

"Because I knew that Paul had more to offer. I was a musician who was just starting out, going out on the road all the time to promote a then little-known debut album. I couldn't offer you stability. He did. He told me about his plans, and he was ready to offer you more than I could ever give back then. I promised myself that the next time you'd see me, I would have to be the successful musician that you always encouraged me to be. I wanted you to be proud of me."

I scoff, "I hear your words, but all they do is spell out how selfish you were."

"I was being selfish? I sacrificed how I felt for you so you could fulfil your dreams. How was that a bad thing to do?"

"You were selfish because you decided that you knew what was best for me … what was best for us, without even talking to *me* about it. This wasn't just about you and what you thought was best. It's *my life*, Atticus. I get to decide what *I* think is best for *my* life! And all I wanted was *you* in *my* life."

He sighs, "I know, Hannah. I fucked up. I fucked up badly. But I saw how much Paul made you happy. I witnessed it for myself. You *loved* each other."

"See … that's the thing, Atticus," I say with a shaky breath, "as much as I loved Paul, and as much as I appreciate how incredible he was with me, I hated myself a little bit more, every single day I was with him, because no matter how I tried, my heart couldn't love him the way he deserved. I gave you my heart, Tic, all of it. But it broke when you left me, and it never healed the way it should have. So I loved Paul with whatever fragments I had left. And he loved me with everything he got. And yet, I could only manage to give him pieces of myself. It hardly seemed fair to him, but he never realised it because whatever love I managed to give him was true, and pure, and unconditional. Those little fragments of my heart were his."

"God, Hannah. I'm so sorry. I never knew …"

"How could you have known? You were living it up with your fame ... money ... women. I'm not naïve, Atticus. I know how it all works."

I gasp when I feel his hands cupping my jaw, "But that wasn't true, Hannah. And even if it was, I didn't give a shit because I wasn't sharing the experience with you. I would give up everything if it meant having a tiny piece of that love back."

"You owned the majority of my heart, Atticus. But it's still broken, and I don't know if it will ever heal or if I'm prepared to risk getting it broken again. And from the way I reacted just now, maybe I'm just not ready yet."

"Then I'll wait. And I'll even help you pick up the broken pieces so you can be whole again. Please Hannah … give me another chance."

I tilt my head downwards. "Why the hell would you give up everything for me? Isn't that why you up and left me in the first place ... because you wanted to have everything?"

"Hannah, I left because I wanted you to have everything," he insists, with both hands now cradling my cheeks.

I swat his hands off my face, "Bullshit. Don't twist this around on me."

"I'm not twisting anything. *I* was dragging you down. Me. I wanted you to be with someone you can be proud of … someone you can introduce to your family as your man."

Oh God.

All this time, I thought he was happy to keep our relationship a secret. But all this time, it hurt him.

He thought I wasn't proud of him.

Oh, Atticus ... if you only knew what I had planned the day after my sixteenth birthday.

"I've always been proud of you, Atticus. And I only ever wanted you. Not the fame, not the money. None of those shit. Just. You. And I was going to come clean to my parents and Brodie the day after my birthday party. I was going to tell them that we're together, and I didn't care anymore if they approved it or not, or if you were leaving eventually. But you never gave me a chance."

"Shit, Hannah ... I ... I didn't know. I thought ... Will you ever forgive me for hurting you like this?"

Forgiveness.

It's an act I can barely do to myself.

"How can I forgive you when I can't even forgive myself?" I ask him quietly.

"Han—"

"Do you want to know why Paul and I got into an accident in the first place ... the *real* reason why?"

I hear him exhale, "All I know was that Paul lost control of the car and slammed against the truck."

I tilt my head towards the part of the room that emitted the brightest light. "There was more to it than that, but you're the only person I'm telling the whole story to. I couldn't bring myself to tell everyone else because ..." I trail off, unable to finish.

I breathe deeply before beginning, "We were actually coming from a friend's graduation party. Paul wasn't really drunk, at least he didn't seem like he was. But I was pretty tipsy, borderline smashed. Anyway, Paul was driving me home, but I didn't wanna go home yet. I wanted to party some more. I mean, I aced the HSCs, I blitzed through high school ... and so did Paul. And you know how I get when I drink; I get pretty touchy feely"

I hear him suck in his breath.

"Sorry, I'm sure you didn't want to ... Anyway, the music was pumping in Paul's car, and just the fact that everything felt so freaking perfect, made me want to do something risqué with Paul."

"I really don't feel comfortable hearing this, Hannah," Atticus tells me, sighing.

"But I need to continue with the story Atticus. Please ..."

"I know, I know. It just feels like a punch in the guts to hear it, that's all. But you're right," he squeezes my hand, "please continue."

My breathing becomes shaky as I recall the next events, "Paul found a spot that was discreet enough. And since this was already in the late hours, there weren't many cars about. But by this time, I didn't care anymore. I just wanted him. We started getting into it, like clothes off and shit," I hear him exhale deeply again, and I start second-guessing if I should continue on or not.

But he needs to know.

Atticus needs to know the whole, ugly truth.

"Things got pretty heated up between us real quick, and I was so into it that I started calling out his name ..." My lips start to tremble, and fresh tears seem to gather in my eyes. "But ... but it wasn't Paul's name I was calling out. I don't know, maybe I was too drunk. But Paul stopped because he said that I ... he said that I was calling for you."

"What? Wait ... what?" even in a whisper, Atticus sounds incredulous.

And my stomach dips, knowing I have to repeat myself, "Paul and I were having sex, and I was calling your name. I mean how *fucked up* was that? How *fucked up* was I?"

Reliving that fateful night, no matter how necessary it is, hurts like a motherfucker because the guilt feels like razorblades cutting through my insides.

"Hannah," Atticus tries to wrap his arms around me, but I shake my head and push him away.

"And you know what? That wasn't the first time. He said that I called for you in my sleep too. And he said that on a couple of occasions when we were messing around, I said your name, and I didn't even know it. You know why? Because Paul just let it go. He let it go because he loved me, and he thought I just needed time to heal. That eventually I'll forget about you. But how many chances was he going to give me? We all have our thresholds. So on that night, while we were parked on the side of the road, practically undressed, he broke up with me. I was shocked. I never expected that he'd ever break up with me. But I guess that subconsciously, I knew this was inevitable. I was just too afraid to let him go and that I couldn't break things off with him myself. He was such a gentleman that he offered to take me home. He could've just left me on that side of the road, but he didn't. He wasn't built like that. But I don't know, maybe it was because we just broke up and we were still emotional, or maybe because he *was* drunker than he thought, but Paul lost control on the curved side of the road and hit that truck. Maybe if we stayed at that rest stop just a little bit longer, this wouldn't have happened. Maybe if I didn't seduce him, he could've just driven me straight home. Maybe if I called his name instead of yours ..." I'm choking on the words as memories of that terrible night begin to engulf me. "I felt so much guilt, and I felt so awful at the way I treated Paul. He didn't deserve a half-assed love, but that was all I could manage to give him. And I tried. I tried so hard to give him more. But do you know what was even more fucked-up? Just before the accident, I remember feeling so relieved. Can you believe that? Relieved! Relieved, even though I broke an amazing person's heart because I was still pining for the guy who shattered my own." I start clawing at my own chest, my body shaking, as I become hysterical, bawling like a mad woman.

"Stop, Hannah. No more, please. Stop beating yourself up," Atticus begs me, holding me against his chest, rocking me back and forth like a child in distress.

"I hate that even after Paul died, you're the one who continues to haunt my thoughts. It's *my* fault that he died. And now I can't even respect his death enough to stop myself from thinking about you," my words are muffled against Atticus's chest, but I'm sure that he heard every word.

He doesn't say anything, but he continues to rock me back and forth in his attempt to soothe me. The only sound in the room is my muffled sobs and the faint crashing of the waves from the beach just beyond the walls of this house.

I know that I should feel comforted by Atticus's arms around me. I should feel some form of relief because I'm finally letting everything out, no holds barred. Atticus finally knows what really happened the night of the accident, and yet he's not upset, he's not despising me. In fact, he's trying to make me feel better.

Me.

Why me?

But I don't feel comforted, or relieved. I don't feel like the weight of the world has been lifted off my shoulders.

I thought that finally telling Atticus the whole story would help liberate me from my self-hate, that maybe I'm on my way to forgiving myself.

But it doesn't help at all.

In fact, I feel shittier than ever.

Because hearing myself speak the words out loud just magnified exactly how awful a person I am.

I still loathe myself, and I still can't trust Atticus enough to feel secure that he won't hurt me again.

One night of passion and a morning's worth of revelations can't change everything in an instant.

But if I'm being honest with myself, I don't think anything will.

I was naïve to think that giving Atticus something so precious like my virginity would make him rethink his priorities; that maybe he'd change his mind and stay...or at least wait for me until I'm ready to go with him. I thought it'd make him love me more and he'd wait.

And since I developed a severe case of amnesia with a side of stupidity, I slept with Atticus again last night because I thought that remembering how we felt together would be the key for me to justify the clusterfuck of events that happened before the accident.

It's Atticus ... my body just responds to him in some cosmic level.

But I was foolish then, and I'm even more foolish now.

Did I really think that making love to Atticus would miraculously heal me? That being with him would cure my damage?

I still feel so broken, so afraid, so ... guilty.

I'm doing this all wrong.

And if I don't approach this the right way, I have a feeling there's a chance that I'll end up an even worse state.

"I wish I can make this pain of yours go away. I wish I had that power, Hannah," Atticus sounds despondent, resigned.

I squeeze my eyes shut, stopping tears from falling down his chest.

I wish you could too, Atticus ... I really do ...

I know now what I need to do to truly make this sadness, this guilt, this *pain* go away.

I know now what I need to do to move forward so I can finally start to live this second chance at life I've been gifted.

I have to let go of everything that seems to be weighing me down.

I have to free myself of all the baggage.

I have to let go. I have to let *him* go.

So I pull away from Atticus's embrace, ignoring the way my body cries for his touch. I turn around and place my feet firmly on the floor so I can stand up.

"Atticus, please take me home. I need to go home now."

"Are you sure? Okay. Of course. And I'll stay with you until you feel better." He guides me near the door where my shoes are, and he hands me my purse.

"Thank you, but I just need you to take me home, please."

It takes him a moment before he answers, "Okay."

I keep my silence while carefully using the walking stick as we make our way to his car. Somehow, it just doesn't feel right to hold on to Atticus, but I do let him hold me by the arm so he can guide me in the right direction.

The short ride home is a welcome relief because the silence between us has become too uncomfortable to bear. He tells me I'm home as he drives up my driveway and finally stops.

"So ..." he starts, sounding a little hesitant, "when can I see you again?"

I try to sound composed, even though my head hurts, and my eyes and throat feel swollen from all the crying.

"Never."

"Excuse me?" Atticus sounds perplexed at my answer, so I close my eyes and breathe deeply.

"The first thing I did when I woke up this morning was panic. I panicked because I thought you left me again without reason."

"I didn't, Han—"

"Please, just let me finish."

"Okay," Atticus relents.

"Thank you," I pause to regain my composure. "When I woke up this morning, and I didn't find you there, I thought you walked out on me again, and it scared the living shit out of me. The first time you left was so devastating, I didn't know if I was ever going to get over it. But I wanted to so badly because I didn't want to live with the pain anymore. I thought Paul was my remedy. He was your opposite, and to me, that was a good thing to me because it meant that he would never do what you did to me. But now I realise that a broken heart can't be tricked into loving someone else. It's like you're taunting fate. I forced this love to happen before I was truly ready, and that, I admit, was my undoing. Looking back now, I've realised I was unfair to Paul. I even fucking cheated on Paul with you, for goodness sake! I was ready to walk out on him, and you only had to say the word. And now … and now Paul's dead because I *could not,* for the fucking life of me, forget about *you.* I'm living with the consequences of that accident every single day because I let myself become completely obsessed by you."

I wipe a single tear that has fallen, continuing, "So I've decided to stop taunting fate. I'm going to help my heart to heal completely first. And only when it's finally whole will I allow myself to move forward. But a big part of healing is learning to forgive. I need to forgive you first before I can even consider forgiving myself. But forgiving you means eliminating your power over me. It just hurts too damn much knowing how much I love you, and knowing how much it scares me when you decide to leave me once again. I *need* to do what I should've done before. I need to learn to be on my own. And when I'm ready to love again, who knows? But I'll be realistic enough to understand that you probably won't hang around for me when it happens."

I hear him whisper my name, but I stop myself from reacting, "So this is it, Atticus. This is goodbye. But before I go, I want to thank you for a memorable night. And yes, I'm even thankful for our heart-to-heart this morning. But you were right in the first place. We *are* better off apart. I was just too stubborn to see it back then." I turn to unlock the car door, pulling the lever so it'll open. But his arm shoots across my chest, and he slams the door shut.

"No. You don't mean that," he tells me adamantly, "hear me out before you decide anything."

I try to remain steadfast, holding my ground as calmly as possible. "For once, I'm going to decide what's good for me. I have to let you go so you can live your dream and finally live your life without constraints. All I ask is that you let me live mine in the same way. After all, isn't that what you wanted for me in the first place?"

"You don't mean that, Hannah. You don't mean to let me go now. Please. Give me another chance."

"I'm giving *myself* another chance. And if you really do love me like you say you do, then you will let me. You will set me free just like you did before. And I will do the same with you."

"Please don't do this," the anguish in his voice almost breaks my resolve.

My hand reaches for him until I'm touching his face, and then I lean forward and I kiss him gently on the cheek. Then I close my eyes and breathe him in for the very last time.

"Goodbye, Atticus. I will be forever grateful that you wrote me those songs. Now go, be the star that you were meant to be."

I don't wait for him to respond. But then again, he stays quiet, which makes me feel oddly thankful. So I open the car door again, and thankfully this time, Atticus doesn't stop me. I unfold my walking stick first before I step out of the car, closing the door behind me. I'm relieved that he doesn't open his car door, but I know that he's following me with his eyes.

I can feel it.

I always do.

I finally make it to the front door of my house. Using my keys, I unlock the door, but quickly locking it as soon as I'm inside, just in case Atticus changes his mind and decides to storm in.

And yet he doesn't.

I stay put, standing right next to the door, and I wait.

I wait until I hear the car engine hum. Then I listen on until I hear the car leaving the driveway. My ear is still pressed against the door as I listen to the distant echo of the vintage engine as it drives off away from me and to goodness knows where.

Once I'm in my bedroom, I pop a couple of painkilling tablets and crawl to bed, needing something to numb the pain I know would take a long while to get rid of. Thankfully, the pills take effect in no time, and before I know it, I'm closing my eyes, and I succumb to a deep, and thankfully, dreamless sleep.

CHAPTER EIGHTEEN

Eight Months Later

Mum is crying … again. This is probably the third time she cried that I know of since we left our home over two hours ago. I'm just counting the ones I can hear, and I think I may have heard her sniffle way too many times in-between.

Now I know why I'm such a damn crybaby. It's genetic.

"Mum, you're breaking my heart here," I reach forward to squeeze her shoulder, but she grabs my hand and keeps it there.

"I can't help it. I'm sorry, but I can't help it, *mi corazon*," she sniffs.

"It's not like Hannah's never coming to visit us, dear. And it's too late to turn back around now, seeing we're a block away from her new home."

I can't help but smile at Dad's attempt to lighten up Mum's mood.

"I texted your friends. They are outside now, and they're waving like crazy," Mum tells me in-between the sniffles.

As soon as Dad parks the car, I ask, "Is it okay to open the door now, Dad?"

"You're good to go, Han," Dad answers.

I let myself out of the car, welcoming the chance to stretch my legs. I haven't even unfolded my stick yet when I hear two sets of squeals, and they're coming from my best friends, the same best friends who stuck by me.

"You're here!" Patty screeches, jumping up and down and taking me with her.

"We are going to have so much fun!" Brook adds straight after. "Group hug!"

"I still can't believe this is actually happening!"

"Okay, how about we all take this inside? Nancy looks like she's about to break down again," Dad tells us laughingly, just as I hear the car boot closing.

"Oh, shoosh, *mentiroso!* I'm trying my best here, but this is my *unica hija* so I will cry if I want to," Mum places her arm around me.

"*Como estas*, girls? I brought your favourite empanadas!"

My friends let out a whoop, then they usher me inside the house— the new home that the girls and I will be renting … just like what we planned to do when we talked about our college life back then.

Except, I'm a little late in the take, a year late to be exact. But that's okay because I'm more ready now to take on this next chapter in my life than I was back then.

Breaking up with Atticus was probably one of the hardest things I've ever done in my life. He was my greatest love, but he was also my ultimate downfall. Not having him around helped me to finally focus on myself, but more importantly, to depend on myself. I finally gave in to Mum's request and checked out the guide dog option, but I decided that having a guide dog wasn't for me. I needed to be able to do this on my own without getting emotionally attached to another living being, especially when I'm rebuilding my emotional state in the first place. I decided to go for this thing called Independent Living Training, which was run by an organization that assists the blind to live with least assistance as possible. They taught me all the skills I needed, and they trained me to do achievable day-to-day tasks without assistance. My trainer even came with me here before my actual move to help me with navigating around the house. She also taught me how to take public transport to travel to and from the university. So even though I'll still be needing some form of assistance in some aspects of my everyday life, I'm feeling quite confident that I can do this in my own capabilities.

I have made my peace with the fate I've been given, and because of this, I'm finally able to feel like my old self again. My *true* self.

And my true self is happiest when I have music in my life.

So I played my guitar more often, and I've started writing songs more. I took my cues, not only from memories both painful and happy, but also from my journey of acceptance.

These original songs I created led me back to Sydney University.

Not the School of Law. In fact, it's far from it.

After an admittedly nerve-wracking audition, I have been accepted at the prestigious Sydney University Conservatorium of Music.

When I told my parents that I've decided to go to uni, I told them both that I wanted to earn a degree in music instead of law.

I was expecting my dad to be against it. He had a precedent—Brodie. But to my surprise, he was proud that I've made this choice, even telling me that he should've been more supportive of Brodie back then instead of pushing for what he personally wanted.

Maybe my own father had his own breakthrough, I'm not sure, but his change of heart was the catalyst that brought us closer once again ... just like we were before the accident.

I've never been this happy in a long time.

Funny what a mere eight months could do.

"So, I placed all of your bags in your bedroom," Dad says. "Did Brodie tell you what time he'll be over, Brook?"

"He's in the studio with the band, so I'm assuming ... in a couple of hours?" Brook answers.

I've got to hand it to Brook. She got my wayward brother in line, and they're still together.

"Okay, well ... maybe we should just allow our daughter to get settled with her friends." I feel Dad's hands on my shoulders, and a wave of melancholy washes over me.

"Oh, but we're in no hurry. I can prepare a little something for the girls. So wh—" Mum's voice goes a pitch higher, and that only happens when she's trying to swallow her feelings.

"Nancy, dear, I know what you're trying to do. But it's time to let go. Hannah's more than ready to do this, and she's got her friends with her."

"Oh, but—"

"Mum," I interrupt, reaching out in her direction until she's holding my hand, "Dad's right. I'll be okay. And you'll come get me after the term ends, won't you?"

"Of course, *mija*. Try and stop me!" she answers back with conviction before practically suffocating me in her embrace.

"*Te amo mucho*, Mum. I'll miss you, but don't worry. I'm going to be fine."

"*Te amo mucho tambien, mija*. Use your phone and call us whenever you can, okay?"

"Okay. I will," I answer back, before feeling Dad's arms around me ... followed by friends cooing at the public display of parental affection in front of them.

I would probably be embarrassed by my parents—if these were normal circumstances, but it isn't. I *will* miss them … so very much.

After several more hugs, mostly from Mum, they're finally in the car and on their way home. That's when my friends and I head to my new bedroom. The layout of the room and where everything is going, have been preplanned so I'll know exactly where everything is. This makes it easier for me, and I won't have to rely too much on Brook and Patty.

"So, are you excited, Han? I know I am!" Patty tells me from one side of the room.

"We should go out to Gilroy's once the boys are back from the studio," Brook adds from the en suite. "Actually, let me text Brodie now."

"Yeah, we should. I don't mind getting to know the local," I answer back, smiling to both of them.

I didn't really bring much, so it doesn't take me long to unpack. Eventually, we find ourselves in the dining room, eating the empanadas that Mum brought for us.

"I tell you what, these empanadas are just bloody amazing. I should learn how to make these. I'm asking your mum for the recipe." Patty loves to cook and has been considering auditioning for the TV show, *Masterchef*. We told her to go for it, but I think she just needs to get over her nerves first. Even with her show of confidence, Patty's probably one of the most insecure people I've ever met.

But girl can cook like nobody's business.

"So did you visit Paul before you left?" Brook asks from out of the blue.

"Yeah. He knows that I finally made it here," I answer contemplatively.

I went to the cemetery and said goodbye to Paul the day before I left Avoca Beach. It may sound a little on the crazy side, but I still went to visit him whenever I had some good news to say, or when I had to vent out after my group therapy sessions or my Independent Living Training. In one of those occasions when I visited Paul, his parents arrived while I was still sitting next to his headstone. It scared me at first. I never had the guts to face them since the accident. The only contact I had since, was a heartfelt letter I wrote a few days after I awoke from the coma. It was a difficult letter to write because I couldn't distinguish the difference between sorrow and guilt. They lost their only child because of me. How can a letter make them feel any better? How can a letter make up for the fact that I lived and their son never even had a chance?

I came to the cemetery that day with Mum. She would usually leave me alone, staying in the car and watching her telenovelas on her iPad or reading another historical romance. She'd give me the time alone so I could talk to Paul. But that time, she came up to me and told me that Paul's parents had just arrived.

I was bracing myself for a throw down. But instead, I got two sets of arms hugging me and thanking me through their tears for the letter. But what broke me down was when they told me how they understood why I never showed up at their doorstep. They said they understood that we all grieve differently, and that I had my own issues to overcome. When I told them that I had been visiting Paul on a regular basis, they were pleased, and told me that Paul would've been happy about that. I made it clear however, that I didn't do it because I was obliged to do so, and that I will continue to visit him because I still love him, and I always will.

That was no lie.

I meant every word.

After that day, we vowed to keep in touch. They even invited me to dinner at their place when I come back home during school holidays.

We're still gathered at the dining table when the front door opens, and I hear the rambunctious laughter of my big brother, followed by my name being called out way too loudly.

"Hannah Banana!" Suddenly, I feel myself being lifted off of my seat and into my Hulk-wannabe big brother's arms.

"Let me go, dickwad!" I yell out to him laughingly.

"Wait, the boys wanna carry you too." And like a freaking pass-the-parcel at a children's birthday party, I'm being passed around and carried by Mike, Shane, and Derek.

"Let me go, you fuckers, or I'll use my stick and shove it up your asses!"

That's when I get dumped unceremoniously on the couch.

"Fuckers!" I yell out to them, but still laughing as I try to make my way back to the dining table.

203

"Mum and Dad left?" Brodie asks, sounding like his mouth is full, presumably from Mum's amazing empanadas.

"Dad had to drag her out of here. If she stayed any longer, she would probably decide to move in. You know how she gets."

"How did Dad take it?" Brodie stands next to me and asks quietly. He's trying to sound casual, but he knows that I know their history too.

"Typical Dad, you know. Trying to be the rock for Mum."

"Yeah, typical," he answers wistfully.

I reach out to him and squeeze his arm.

"He gets it now, bro. And he's truly sorry for being such a hard ass on you."

"Did he say that in verbatim?" he asks sarcastically.

"I'm not quoting him word for word, but I'm not lying either. He's proud of you for real, Brodie."

Brodie doesn't reply, but he wraps an arm around me and kisses the side of my temple before announcing to everyone, "Okay people, Gilroy's in half an hour!"

The atmosphere at Gilroy's is buzzing, and the music is pretty decent. Patty orders a shitload of food for us to share. I don't even realise it is practically dinnertime until I ask her what time it is.

Brodie's sitting next to me, which is good because we need to catch up on life.

I just wish I could pay more attention to what he's saying.

The truth is, I want to ask him about the one person I know I shouldn't ask about.

I've held back in the past months. I really did, because I needed to focus on myself alone. I even asked Brodie not to mention his name around me. It worked most days.

But I slipped up in between. That was when Atticus filled my thoughts.

And I'm having one of those days right now.

There is a lull between our conversation when I suddenly blurt out, "So, how's Atticus?"

Brodie sounds like he's clearing his throat, "Are you sure you wanna talk about him? I thought you've banned him from our conversations."

Oh. Good point.

Am I sure I'm ready to find out how Atticus is doing?

Who am I kidding, anyway?

Because as much as I've been doing all that I can to remove him out of my life, it's just not physically possible. He's ingrained in my thoughts, under my skin, in my heart.

And I know he'll stay there for as long as I'm breathing.

I try my best to sound casual, shrugging, "He's bound to be included in our conversations now anyway, since we'll be seeing each other more, and he's like, one of your best friends."

"But we don't have to talk about Tic if you don't want to. This is your first night here, and I don't want to ruin it by getting you distressed."

"Look, I just wanna know that he's okay, that's it," I try to laugh it off, but I'm not sure if I've convinced Brodie enough. "I'll be fine. I've been fine about a lot things if you haven't noticed."

"Alright. I can give you a quick update, but tell me if you want me to stop, and I'll talk about something else, okay?"

"Okay. But first, let's do one round of shots!"

Brodie doesn't seem to know what happened between Atticus and me after we left Peak. What he *does* know is that I broke my ties with Atticus permanently, that's it. It explains his initial hesitancy to talk about Atticus with me.

But after downing a few shots of tequila, Brodie loosens up a bit and begins to talk about Atticus.

He tells me that Atticus decided to leave Sydney after we last saw each other, making Los Angeles his home base while he prepared for the tail-end of his concert tour with Halcyon.

Well, the tour finished five months ago. Brodie and the rest of the band have been back home working on some new material since then. They're all sharing a house over at Bondi, which is only a suburb away from where my friends and I are currently living.

But as they were making plans to go back home after the tour, according to Brodie, Atticus, on a whim, decided to stay in the U.S. for longer. I want so badly to ask Brodie why he decided to stay back. I want to know if he's staying there for work or because he found someone worth staying for. But I can't even open my mouth to ask him that question. I'm just too afraid that Brodie might tell me that it's the latter, that he's found someone else.

I don't know how I'd feel about that.

No, I do. I'd be utterly devastated.

Because I still miss him, and I still feel an ache every single time I think about him. But I didn't give him much of an option when I said goodbye. Maybe he's moved on with another woman, maybe he's sleeping around with a lot of them. Maybe he's doing his best to forget about me. After all, he has every right to do that so he can move on.

He let go of me a couple of times before, so I'm sure that he can do it again, and maybe it would truly be the best for both our sanities.

We may have been amazing together, but we were amazingly volatile together as well.

We were too much … too soon.

Two precarious beings are better off apart.

Then how come my heart still aches for him?

That's the thing about meeting your greatest love too early in your life. Once you lose your great love, you just feel lost because a gigantic piece of yourself is gone.

"So he's not coming back, huh?" I ask Brodie.

"No, at least not for a while. But that's what you wanted for him, right? To follow his dream so you can follow yours? This is a good thing. Having him around might just hurt you again. Now's your chance to enjoy your life, and who knows? Maybe you'll meet someone special again, right?"

"Yeah … we'll see," I answer back wistfully before taking another, much-needed shot of tequila.

I'm back home, in bed, headphones over my ears, listening to a new playlist I created to hopefully help me to sleep.

But it's not working, and I'm sure it's because my thoughts keep returning to what Brodie said to me earlier.

I'm still young. I still have this new life ahead of me.

And I'm proving how being blind isn't holding me back.

Sure, we all have our demons, we've all been wounded and scarred in one way or another. But we try to get past it, we try to learn from it, and we try to better ourselves so it doesn't happen again. And if it does, we learn to get back up and try again.

I'm determined to win despite this blindness, despite the scars, both inside and out.

And I know that in time, I will win over this pining over Atticus.

Yes, it's easier said than done.

But it's doable.

It's. Doable.

And maybe if I say it enough times, there will come a time when I'll actually believe it.

CHAPTER NINETEEN

Blindness perk number nine: Winning at independent living as a blind person is equivalent to not only winning the lottery, but also winning in life.

I'm feeling particularly cocky today, waking up with a smile on my face.

It's the last day before our two-week school holiday. I've spent three months at university, working harder than most in my class, just to prove to my peers and my music teachers that my blindness should not be treated as a hindrance, but an actual advantage. I went to and from my university on my own, catching the bus, even catching the train once in a while if the need arises. Admittedly, it wasn't smooth sailing most days, and I've had my share of mishaps, but I always seem to have a random person who's able to help me. I've survived my commute, and I know that it's also because of the kindness of strangers.

I've also made a few new friends in my class. There's actually one guy in particular, Joshua, who's been particularly nice. He's a multi-instrumentalist, but he plays the piano like a genius possessed. With the kind of passion he has, you'd think he'd be highly competitive, but he's far from it. In fact, he has been quite accommodating when I've shown interest in learning how to play the piano. He'd patiently teach me each step, since I'm only able to learn by feel. A week before the end of term, he asked me out to an outdoor jazz concert at the university grounds. I said yes, but it had been close to two years since I last went on a proper date, and that was technically with Paul. So I could be forgiven for being a nervous wreck. But Joshua was a gentleman through the whole night, and he made me feel comfortable and safe. He kind of reminded me of Paul with his demeanor, but according to Patty and Brook, although Joshua has the same height and lean physique like Paul, he has dark copper-coloured hair and pale skin. They did, however, confirm that he's quite good-looking, like a slightly geeky version of Michael Fassbender. They didn't have to convince me further.

Why? Because Michael Fassbender, that's why.

No further explanation needed.

After our date, he took me straight home, and he kissed me. Our first kiss was pleasant, gentle. He did ask me if we could see each other again after the break. I just smiled and said *'Maybe.'* I wasn't trying to be coy. Because even though I had a wonderful time with Joshua, I felt like I needed the break to think things through.

And if I'm being honest with myself, I think I know why.

Atticus is still in my thoughts, no matter how hard I try to occupy myself with my studies and being social. Also, once in a while, at the most random of times, I would get this warm, tingly feeling coursing through me, and it was the type of feeling I'd always associate with Atticus. Sometimes I welcomed it and thought of the happier times we shared, because we did have so many. But most of the time, I dismissed it because at the opposite end of the spectrum, dwelling over him also meant bringing back memories of the times he broke my heart, not once, but twice.

It's just not healthy, this borderline obsession I'm still harboring over Atticus.

Tomorrow, the girls and I are taking the country train home. Mum and Dad were supposed to pick me up, but I called them and told them of the change in plans. They're picking us up from the train station instead and will take the girls home since we all live close by.

I am *so* looking forward to this break. And seeing as the weather has been warmer than usual for autumn, I've decided that I'll try my hand at surfing again when I get back home. It's one of the things that I missed doing since losing my eyesight. Unfortunately, a busy schedule from my music degree meant using up most of my weekends studying and practising.

But I think I'm ready to surf the waves again. I think that I'm ready to tackle that bull by the horns and ride those waves like I was born to do it.

The thought scares me and exhilarates me at the same time.

My bags are packed, and I'm just zipping it up when I hear a knock on my bedroom door.

"Babe!" It's Patty. "Let's have a girls' night out tonight. There's this new club I wanna check out. You're coming, okay?"

"We're catching the train tomorrow morning. We might not make it if we're hung over."

"Come on, loosen up! It's gonna be fun. And we won't have to catch our train home until ten in the morning. That's plenty of fucking time! You've packed already, haven't you?"

Sighing, I answer back, "Yes ... okay fine. So what time are we going?"

"Girl, it's six now, so let's be ready in an hour for dinner out, then go to Ruby Red's. All good?"

I've heard of Ruby Red's. They play dance music on one floor but have a live band perform a set at the basement and bar. The bands are usually up and comers, so I'm looking forward to listening to some fresh music.

I wonder if they'd let someone like me perform in a place like that. Not that I'd have the guts to perform in front of these big city folks. That one night at Peak was nerve-wracking enough, and over there, I was playing in front of people who mostly knew who I was. That was supposed to make it easier for me.

"I'll be ready!" I yell back, shaking my head and smiling at the same time.

"Tell me what it looks like, girls." I'm arm in arm with Brook, with Patty walking next to me. I'm not using a stick tonight, but I do have it in my purse just in case. I made them promise on their favourite pair of stilettos that they'll never leave me all alone. We usually go to bars or clubs in a bigger group so there will always be someone around to assist me, just in case. Tonight, it's just us three, so I can be forgiven for being a little clingy.

Patty answers, "Well, the sign is bright red of course, and it looks like a handwritten signature. There's an old-school pinup girl right next to it, really sexy, long hair, slim legs and a bubble butt, kinda has a striking resemblance of you."

"Shut up!" I elbow Patty playfully, "I *totally* blame my mother for my big Latina ass."

"Please, no offence, okay? We know that you won't see it anymore when men stare at your hotness, but Brook and I still have working eyes, and girl, we see these men looking. And hey, you're single. Embrace it! Take it as a compliment!" I hear Brook agreeing wholeheartedly, and I shake my head at them. I know I should feel offended at being objectified, but for some reason, the thought of other men noticing other parts of my body and not my eyes or my scar is surprisingly doing wonders to my ego.

"Have a good night, ladies," I hear a deep voice telling us before I feel the air swoosh in front of us, which I assume is coming from a heavy door opening.

"See! That bouncer was checking you out!" Patty nudges me while Brook ushers me inside. "And he's cute, in that rugby player sort of way, you know, tattoos, all muscles …"

"As if a rugby player lookalike would be interested in me. It's dark, he probably didn't see my scar. And you know that I won't be able to tell if you're telling me the truth, right?" I scoff. As much as I'm feeling secretly flattered, I couldn't help but feel like my friends are just fibbing to make me feel a little better about myself.

Brook answers, "You know we're not gonna lie to you about those things, babe. We seriously want you to have fun. But don't you worry. We got your back, right? And if you do wanna hook up with a guy, we'll make sure you're hooking up with a hottie. *But*, we'll Facebook stalk him first in case he's married or a serial killer in the making," Brook giggles, and we giggle with her.

"Okay, let's not get ahead of ourselves. I'm not going to hook up with anyone, just so we're clear. I plan on focusing on only two things: music and dancing. That's it."

"Plus it's pretty obvious that you're still not over Atticus. Not by a long shot."

Patty totally pulled the rug under me on that one.

How totally random!

It may be a true statement, but it's still random and uncalled for.

"It doesn't matter how I feel about Atticus anymore, Patty. He's gone from my life, remember?"

A moment passes before she answers, "Of course … of course. Sorry."

The odd tone of her voice leaves me puzzled. But whatever and whomever I've been thinking about is quickly pushed out of my head by the blare of the dance music.

"Swear to me you won't leave me alone, okay?" I hook my arm on Patty as well, suddenly feeling a lack of confidence as the music gets louder, and I'm finding it harder to distinguish certain noises.

"Hannah, trust me when I tell you that you will never be left alone, okay?" Brook tells me reassuringly, "Just trust me and dance!"

I hear Patty whoop it up, and I give in to the thump of the beats. The pulsating rhythm sears through my body and in a little while,

I'm dancing, raising my arms up and just … feeling … free.

Free.

Free from fear, guilt, anguish, and Atticus.

Wow, thinking it aloud somehow still doesn't give me comfort whatsoever.

But I'm still dancing, and I'm loving every single second of it.

After the third song, we all agree that our heels are beginning to murder our feet one toe at a time. Well, my shoes are practically flat, and the tiny elevation is just a wedge, but my throbbing feet tell me they've had enough too.

They guide me to what they say is a small booth. Patty continues to describe the interiors of the club, which I am now picturing as something out of a comic book from the fifties.

Brook tells us that she's buying us super-girly cocktails. I eagerly agree, ignoring the fact that I'll probably regret it tomorrow morning when we try to make it to our train home.

But I did work hard and overcame a lot of my personal obstacles, so I'm taking my friends' advice, and I'll loosen the fuck up.

I don't even know how we've made it back to the dance floor, but after downing our sweet, alcoholic concoctions, we're busting a move again like we're all that.

We dance to one more song, then we agree to check out the basement to watch the bands play.

All of a sudden, I feel a hand grip me on my hip, followed by a rough-sounding male voice slurring against my ear.

"Hey, beautiful! How about a dance?"

Too stunned to respond, he tries to spin me around, still gripping me tightly. The stink of beer on his breath is making me want to retch.

Patty grabs hold of my hand and tries to pull me closer to her, "This is strictly a girls' night out, mate. Go find someone else to annoy."

"It's alright," he slurs back, "I only want one dance. So what do you say, babe?" The creep grips my waist, and I yelp when he pulls me back to him and drags me like a fucking cave woman. I raise my arms and try to reach out for my friends in panic, waving my arms towards them like a mad woman.

I hear Brook's voice, but I can't understand what she's saying over the loud music.

Oh my God!

"Patty! Brook! Where are you?" I cry out. "Let me go, asshole!" I try to loosen his grip, but he's too damn strong.

"I'm here, Han!" I hear Patty call out, but her voice sounds worryingly distant. "Let go of her, or you'll regret it, you fucker!"

I feel them struggling to get me, but he's too strong and Patty loses her grip on me.

"Oh, shit! Hang on, hang on, are you blind? Well, I've never danced with a blind chick before," he laughs as I try to struggle from his clutches. "Actually, I never kissed a blind chick before either. Well there's a first time for everything, isn't it, baby?"

I can smell the awful stench of beer from his breath as his face seems to come closer.

Until it's not anymore.

He is pulled away from me with so much force that I lose my balance.

"I got you, Hannah. I got you," I hear Brook's reassuring voice as she takes hold of me. I hear scuffling and a loud grunt, then people cheering.

Why are they cheering? What just happened?

"That asshole's knocked out, Hannah. And he's currently being dragged out by security. I told that fucker he'd regret it," Patty's livid tone matches the words that came out of her mouth, but the relief I feel, knowing I've avoided something that could've turned into something horrific is too much to keep in. I felt so helpless, so vulnerable. I sob, and I break down in her arms.

That's when I feel another set of arms around me, "Shhh, Hannah. You're safe now," Brook tells me in a gentle tone.

I turn to Patty, suddenly realising that I didn't even ask how they got rid of him.

"Did you do that? Who took care of him?"

They both laugh nervously.

"I didn't do it. I asked for help."

"Who helped me? I'd like to thank that person. Is that possible?" I ask, straightening up, trying to wipe the tears from my eyes.

Brook answers, "Uh … I don't know if it's a good idea to speak to him—"

Patty cuts her off, "Because he's left already. He was there, but now he's gone, right, Brook?"

"Yeah, sorry, Hannah. But how about we just call him your guardian angel?"

I scrunch my brows together.

Why do they sound weird like they're not being completely upfront with me?

But I push out my suspicions. Maybe I shouldn't read too much into this. It could be some random guy who was just plain nice enough to help.

It could also be the club's security.

Still, it would've been the right thing to do to offer him my gratitude.

Times like these make me wish I wasn't completely blind.

It would be nice to see this so-called guardian angel's face and thank him personally.

Maybe it's a good thing we don't end up staying at Ruby Red's. After the incident, we are all too shaken to stay. We decide to go home and have a relatively early night.

But before I go to sleep, my thoughts return back to the stranger who punched the lights out of that drunk shithead.

In the morning, we make it to the train with lots of time to spare. I use that time to listen to an audiobook of a best-selling novel. I used to love reading, used to love the smell of books both new and preloved. But now, it's either reading a book in Braille, or listening to an audiobook. The audiobook wins out, only because there are more titles to choose from.

Halfway through the third chapter, my thoughts drift back to the events of last night. I press Pause on the player and take my headphones off.

"Patty? Brook? Any of you awake?"

"Hmm? Yeah. Why?" Patty answers.

"What did he look like?"

"Who?" Brook asks.

"You know, that guy who helped out last night? Was he one of the security guys? Or was he that rugby player look-alike?"

"Why are you curious all of a sudden?" Brook asks again, before she sighs, "Would it make a difference if you knew?"

"No, not really, I guess," I shrug, "It's just nice to have a picture in my head. And I mean I just found it a little weird that he just up and left without waiting for a thank you."

"Maybe that's what makes him your guardian angel. I'm sure that angels don't perform good deeds for the glory. They do it out of a basic compulsion to help somebody in need. Sometimes they do it out of sheer selflessness …"

"Or," Patty adds, "sometimes they do it out of love."

"Love?" My head turns in her direction, "What do you mean by love?"

"Uh, I guess in your case, it's option number one: sheer selflessness," Patty quickly answers.

I pause for a moment before nodding, "Yeah, definitely option number one. Unless my guardian angel saw me and fell in love with me at first sight."

An awkward silence fills the space, and I wonder if they're thinking I am being serious. Thankfully, Patty blurts out, "Yup! That must be it!" then she starts laughing, and we all laugh with her.

"Okay, okay," Brook sputters out, "if it helps, your guardian angel doesn't work for the club as security. He was just a really hot, good-looking guy who just happened to be at the right place, at the right time. That's all I'm gonna say."

My heart skips a beat for some reason, as I try to mentally build a picture in my head.

Good-looking, huh?

"Tell me what he looks like."

"Nope. There's no point in it," Brook says firmly.

"Patty?"

"I'm with Brook on this one."

"Why can't you give me a freaking mental picture?" I ask, getting increasingly frustrated.

"Babe," I feel Brook's hand take my own, "we're not trying to be cruel or anything. But to be perfectly honest, I don't think we can perfectly describe that guy and still do him justice. But know this. If we do get a chance to see him again, we will let you know, so you can personally thank that person yourself, okay?"

My brows furrow, "You'll really do that?"

"Of course, we will."

I nod back, smiling gratefully, "You've no idea what that means to me. Thank you."

Afterwards, I put my headphones back on, and I listen to the rest of the audiobook.

After over two hours inside the train, the train conductor announces that our stop is next. I put my backpack on, plus a carry-all over my shoulder. Patty places my hand on her shoulder and guides me towards the exit, just as the train slows to a stop.

As soon as we're off the train, I unfold my walking stick, walking carefully while my hand is still on Patty's shoulder. Not long after, we hear Mum calling for us in her not-so-inside voice.

After being away for so many months, one of the main things I missed the most was my bedroom. I stayed inside this bedroom for so long after the accident. This became my refuge, my sanctuary. I used this room to lock everyone out and push people away. I felt that I was all alone in this turmoil, that no one could possibly understand the struggle I'm going through.

But I was wrong.

And I'm so glad that I was.

I feel like I've come a long way from that broken girl who closed herself off in this very bedroom a year ago. But I'm also realistic. I do know that who I am at this very moment is still a work in progress. But I'm getting there. I'm building myself from the ground up, and I'm getting there.

Mum told me earlier that she'd be cooking up a feast for dinner tomorrow night to celebrate my return. I thought it was a little too much. It's like I've been gone for years instead of three months. But I have a feeling she's not just celebrating my return, but also the change she's seeing in me. Brodie's still in Sydney, working on a song with his band. But he promised he'd be home by tomorrow afternoon. Patty and Brook were invited, along with their respective families. But I also asked if I could invite Nicki and her family. She has become a good friend since I joined the support group, and we've been in touch ever since.

I'm lying in bed, just listening to some new music from one of the playlists I've been following. My heart jolts when I suddenly hear the unmistakable voice of Atticus Foster. But my heart starts beating like a jackhammer when I realise that he's singing "Once Again."

I didn't even know that he released that song.

I know that it's probably best if I press the remote button Forward, but for some reason, I keep listening. The words weren't changed, with only an acoustic guitar as its instrument, just like how Atticus played it in public for the first time at Peak … the night before I ended things with him and told him that I never wanted to see him again.

Dammit. Why did Atticus create such a beautiful song? It's giving me the feels, with stupid goose bumps to match.

I listen to the whole song, and press Stop as soon as it's finished.

I don't know why I feel a tinge of guilt for loving that song.

I think I might have to see Paul. I need to talk to him to hopefully clear my head.

After getting out of bed, I head towards the door, yelling out, "Mum? Is it okay if I visit Paul?"

"Hey, Paul. Guess what? I'm back! Duh … you obviously already know that."

I'm kneeling next to Paul's headstone, my fingers absentmindedly tracing the indented script of his full name. The first thing I notice is how calm I feel on the inside, being here next to Paul. I've had a roller coaster of emotions every time I came and visited before, and this is actually the first time I feel calm … at peace with myself.

I clutch my chest and notice that it feels lighter than usual.

"Are you doing this?" I ask Paul in a whisper. "I never felt like this whenever I came and visited you. But today, I feel lighter, happier. It's kind of weird, but not in a bad way. Does this mean you're in a happier place, and you're letting me feel it?"

I shift my position, crossing my legs in front of Paul's headstone, and I raise my head upwards, feeling the warmth of the sun on my face and delighting at the hint of light coming through the darkness of which I've grown used to.

With a smile, I tell him about all my adventures in the big city, from the mishaps, to the new friends I've met. I divulge about how random people had helped me when I was lost, or when I stumbled when my walking stick missed a crack on the ground. I also tell him about what happened last night at the club and how one brave, anonymous stranger helped me out. But I skip the part about Joshua.

217

It just feels odd talking to Paul about a guy I started dating who reminds me of him.

"One thing's for sure though, Paul. You would've loved it over there. And even though I didn't end up studying law, I know in my heart that I've chosen the right degree, and if you were still around, I know you'd understand why. That's just who you are. So I may not earn anything from this after I graduate, and I'll probably end up penniless and living in Mum and Dad's house, but who knows, right?"

I place my hand on top of the smooth headstone. "Sometimes I get this feeling, like someone's looking out for me, guiding me so I'm always safe. I don't know if I'm just imagining it, and I don't know if you have anything to do with it. But … I'm grateful … to you and to the powers that be. Heaven knows I probably don't deserve it, but I feel it. I feel like everything's going to be okay from now on. If this is your way of telling me that you've forgiven me, then thank you, Paul … thank you so much."

And as I blink, a stray tear escapes my eye, down my cheek, and onto the ground, mere inches from Paul's headstone.

It may just be a solitary tear, but it represents something far greater than that. For amongst all the tears of grief, guilt, and even self-hatred that I've previously shed on this ground, I have finally shed a solitary tear of joy.

And for the first time since I first visited Paul, I'm finally leaving the cemetery with a smile of gratitude on my face and a huge weight lifted off my shoulders.

CHAPTER TWENTY

Mum definitely outdid herself tonight.

I'm making my way out the back door, needing somewhere quiet from all the loud music and the chattering. As happy as the atmosphere can be, and as much as I wish that I could be in the middle of it all, sometimes it gets too much, and my head starts to hurt. It's just one of the things I have to live with now.

Plus I need to sit down and digest all the food I just ate. I don't even know how I managed to fit so much food in my stomach.

The dinner party is in full swing, and it's much credit to my mum. She was cooking and cleaning like a mad woman the whole day today. I knew it from the moment I hear her playing a *Buena Vista Social Club* album that she's going to be in her element.

I'm pretty pleased about the turnout. Brodie and the boys came home after lunch, earlier than we expected. Now they're all here, including their parents, since my parents have been friends with them since they were kids. Same goes with Patty and Brook. Their parents and siblings are here as well. It's a small community, so everyone knows each other, and most friendships are long-term.

I guess this party is a good excuse to gather everyone together in one place, since all of us actually being in one place hasn't happened in a long while.

But now I have a headache, so I need to get away from it, even if it's just for a few minutes.

I plant myself on the swing bench, which overlooks our backyard where a small swimming pool sits to my left, and the converted shed is just a few steps to my right.

At least, that's what I'm hoping it still looks like, since I'm only recalling it from memory.

The gentle breeze feels cool on my skin, and it helps me relax and reflect on how so many things have changed in my life these past months, but some constants remain as well.

I still feel melancholic about Paul's death, but I'm also beginning to feel at peace about it. I've come to accept now that the accident was just that: an accident. I know now that I can't live my second chance in life, dwelling over something I have no control of.

The earth will still rotate on its own axis, day will still turn into night, and life still goes on.

It just does. And I've made a conscious choice to finally *live* it.

And then there's Atticus Foster. I can't lie to myself anymore. I still miss him. He invades my thoughts every single time. Saying goodbye to him felt like the best thing I've ever done. But now, in retrospect, saying goodbye to Atticus is something I wish I didn't have to do. I feel it the most, whenever I achieve a personal goal, and I find myself wishing he's a phone call away, or just around the corner, so I can tell him everything. And most times, no matter how much I want to deny it, I find myself wondering if he's doing okay in his part of the world. And then I just end up torturing myself when I start to imagine him in the arms of another woman … maybe even the new love of his life.

I don't know what it is about him … about us, because we are two completely different people. But somehow, we found ourselves deeply in love with each other. And no matter how much he hurt me, no matter how much I wanted to hate him for breaking my heart, I just can't do it.

I'm still madly in love with him.

Atticus Foster has been and will always be my constant.

Not that it matters now, anyway. He's gone from my life because I drove him away. And I've come to accept that maybe he will never come back. I mean, he can have any woman he sets his eyes on. Why would he come back to a blind and badly scarred small town girl like me?

I sigh out aloud, just as I hear the back door creak open.

"Well, that's a mighty big sigh you just expelled there, sis," I hear the wooden floors of the deck creak from Brodie's weight as he walks towards me, pushing the swing to move as he sits next to me.

"So you think you're ready to surf tomorrow?" He asks.

"I'll certainly give it a shot." I shrug back.

Then Brodie lets out a massive burp.

"Ugh! Gross!" I cry out, making a gagging sound.

"Better in than out, that's what *Abuelo* used to say," then he lets out another burp.

I can't help but laugh now. *Abuelo*, Mum's father, was a straight shooter and uncompromising in the way he lived his life. But to us, his grandchildren, he was a teddy bear with a gigantic heart. He used to give us lollies when my parents weren't looking, telling us to keep it our little secret. Sometimes he'd pick us up from school so he could take us to the playground, then milkshakes straight after at the local café. He kept reminding our friends to call him *Big Swanky* because the nickname, plus his signature suspenders and newsboy cap, made him sound cool and hip. Our friends loved him. You would've been an idiot not to be drawn to him. He was an amazing human being, and loved by so many people. When a complication from pneumonia became too much for him to bear and he left this world, all of us were shattered with grief. It felt like the world we're living now has lost a little bit of its colour.

It makes me wonder now if he's also my guardian angel, watching over me and keeping me safe.

"I miss *Abuelo*," I tell Brodie, sliding closer to him and placing my head on his shoulder.

"Yeah, me too," he replies somberly, as he sways the swing bench gingerly.

After a few moments of contemplative silence, I speak up once again, "I visited Paul yesterday."

"Yeah, Mum told me. How'd it go?"

"It felt different visiting him this time. I actually left happier than my previous visits, and the feeling was startling, but in a really good way. In fact I'm actually feeling relieved."

"That's great, Han. Maybe you're already at the final stage of your grief … you know, acceptance."

"Maybe."

"I *have* noticed big changes in you."

I snort, "Good or bad?"

"All good, of course. Looks like you've won the battle to reclaim yourself, and I've never been more proud of you."

"That sounds so profound, big brother."

"I'm not just all about good looks, I'm also a songwriter, dum-dum! Of course I'm profound."

"Do you want me to remind you that your last hit song was penned by *me*, and not you? So who's the dum-dum now?"

"It's not like I'm gonna say no. You and Atticus are probably the most poetic songwriters I know."

"I am? We are? You're not shitting me?" I look up at Brodie, smiling from ear to ear.

Me and Atticus. Gosh, I don't even know how to react to that. Atticus is a phenomenal songwriter. He wouldn't have this meteoric rise to fame if he weren't so talented.

"So, um, speaking of Atticus ..." I swallow hard, "I never asked you if he was seeing anyone ..."

"You sure you wanna know?" Brodie asks cautiously.

"Yeah. I guess. I'm a grown woman. I can accept it if he's seeing someone. I'm seeing someone too, so ..." I tilt my head up to him. "So, is he? Seeing someone, I mean?"

I hear him exhale out aloud, "To answer your first question, yes, I guess you can say he *is* seeing someone."

Wow. I did *not* expect that to hurt as much as it's hurting now.

Of course he'll be seeing someone else by now, why did I bother asking such an idiotic question?

I remain quiet, nodding back and trying my best to swallow my feelings. But in actual fact, I feel like I'm being choked by it.

"Hey, say something. You wanted to know, right?" Brodie shakes my shoulder, urging me to speak.

"I'm glad that he's happy," I lie.

"Not sure if he's happy. This girl he's seeing, he's not even certain as to where he stands with her."

I pull away from Brodie, facing him with a frown. "Well, if this girl ... whoever she is ... can't see how much of a catch Atticus is, then she's either fucking stupid, or she's blinder than I am."

Brodie chuckles, "Or maybe she's a little bit of option one, and a little bit of option two."

"Damn straight. What an idiot," I sniff, pausing, knowing I'm saying this more to myself.

"When I talk to Atticus again, do you want me to tell him you said so?"

I jerk back, "What? No! I mean, don't tell him anything. Don't even mention that I asked about him. If he's busy chasing another girl, the last thing I want is to be that desperate chick that gets in the way. I just wanted to know that he's okay, that's all."

"Well ... if that's what you want. But there's no harm in actually talking to him, Hannah. I have a strong feeling Atticus still cares about you."

Brodie's words make my chest expands, letting little butterflies in, making my stomach feel funny.

But I'm reading too much into Brodie's words. He only has a strong feeling that Atticus still cares about me. It's not based on fact.

And just like that, my chest closes tightly once again, killing all the butterflies in its way.

"Hey, Hannah Banana!" Brodie shaking me by the arm brings me back.

"What … what?" I respond impatiently.

"You know, we haven't played together in ages. You know that's guaranteed to put a smile on your frowning face. Let me set up the studio then I'll come and get you. What do you say, sis? Ready to show me what a conservatorium student can do against a dropout?"

Was I frowning that badly because of Atticus?

Maybe playing some music with Brodie is exactly what I need.

"Ha! You're on," I answer back with a beginning of a smile, "I say let's do it, big bro!"

And as the night progresses, what started out as a jam session between brother and sister, progressively becomes a mini concert, with Mike, Shane, and Dylan joining in as the rest of our friends and families move from the house to gather around our humble converted shed.

It really has become an amazing night.

And before I can even stop myself, I'm already wishing that Atticus were here to make tonight even better.

CHAPTER TWENTY-ONE

Atticus Foster

She doesn't know.

And I have no choice but to keep it that way.

At least for now … until she's ready.

I understand why Hannah doesn't want to have anything to do with me anymore. She must have totally given up on me for her to think that I'd just accept her decision without a fight. I want her to take back those words. I want her to hear me out because I'm willing to do whatever it takes for her to change her mind. I need her to understand that the coward who left her three years ago is not the same person she drove away and who she was willing to let go.

I made a lot of bad decisions in my life, and two of those decisions hurt Hannah in the worst possible way. But to my defense, I'd rather sacrifice my feelings and stay away from her if it meant giving her a chance for a more secure future.

I had nothing to offer her. I came from a shitty home, had a father who despised me so much he'd beat me constantly to make himself feel superior, and I wasn't as smart as her. I had no contingency plans, I wasn't skilled enough to do anything else but write songs and sing. All I had that mattered were my music … and Hannah.

What would happen if I failed to get a break? I would have been a complete failure, just like what my father thought, and I would have dragged Hannah down with me.

I couldn't live with myself if that happened.

The night of her sixteenth birthday, after Hannah gave herself to me, I was torn to pieces. It was the most incredible moment—to see the look in her eyes as I made love to her for the first time. But it was that same look that frightened me as well. She looked at me with so much love, with so much hope, with so much expectations that I knew I couldn't fulfil if she stayed with me. It wasn't her fault that I felt petrified at the thought of failing her. I just didn't know how I'd cope if that look of love she gave me would morph into disdain, disappointment, or worse, pity.

That would just kill me.

So I thought I did the right thing by giving her up.

I'd rather that she hated me then.

I could work with hate because hate could be temporary.

Hate might eventually turn to love.

And she might not be aware of it, but I saw that same look of love on her face when we made love that night after we left Peak.

I knew she still loved me.

The kind of love we had couldn't just disappear like that. It was in our bones, in the blood that flowed in our veins.

Hannah … she'd *always* be mine.

She said she needed to be on her own, to learn how to cope with her blindness and become independent without anything or anyone complicating her process. She needed time, and time was what I gave her. I could be patient. I could wait.

But I wasn't always patient when it came to her.

I used to think that I was leaving for the city to become a successful musician, so I could prove to my father that I wasn't a worthless piece of shit while he slapped me around for good measure. But my purpose changed when Hannah came into my life. I still wanted to become a successful musician, but I also wanted to leave for the city so I could be successful for *her* … so I could be someone she would be proud to call her boyfriend—to call her man.

So I hustled. I worked hard on my craft, sang in pubs or whatever gigs I could get, I peddled my CDs while busking during the day, and tried to speak with people in the music industry, hoping for a chance to be heard. But all they did was slam their doors in my face without even hearing my music. When shit got too bad and I was close to giving up, I would gather whatever money I saved and I'd make my way back to Avoca, just to be able to catch a glimpse of her. I knew it was crazy, but Hannah centred me. She was my light. She radiated it, and she didn't even have to try. I never approached her because I didn't want to complicate her life, when my own life was snowballing into a disaster.

Once I've had my Hannah fix, I'd return back to the city so I could hustle my music all over again.

Then one day, while I was busking at Pitt Street Mall, I got lucky enough to be heard by a highly reputable music producer. Finally, a door opened for me, and it changed my life.

When I returned back to Avoca for a much needed break with Brodie, Shane, Mike, and Derek, I was already on my way to the top of the charts. I couldn't wait to see Hannah, so she could finally see me as the Atticus Foster she had always thought I could be.

But I wasn't expecting to witness just how happy she was with her new boyfriend, Paul. And as much as I wanted to hate the guy she was with for holding on to my Hannah, Paul was genuinely a good person, and he loved Hannah the way she should be loved ... the way I should have loved her.

Seeing them together magnified all of my mistakes, my shortcomings. Compared to Paul, I still fell short by a long shot.

My pride couldn't take it. I wanted to know if I still had a chance with Hannah, that even after what happened between us, she still had some love for me. So like a gigantic asshole, I tried to win her back, and I was blown away when she showed me that my instincts were right. She still loved me, and she was willing to end things with Paul to be with me again.

I had my opening. I could've gotten her back.

But my father's words came rushing back in my head when he told me I was, and would always be, worthless. And when I looked at how Paul and Hannah were together, I felt I was every single degrading word that my father had ever called me.

I felt like a piece of shit back then for trying to break up Paul and Hannah. I let my ego take over, and I couldn't accept the fact that Paul was the better man who would never break Hannah's heart.

I, on the other hand, already did that to her once.

So just because I *was* an asshole, I broke her heart for the second time, trying to justify it by convincing myself that it was the right thing to do in the long run.

After all, wasn't a short period of sadness worth it for her, if it meant spending a lifetime of complete contentment with a man who was perfect for her?

That was what I wanted for Hannah. And I didn't care if it meant spending my lifetime with a big chunk of my heart missing, and knowing I'd never get it back.

When Brodie told me that Hannah and Paul were involved in a fatal accident, my whole world stopped and what remained of my heart completely shattered.

Unfortunately, Paul didn't make it, but Hannah did survive, thankfully. But because of the extent of her head injuries, she had to be placed in a medically induced coma, just to give her a better chance of recovery.

I fucking dropped everything, packed some clothes, left the city, and went straight to Central Coast Hospital. Seeing Hannah lying on the hospital bed for the first time almost left me legless. She was almost unrecognizable, her head was covered with a heavy bandage, and so was her whole jaw. Whatever part of her face I could see was swollen and bruised. She also had tubes and wires attached to her, with a machine that beeped to mimic her heartbeat.

Whenever I was allowed to visit, I always brought my guitar with me so I could sing her familiar songs, in the hope that she'd hear me and she'd open her eyes. I think I sang "Songbird" more times in the span of six days than I ever did in my live performances. I was just thankful that the nursing staff never called security for noise pollution.

But I somehow needed her to know that I was there. I needed her to know that we were all waiting for her to wake up, that we *knew* that she had it in her to wake up.

And she did. Hannah finally opened her eyes. But whatever relief we all felt was obliterated when the doctors confirmed that she lost her eyesight. I wanted to comfort her and to be there by her side, but I ended things badly between us—twice, and I was afraid that my presence would cause her more pain. So when Brodie asked me if I could give Hannah some time to let her come to terms with Paul's death and her blindness, I didn't protest. I was willing to do whatever it took to make sure that she recovered without any problems. I even asked them not to tell her that I visited her almost every day, in case it aggravated her further. By that time, I was about to have my first concert tour, so I buried myself with work, and it shaved off some of the edge I felt for not being able to see Hannah.

Unfortunately, relinquishing my time with Hannah meant standing idly by as her resentment for me grew as well.

I just couldn't get it right with her. I kept making the wrong decisions.

I caught a glimpse of her resentment towards me when I came back from a break in our tour. The look of hatred on her face felt like a thousand knives being shoved through my chest. I thought that was easier to see than pity. I was so fucking wrong.

227

But when I picked her up from her first group therapy session, I felt a spark between us that was so strong, it manifested through her clear anger towards me. And strike me down if I was wrong, but I was pretty sure Hannah felt it too. The attraction was so palpable I could practically touch it.

And God, when I touched her …

She felt amazing, just like I remembered, but a thousand times better.

I had a moment of weakness, and I kissed her. When she kissed me back, I knew. I knew it wasn't over between us.

She tasted so sweet and so addictive that when she told me I couldn't kiss her anymore, it felt like being fed an expensive lobster meal before I was about to be led to my execution.

But I'd gladly die to have another chance at kissing her again. I'd die with a smile on my face.

And that chance to kiss her again came a few days after. That night she sang at Peak made me fall in love with her all over again. Her song was something she wrote for Paul, and hearing her sing it in front of the crowd made me feel immense pride of her but jealous of Paul at the same time. It reminded me why I had to give Hannah up the second time around, but also why I wished I didn't have to.

After her song was over, I knew I had to grab the chance to talk to her. She thankfully agreed. I was so eager for my chance to be alone with her that as we were about to leave, I was called onstage. I planned on singing to her as a last ditch effort to hear me out. It was a chance for me to tell her exactly what I wanted to say so I could finally redeem myself.

I wrote her a song on the same day I picked her up from the group therapy session, the same day we kissed, and the same day she told me she was never going to kiss me again. I wrote a song about forgiveness and a second chance. The words mirrored my heart and my soul, and they flowed out of me and onto my lyric sheet. The song was my desperate *Hail Mary*, my last chance for her to hear me out.

She sat across from me as I sang "Once Again."

And when I was done singing the song, Hannah did give me another chance.

But for that night, all she gave me was a chance to touch her again.

She just wanted to *feel* me.

I jumped at the chance. I'm fucking human.

After all, it was Hannah Mackenzie ... *my* Hannah Mackenzie.

If she only wanted me physically that night, then physical was what I'd give.

And that night, we touched, we kissed, and finally we made love.

We didn't fuck. We didn't have sex.

We made love.

She said she wanted to remember that moment. I made damn sure she remembered it so much that she would never forget again. I wanted her to feel me like I was tattooed on her skin.

Then afterwards, we fell asleep with her in my arms. Before I closed my eyes, I thought that if this was how we'd be living the rest of our lives, then I'd be more than happy to do so.

Heaven was literally wrapped in my arms.

I thought this was my redemption day.

But I should have known that it was too good to be true.

The next morning, after I snuck out to buy her breakfast and coffee, I was shocked to find her scrambling on all fours, frantically trying to find her things, tears streaming down her face. Her reaction— from petrified when she thought I had left her again, to absolute relief when I came back, completely and downright broke me.

I was a fucking idiot for sneaking out like that, knowing I had a history of leaving her at the worst times.

She must've thought I left her again, and after just losing Paul, she felt like she's been abandoned again. Her panic must have been amplified because she couldn't see to actually dispel her fears.

It must have scared her so much.

Because I did that to her before, and even after so long, it's obvious that it still affected her.

I felt like I was the worst human being who ever lived.

It didn't matter that I just wanted to surprise her with breakfast and a good cup of coffee.

I apologised profusely, and I reassured her that I'd never leave her again ... because I know in my heart that that was the truth. I was done running away from her.

But that was when she tore down the walls and finally told me everything. She told me why she felt she was the reason why Paul was dead, and it involved me. I felt gutted. Gutted for the pain I've caused her, and the guilt she couldn't seem to shake off. I wanted to tell her, to sing to her, just … to convince her that she was in no way at fault. I wanted to take the remorse that had broken her spirit and keep it inside of me instead. After all, Hannah's love enabled my spirit to heal after years of beatings and tauntings from my father.

I desperately wanted my love to heal her pain.

But I found out the hard way that it wasn't enough anymore.

Nothing prepared me from her telling me goodbye … that she loved me but she had to let me go.

She used my very own words against me.

And the worst part was that I had a chance to change her mind, but I didn't fight tooth and nail for it.

How could I, when she needed to heal? I had to put her first, and being with me would just make things complicated.

So I tried this patience thing and I waited. I was willing to wait for as long as it took until Hannah was finally ready for me to love her again.

And yet now, here I am, sitting by the bar at Gilroy's, my eyes fixated on her.

And I have been keeping an eye on Hannah since the first day she moved to Sydney to study at the Conservatorium of Music.

But no, I'm not stalking her. It's far from it. I only want to make sure that she's safe. I won't interfere but I'll assist if I need to, without letting her know it's me.

How I do this without getting caught, or without her noticing I'm around will not be possible if everyone isn't in on my plan.

My plan was elaborate, and frankly, pretty fucking crazy.

I came up with the cover of living in America, and I asked her mum, dad, Brodie, Brook, and Patty to help me. I spoke with my manager and my agent, and I let them know that I needed to keep a really low profile right after the world tour so I could write some new material. It's not exactly a lie, anyway. Hannah has always been my muse, my inspiration. I write better songs when I'm closer to her.

The one thing I was adamant about, however, was that Hannah should not know that I was around. She had to be able to go about her day-to-day life independently. She had to feel that sense of pride because she had come a long way, and she truly had. I may have looked out for her, yes, but I did my best not to interfere.

And it was fucking hard. There had been so many instances when she had inadvertently placed herself in dangerous situations, so

I had to make sure the dangers were averted. I took care of that pervert who tried to take advantage of Hannah's vulnerability at Ruby Red's. He was lucky that security took him away, because otherwise, I would've probably castrated him for even laying his hands on her. Hannah was completely oblivious to who rescued her, and that was how I wanted it to remain.

And tonight, Hannah is still completely oblivious of me being here at Gilroy's as well. I know I don't have to be here tonight since she's with Brodie and her friends, anyway. But Hannah invited Joshua as well, and he's seated right next to her.

I don't like him. I have a bad feeling about him.

Joshua. I don't need to know his full name. He may seem like a nice guy to them, but I've known assholes like Joshua all my life. There's just something not quite right about him.

That's why I'm here, seated by the bar, drinking my beer while watching Hannah and Joshua together. I want to punch him in the throat whenever I see him try to cop a fucking feel of her.

I sit up when I notice Joshua excusing himself from the group, his lanky legs taking him to the bar. And now he's standing at the empty space right next to me.

Great. Just fucking great.

He raises his hand, and the bartender approaches him.

"What would you like?" she asks.

My blood begins to boil as soon as I see Joshua's eyeballs pop out from staring at that bartender's ample breasts.

"Hello, gorgeous. Can I get twelve tequila shots, please. Put it on this," he hands her his credit card with a wink.

Fucker.

The bartender barely blinks as she prepares his order, then finishes the transaction and hands Joshua his card and a receipt. He must have felt my eyes on him, and he turns towards me.

"Hey mate, how're you going?" he greets me with a fake smile. Only, that fake smile turns into a smile of recognition.

Shit on a brick.

"Holy shit, wait … you're Atticus Foster!" he exclaims.

Not needing the unwanted attention, I answer quietly, "No, I'm not," swivelling the bar stool so I can focus my attention again on the one person that matters to me the most.

Hannah's laughing at a joke Patty just said, and the sound of her melodic laughter travels towards me, and I can't help but smile with

231

her. Her hair sways to the side when she tilts her head back, and the light illuminates the scar running across her jawline. My chest swells at the reminder of her survival, but when she hurriedly tries to cover it back, I want to run over to where she's sitting and tell her it's beautiful. Then I'll kiss it, like how I did that night we—

"Yeah, she's a pretty little thing, isn't she? Well, other than that scar, she's pretty. Oh, and I'm dating her so I'd appreciate it if you stopped staring at her."

My jaw clenches with Joshua's words, trying my best not to jump off my seat and bang this fucker's head on the solid, wooden bar. But instead, I continue to stare at Hannah.

This idiot doesn't deserve her. *I* don't deserve her. But I want to be, and I'm doing everything I can to be the man Hannah wanted me to be in the first place.

"If you keep staring at her like that, you're not going to like what I'll do next. You're staring at the girl I'm taking home with me tonight."

My teeth clenches, and I'm gripping my beer way too tightly. But I try to ignore him.

I'm *really* trying.

But the whole patience thing worked for only about five minutes.

"Fine. You wanna stare? Go ahead. She won't know anyway, since she's blind. I heard blind people are great with their hands 'cos they overcompensate. Maybe I'll let her massage me—"

That was it for me. The fucker doesn't get to finish what he has to say because my fist on his mouth cuts him off.

"Don't you *ever* talk shit about her, do you hear me?" I roar down to him, his body now splayed on the floor, ignoring the gasps of horror from around us.

Joshua's cupping his jaw, wincing in sheer agony.

Good.

"What's the matter with you? Who the fuck do you think you are?"

"Who do you *think,* motherfucker?"

"Tic? Mate, what are you doing here? You didn't have to be here tonight."

I turn my attention to Brodie, whose hand is now on my shoulder. He stares down at Joshua with a frown, but doesn't bother to help him up.

"Good thing I was. He disrespected her and started talking shit. I just showed him what happens when Hannah's disrespected."

Just then, I notice Hannah approaching, with Brook guiding her closer to us. My heart was already beating fast from the adrenalin rush of punching Joshua. But seeing her approaching is making my heart beat out of my chest.

She's so damn beautiful, and I ache at the look of concern on her face, knowing that concern is not directed towards me.

"Oh my God, Joshua, are you okay?" Hannah stops next to the fucker, carefully kneeling beside him, trying to help him as he tries to get back up. "Who did this to you?" She looks up to us, and my heart seems to stop as her eyes seem to stare right at me.

"I had to, Hannah. And I'll do it again," I don't know what made me speak up.

Oh shit.

Hannah isn't supposed to know that I'm here.

But I can't stand it anymore. I can't stand the hiding behind the shadows. I can't stand not being able to touch her, and I especially can't stand seeing her with another man.

"A-Atticus?" she whispers, eyes widened, face depleted of colour. She stands up, forgetting to help Joshua who is now trying to stand up on his own.

"So you know him? Of course you do, your brother's from bloody Halcyon! I knew he was Atticus Foster!" Joshua yells out, gaining us even more unwanted attention.

Brodie grabs Joshua with both hands bunched on his shirt, "C'mon, asshole. You need to go." He nods back at me, and he drags the other guy towards the door, stopping only to hand him to the two security men who are approaching us.

I look back at Hannah, and I see the panic and confusion in her face. Her eyes are downcast as she tries to hear what the hell is going on around her.

Brook steps closer. "You guys need to talk," she turns back to Hannah, "Han, we'll just be at the table. If you need us, just call out."

"No, Brook. Please stay," Hannah beseeches Brook.

My heart is beating into overdrive, my palms sweaty. I've never been this nervous in my life, and I've sung at sold-out venues that seat thousands.

Hannah turns back towards me, still looking confused, "I don't understand. What's going on, Atticus? What … what are you doing here? I thought you were in America."

I look around me, and I see the curious stares not only from our friends, but also from other patrons.

"Can we talk somewhere more private? People are staring, and—"

"I don't *care* if people are staring. I *want* to know what's going on. Why are you here, and what did you do to Joshua?" Hannah's voice is rising, and it's obvious that she's becoming highly irate.

Shit.

This isn't exactly how I pictured it in my head when I finally admit to Hannah that I've been with her all along, keeping an eye on her, trying to prove to her that I do want to stick around for her. I pictured her wrapping her arms around me after I finally give her my confession. But her reaction makes me wonder if she'd rather slap me in the face.

But I should come clean now. I have to tell her the truth.

"I'm not doing anything wrong. It's Joshua who's been an asshole. He doesn't deserve someone as good as you."

"But *you* don't get to decide that. I do! It's my life! How long have you been in here?"

"Han, maybe I should go …" Brook chimes in.

"No!" Hannah answers, her expression thunderous now, "Atticus is going, not you. But not after he tells me how long he's been here watching."

"It's … it's not exactly the only time I've kept an eye on you," I tell her softly. "Please, Hannah. We need to talk about this … preferably somewhere more priva—"

"Wait! What do you mean this wasn't the only time? Have you been *following* me? For how long?"

I swallow hard, feeling cold sweat line my forehead. "On and off when the tour finished, almost every day when you moved to the city. But I only did it because I wanted you to be safe, Han."

"Oh my God. Oh. My. God," Hannah clutches her stomach with one arm, and Brook's shoulder with the other, seemingly losing her balance.

I try to take her in my arms, unable to help myself.

I want to be the one she looks to when she needs the strength.

But she won't even give me a chance.

"No! Let me go!" Hannah pushes me away.

She's upset with me, and I'm not going to fight her on this.

"Let me explain everything, Han," I plead softly, "Please …"

Her eyes are downcast, "All this time you watched me … since I moved to the city?"

"Since you started your music degree," I answer quietly. "I did it because I wanted to keep you—"

"Safe. You wanted to keep me safe, right?" Hannah cuts me off sarcastically. "Repeating it over and over doesn't make it right." She turns to Brook, "Did you know about this?"

Brook looks resigned as she answers, "Yes. But Atticus only meant well, hun."

"Oh! He only meant well! Okay then. So does this mean I have to thank you, Atticus?" she sneers, and it makes my chest ache.

I reach out for her arm, but she swipes my hand off roughly, making me wince.

"What you did … no, what you're doing right now is messed up, you hear me? So you pretend to be in America, when all this time, you were stalking me? What are you trying to prove, Atticus? Don't you have anything better to do than mess with me? I've been trying to move on without you in my life. Why can't you just respect that?"

"Because I still love you. I never stopped, and I know I never will. I tried, Han. When I was on tour, I tried to forget you. I had women throwing themselves at me for fuck's sake … and I meant that in its literary sense."

"Oh, spare me!" She raises her hand at me, disgust on her face.

"But I didn't do anything with any of them. It's always been you."

"Until you decide that either you're not good enough, or that you need something more. Then you'll leave me again, right?" she tells me so bitterly that it makes me cringe. "So let me be clear once and for all. We will *never* happen again, Atticus. Never. Get that through your thick head. We. Are. Done."

"Please, Hannah. Just give me a chance to explain." I feel like I'm about to throw up my heart.

I can't believe this is happening.

She vehemently shakes her head, "I've been through enough. I can't do it anymore with you. You need to stop deciding for me because you have no fucking right to do so. This is *my* life. And I do not *want* you in my life. So you need to stop stalking me. And if I need to get an AVO to keep you away, then I'll do it."

"You don't mean that. Please, Hannah. All I ask is just one chance. One last chance. I'll never hurt you again, I promise." I start to blink like mad, trying to stop the sting in my eyes that comes from hot tears welling up. I know how pathetic I look right now, but I don't care. I just care about her.

That's why she can't be saying these things because it hurts. She can't mean the ugly words coming out of her beautiful mouth.

"Don't you get it? You *are* hurting me. You continue to hurt me by trying to run my life. You hurt me by not respecting my decision to be alone. No more, Atticus. No more. I'm done. Now it's either you leave or I leave. Either way, I want you as far away from me as possible," she raises her chin up as she takes her stance, but I notice the tremor in her voice, and I notice the tears streaming down her beautiful, haunted face.

"I'll leave … okay? I-I'll leave. But before I do, I need to know one thing. Do you still have some love left for me at all? Even if it's just a little bit?" I ask in hope.

Hannah looks away, wiping her tears with eyes now downcast. Then she shakes her head, "I can't love someone I know in my heart can hurt me again. So no. I don't love you anymore, Atticus, because I would be pretty damn stupid to do so."

"Oh," I nod, swallowing the big lump in my throat, feeling devastatingly defeated. "I guess you can't be any clearer than that."

I step closer to her, planting one last kiss on her cheek, wishing in my heart that she'd let me linger my lips on her skin, because that would give me some kind of hope.

But instead, she pulls away quickly, yanking my heart with it.

I try to choose my battles. I always have. I choose to fight the battles I know I'll win … like I never fought against my father because I didn't want to prove him right.

But fighting for Hannah's love was a battle I was willing to fight for, and succeed in because I thought that in the end, when she's finally stronger enough to love again, she'll tell me that the war is over, and that I've won … we've won.

But I guess this time, I'd have to wave the white flag and surrender in defeat. I can't fight for a love that she basically nuked and destroyed.

I guess no one really wins a war.

"Goodbye, Hannah Mackenzie," I whisper.

And with feet made of lead, I drag my embattled body out of Gilroy's and out of Hannah's life.

CHAPTER TWENTY-TWO

Hannah Mackenzie

My heart is beating right out of my chest.

I can't believe what just happened. I can't believe the sheer audacity of that man.

What makes him think that he can get away with something practically predatory?

I am so angry at the way he used my disadvantage to *his* own advantage.

I turn towards my friend, something I'm not so sure of now, since she'd been conniving with Atticus to do this to me. "Be honest with me, Brook. Is he gone?"

"Yes," she sighs.

"It doesn't matter now. I can't stay here anymore either. Please take me home."

"Are you alright?" I feel Brodie's hands on my shoulders, trying to comfort me. But I shrug them off, still quite upset at being made to feel like a fool.

"Other than the fact that you all played me, yeah I'm alright," I answer sarcastically. "I'm going home." I start walking off, not even caring anymore if they come with me or not. I wish I didn't have to depend on them so much. I just don't want their company right now. I just want to be alone.

"We're both taking you home, hun. Patty and her date, Dan, I think that's his name, will just follow us after. They're just sorting the bill," Brook says, but I don't answer. I just continue to walk, banging my walking stick on chairs and walls, knowing I should be careful, but right now, I just don't care.

Thankfully, our place isn't too far, and after enduring a few moments of uncomfortable silence on the way, I finally make it home and in my room. I try to close the door so I can lock everyone out, but I don't realise that Brook is right behind me.

"You should have allowed Atticus to explain himself," she tells me all of a sudden.

Is she seriously taking his side? Of course she is. She's in on it just like everyone else.

"I don't really feel like talking to you, all of you for that matter. Can you close the door, please, and leave me the fuck alone?" I place my walking stick by the door, next to my guitar case, before sitting at the edge of my bed, my back facing the door.

"Hannah, that was uncalled for," I hear Brodie's voice coming from the same direction as Brook's.

"Fuck off!" I yell back at them.

"I'm going to blame the margaritas you drank tonight for your shitty behaviour, but I cannot deal with you right now," I hear Brodie whisper something indecipherable to Brook before I hear his heavy footsteps on the floorboards as he walks away.

"God, you are such an asshole sometimes, you know that?" Brook tells me, sounding exasperated.

Appalled, I stand up to face her, "I'm the asshole? Atticus was stalking me, he also hurt Joshua, you know, my *date*? And yet, you are *all* backing *him* up. I'm not the asshole here. You *all* are! How can you do this to me?"

"Jesus, Hannah, stop it with this whole *I'm a victim* act and get a grip. There's a difference between what Atticus was doing *and* stalking. All he did was made sure nothing happened to you. He didn't want to be found out. Atticus never wanted you to know until he knew you were ready to have him back."

"Have him back? Why? I'm no longer that lovestruck idiot. I know that he will end up leaving me in the end, Brook!"

I hear the door close, then her heels clacking as she comes closer, "Of course, you'd say that. You are so hung up on the possibility of him leaving you that you fail to realise that everything he's done, misguided or not, was because he loves you. Did you know that he got an offer to perform at *The Tonight Show* and *Saturday Night Live* over in America to promote his new song? But he declined. You want to know why? Because it meant him leaving you, Hannah. That man is bending over backwards to be there for you. All he wanted was another chance … and that's why we decided to help him when he asked. Even Brodie helped out. Brodie. You know, the one person who came between you two before."

I'm sitting on the edge of the bed. My chest hurts, and I'm getting light-headed. I'm pretty sure this isn't from the two margaritas I downed over an hour ago.

Brook sighs, and I feel the bed dip next to me as she sits down, "Atticus took it hard when he found out about the car accident. He was here in the city, but when Brodie told him, he didn't hesitate to come back so he could visit you. I bet he never told you that he sang to you almost every single day while you were still in a coma, did he? Of course, he didn't. But he *was* there for you, and he never left your side. He wanted to stay when you woke up, but he realized how badly he hurt you. So he left, just in case you freaked out. When he found out that you lost your eyesight, it devastated him so much. I saw it myself. Seeing you suffering tore him apart, and I think he took it the worst because he couldn't comfort you. But he understood that you needed to grieve. He also had a tour to prepare for. He couldn't back out of that because he didn't want Brodie's band to miss the opportunity as well. Babe, that man *loves* you. And just because you can't see what he does behind the scenes doesn't mean it's not happening. If you still think he's selfish, I hope that what I just told you, helped. So I suggest that you get your head out of your self-righteous ass and stop overanalysing his faults and why you shouldn't take him back, because deny it all you want, we all know you never stopped loving him either. You only lost your eyesight, Hannah, you still have your heart."

"But my heart is broken, and I don't know how to fix it," I answer despondently.

"Your heart is beating, Han. And I'm sure it beats the strongest when Atticus is around, am I right?"

Does it?

Why do I even have to ask myself? Of course, it bloody does!

But I don't know what to say. I am literally at a loss for words after Brook's revelation.

"I need to process it all ... I'm sorry, I just ... I can't, right now ... I'm ... I'm sorry ..." I stammer, my head down, a mix of emotions overwhelming me.

"I didn't mean to sound so harsh. But you're a stubborn cow sometimes, and it's the only way to get through to you."

I give her a small smile, "And I needed the kick in the ass." I turn to face her before continuing, "If you don't mind, I just need to be alone right now. I have a lot to think about ... God, I don't even know where to begin."

"Yes. Yes, of course. If you need anything, just yell."

I nod back, and Brook gives me a brief squeeze before getting up from the bed.

But a question pops in my head, "Brook?"

"Yeah?" I hear her pause mid-step.

"How did you know all of this? I mean, about Atticus and what he's done for me?"

"Atticus enlisted your family's help, and then your brother told me and Patty about Tic's plan. Brodie and I try to tell each other everything. Secrets just ruin lives."

"Don't you ever get scared that Brodie might leave you? He's bound to live the same life as Atticus's. There will be girls who will try to get his attention."

"I think about that a lot, I'm not gonna lie. But I trust Brodie, and he's never given me any reason to doubt him."

"But I trusted Atticus too, and he still broke my heart."

"A couple can be married with children, work stable jobs and one or both of them can still end up being cheated on and suffer a broken heart. The risk of getting your heart broken will always be there. But most of us have only one life to live, so we should take that chance and *live* it. I'd rather love and get my heart ripped to shreds, than live my life not feeling anything at all. The only time I'd allow myself to feel nothing, to feel numb, is when I'm dead. You have a second chance at life, Hannah. *Live* it."

My tears well up, as I give Brook a nod in agreement.

"When did you become so profound, Brook?" I ask, chuckling weakly.

"I've always seen myself as the group sage," she laughs, elbowing my side. "Patty's the hilarious sex kitten, and as for you … you've always been the brave one. You've always been fearless."

I smile back, feeling warmth on my cheeks, as I remember back when we were younger. I was always the one who tried something first, the one who led a debate team, the one who competed in sports, and eventually had a thick enough skin to perform onstage.

"I wish I kept the bravado, but I must have lost it along the way."

"Hannah," Brook kneels in front of me, her hands planted on my knees. "Look where you are now, and what you've already accomplished. You've managed to become independent and kicked the stigma of blindness in the ass!"

"Well, that's not entirely true. Atticus helped too, didn't he?"

"He only helped when he had to. But otherwise, it was all you. I think that not only makes you brave but also inspirational."

"Ugh," I react sheepishly, "that outburst I had towards Atticus was hardly inspirational."

"Yeah, that was just tragic and painful to hear."

I picture her cringing at that scene I caused earlier, and I can't help but chuckle. Thankfully, she joins me.

We take a few moments to settle down. Then I feel the bed spring back as Brook gets up, her heels clacking on the hardwood towards the door.

"Remember … just yell," she reminds me.

"I will. But I think I'll turn in shortly. I've got a lot to think about."

"Yeah, I know. I hope I didn't make it too overwhelming for you." She pauses, and I hear the door open, "I love you, Hannah," she tells me softly, and I look up to give her a smile.

"Love you too," I whisper back. Then I hear the door click upon closing.

Two days have passed, and I've barely left my room, my mind consumed by Brook's revelation.

Well, I did eat when my hunger pains became too hard to ignore. But I stayed mostly in bed, and even skipped my classes today.

And it's not like I can distract myself by going to the movies, or people-watching in a café. I had no choice but to confront my thoughts and process what my ball-breaker friend said that night.

Brook was harsh, but maybe I needed to be slapped in the face with her words. I've been so angry and so hung up on the ugly fragments of my past that I allowed it to foreshadow all of the positive aspects that, in reality, are more constant than the negativity.

Like my family—my family is amazing. Yes, my father and I are still figuring things out, but we're on the right path, and we're walking on that same path together. My mother is a phenomenon in patience and *unconditional* everything, and my brother is just the shit, really. We may not see eye to eye sometimes—pardon the pun, but I can't ask for any brother who's more patient and caring, and who makes me laugh the ugliest, pee-inducing laugh … plus he's dating one of my best friends, which …

242

Leads me to two human beings who, among all of my current friends (which I can now just count with my fingers), have been the most loyal friends in the history of friendship. They never gave up on me, even when I did the 360 degree on them at my very worst.

And then there's Atticus.

How did I get it so wrong with him?

I wasted my time thinking he was selfish, that he didn't care about anything and anyone but himself, when in fact, he cared. He cared way too much for someone who pushed him away. He was too selfless, sacrificing his own career especially at the time when his popularity was soaring. But most of all he was there.

He was there.

He never really left me.

I was the impatient one.

I was the one who lost hope.

I was the one who gave up.

I didn't fight for him hard enough, so much so that I jumped at the chance of regaining what I've lost, with another man who loved me more than I could ever bring myself to. But I did my best. God, I tried so hard to love him the way he should be loved.

I never realised how blind I've been, way before I actually lost my ability to see.

When Atticus left me, it wasn't because he gave up on us. Now, as I start to see him more clearly, I'm beginning to realise the value of his reasons, the same reasons I previously dismissed as mere excuses.

The sacrifices he made, the risks he took throughout our relationship, he did them all because of his love for me. And instead of being grateful, I ended up thinking the worst.

That was unfair to Atticus, but it was even more unfair to Paul because he got caught in the crossfire.

I know now that the only way I can atone for my mistakes is to live this second chance at life to the fullest, and not to waste it with self-doubt and suspicion.

There's a reason why I was given another chance at life.

I have to right my wrongs.

And I'll start by giving Atticus another chance.

Finally, it feels like the grip of the darkness inside of me is loosening its hold and light is beginning to stream through the cracks.

I may be blind forever, but for the first time in a long time, I can finally see clearly.

CHAPTER TWENTY-THREE

I don't think I've ever woken up with such dogged determination in a long damn time. But as my alarm clock chimes the time to wake me up, what usually makes me want to throw my phone across the room makes me rise up eagerly like I have some kind of spring on my back.

I've decided that I'm going to meet with Atticus today.

I'm going to tell him that I know what he's done for me.

Then I'm going to apologise to him for being so callous, for not giving him another chance, when I was given another chance at life myself.

And lastly, I'm going to tell him that I love him and that I've never stopped.

No matter how much I tried, and God knows I tried, he's managed to get under my skin, seeped himself through my veins and into my bloodstream.

I'm going to tell him that my heart beats only for him.

It always has.

And it always will.

I see that now.

I just hope I'm not too late.

Yesterday, after coming to terms with what Atticus has done for me all this time, my first thought was to call Atticus, so I asked Brodie for his phone number. I deleted the number I had of his over a year ago. That was when he left me again for the second time, so I decided that I didn't want to have anything to do with him whatsoever. I wiped him off from my Contacts list, as well as in all of my social media accounts.

It felt satisfying at the time.

But in the last minute, however, I decided to hold back on contacting him by phone. I couldn't just apologise to him like that after threatening him with an Apprehended Violence Order if he ever came near me again. I knew that the right thing to do is to meet with him so we can talk to each other face to face.

But to arrange a meeting with Atticus, I still need to make that phone call.

Okay ... here goes nothing.

I grab the phone off the charger on my nightstand table, my palms suddenly feeling sweaty and my heart gradually pitter-pattering at a fast rate.

"Call Atticus Foster," I enunciate as clearly as possible, after pressing the button on my phone and hearing the beep, signalling me to speak.

I let out a big exhale as I press the phone against my ear. It's dialing, but after a few seconds, I hear an automated message telling me that the phone is switched off.

Not wanting to give up so easily, I try again, and again. And after ten more attempts, the smile I had on has been replaced with a worried frown.

I get up from the bed, phone in hand, and I leave my room, heading straight towards Brook's room, which I now know where by heart.

"Brodie?" I knock on the door several times, my ear plastered against the door so I can hear if he's getting up.

"Brodie!" I try again.

"What?" Brodie answers, and I step back from the door as soon as I hear him approaching.

"Yeah?" he gruffly answers after opening the door.

"Morning, babe!" I hear Brook yell out sleepily.

"Morning," I call out to Brook before turning back to Brodie. "He's not answering," I whisper.

"Who? Oh. Atticus?"

"Yeah. I tried several times," I didn't want to admit exactly how many, "but I think his phone is switched off, and I'm kind of getting worried."

"Right. Okay. I'll see if I can call his manager. Maybe he knows what's going on with him," Brodie sounds oddly calm compared to my near panicked state.

"I just hope he's okay," I know I sound worried, because I am. It's the fear of the unknown, and I know I have to get over it.

Brodie squeezes my shoulder, trying to reassure me, "I'll let you know as soon as I hear something, alright? He probably just needed to be alone after what happened at Gilroy's that night."

My chest squeezes tightly, but I nod and force a smile.

"I might as well make some coffee since I'm already up."

"We'll join you shortly."

"Yeah … yeah, alright." I turn away from him, and I head to the kitchen, my fingertips trailing along the wall of the hallway that leads me to where I need to go.

I turn on the TV, needing some sort of distraction to take my mind away from Atticus while I prepare my coffee. I know where everything is, and since the girls always make sure to put everything in its rightful spot, I pretty much know my way around the kitchen.

It also helps that I labelled all the essential items with my Braille labeller.

I'm already eating my cereal when Brodie and Brook join me at the table.

"Do you want anything else, Han?" Brodie asks. "I can make us some of my world-famous, buttermilk pancakes?"

"And I'll cook some maple bacon too," Brook chimes in.

I smile politely, shaking my head no, "My cereal's fine, but thanks."

"Okay, pancakes next time then," Brodie answers. "What's this shit show you've got on, sis?"

I shrug. I don't even know what the hell I had on, but the TV show isn't really helping me drown out the anxiety wreaking havoc in my guts, making even my favourite cereal taste like cardboard.

"Have you made contact with Atticus yet?" I finally ask.

"Nah. Phone's still off," I hear him approach, followed by a scraping sound as the dining chair next to me is being pulled back. "But I did speak to his manager."

"And?" I ask, facing him.

He sighs, "*And*, apparently Atticus told him to confirm the gigs for *The Tonight Show* and *Saturday Night Live*. So if the rescheduling pulls through, judging by how keen the producers from these shows want him, he could be leaving as soon as the end of this week for meetings and rehearsals. And I don't know when he's coming back."

"What?" My body feels like it's been drenched in icy cold water, and I'm going into shock.

"Yup."

"He's leaving me again? He's leaving indefinitely?"

"Technically speaking, Hannah, you let him go. You threatened him with an AVO, for Christ's sake."

"But I didn't mean it though. I was angry and confused, and …"

"Maybe he's just respecting your wishes."

"Well, you guys aren't out of the woods either. I felt like such a fool. Why didn't you tell me Atticus was with me all this time?"

"If we told you that he still wanted to be a part of your life, would you have said yes?" Brooks asks from the kitchen.

"No," I answer instantly. I'm not even going to deny it.

But now I wonder what would've happened had I said yes.

Hannah, you have to stop dwelling on the past. Mistakes or lessons learned, and the decisions you have made, would have to remain in the past if you even want a chance to move on.

And live.

Just *live* right now.

"Well, you people owe me, and you owe me big time! So I'm going to need you to make up for it as soon as possible. Maybe tonight?"

"Tonight? What do you want us to do?" Brodie asks.

An idea starts formulating in my head, getting clearer as my impromptu plan begins to take shape.

I'm using what Atticus did and turn it around on him.

"If Atticus is really leaving soon, do your best to make contact with him. But make him believe that he should still go ahead with his promos in the US. I don't want him to change his plans again for my sake. But definitely do *not* tell Atticus that I want to talk to him. I want him to have no doubts whatsoever, that he should still leave."

"Okay …" Brodie acknowledges, but obviously sounding confused. "I'm sure you have a point to all of this. Care to divulge?"

"Take him back to Ruby Red's tonight for some farewell drinks."

CHAPTER TWENTY-FOUR

"Is he here yet? What did Brook say? Did she send you a text yet?" I ask Patty, my nerves starting to give me cold sweats all over, from the palms of my hands and down my back.

"Um," I hear her unlocking her phone, "Oh! Oh yes, they're here, and they're just taking their seats now."

"Are they close? You know, will they see me?"

"Wait, let me ask …" I hear her tapping away on the screen's keyboard, followed by a *woosh*, indicating that she sent a message.

Not long after, I hear a beep. "Yes, they're sitting super close."

"Great … great … okay …" I breathe out, stammering, somewhat hyperventilating.

Why did I think this was a good idea?

"Babe, just breathe," Patty says, as she tries to calm my nerves by rubbing my back in a soothing motion.

It's not really working. But I just let her do it anyway.

Maybe it will help eventually.

But obviously not right now.

Definitely not right now.

We both jump when we hear a knock on the door.

"Hey, guys. Are you ready? You're up," a rough-sounding man asks us through the door.

Am I? Am I? Oh shit, oh shit, oh shit, oh sh—

"We don't have to do this if you're not comfortable, babe," Patty says, still trying to comfort me with her words.

But it's now or never.

Time to take another leap.

Time to live.

"I want to do this. I'm ready," I answer back with a steely determination I wouldn't have thought would be in me.

"Right. Let's do this." Patty gives me a firm pat on my back, jolting me up.

"Let's do this!" I yell back, trying to psyche myself.

"For love!" Patty yells again.

"For love!" I repeat, my adrenalin now released, making my heart beat like a drum doing an awesome solo.

"For Atticus!"

"For Atticus," I whisper out, turning to Patty and beaming.

I'm ready.

No I'm not.

I'm fucking not ready.

We're standing behind the curtains, and according to Patty, the material is thick enough that no one can see us through it on the other side. I'm just waiting for the guy to signal to us that we're ready to go.

"Okay! The wickedly hot, bearded dude just signalled that we can go. I can't believe this plan of yours is working!" Patty holds me by the arm and starts to guide me forward. But I refuse to move, my feet suddenly feel like they're stuck permanently on the sticky stage floor.

"It's not working yet until I get the outcome I want," I exhale out aloud, then a thought hits me, "Shit! Wait. God, Patty. What if he rejects me?"

"Atticus rejecting you is basically like Chris Hemsworth marrying me and having my litter of babies. In other words, impossible."

"Babe, I'm sure if Chris isn't married to a hot actress, doesn't have a family already, and doesn't live in Hollywood, I'm sure he'd drop everything to be with you."

"And this is why I love you, Han. Now go and take back that man who *actually* dropped everything just to be with you," Patty nudges me forward again and just like that, my feet feel lighter, like feathers have just replaced the lead that was weighing me down.

I feel the brush of the curtains against my skin as Patty opens them for me, whispering for me to walk five straight steps forward. The noise beyond the curtains is louder than I expected, disorientating me and throwing me off-balance.

I guess I'm not in Avoca anymore.

Thankfully, Patty's hand is back on my arm, and she guides me forward. My head is angled down, trying to ignore the not-so-whispered remarks from the crowd, like *"OMG, is she blind?"* or the *"Aww, poor thing."* or even the *"Oh shit, I hope she doesn't fall off the stage."*

My outstretched hand finally reaches the microphone stand, gripping it like my life depends on it.

"I got this," I whisper to Patty.

"You always do, babe. Oh, and he's seated to your right, and he looks like a stunned, but still hot, deer in headlights. Now break a leg. Or don't. Actually, stay intact. I love you!" And with a quick peck on the cheek, Patty lets me go.

And I'm all alone onstage.

I'm standing still, clutching my guitar a little too tightly, as I hear people telling others to shush, until finally, terrifyingly, the room is quiet.

Except for the muffled sound of dance music from upstairs.

Inhale.

Exhale.

"Hi …" I manage to squeak, clearing my throat and managing to magnify the awful sound with the microphone.

"Uh … hi, everyone. I'm uh, Hannah. This is my first time here onstage at Ruby Red's."

"You can have another first time with me, sweetheart!" a heckler yells out, making me cringe.

"Thanks, mate. But I have standards, even for a blind chick," I answer back, surprised when the crowd actually laughs and cheers back.

This is good.

If Atticus doesn't want anything to do with me after this, then at least I can probably have a career in comedy.

Focus, Hannah.

"I asked not be announced before going onstage like the other acts because I wanted this performance to be a surprise to someone very special to me, so … surprise!" I chuckle nervously, facing the crowd on my right, wishing that even for a second, I can see Atticus's reaction.

I feel my guts tightening from the nerves again. I have to get this over and done with, like waxing. It'll be fucking painful, but at least it's over and done with.

"Since this is my last ditch chance to make this person change his mind about me, I wasn't able to get a chance to write this person a song to express my true feelings. But the song I've chosen sums up everything I'd like to say."

"Who's the lucky man?" I hear a girl yell out.

"Uh, I think I'll save that person, and consequently myself, from complete and utter humiliation. Therefore, I think it's best if I leave him nameless. This is an acoustic cover of "When I Look At You" by Miley Cyrus." I hear groaning from the crowd, but I hold off the panic trying to rear its ugly head. "Yes, I know, it's a Miley Cyrus song, but just humour me please and keep the jeers 'til the end of the song. My poor ego can only take so much."

"Sing it, girl!" I hear an all-too familiar voice yell out, before the crowd starts cheering again.

Thanks, Brook.

"Thank you. Okay. Well, here goes nothing."

And as the crowd begins to hush, I close my eyes, I take a deep breath, and then I strum.

It always surprises me when a songwriter can create a song that people living on the other side of the world can connect to. It's something I'm aspiring to do in the future, and hope to succeed in on my own.

I especially connected to this song the moment I heard it, albeit by chance because it was in the playlist I was listening to. I never thought I'd be able to hear a song so perfectly aligned with my own thoughts and experiences. Word for word, verse for verse.

Because in reflection, I know that each and every word of this song are the exact same words I want to tell Atticus.

I may be blind now, but it's now that I can see him more clearly.

So I sing every line like I'm writing him a letter. I sing with my heart attached to my fingers as I pluck the strings of my guitar.

I sing like it's my last day on Earth.

Because I'm singing for my life.

And my life is literally sitting only a few metres to my right.

Imagining him watching me while I'm possibly making a complete fool of myself makes my blood pump increasingly faster, my nerve forcing its way through until I know I won't be able to stop it from spilling out.

But I manage to make it to the last verse, to the final chorus, and finally, to the last note.

And then all I hear is silence.

Silence.

The *I-wish-the-earth-can just-swallow-me-whole* silence.

And then I hear gasps and shrieks from women. Followed by loud whispers I cannot seem to hear clearly.

By this time, a few beads of sweat are sliding down my temple, and my guts are twisting so tightly that I'm beginning to feel nauseous with the thought that he might have walked out on me.

They all hate it. But it's not why I want to just run off the stage.

Atticus must've hated it.

He fucking hates what I did, and he hates *me*.

And just as I'm about to stand up and end the soul-crushing humiliation, I hear a pair of heavy footsteps on the stage.

And then I smell him.

I smell that same cologne, mixed with his very own distinct musk.

And he's close. Like inches from me, so close that he's touchable if I try to reach out to him.

Atticus.

"So … Miley Cyrus, huh?" I knew it was Atticus. And yet my heart leaps out of my chest as soon as I hear his voice.

God, it doesn't matter if he's talking or singing. All I know is that I love that voice of his.

I can't control my bottom lip from trembling, so I just nod, my head tipped down, unsure if I should be embarrassed or proud of my song choice to get Atticus back.

I feel his finger under my chin, tipping my head up to face him. That single touch sears over my skin, the heat from that single contact is enough to make my trembling lip stop.

"Was this your plan—to ambush me using your brother's help, with a cover of a pop song like that, hoping that I'm going to change my mind and not leave Australia indefinitely?" he speaks to me in a monotone, and it kills me that I can't tell if he's happy or disappointed at my efforts.

"Please … just spare me the humiliation," I whisper, suddenly feeling exposed and unwanted. "I understand if you don't think I deserve a chance."

"You shouldn't ask me for a chance, Hannah."

A lump gets stuck in my throat.

Any hope of avoiding humiliation in front of all these people has gone to zero percent.

"If you don't mind … I just want to leave the stage and not show my face in this place again for the rest of my life. So if you just came over to tell me that I lost you forever, then—"

Atticus interrupts, his tone laced in mirth, "I came here to kiss you, so I'm the only one asking for anything here. May I kiss you now?"

Oh.

Ohhhh....

"Yes," I answer, nodding back, grinning uncontrollably.

Have you ever seen those cheesy romance genre movies where, before it cuts into the credits, the girl and the boy finally kiss each other regardless of who witnesses it? Because at that very moment, it's just the two of them in the room, and everything and everyone else is inconsequential. That's when the chorus of the movie's theme song plays to a crescendo, and the crowd erupts into cheers and cries of encouragement, nodding to each other as if agreeing that yes, they finally find each other, they finally figure out that they love each other. It doesn't matter if they are strangers to the couple because even the most cynical person is a sucker to a happily ever after, whether they admit it or not.

It's cheesy, and heart melting, and amazing, and it fills you with a warm, gooey feeling that only a satisfying end to a love story can bring.

As you can tell, I'm a fan of cheesy.

And as Atticus and I kiss, I can't help but feel that spark of hope that maybe, like in those super cheesy but awesome movies, we are finally taking our first step towards our very own happily ever after.

As anticipated, the crowd slow-claps at first for us, then they're whistling like crazy, and pounding their hands on their tables like hungry prisoners waiting impatiently for their meals.

But even through the deafening sound, I still focus all of my senses into the one person who has owned my heart from the very beginning.

"Let's get out of here," Atticus whispers after coming up for breath. He lifts the strap of the guitar up and takes the guitar from me.

Too giddy to answer, I only manage to nod back, biting my bottom lip to stop myself from giggling like I've never been kissed before.

And before I know it, I'm being hauled off the stage floor, and I squeal as he throws me effortlessly onto his shoulder, the same way he carried me when I adamantly refused to go with him after my first support group session. Only this time, there's no place else I want to be.

"My guitar!" I squeal once again.

"Brodie's got it. Let's go, woman. We have a lot of catching up to do!" I laughingly cling onto him as he hops off the stage, and I drown in the roars of the crowd.

For some reason, the image of one of the most classic, fictional movie couples, Zack Mayo and Paula Pokrifki, comes to mind. I can't help but giggle. This may not be an exact ending straight out of *An Officer and a Gentleman,* but it sure feels close enough.

I get caught up in the whole, sweeping me off my feet whirlwind, that before I know it, Atticus has taken me to his place, somewhere in good old Bondi.

As soon as we make it to his bed, our lips find each other once more, then our clothes are off and probably in a heap all over the floor. We're touching each other in places we've waited so long to rediscover, and I feel my hunger for him grow as I feel every sinew, every movement of his muscles.

I don't know how I lasted this long without his touch, how I thought that living without feeling his body against me was even living at all.

My whole being longed for Atticus all this time, and yet, I was so damn blind to see it.

But now, as I feel him, hear him, smell him, and taste him, everything that I have missed about Atticus is coming back to me … and yes, I see him.

I. See. Him.

And God … he's beautiful. Just like he always has been, just like I used to wish he wasn't at my angrier moments.

We make love with complete abandon, our passionate duet building towards a feverish climax so mind-blowing that after we reach that peak, it takes us forever to catch our breaths.

Afterwards, he gently tucks me inside the sheets and wraps me securely in his arms.

God, I missed this.

I nuzzle in the crook of his neck, a smile set on my face, and I let my fingers trace every muscle on his torso.

I feel his fingertips run across my jaw, right where my scar sits. I reach for his hand, but not to stop him from going any further. I know that it will take me awhile to get used to the scar, and I know that a big part of it is not knowing exactly what it did to my face. It's the fear of the unknown, a kind of fear that naturally comes with the inability to see. But it's a fear that I'd hope to eventually be at peace with when the right time comes.

I take Atticus's hand, and I turn to leave a lingering kiss on it's palm, hoping that the small gesture will show him that I remember every beautiful thing he said about my scar.

"How did you do it?" I ask, finally finding my voice.

"Did what?" Atticus asks, his forefinger drawing lazy circles on my upper arm.

"You know, how did you manage to follow me without being caught out?"

"It's not hard to be around you when you know I'm in America."

"True. Although I did get that feeling sometimes. I can't explain it, but it felt comforting," I pause, trying to remember instances when I either felt goose bumps or felt enveloped in warmth. Then I continue, "How did you help me?"

I feel Atticus's chest rise and fall as he breathes deeply, "Hmm … I guess the most common thing I used to do was make sure that I cleared a path for you to walk through. But not always, since you were pretty capable to weave your way through a crowded sidewalk or a crossing. It was just when it got too crowded, or if there were rowdy kids who might cause trouble for you. I also made sure to catch the bus with you, but I would be a couple of seats away, in case someone tried to take advantage of you. As much as this city is relatively safe, I'd be damned if I let you out alone. Sick perverts exist in even the safest towns," he snorts. "Speaking of sickos, I remember that night you went to Ruby Red's to go clubbing—"

"Wait!" I lightly smack him on the chest, cutting him off, "Was that you? Were you the guy who punched that sleazebag?"

"I've punched two sleazebags for you. And I'd gladly do it again. I want to be the one to keep you safe."

My insides tighten at his admission. I know that what he's admitting to is practically caveman in nature, but he acted like a caveman only because he wanted to keep me safe.

Call me crazy, but I find Atticus in caveman mode extremely desirable.

But he has a burgeoning career that could easily be taken away by a single punch.

"You could've gotten yourself hurt. Not only that, but you also have a singing career to take care of so you have to take care of yourself. Why didn't you just get someone else to do it, if you were so adamant at steering me away from harm?"

"I couldn't care less if I got hurt. You know about my past. I'm used to the pain."

"Atticus ..." I close my eyes momentarily, recalling the shit he's been through from his father,

"It had to be me, Han. I had to be the one to take care of you because it means I get a chance to be near you. I know how that sounds. It sounds creepy, right?" he pauses once again, and I take that chance to speak up.

"Now that I know the whole story, no, it isn't creepy. Not at all. And I think it's quite chivalrous, actually."

I feel his lips on my temple, and he squeezes me tightly. "Don't tell your brother this because I love him like my own brother, and I'd hate for him to be upset with me over this. But one of the reasons why I wanted Halcyon to be the front act on my first tour was because he was my connection to you. That connection meant hearing about you from Brodie. Of course I pretended to be nonchalant about it, even though it killed me like a motherfucker when he used to talk about you and Paul. But I listened to every word because hearing him talk about how happy you were, in a weird sort of way, made *me* feel happy as well. I was just glad that Paul gave you happiness when I so clearly couldn't do it."

My arm stretches across his chest, trying to hold him tighter, closing my eyes again to stop premature tears from falling.

This boy ... no ... this man. How do I even come close to making up for all of his sacrifices for me when I didn't do anything to warrant any of them?

"I'm sorry about how I reacted that night," I tilt my head up to him, wishing that somehow he'll be able to see through my broken eyes and know that I'm being sincere.

"Hannah, you had every right to be angry. I'm the one who should be sorry, and I still am. But I got desperate. And I thought that following you and making sure that you're safe from point A to point B would somehow give me the peace of mind I so desperately needed."

257

"But is it peace of mind you're after, or is it penance?"

"Both … I guess."

"I know it took me awhile to get there, but I've forgiven you already, Atticus. I think I forgave you while I was still with Paul, but I was still hurting and lashed out even after the accident. And I also knew that I couldn't be with you if I wasn't even close to that point where I could forgive myself for what happened to Paul."

"But Han, it's not your—"

"Fault? I know what you're saying because everyone told me the exact same thing. But there were only two people in that car, and only one of us survived."

Atticus shudders, then he squeezes me even tighter in his arms.

"But I've made peace with being the only survivor. I'm on my way to accepting the fact that I didn't come out of the wreckage unscathed. And that I will carry the scars for the rest of my life … and I'm not just referring to the physical but the mental and emotional scars too."

"But you're not alone in all of this. Yes, you were the lone survivor, but you're not carrying this burden alone. I'm here, Han. I will always be here for you, whether you want me to or not."

The conviction in his voice sets me off, and before I knew it, the tears I've been trying to hold back are falling. "I want you to … be here, I mean … for me? Sorry … I'm a hot mess right now," I try to laugh it off, but my voice is cracked from choking on the tears.

I feel his thumb wiping my tears away, "Shhh … baby," he tells me gently, "trust me, you're not a hot mess, but you are fuckin' hot. Very hot."

Giggling, I pinch him on the side, making him gasp, and making me giggle even more.

Ah, so he's still ticklish there. Good to know.

He shifts his position so that he's lying on top of me, his bottom half in-between my legs. He props his arms on both sides of my head, and as I feel his warm breath tingling my forehead and my nose, I know he's staring at me, studying me.

I can't see him, and yet I feel my cheeks heat up so I turn my head and close my eyes.

"You're beautiful, Hannah, so there's no need for you to hide in the darkness."

I open my eyes, though I know it's a futile effort. But I turn to face him again, because I still don't know exactly where we stand.

"Is it true … what Brodie said? Were you really leaving for the U.S. soon to do some shows?"

He sighs, and I feel the skin on my cheeks tingling because of it.

"Yeah, I cancelled once already, so I asked my agent over there to reschedule. I guess the producers were keen and booked me for next week. I need to fly over there in a couple of days to meet with them and work out some shit. But I will be coming back straight after."

"But were you really planning on staying over there indefinitely if, you know, if *this* didn't happen?"

"Probably."

"Oh."

"Hannah, you said you didn't want me in your life anymore. Then there's the AVO threat. I didn't know what else to do."

"I was an asshole to you after everything you've done for me. I guess you had every right to leave if you wanted to."

"I didn't want to. And I don't think I can really be away from you for too long. I'll always come back. And I will keep coming back because I just can't help it. I am so in love with you, Hannah. I always have and I always will. It has been, and will always be, *you*."

"Oh Atticus …" I choke out, my heart feels like it's about to explode. I reach for his face, trying desperately to trace his features with my fingers, "I would do anything to see your face when you tell me you love me."

"But Han, you don't need your eyes to know how much I love you. Listen to me speak the words. When I sing to you, listen to the lyrics because I wrote them all for you. Smell the flowers that I will give you, or your intoxicating scent on my skin when we make love. Use your hands to feel the way my heart beats every single time you're around. And when I kiss these lips of yours, I'll make damn sure that even the deepest part of your being will never have an iota of doubt. Trust me, you'll feel it in spades, that seeing me speak the words will just become redundant."

"Wow … you—you love me that much?" I ask, completely stupefied.

"No, my beautiful Songbird. I love you *a lot* more than that."

"You've no idea how crazy happy I feel right now. I love you with everything I have, Atticus, and it never changed after all these years. Not one little bit," I whimper out. Unable to fully contain my happiness, I pull him down, and I press my lips against his. He kisses me deeply, reverently, practising what he preaches and making my toes curl at the same time.

And just like that, my heart does explode with happiness. And in my darkness, I imagine the bedroom now lit up with fireworks and bright confetti.

He pulls away, breathing heavily. "Come with me. Come to America with me."

Taken aback, I ask, "Are you sure? But I will just be in the way. Plus I have school to worry about."

"But Hannah—"

"It's okay. Don't worry. I'm not going to get upset because at least I know you're coming back," my brows furrow. "When will you be back exactly?"

"I'll be back in a fortnight."

My heart sinks, "So … that long, huh?"

"I don't have to if you don't want me to."

"I love you, Atticus. That's why I'll never hold you back from your dreams because this is who you are. I knew that all those years ago, and I still know that now."

Atticus buries his face in the crook of my neck. "Sometimes I wonder if you would have waited for me had I asked you to, all those years ago. Maybe none of this would've happened."

I lean my head against his, eyes wide open, imagining exactly the kind of life we could have lived if we stayed together. And then I see Paul, alive and happily in love with another girl who truly deserves him. The accident never happened, and all is well.

It would have been an amazingly happier version of the now.

But all of the 'could haves' and 'would haves' will never change what our actual present has become.

And I'm learning to be okay with that. I'm learning to leave the past where it belongs instead of dwelling on it.

Sometimes we hold on to the past so tightly that it becomes difficult, even painful, to let go. Because we get so used to it that it becomes our object of comfort. But it's deceiving. There is no comfort in holding onto the past, only more pain. But if we don't force it, and if we do it slowly, one step at a time, then letting go will not be such a daunting task.

Eventually we'll be free to welcome the future in front of us with open hands.

I don't really know exactly how our lives would have ended up if we both did something differently. But good or bad, fate always has its way of catching up to us. Who knows? Maybe this is where we'd still end up because this is where we have to be.

I feel his lips on my neck, travelling upwards to my cheeks, my nose, and finally on my lips where we kiss with an emotion we need not have to speak of. And as he pulls away, Atticus touches his forehead on mine, where we breathe together in synchrony.

"Wait for me." Atticus murmurs, "Promise you'll wait for me."

I smile back, "I promise, Atticus. I'll even pick you up at the airport and everything." I answer, smiling.

"I'm holding you to that. But I'll send a driver to pick you up so you can pick *me* up at the airport," he responds back, before his lips begin to tell me exactly how happy I've made him.

There is no rush as we make love the second time around, taking our sweet time with each other because frankly, we really do have a lot of catching up to do. But our bodies can only take so much pleasure before giving in, seeking release. We climax in unison, crying out each other's name, clinging to each other until the last tremble ebbs away.

Exhausted, it doesn't take long before sleep finally takes hold. And as we lie down with our limbs tangled lovingly, I cannot help the sigh of contentment that softly escapes my lips, safe in the knowledge that I no longer have anything to fear when I wake up tomorrow.

CHAPTER TWENTY-FIVE

Three Years After

"It helps to imagine them all naked," Atticus tells me in his lame attempt at comforting me.

"What? No!" We're about to go onstage, our first official show in conjunction with the release of our self-titled debut album.

Yes, our debut album.

As a duo.

As a couple.

And now we're about to headline a show … together.

Did I just blow your mind or what?

I still can't wrap my own head around it either.

It all started pretty much after Atticus returned from his guest appearances in America. People loved him over there. There was just something about Australian men in general that got those American women swooning. But all the attention never worried me. In fact, I was extremely proud of him and the reception he got across the ocean. He deserved all of it.

And to think that he was willing to give them all up for me.

I couldn't let him do that. I could feel the depth and the extent of his love for me, and I wanted to prove to him that I loved him just as much by supporting his flourishing career.

When he returned from his trip, it was like something switched on between us. He asked me to move in with him right at the airport, and I said yes without hesitation. It felt like we were caught up in this whirlwind romance that was six years in the making.

And how we made up for our lost time. We'd spend every single moment we could, together. He drove me to and from the conservatorium in his Mustang. But every other day, I insisted on going at it by myself. I knew that he followed me around like he used to, but I just let him. I made him think that I didn't know … or maybe he knew that I knew … I didn't bother to ask. Then we'd spend our nights together, making love, or making new music. Either way, we ended up sleeping in each other's arms completely satisfied.

And happy. We've been just. Happy.

Not just the laugh out loud kind of happiness, but the kind that warms you up from the insides, reverberating outwards, and making you want to be kinder to people ... even kinder to yourself.

It was like I was reborn, like finally, after being in the darkest tunnel alone, I finally made it into that proverbial light at the end of the tunnel.

The light I used to take for granted when I still had my eyesight is now something I may not experience anymore, but I am happiest where I am now because the kind of light I am basking in was borne out of love ... out of Atticus's love.

My life after light …

It was at this early stage of my rebirth that Atticus and I started writing music together. The process was organic, he started playing a made-up tune, or I'd start, then one of us joined in. Lyrics got thrown in, verses got formed, and choruses fashioned to suit both of our voices singing in harmony. Our songs began to take shape. And they were, in their truest sense, a collaboration.

And gosh, the songs were honest, and they spoke for us.

Then one night, as I was suggesting a line for Atticus to use, he suddenly blurted out that we should record the songs in his recording studio. His studio was basically the second bedroom of his bungalow, converted and soundproofed into a small recording studio, but with professional-grade equipment. I agreed to record without hesitation, just for the shits and giggles, anyway.

We had ten songs in total: six duets, and two solos each, with one singing back-up for the other. We had no band, no extra instruments. All we had were our acoustic guitars, and nothing more. After we finished recording all the songs, we decided to invite just our closest friends and surprise them with an intimate listening party.

Thing was, no one really knew how we truly sounded together because we never performed for anyone before. Atticus and I just mucked around every time our friends came over. It was only during days when Atticus and I were alone that we took it seriously.

It was nerve-wracking, trying to gauge their reactions as they listened to our first recorded duet. And when that song ended, Atticus pressed Pause and asked them what they thought. There was silence for the longest time, until I heard Brook sobbing, and then Patty.

That was when I realised that they felt what Atticus and I felt when we recorded the songs.

Brodie suggested that maybe we should get the record company involved because our sound was unique, and it needed to be heard. The idea of someone, or a group of people I didn't really know, listening to our songs and judging them, freaked the shit out of me.

But Atticus, however, thought it was a great idea.

I argued on the contrary and continued to argue with him until all our friends left. For me, the songs were just supposed to be meant for us, like a journal of our most cherished thoughts.

Then Atticus told me that our story might inspire others to be braver. That maybe, in another town, or in another part of the world, some other people with a broken heart would hear our songs and would realise that it was okay to feel the pain that life brought to them because it meant that they were still able to feel love.

Just like us.

And although he said that I still had the final word, I knew that I was going to agree with him and let him speak to his record company.

The reception to our debut album as a duo was bananas. The critics opined that our sound was a cross between He & She and The Civil Wars, but the edginess that Atticus Foster brought to the songs apparently made our sound stand out over the rest of the duos.

People loved our music. I was in a weird limbo, still trying to grasp what was happening. But Atticus was there to hold my hand the whole time, and he held on tight.

Five number one hits, a couple of Aria wins, a Grammy nomination, and guest appearances in quite a number of countries later, the rest was ... well ...

I can hear the crowd chanting our names in this venue that has a capacity of about four thousand.

It's a sold-out show.

So I guess it's completely understandable why I'm nervous as all hell. Sure, we've done gigs at smaller venues on our promo tour, but they only seated about five hundred, tops. There are literally ten thousand people who used their hard-earned money and bought tickets to this show. *Our* show. I don't want to let them down.

"Hannah, just try it. It helped me on my very first arena concert."

"Babe, I'm blind. I can imagine whatever I want. Maybe I'll imagine a peaceful beach somewhere to help me relax. And seriously, I really do not want you picturing anyone naked anymore, especially naked women!" I wag a finger at Atticus, but he grabs my wrist and kisses the tip of my wagging finger.

And just like that, I begin to feel a little more relaxed.

"You know there's only one woman I love picturing naked," he says, his voice deep and utterly sexy, "especially when she's underneath me, bent down in front of me, on top of me, her perfect tits bouncing up and down, her fingers scratching my skin as soon as she co—"

"Yes, yes! I get it. You picture me … us!" I grit my teeth at him, covering his mouth to stop him from embarrassing me even further. "Seriously, there are people around us!"

"Babe, it's not exactly a secret that I love you and your fucking hot body."

"Okay, okay! Just … just let me find my happy place." I playfully push him away, unable to help myself from giggling.

Blindness perk number one hundred and twenty: I've developed quite a vivid imagination.

And that imagination takes me back to the beach with Atticus, surfboards in hand, watching the waves together, the sun making the water glisten.

That's when I actually feel Atticus's fingers tangle with mine, holding me firmly in warmth.

"Are you ready?" he asks.

I turn to him, smiling, "With you? Always."

Then we walk together onstage, one we've practised so many times today so that I know where everything will be. With my guitar securely across my body, I reach for the microphone stand.

"Good evening, everyone! Hope you're ready for some good times tonight. By the way, I am Hannah, this is Atticus, and we are Mac and Foster!"

EPILOGUE

One Year Later

I picked a good day to do this.

I'm being sarcastic.

The forecast is supposed to be sunny, but as I'm driving to Avoca Beach, the sun well and truly disappears behind the gray clouds that cover the whole expanse of the sky, well, as far as I can see, anyway.

And it turns for the worse as soon as I'm exiting the freeway, as fat drops of rain start hammering down on the windshield and on the roof.

But I push away any niggling doubt that I'm making a big mistake, that this is some sort of an omen.

No.

After everything that had happened in the past years, I know that for me to even attempt to live the next chapter of my life with the person I want to live the rest of my life with, I need to do the right thing.

It doesn't make it any less daunting though. And this fucked-up weather doesn't help.

The rain doesn't let up when I turn towards the gated entrance of my destination. I know exactly where I'm going because this isn't my first time in here. The nervous tightening building up in my guts tells me I'm closer, and by the time I park the car I feel like throwing up.

"You're doing the right thing," I tell myself repeatedly, stopping to silently curse because I have no umbrella, and I'm drenched like a wet dog.

But as soon as I stop in front of it, my nervous energy transforms into a sense of purpose.

"Hi, Paul," I call out, squinting to see his headstone through the veil of heavy raindrops. "It's been a while ... a long while, actually."

I pause, trying to form the words in my head into something coherent.

266

"I'm just going to get straight to the point, if that's okay. I know that nothing I say or do will ever take back what happened all those years ago. But I want you to know that I love Hannah. I always have. And I will do all that I can to make her happy. That's why I came here, Paul. I want to do the right thing by you. I want to ask Hannah to be my wife. I don't know if she'll say yes, all I know is that I want to make her happy for the rest of her life. And I can't ask her without your blessing. I know how she still feels about you, and I completely respect that. You made her feel so loved at the time when she truly needed it. That's why I'm here. Out of the same respect for what you've done for her, I'm here. All I need is a sign, Paul ... a sign that you're okay with this, and that you've finally set her free."

For a moment, I forget how hard the rain is, until I realise how drenched my clothes are. I squeeze my eyes shut, turning my head up at the dark clouds and letting my face bear the solid drops of rain.

I don't know what I was thinking earlier, coming here expecting a blessing from Paul, knowing how badly it ended for him and Hannah. Now I just feel stupid ... foolish.

But that was years ago. Paul was a good person. He's in a happier place now so he can't hold grudges.

I shake my head in resignation. I know what I just said to Paul. But I'm an impatient fuck. I've waited way too long to have my forever with Hannah. So I'm stuck between doing what I want and doing the right thing.

"I guess I have to let you think about it, mate. I don't even know if I'm waiting for something that's probably impossible to happen. But I think I've proven that I'm worthy of her, and I won't fucking stop proving myself to her so you might just as well ..." my voice is rising, and I need to get a grip.

"Well, I think I've said my piece. I'm going now before I make an even bigger fool of myself, not that anyone would see anyway, especially in this rain." I take a few steps back, mud slushing on my favourite, worn-down Chucks.

"Goodbye, Paul," I sheepishly give his headstone a brief nod, before turning and walking towards my car feeling battle-weary but not defeated.

Caught in my thoughts of what to do next, I wince when I feel the stinging heat on my back. When I lift my head up, that's when I notice that the rain has stopped, and the sun has broken through the thick, gray clouds.

Impossible.

This doesn't happen in real life, especially to someone like me.

Or does it?

After all, I have Hannah in my life when I thought I lost her forever … twice.

But it's how brightly the sun is now shining, not to mention how hot the sun's rays are on my skin that it leaves me with no unfathomable words to say.

Well, except for these: "Thank you, Paul," I call out onto the heavens. "If this is what I think it is, then thank you … thank you."

I leave the cemetery knowing exactly where to go and what to do next. I still have to ask Hannah's parents for their blessing for Hannah's hand in marriage. Then I will visit my own father and tell him I forgive him. If Paul can forgive Hannah and me from beyond the afterlife, and if Hannah can forgive my mistakes, then I should be able to forgive my father in this life. Things may not have been as I had hoped would be between us, but I'll try my best to build that bridge if I have to, and hopefully, before it's too late, my father will be willing to cross that bridge and forgive me for the sins he believes I have to pay for.

Hannah Mackenzie.

Her name instantly lifts my spirits.

After doing whatever else needs to be done in here, I will go back to the woman I love. I thought I lost her forever, just as she lost so much in her life.

But now, she is stronger than ever, and she has grown to accept her losses and even managed to use them as a source of strength.

I want to spend my days as her biggest fan, and if she lets me, her devoted husband.

She brings the light to my darkness, and I plan to be the light that she needs, for as long as she wants me to, for as long as I live.

I grin to myself as I make my way to my next stop, my heart pounding excitedly at the prospect of what's next to come.

Forever with my Hannah.

Sounds like music to my ears.

~THE END~

LIFE AFTER LIGHT PLAYLIST

"Rock Star" ~ N.E.R.D.
"Be Still" ~ The Fray
"Storm" ~ Lifehouse
"Waves" ~ Mr. Probz
"Gone, Gone, Gone" ~ Phillip Phillips
"Let You Go" ~ Alex G
"Hurricane" ~ Mindy Smith
"For You I Will" ~ Teddy Geiger
"Holding On and Letting Go" ~ Ross Copperman
"Same as the Sun" ~ Jesse Cole
"I'm Fallin for You" ~ Chester See
"Perfect for Me" ~ Ron Pope
"Touch" ~ Daughter
"Stay" ~ Miley Cyrus
"When I Look at You" (Cover) ~ Julia Sheer
"The Light" ~ Sara Bareilles
"Light Outside" ~ Wakey!Wakey!
"The Beautiful People" ~ Marilyn Manson
"Light Years Away" ~ MoZella
"Forever Like That" ~ Ben Rector
"Crazy in Love" (Cover) ~ Daniela Andrade
"Words" ~ Skylar Grey
"Undone" ~ Haley Reinhart
"Dancing" ~ Elisa
"Lover of the Light" ~ Mumford & Sons
"Falling Slowly" ~ Glen Hansard
"Strong" ~ London Grammar
"World Spins Madly On" ~ The Weepies
"Shiver" ~ Lucy Rose
"The Reason" ~ Hoobastank

ACKNOWLEDGEMENTS

Third book done and dusted. Three books in two years. Wow! I can't believe it. Sometimes I just stare in space and wonder how, between a full-time career, a family with two kids, and pounding on the words, do I even have time to shower or do any bodily functions for that matter. I know that I won't be able to do all of these without a lot of help and a lot of love from an amazing group of people in my life.

First of all, I want to thank something that's closer to home: my brain. Thank you, brain for not giving up on me, for functioning even in the wee hours of the morning after already exhausting you during the day. Your resilience and never-give-up attitude is admirable, especially when you don't shut down on me when I need you the most. Sure, sometimes you forget certain things, but that's okay. It happens. We all have our bad days. But trust me when I say that without you, I cannot literally function. For reals.

I also want to thank my heart. Thank you for working with my brain and helping me find the correct emotions when I'm writing certain scenes of the book. Thank you for letting me know that I'm on the right track by beating fast when I've written something on point. We have had our little spats, and you made me think I was having a heart attack on a couple of occasions, but I've got nothing but love for you. Sometimes we just let our emotions get the better of us. But always know that I love you as much as I love my brain. At the expense of sounding corny, I can't live without you two. You guys rock.

To my dad, I love you, and I'm sorry I don't cook as much as I used to. But I promise to do more when I'm in-between my writing breaks, though I doubt if my standards are as good as yours because the food you cook is amazeballs. To my mum-editor, thank you for the feedback and for not being so liberal with your red marks as you used to. Does that mean I'm improve and I ken acchually write English proper? Maybe not, but thank you for correcting them so they're understandable. But seriously though, I love you and Dad so much, not just because I have to say that, but because I'm lucky to be your daughter, just as my kids are lucky to have you two as their grandparents. Sorry about my hubs though … just bear with him, his pranks are just his cheeky way of showing how much he loves you … I hope.

Which leads me to my ex-boyfriend. Thank you for breaking up with me so you could propose and marry me. You're so damn lucky to have me as your wifey, it's not even funny. But if it makes you feel any better, I hit the jackpot with you. Thank you for your help, your support, for your unconditional love, and like I said before, for buying me sushi when I need it the most. You are my BFF and BBF all rolled into one, and so easy on the eyes I can stare at you all day. But if I do stare too long, I'm probably just procrastinating so please tell me to get back to my work immediately.

To my children, Thing One and Thing Two, I love you more than I love myself, or sushi. Thank you for giving me space when I'm in the zone, also 'you're welcome' every time you distract me and I don't get upset. And if I do get upset, I'm so sorry. Mama needs to hustle sometimes. I'll explain what the word *hustle* means when you get a little older, and I'll try to explain it in good context.

To my golden girl, Latifah, thank you for being so gosh darn cute!

To my fantastic betas, Di Ainsworth, Tonette Davis, and Kitch Ponce, thank you, thank you, thank you for the feedback, the suggestions, and for the positive encouragements that helped improve the story. And Kell Donaldson, you believed in me since Autumn Falls, and have continued your unwavering support. You've no idea how precious that is to me. I mean it. I'm blessed to have you amazing ladies in my life and I'm forever grateful that you spent your precious time on my work in progress. I don't know how to return all of your efforts, except to promise to continue to deliver quality stories for you ladies to read … or maybe a bottle of vodka or tequila each? You're choosing option two, aren't you?

Obsessive Pimpettes Promotions, especially Maria Lazarou, thank you for pimping my book to the best of your abilities and for being super nice and easy to communicate with. You all do an amazing job!

For the bloggers and readers, new bookish friends and lovers (maybe not that so much) who have or have not read the book, thank you for your support, for the shares, for the comments, and for the feedbacks. You make all of the long hours and sacrifices worthwhile. Truly. If you haven't read the book though….c'mon, help a sister out!

Life after Light was not an easy story for me to write because it's emotionally charged, and deals with loss of a loved one. Some parts of the story are true to my own experiences of loss, but in our lifetime, we all go through some kind it one way or the other, and we all deal with it differently … some better than others. I've shed many a tear in-between paragraphs and chapters that sometimes I had to close my laptop and just step away from it. But even through all of that, I can honestly say that I love every character, every phrase, every word in this book. I hope you'll love Hannah, Atticus, Paul, Brodie, Brook, Patty, and even Mum and Dad Mackenzie as much as I did. I hope you find little bits of yourselves in them, just like I did. And I hope that after reading this book, you will take away something good, something positive … just like I did.

I love you all greater than the universe!

Me out.

Drops mic

ABOUT THE AUTHOR

E.S. Maria is the author of The Autumn Series: *Autumn Falls* (her debut novel) and *Autumn Reigns*.

Happily married with two kids (a boy and a girl), she crunches numbers by day and counts her words at night. She lives in Sydney, Australia and loves to satisfy her wanderlust by travelling with her family. You'll most likely see her tapping away on her phone, noting down book ideas or scenarios to add to her works in progress.

If you would like to know more about her, and her upcoming novels, please check out the links below. Your feedback and comments are more than welcome. She would love to hear from all of you!

Website: esmariawrites.wordpress.com
Facebook: https://www.facebook.com/ESMariaAuthor
Twitter: https://twitter.com/AuthorESMaria
Instagram: https://instagram.com/evette88/
Email: author@esmaria.com
Goodreads:
https://www.goodreads.com/author/show/8058885.E_S_Maria